A BUXTON TRILOGY

Buxton is a town that has been inhabited for over a thousand years. It exists for no other reason than a remarkable spring bubbles to the surface alongside the river Wye and has been a place of both religious and secular pilgrimage since the Roman legions occupied England. Watering places have always attracted interesting people who, apart from seeking relief for their ailments, will gossip and write of what they hear and see in letters, diaries, books and travel guides.

A Buxton Trilogy tells of events in three distinct periods of Buxton's history; the visits of Mary, Queen of Scots between 1573 and 1584, the great holiday resort that was the newly built Crescent in the 1790's and the place of tranquillity and treatment in the early 1920's.

Each story is based on actual tragic events and each is very different in the telling.

Marie of Buckstones recounts the five visits undertaken by the hapless Mary who came to seek comfort for her aches and pains. Central to the story is her fractious relationship with her 'gaolers' George Talbot, the Earl of Shrewsbury and his dominating wife, Bess of Hardwick. Shrewsbury had built the Hall in which Mary was lodged and it is no coincidence that many of Elisabeth's courtiers made the arduous journey up through the Peaks to take the waters here. Letters written by many of them give an account of the state of the town and its most famous invalid as well as scratching short messages and verses on a window within the Hall.

John Kane, an actor comedian, performed here every season for ten years until he sadly mistook hemlock for horseradish one mealtime in 1799, with tragic results. The 1790's saw the completion of the Crescent with its hotel, shops and assembly room and was the height of fashion. John Kane, by all accounts was a moderate actor, excessive drinker and great good fun amongst his friends and acquaintances. The story is based on factual accounts written up by visitors and travellers and gives a vivid picture of theatre people in this popular spa.

Pro Patria tells of three people who are entwined through the tragic suicide of one of them, Albert Gibson, in a small cottage in Buxton in 1922. Post traumatic syndrome was little understood after the First World War and Albert's death affects all of those he touches; Trudie Polesden the young woman he meets in the Pavilion Gardens, racked with guilt over his death and Percy Bradstone Smith, his emotionally cauterised commanding officer at the Front. From Buxton and Derbyshire, to the art world of London and the horrors of the Front, the story relates the impact of one mans nightmare on the lives of others.

A BUXTON TRILOGY

BY
PATRICK CHAPMAN

COUNTRY BOOKS

Published by Country Books/Ashridge Press
Courtyard Cottage, Little Longstone, Bakewell, Derbyshire DE45 1NN
Tel: 01629 640670
e-mail: dickrichardson@country-books.co.uk
www.countrybooks.biz

ISBN 978-1-906789-48-0

British Library Cataloguing in Publication Data.
A catalogue record for this book is available from the British Library.

Printed and bound in England by Berforts

DEDICATION

With all my thanks to the Buxton Writers Group who kept me up to the mark, Tim and Suzanne, for helping to fix the errors, Ros Westwood for finding things in archives and my wife, Joan who brings me back to earth with a bump.

THE AUTHOR

Patrick Chapman has had a long and varied business career which he gave up ten years ago to run a B&B and write.

CONTENTS

MARIE OF BUCKSTONES

Mary, Queen of Scots

PREFACE

There are not many people in British History who evoke such curiosity as 'Mariae Scotorum Reginae', as she signed herself on a window pane at the New Hall in Buxton. Better known as Mary, Queen of Scots, she was a queen of France, Scotland and pretender to the English crown; staunch in her Catholicism, a poor judge of marriage partners and prisoner of Queen Elisabeth 1st from 1568 to 1587. The Earl and Countess of Shrewsbury were charged with keeping her close confined and well away from troublesome plotters for fourteen of those years. It nearly drove poor George Talbot mad as he juggled the demands of his royal captive, his increasingly estranged, dominating wife, Bess Cavendish, and the suspicious Queen Elisabeth who was ever sending him instructions.

During her captivity, Mary's health deteriorated and after much nagging, she was granted leave to visit the 'Buckstones' tepid water baths which had recently been popularised by Doctor John Jones. The commercial potential did not escape the attention of the Earl and Countess of Shrewsbury either and a number of the most senior court figures trekked up to Derbyshire to avail themselves of the curative waters and a possible meeting with the 'celebrity'.

Mary visited Buxton on five occasions but records of what she did whilst in residence are sparse. We know who visited and when, through various letters and most intriguingly some of their thoughts, written on a window pane at the Hall. We also know that Queen Elisabeth planned a visit whilst Mary was here but it was cancelled and they never met.

Mary Stuart is known as a 'tragic' queen who was beheaded because she posed a security risk to the Realm. She was always at the centre of some feud, conspiracy or bloody revenge and was the beacon that kept alight Catholic hopes of re-converting Protestant England. Buxton was her oasis of calm whilst all around were plotting and scheming. She suffered recurrent bouts of severe abdominal pain and debilitating pains in her side, arms and hip which would leave her as quickly as they came. This has led some doctors to speculate that she suffered from porphyria, a condition she may have genetically bequeathed to her descendent, King George III who suffered similarly. We shall never know but we may also speculate that her visits to Buxton did have a beneficial effect and the remote surroundings enabled her to reflect on a world that was not kind to her.

'It is enough that I am alive'
21st August to 27th September, 1573

Bastian Pages snatches at the reins which she throws to him and steadies the horse. She looks tired after the ride over from Chatsworth. He has placed a stool ready for her to dismount which she does a little stiffly and then winces with the pain in her side. She smiles her thanks to her faithful *valet de chambre* and brushes her dark riding habit. For a while she stands looking at her surroundings, ignoring for a moment those few who have come out to welcome her. Many of the inhabitants and visitors have been moved away from the Hall on the instruction of Queen Elisabeth who does not trust Buckstones, situated as it is in the high hills where unseen rebellion can be stoked.

Robert Newton, the Earl's Hall keeper, steps forward and bows low. 'Welcome, Your Majesty. May Buckstones be blessed with your coming.'

'Thank you. I believe the waters will do me good. And my visit is welcome.' Her accent is heavy still with French. 'Is my Lord Shrewsbury here yet?' she asks.

'No Your Majesty, he is but a few miles behind and will be here within the hour.'

In the background she sees a young woman drop to her knees and surreptitiously cross herself.

The snort of horses and the cry of ostlers are mingled with those of the guards who have escorted the Scottish Queen the fifteen miles from Chatsworth. They are Shrewsbury's men, all hand picked and solidly loyal.

Her own attendants bustle around with practiced ease; they

have become used to moving from place to place, prison to prison, these last four years.

Marie is escorted through the entrance and into the long gallery, where a table has been laid with food. Robert Newton is surprised at her height, but she is not quite the beauty he had heard about. Her mouth has saddened and she has flesh under her chin but her eyes are bright and for now she is composed and regal. She is dressed modestly in black with a simple white embroidered collar and her hair, once so russet, is covered in the old way with a French hood. At thirty one she has more weight than when she was in Scotland. Imprisonment has meant fewer opportunities for hard riding and hunting which kept her lithe.

'Will you take food and something to drink Your Majesty?'

'A little water if you will. That is what I am here for.' She smiles at Mr Newton and he feels a stab of compassion. She carries her head high, as expected of a queen but there is no arrogance in her look; no disdain for his meagre effort at a welcome.

'My rooms…?'

'Ready sweetened Your Majesty.'

Mary, Lady Livingston enters and addresses her. 'A small place Your Majesty but warm enough. And close enough to the bath without encountering the weather.'

'Mr Newton here has done what he can to ensure we will be comfortable, Mary.'

Mary Livingston is not quite as sanguine and sniffs at her surroundings. The new Hall, especially built for visitors, and in particular the Scottish queen, is a large rather austere square structure of four storeys. A high wall surrounds the building which gives the place a less than tranquil feel. Beyond the wall stands the old Hall, now no more than one of a number of outhouses, cottages and farm buildings. Nestling under the cliffs is the well, blessed by St Ann, whose waters have miraculous healing powers.

'We will retire now. I will rest until His Lordship arrives.' She rises still a little stiff from the journey. Her ladies in waiting have preceded her up the stair and Mary Livingston follows a couple of steps behind. Mr Newton watches interestedly. He is not the first to be intrigued by her on first sight.

George Talbot, the Earl of Shrewsbury and his wife Elisabeth, known as Bess, arrive with yet more hustle and bustle. Never has there been such dramatic anticipation in Buxton since Cromwell's order to dismantle the little chapel which stood over the well, almost one hundred years ago.

George Talbot marches into the Hall and looks anxiously around him. 'Robert, is she arrived well? Is she attended?'

'She is my Lord. She is at rest in her rooms.'

'Good. May she stay there awhile until we are set. Lord Burghley arrives shortly as well.' He turns to his wife. 'And we all know why, don't we?' He slaps his gloves against his thigh nervously.

'He is as welcome here as any to take the waters I suppose. His hands cramp him with rheumatics,' she says curtly.

'The Scottish Queen cramps him you mean! And he does not trust me to keep her safe. Not after the Norfolk trouble last year.'

'Fie my Lord. She is held as tightly as if she were at Tutbury. You have banished half the county from entering the town. Don't fuss! If Cecil has come to check the arrangements he can take nothing but good reports back with him.'

'But I will satisfy myself,' he says huffily. 'Where is the Sergeant of the Guard? I will review what has been put in place.'

George Talbot is a man not best suited to the task of looking after Marie Stuart. He is a worrier. He is also terrified of Queen Elisabeth who has charged him with this unenviable job. It makes him anxious and short tempered and his wife does little to ease his discomfort. She turns and makes her way upstairs to Marie's rooms.

The two women have got to know each other very well since she came into their keeping. They grew closer when Bess helped ease the pain of loosing the prospect of marriage to the Duke of Norfolk. It was never really on but Marie saw it as her means of escape and Bess spent many hours consoling Marie; the two of them embroidering, chatting and playing at cards together. Bess, twenty years her senior, knows Marie well; her moods, her wishes, desires and frustrations. She almost has the advantage of her, but not quite. Marie Stuart is wary, and although she wears her heart on her sleeve, there are humours deep within her soul which she herself does not understand.

The door is opened on her knock and Bess sweeps in to find Marie sitting quietly by the window, looking at what is now a dull day with the promise of rain on the wind.

'Your Majesty. I trust you are recovered from your journey. The ride from Chatsworth can be tiresome.'

'Oh, that did not trouble me. It is this pain, here in my side which is the torment. But then it is the reason for the journey. If it were not for that, you would not be so inconvenienced.'

'George welcomes the opportunity to come here to Buxton as much as you. He suffers too you know. And Lord Burghley, who is to be our guest as well. It seems the whole court suffers rheumatics, or gout or a vomiting sickness or something that needs these waters to cure them.'

'And you? Do you need the cure, Bess?'

'Me! Oh no. God has been pleased to make my bones of iron and Buckstone's waters must be in my blood, for I suffer rarely.' Bess stands straight backed in front of Marie, hands clasped in front of her. The two women are not dissimilar in appearance; both have rich russet hair colouring and both are tall. But Bess has the sharper features that are not easily prone to laughter.

'You are lucky.' She looks out of the window and watches the people below. One of the guards has already struck up a conversation with the young woman who knelt and blessed herself on her arrival. Piety, it seems, is soon supplanted by stronger emotions when the opportunity arises.

'I will leave you then to your rest,' says Bess, looking around the room which is being readied by the servants. Hangings sent over from Chatsworth have been put up, tables conveniently placed and set with posies and herbs. She notices the rosary and bible lie near the Queen, her constant companions.

'Well, the carts should be here in good time with provisions, although we cannot expect too much.'

'And instruction was given for my little dog to be brought over?'

'Yes Your Majesty, your dog will arrive too.'

Marie looks on her custodian with a sad pleading expression. 'There will be opportunity for riding, I trust. I am so becalmed all the time and riding is more than a pleasure. It stimulates me. With the water treatment and fresh air, I will find a new strength.'

'Indeed. I will ask George what arrangements have been made.' As she leaves she knows that George will panic at the thought of having Marie riding freely across the moors. She also knows that under the pressure of Marie's pleading and tears, he will give way once more.

William Cecil, Lord Burghley, Secretary of State and Privy Councillor, is a man with darting eyes and a keen interest in the company he finds at the table. At the head, sits the disgraced Marie Stuart, once Queen of France, Scotland and still in line to succeed to the English throne. On her right hand sits George Talbot and on her left, Bess. William Cecil sits opposite, the better to observe. Mary Livingston, sits ready to charm him. She was not known as 'Lustie' for nothing in Scotland.

The company is quiet and the conversation lifts no higher

than social pleasantries. George Talbot, ever anxious to hear news of London and the court, asks as to the health of his Sovereign and sundry other courtiers. Cecil in turn asks of progress with the building of Chatsworth. And from the corner of his eye he glances continuously at Marie who refuses to be drawn in. She still has too much bad feeling towards this man who has dogged her every move since the death of her second husband, Henry Stuart, Lord Darnley, and still questions her part in his murder.

But Cecil is not so reticent and asks in a friendly way. 'I trust Your Majesty will find comfort in the waters here. I myself hope to cure the pains in my hands.'

She looks at him steadily. 'And I hope you find comfort here my Lord.'

'I can stay but a short time only. Duties call but I will make the most of the waters whilst here.'

'I am sure you will.' She turns to Bess. 'If you will excuse me I will retire to my room.' She has eaten little and taken no wine. She rises swiftly without looking at Cecil and Mary Livingston abruptly puts down her fork to accompany her up stairs. George half rises, but his wife restrains him with a 'stay where you are' look.

The conversation resumes after the interruption and more food is passed round the table. William Cecil asks George 'How does she?'

'Well enough. She is often ill or claiming so…'

'I mean in her mind. I do not expect her to be reconciled to her position, but the Queen is always anxious to know how she is in herself.'

Bess cuts across her husband. 'She is often exasperated and bored. Sheffield does not offer much in the way of recreation and as we are bidden to keep her close, we cannot allow her much exercise. She is removed to the Manor when the castle is cleaned and at Chatsworth she is able to ride…'

Cecil smiles archly again, reminded of the plot not two years ago which would have spirited her away on one of these rides she was so fond of.

'Does she talk much about what is in her mind? Has she softened towards us any?'

'The fiasco with Norfolk shook her badly,' says Bess. 'As you know she laid great store by that match.' George does not care to be reminded of the events which saw the Duke of Norfolk beheaded for his part in the plots to have Marie and the Duke on the throne of England and an invasion of Spanish troops. He coughs and covers his discomfort with a fork full of chicken.

Cecil puts down his fork and wipes his mouth slowly before replying. 'Well, George, I did try to find some reconciliation as you know. She is a stubborn woman. And a foolish one. She could have married Leicester with the Queen's blessing years ago when she was just returned from France, but chose that deviant Darnley instead. She could have had Norfolk if she had not insisted on her right to the English throne and not stirred up the Catholics here in the North. And the letters...'

'There was nothing proven convincingly in the letters, William,' says George who is ever ready to say something in favour of his charge. 'We all know they were tampered with and forged to place her at the heart of the murder.'

'George, please,' Cecil says condescendingly 'The letters presented may not have been honest, but sufficient doubt still remains about her complicity in Darnley's murder and her adulterous relationship with Bothwell for us to be sceptical.'

'But she was not allowed to defend herself; to answer those accusations. It was not well done. The Scottish Lords are a barbarous rabble who will do anything to remove themselves from the light of condemnation.'

'It is *our* realm that concerns me, George. We will do what we must to protect it, from Scots or French. The massacre last year of fellow Protestants in Paris tells us all we need to know of the intentions of Catholics; her own family Guise were the perpetrators.'

William Cecil does not wish to drag up issues that no longer play the main part in her captivity. It is the secret proselytising Jesuits and meddling Catholic Kings in Europe that concern him now. 'Does she have a priest in her party?'

The question catches George Talbot by surprise. 'No, on that I can assure you.'

'But I hear in these parts there are priests and recusants who hear Mass secretly. The college at Douai is already sending in Catholic priests to turn the country.' He says this with a curl of his lip. 'Not that it will get them very far but your ward is a magnet for such malign forces.'

'I have a force of forty horsemen placed around the town to deter any unknown person from entering the boundary,' he replies curtly.

Cecil smiles at George's naivety. He knows the ways of the secret priests, dressed as beggars and tinkers. Her retinue is numerous and any priest could be disguised as a groom or kitchen porter, able to deliver a Mass in some dark corner.

'Good. I am sure you would entertain only people of good standing and loyalty here. Perverse influences are kept out, hey George?'

'She holds herself responsible for Norfolk's death,' says Bess. 'Many letters were exchanged between them and she is most distressed that she may have written words that condemned him.'

'He was tried fairly by his peers,' says George. 'Her very presence in England was enough to condemn him, whatever she may have said by word or letter. She was ill served by her envoy, Leslie, who traduced her most harshly at the hearings.'

'Do I detect some slight pity towards her, George? They do say she has a beguiling way with men.' Cecil pushes away his plate and a steward places a leg of pork in front of him which he waves away. 'I am here for my health. That will bloat me and the journey will be wasted. But I will take more wine.'

Bess is watching carefully for her husband's answer. 'I perform my duty without prejudice,' he says feeling chafed.

'And if I were to say that Elisabeth thinks that duty is to, how shall I say…. keep her off balance?'

'I do not think it is meet of me to determine the wishes of our Sovereign Queen who is most particular that Marie is kept secure and in good health,' he says stiffly.

'And should our Queen Elisabeth die without issue? Where will your duty be then George?'

'Where yours will, William, ever serving the Sovereign Ruler of England, whoever that may be.'

'Well,' says Cecil, 'in that case you had best make sure a doctor is in attendance and she finds comfort in the waters. Queen Elisabeth has little close family and would hate for anything to befall her cousin. Unless of course it is proven that she has traitorous intentions.'

In her room Marie walks agitatedly back and forth and confronts Mary Livingston. 'Why has that odious man come to disturb me? Have I not enough to put up with? My distemper will not be cured with him staring at me. Has he not done me sufficient harm?'

'Calm yourself Your Majesty. There is little to be gained by agitation. He will be soon gone.'

'He has come here to spy on me. I know it. He will report back to my cousin that I am contrary; that I am angry. Well I am! As a sovereign queen I have the right to my own life and that of my son. I am held illegally and have a right to seek help where I may, even in the face of Burghley and the Council who would have me dead!'

The light is poor and the candle lit shadows creep along the walls as she moves about the room; ethereal spectres which seem to haunt her as she paces. She stops. Two perfect tear trails fall either side of her face and her companion is moved to cry with her. 'Your Majesty, please sit awhile and let me get you something to eat and drink. You have had nothing and the day has been long.'

'I am not hungry,' she says defiantly and wipes away the tears and dabs at her nose with a scented handkerchief. 'I will go to bed. Please call Catherine and Jane to help me.'

Mary Livingston returns to the supper table and they all look at her expectantly. 'She has retired for the night,' she says quietly. 'She will be calmer tomorrow.'

'Good. I have made arrangements for her to bathe in the morning and then if she feels able, a short walk. The river affords a pleasant view and she may wish to visit the big Hole at some time.' George Talbot is ever mindful that Cecil will write in fine detail all that is being done for Marie and carry it back to the Queen.

'I hope that she has not taken against me entirely for I would dearly like to converse further before I leave,' says Burghley. 'We are still seeking ways to resolve this…impasse. Something that will satisfy all of us and not raise false hopes amongst our enemies.'

'She still has the expectations of a sovereign queen and craves nothing more important than an audience with Elisabeth,' says George.

'But she abdicated her throne in favour of her infant son, James…'

'Which she has since retracted…'

'…and the Queen will have no audience with a woman who is suspected of murder, even if they are kin. Her rights as a legitimate sovereign are diminished and those who support her in Scotland are diminished too. She is become a thorn in the side of all of us.' Lord Burghley stabs at the table to emphasise the point. 'And every Catholic zealot looks to her as a martyr!'

George Talbot rubs his face in exasperation. 'So, where do we go from here? Are we simply to hold her in confinement and await events?'

'For the time being, yes. Queen Elisabeth will have her treated as a sovereign, and so should we. It is the forces that surround her which are the problem; the plotting and scheming, particularly up here where people are, shall we say, more impressionable. There is always the fear of an uprising amongst Derbyshire folk, hey George?'

George squirms and Bess says, 'I have talked with her often. She is naïve but has no serious intent to march at the head of a Catholic army. All she craves is to be free.'

'But where can she be free?' says Cecil, biting into an apple. 'The Scots don't want her. Her French relations hardly want her back. Only Philip of Spain would be willing to take her if she can give him England as her dowry and that's not going to happen!'

'But we cannot keep her indefinitely. The expense for one…'

Cecil has wondered when George will raise the matter of how expensive it is to keep Marie. 'Things getting tight, are they George?'

'You know as well as I that as a sovereign queen she expects a household. At present she has over forty in her retinue, all of whom need feeding, not counting my own staff. What we get from the exchequer is inadequate to pay for all of them and their servants as well. And she gets precious little from France, as is her due. Not to mention the cleaning of …'

'I get the picture, George. If you wish, I will ask Her Majesty if she is willing to increase the allowance, but don't hold your breath.'

'I can furnish you with the details.'

I'm sure you can, George,' Cecil also knows that the rebuilding of Chatsworth is sucking money out of George Talbot's estates, despite the fortune Bess brought with her when they married. They are not short of funds. He knows that the Queen will not look favourably on George's whining and grumbling about the cost. After all, it is an honour to be the custodian of a queen!

The table is cleared and Cecil decides he too will retire. He has letters to write and papers to read. He bids his hosts good night and makes his way up stairs to a room a few steps from that of the Scottish Queen. He stops on the landing and looks at the closed door and shakes his head.

'It would be better for all if she were no longer amongst us.'

Downstairs Bess is instructing the household staff on the requirements for the morning. George sits, stroking his beard and wonders why he was chosen to take on such a burdensome task. The stress is taking its toll on his health and his marriage. Bess now watches his every move when he is in Marie's company.

Suddenly he is conscious that there is an agitated conversation taking place behind his back and he turns to find the sergeant of the guard and a messenger looking concerned.

'What is it?'

The sergeant approaches. 'A message for Lord Burghley, my Lord. An urgent message. From the Court.'

'Well?'

The sergeant looks uncomfortable and hands the letter to George. It bears the Queens seal.

'Ah.' He murmurs and taps the letter. He strokes his beard and blinks hard, fearing that the note may not be to his advantage; another instruction on how to manage his captive.

Bess comes over. 'A message has arrived in great haste for our guest, from Her Majesty, my dear.'

She looks at the fine paper letter. 'We had best get it too him before he goes to sleep.'

She looks around and summons an usher who stands near the door.

'Take this to my Lord Burghley and report back.'

The boy races up the stairs and knocks on the door.

From her room, Marie hears the hurried knocking on Burghley's door and wonders what could disturb the evening. She hears muffled words and the door slam. She is frightened. Are they coming for her? She lives in perpetual fear that she will be snatched away against her will. Are they soldiers at her door? Once, they dragged her out of her room to see the murdered Riccio, her precious friend. And most horrible memory, her trusted James Hepburn, Lord Bothwell forcing himself on her in rough manner against her will. Huntingdon, cruel mouthed, searching her rooms at Tutbury. So often she had been disturbed and roughly handled in the night. She shuts her eyes and clutches her rosary and prays. '*Father who is all merciful, keep me from harm….*'

But it is not soldiers at her door but Lord Burghley who is being disturbed. He reads the letter quickly and curses silently under his breath. He goes down stairs and finds George and Bess waiting expectantly.

'I have been summoned back to London.' There is a hint of embarrassment in his voice. 'Her Majesty requires me on urgent business so I will not be able to take advantage of the waters, or your hospitality.'

'But you will wait until morning?'

'Yes, but I will leave early. Could we make preparations now? I will travel light. My things can follow.'

Bess sees that Cecil is disturbed and guesses that Queen Elisabeth has used strong words with her Chancellor. She smiles secretly. 'We are sorry to hear it William. I was looking forward to your company.'

'Please assure Her Majesty that Marie Stuart will be closely kept. And safe from harm,' says George, ever anxious to send good accounts of his stewardship by whatever means.

Early the next morning, just as light is creeping over the cliffs in front of the Hall, Lord Burghley sets off in the company of six guards and three of his staff who have caught the whip of his angry tongue. But it is with himself that he is annoyed, for his Queen had given him no leave to come to Buckstones and she is angry with him. He should have pre-empted such a reaction. She worries that he might become too friendly with Marie. She will not have her chief minister meddling without her agreement.

It has taken two years for Maria to get to Buckstones. Two years in which Elisabeth had refused permission, fearful that Catholic factions will snatch their figurehead away whilst she bathes in this little unguarded town up in the high hills. George Talbot has assured her that Marie's health will be improved by the waters and it is Lord Burghley who has acted as intermediary between himself and Elisabeth to push the case. Permission was finally granted under the Queen's hand, with strict instructions as to how Marie is to be guarded. George Talbot hopes that once she is here, Marie's constitution will improve and the lamentations subside. His own peace of mind might improve as well.

And so it proves. Each morning she goes through the passage in the Hall which leads to the baths and there, surrounded by her ladies, takes off the cloak and in nothing more than her undergarments, sinks into the tepid waters. She sighs deeply and looks up to the barrel vaulted ceiling; grey, unadorned but to her, a blank canvas on which she can paint her hopes. She lies quietly, her head propped up on a stool which has been lowered into the water. Her ladies sit on the bench along the wall, watching silently. A fire has been laid and lit in the grate at the far end which gives comfort to an otherwise damp atmosphere.

She wishes Mary Seton had accompanied her to Buxton, but she was left behind in Sheffield to prepare the rooms for her return. Mary Seton would have joined her in the water.

'There should be stars painted on the roof,' she calls out, her voice echoing along the bath. She floats for half and hour, musing on how she has come to this place.

'Are you not too cold, Your Majesty? I have towels ready for you,' says Jane Kennedy, her most reliable of serving ladies.

'Thank you Jane. A few minutes more and then I will come out.' She looks at her fingers which are now crinkled and growing cold. She remembers long ago, in France, before she married the little King Francois, how the two of them were taken on a boat on the river and how she trailed her fingers in the water. They were like brother and sister, so happy together.

She rises slowly and Jane wraps her in a large towel. 'And do you feel better, Your Majesty?

She laughs. 'I do not think one dip alone will cure me. The pain in my side is less, so perhaps with a little fresh air this afternoon, I will improve.'

Marie returns to her rooms where Mary Livingston is waiting.

'Lord Burghley has gone. He left urgently this morning,' she says triumphantly.

'Oh? I hope he did not leave on my account.'

Lady Livingston purses a smile and Marie says disingenuously. 'I was so looking forward to discussing matters of state with him.'

'There will be other occasions I am sure.'

'I trust not. He fears and detests me. He has ever been my enemy and supported anyone who was against me both here and in Scotland. He is so afraid that I will end up on the English throne and that I will have him beheaded!'

Lady Livingston knows that Marie's very existence threatens the Queen of England every day. One slip, one fever, one murderous action and Elisabeth dies without any other rightful heir. Marie and the whole Catholic nightmare would rise up and slaughter innocent Protestants in their beds.

'Well, if Lord Burghley is not here to entertain us we must find ways to enjoy ourselves. Is that not so, Mary?'

'It is Your Majesty.'

That afternoon, it is agreed that Marie can walk beyond the walls of the Hall and Bess joins her.

'You must go with her! We cannot have her out of sight for a minute!'

'If you insist, George, but I am not her nurse maid!' says Bess angrily as she prepares for the walk.

Marie, Mary Livingston, Bess and Jane Kennedy, some steps behind, walk along the river, through the trees. Three guards follow at a distance, accompanied by their swords and muskets. The air is softened after a light shower and the leaves glint and sparkle in the sun. Marie sees the horizon without walls and hears the silence; a wisp of peace which enables her to feel the breeze on her face and see the colours of the uplands.

'This reminds me of Scotland, up near where I was born. The hills are the same but I believe we had more trees. Do you like this place, Bess?'

'I favour it for George's health and it has been approved by various medical men who are thought of highly, Dr Jones in particular. It is now very popular with people of all fashions although I do not think the waters are miraculous, as some have said. We do not tolerate the waters being used by the ignorant and superstitious.'

'But the country, Bess. There is something stark and rather unforgiving, as if the hills are protecting this little oasis of healing water… as if they resent people making the arduous journey to get here. Do you not think?'

'It is not a place where one would wish to remain long but it is good for hunting as well.'

'Quite so, although I am sure no hunt will be got up for me,' she says with a sidelong glance at Bess.

The ladies walk slowly along the river, stepping gingerly where the ground is damp. Marie stops now and then and holds up a hand to shush them, whilst she listens to the river and a stray bird song. It is quiet and her heart is gladdened.

'It is a long way from the Court,' says Marie. 'George must miss attending the Council.' She senses Bess tighten.

'He knows his duty. He is charged with your well being,' she says curtly.

'But I am a burden am I not? To you and George. Would that I could grant you your freedom...'

'None of us is truly free. We all have our obligations and I bear you no ill will. George and I will do what is best for us all.'

'Oh, I do not mean to decry what you do for me. It is not you who have put me in this position, I know. My cousin is obdurate. Perhaps it is a family failing. Why do you think she will not face me?'

Bess for once is stuck for words. 'I know not...'

'Do you suspect she is jealous? I know Lord Burghley and many on the Council will have me dead but Elisabeth stays them. She must have some feeling for me?'

'Oh, she does, Your Majesty, she does indeed,' says Bess sardonically. 'You are the closest family she has...'

'Then why?'

Bess says nothing. She knows that the Queen of England is afraid of no one but she will not trust herself to look upon her cousin for fear that her strength will be sucked from her. Elisabeth is all that stands between the sanctity and peace of the nation and anarchy, or so she believes. The Queen will make no decision about her cousin and let no man harm her, for it would be their blood, the royal blood they both share, which would be spilt.

They walk in silence and Bess spots a movement along the river bank. 'Look, is that a kingfisher?' She points up stream where the light catches a flash of blue and green before it disappears.

Marie cranes her neck, but there is nothing to see. 'Just my luck. The prospect of something beautiful snatched away from me again.'

There *will* come an end to this you know,' says Bess. 'I want my husband back and you want your freedom.'

'But what end?' Marie looks at Bess and feels her resentment. Bess knows that George is a weak and jittery man, easily swayed by this unwanted visitor. What is it that men find so intriguing? She is an abandoned woman, one who is tainted with suspicion of murder and lust. Innocent men would throw their lives away for her and the ambitious would attach themselves for their own dishonest reasons. 'They make me sick, the lot of them! She is the architect of her own sorry life!' she thinks in a rush of anger.

'We must all be patient,' she says without a hint of compassion.

'I am four years patient! I wait only to have what is my divine right, as bestowed by God and the right of my son James!' She is filling up again. She is ever on the edge of tears. The peaceful moment is passing.

The two of them have walked some way and reach the point where the river begins to fall from the high moors and cascade down stony steps before it flows on down past the Hall.

'Up ahead is the big Hole which we could enter if you so wish,' says Bess who wants to keep the peace and diverts her attention by pointing to the slopes of Grin Low.

'I have heard of it. Perhaps another day, when the skies are grey. I would rather be in the open. And I am now in some discomfort.'

And as if to bring this brief happiness to a close, the sun dips behind the high moor as the party turns back towards the Hall.

Marie's days are spent with the routine of bathing in the morning and walking in the afternoon. If the weather is not good, she stays in her room with her needlework and her letters, sitting with her ladies.

But then the routine is broken by the arrival of Mary Seton, her most loyal of 'Maries' and the last of the four who had sailed away to France with her when she was no more than six years old.

'Mary my dear, I have missed you.' They speak in French, not to hide their conversation from others, but because it is their habit, learned from childhood. Mary Livingston, one of the other 'Maries' is also pleased to see her and the three old friends sit to hear what Mary Seton has for them with Marie's small dog yapping it's enjoyment at their heels.

'Have you bought clothes and papers with you? Have you letters?'

'I have. And some new hair pieces have been made up which I will fix for you.'

She is as excited and happy as her mistress, for they have not seen each other for the four weeks Marie has been in Buckstones.

'And what news do you have for me? Come, sit here by the window and tell me.' Marie is anxious to know of the outside world and her eyes gleam with anticipation.

'Well, I hear as little as you but I have heard from Scotland…'

'Oh, that can wait! I want to know what Andrew Beaton has said to you. Has he proposed yet?'

Mary Seton twists her fingers and furrows her brow. 'He has.'

'And?'

'I have given him no answer. Oh, Madam, please do not be angry with me! How can I marry now when you are held captive? It would be breaking a bond to make a bond and I could not break that which has endured so long.'

Marie takes her hand and looks into her face. It is not a pretty face, but it is guileless, dependable and when she wants to, a radiant smile shows her true worth.

'But it is your happiness I want! You cannot refuse him.'

'I have decided to wait. I have sworn a vow of chastity and will not marry Andrew Beaton until you are free and safe.'

'But that is not my wish! Oh Mary it would sadden us if I were ever the cause of such an unnatural act. I have married off all of you; Mary Livingston here, Mary Beaton and Mary Fleming. You are the last of our happy little band. Do you not love him?'

'Yes, I think so, but my heart and soul are not my own. Mother church and you have the greater hold...'

'And your father? Has he knowledge of your feelings?'

'My father has counselled caution.'

'If I know your father, he does not think Andrew is a fit person for his daughter...'

'No that is not so. He may be proud but he would not go against my wishes.'

There is a silence as Marie rises, crosses the room and picks up her bible. She leafs through it until she finds what she is looking for in Corinthians.

'There is much here on marriage, Mary, you must read it. It is no sin to be chaste and neither is it sinful to marry. But if you desire him, it is better to marry than to burn. Mary here, married well and is happy, are you not? Why, we were all at the wedding and you, Mary Seton, were the first to shower good wishes on her!'

'I know my bible, and the only sin is to keep Andrew Beaton waiting. He has sworn a vow of chastity as well, in the hope that I will think the better of him. But I do not want him to waste his life in perpetual chance; I know not when I will be able to go to him, if ever.'

'Well, I cannot ask you to follow my example for I have poor judgement with choosing husbands. Francois I knew only as a boy, but Henry Stuart and James Hepburn were great sinners.' She puts down the bible and returns to sit next to the two of them. 'Both of you are my dearest friends, closer than any sisters could be and I wish only that you will find happiness.' Her eyes glance rapidly from one Mary to the other. 'You will not find it with me. I am a prisoner and likely to die a prisoner and I will not have you sharing that burden.'

'But it is my duty, Madam,' says Mary Seton anxiously. 'I will not leave you!' The look on her face tells Marie that it is useless to argue any further. She looks to Mary Livingston and shrugs her shoulders at the failure to persuade the stubborn, chaste Mary. She takes her in her arms and kisses her. There are tears on both their faces.

On a day which starts bright and sunny, George Talbot leads Marie and several of his guards on a ride up through the village of Fairfield and out along the old Roman road through the fields and farms to Peak Dale. They keep to the open spaces so they can see anyone approaching from a distance. It is a rare treat for which she thanks George profusely as she feels her body respond to the demands of her horse and the terrain. She kicks on and reminds him of what a good horse-woman she used to be. They return in the afternoon and Marie goes down to the baths to soak away the ride with a rare show of happiness.

She writes often to her family in France and to young James in Scotland who rarely replies. She writes to anyone who can help her, beseeching them to search for her freedom. Some of those who would help her are no more. Maitland, faithful at the end, husband to Mary Fleming, is dead. John Beaton, Andrew's brother, also long gone. Leslie, Bishop of Ross her envoy to the Court and most reliable intelligencer, now no longer trusted. Moray, her half brother, along with the Protestant faction, is the last person who would want her back for he now rules in Scotland. She is helpless to be at a distance from those who might act for her in France or Spain or Scotland. There are many who pretend friendship; the greedy and ambitious, who would use her but she cannot tell who is true and who is false. She keeps writing; it is the only way she has to keep her hopes alive.

Often she writes for herself; poems and lines which tell of her innermost thoughts. She has always written poetry which has been favourably commented upon. But with captivity has come a darkening of her soul and an urgency to her words. She leaves some of her torment in verse, scratched on the big window in the Hall, that is set near the entrance to the baths.

> *L'envieux peult me porter prejudice*
> *Le mal disant peult dire mal de moy*
> *Mais ja poutant ne fauldray en la foy*
> *Ny ne feray jamais de virtu vice*
> *Basta ch'io vivi.*[1]

The words are cut with one of her diamond rings that have not been stolen by the Scottish Council. She finishes the lines and sits awhile, looking through the window onto the rain spattered yard. Today is Sunday and she will take Mass. The priest, Durham, has smuggled in and has got word to Mary that he is here to take the service.

She gives orders that she is not to be disturbed in her room, save for the presence of Mary Livingston, Mary Seton, Jane Kennedy and young Robert Tunstead who is recently come into her employ and is strong in the Roman faith.

George Talbot and Bess know that she takes Mass and turn a blind eye. George has spoken with her about her devotions and they have come to an understanding that she be discreet and not abuse the privilege. He has suggested that she attend the Protestant service as it will show people and most

---

[1] The envious one can bear false witness against me
The one who speaks evil can speak evil of me
But I, however, will not lack faith
Nor will I ever make a vice out of virtue
It is enough that I am alive

importantly Elisabeth, that she holds no animosity towards her captors. This she declines. 'I was born into the true faith and will die in it. Others may cover their faith in false words, but I cannot.'

The priest, Durham, has with him his communion box, a small wooden cross and cloth and a silver bowl which he lays out. The service cannot be long or elaborate and, almost in whispers, the Latin liturgy is spoken and answered. When it is over, the priest disappears down stairs at the back of the Hall, and resumes his tasks in the stables. He will go on elsewhere to houses in the area, knowing there are priest takers who have marked his name and his time will be short.

And so, Marie regains some of her health and composure at Buckstones. The pain in her side subsides and she is able to mount her horse with little discomfort. She and Bess finish a small embroidered cushion which will serve her back at Sheffield castle. Bess is also dexterous with a needle, but is secretly envious of Marie's better skill and uses her age and eyesight as excuse.

'How quickly our time here has passed. I will come back though, will I not?'

George Talbot is in his usual distress at the thought of Marie returning across the moors. 'Sheffield has been cleaned and fixed for your return. At no little expense, I might add.'

She smiles. 'Thank you George. You are ever solicitous of my wants. I had hoped that my cousin would have paid us a visit whilst we were here, out of harms way.'

'Her Majesty has not ventured as far north this season. There was no opportunity. Besides, I am not hopeful that she would wish to ...' he searches for soft words.

'....she does not think it diplomatic to meet another sovereign without the understanding of her Council,' he stammers.

'And the Council would override her wishes?'

'No, but...'

'Oh, never mind George! I have been waiting four years to look my cousin in the face and I hold out no hopes for this year. I must ready myself for the journey back. Will we stay at Chatsworth?'

'I think not. Sheffield is ready for you.'

Mary looks around the gallery and sighs. 'Will I return?'

'Oh yes,' he says with what for George is an optimistic note. 'Should you require the baths again, I am sure you will return.'

'I would that I was as confident. But just in case, I have left my mark. See there? The window?'

'Yes, I have read them. All of them. Your Majesty… I will do all I can to help you return when the need arises.'

'Thank you George but I do not need to manufacture an illness, for the chill of Sheffield Castle will soon have me back here.'

Time than Fortune should be held more precious
For Fortune is as false as she is specious.[1]
June and July, 1576

Claude Nau sets out paper, ink and quills, ready to write the letter she wants him to send to her envoy in Paris. Claude is a proud man, self confident, 'peacockish' and knows that the Queen has come to rely not only on his secretarial skills but upon his intellect and conversation. She had much love for Augustine Raullet, his predecessor, who died the previous year and was, by all accounts, '*un type ennuyeux*'

He has also started to record her life; more than just a diary, for she still harbours the illusion that one day she will reign with her son James. She wants to record everything; her battles with the Scottish Lords, the murder of her husband, Lord Darnley, the flight into England – a record of who has done what to her as sovereign and captive. She knows that Claude, who has worked for her uncle, the Cardinal of Lorraine, will ensure the story is placed in the right hands.

A room has been set aside for Marie Stuart to write and sew when the mood takes her. Writing, endless missives to anyone who will listen, has become a daily task.

It is early morning and Marie will go to the baths after she has written these letters.

She glides in, with Mary Seton and Barbara Mowbray in attendance. She is in her usual black and since her visit three years ago, a little more worn down with the banality of captivity. She leads a sedentary life and has grown thick around the waist.

---

[1] Book of Hours, 1579

'Good morning Claude. Can we begin please for I am not feeling so well. I ache in my arm and hope some time at the bath will help.'

'Of course Your Majesty. We are ready.'

She sits and dictates whilst Nau writes. The letter is to her Guise uncle, importuning him once more to release money that she may pay her servants and officials. Nau glances at her dubiously. He has penned such begging letters before and he is one of those unpaid.

'You will, no doubt add an entreaty in your own way Claude. Perhaps you have more influence than I do after all these years.' She is growing cynical and weary. There was a time not so long ago, when hope was on her side but with the passing of the years, it has receded to become a dot on the horizon. She rubs her stiff fingers and looks at the back of Nau's bent head as he scratches away at the letter.

'Indeed Your Majesty, but it is your seal that carries the weight and I have not been in France recently. But, we must continue to do what we must...'

'Can you also write to the Bishop of Ross again and ask how the petition in Paris goes?' Frustration is in her words. It is some months since she has heard from her emissary to the Pope to seek the annulment of her marriage to James Hepburn, the Earl of Bothwell. She wonders briefly how her husband is. They say he is locked away and rotting in Denmark, with only the memory of what might have been for company.

'If I am ever to be rid of the stain of my Lord Bothwell, we must have short answer.'

Claude Nau takes another sheet and prepares to write. He knows that his future lies in the success of the petition. She would be eligible once more to marry. Don John of Austria? Phillip of Spain himself. What riches that would yield!

'Where will you have me begin Your Majesty?'

She hovers over a start. 'Have all the depositions been accepted? Is it proven that he was still married to Jean Gordon when we…? You know what to ask Claude'

The memory of that terrible time still haunts her with feelings of guilt and despair. Bothwell was her dearest friend and champion who would defeat her enemies. But she was deceived and Bothwell took advantage of her weakness. No one came to her aid. Yet, for a brief moment, she loved him; looked to him as her saviour. Oh, unhappy chance! That he should be so weak and she the deceiver of her own soul.

'Can you also ask my ambassador in Paris to get some little pictures of me? People are asking for a likeness and I would like to give something to those who have not forgotten me.' Marie is not vain but a queen must be ever mindful of her standing. In days gone by conquerors had their effigy carved, stamped and printed for the benefit of those they would rule and she knows that all things are possible. It is a small gesture of defiance and should she be rescued people must know her likeness.

'Of course,' he says expansively. 'Although we may be able to have you sit for a portrait when you get back to Sheffield, Your Majesty. The Countess of Shrewsbury has been sitting for Master Hilliard and I will ask discreetly if he would be available.'

'That would be most kind, Claude, although I fear she would sabotage it. Perhaps you could arrange something when she is away. She is more at Chatsworth than anywhere else these days.'

The two of them smile at this small conspiracy and Claude thinks it would cheer the Queen if she could do something for herself. He knows that if her portrait were to be sent out into the world, it would be treasured most dearly by all those who still see her as their true Catholic Queen.

Just then there is the rattle of voices outside the door and after a discreet knock, Lettice, Countess of Essex puts her head round the door and enquires if Mary is bathing this morning.

'I will be, shortly. Once I have completed my correspondence.'

Lettice is a breath of fresh air. Young, vivacious and the subject of much gossip, she takes it as her duty to cheer up the Queen. Marie suspects that Lettice is here in Buckstones to be closer to the Earl of Leicester who is a frequent visitor at Chatsworth and has been recently at the baths for the swelling in his leg. Whilst Marie is only too happy to enjoy her company, she is not fooled. Lettice is too attentive; too ready to explain her presence here in Buckstones, when there is hunting to be had at Chartly, her home. Perhaps Leicester will come this summer now that her husband the Earl of Essex has been sent back to Ulster?

'I hate hunting alone. I would much rather enjoy your company than try to fall from a horse, Your Majesty. Besides, there is little comfort at home when the Earl is away.'

Marie smiles quietly to herself. She has heard the rumours that young Lettice, pretty Lettice, has been the comfort of Robert Dudley; that he treasures her above all the other women he knows, including his Queen. They say she has already born him a child, but then they say that about herself and George Talbot!

Claude Nau is completing the final letter of the morning. He chalks it, blows away the residue, folds it carefully and stamps her seal in wax.

'Those will wait until we leave here I suppose, Claude.'

'I can send them at once Your Majesty.'

'As you like. I have waited long enough and answers will not be forthcoming before I leave here. It will do me good perhaps to forget the outside world and indulge my aches and pains. And Lettice here will find things to amuse me, will you not?' She holds out her hand to Lettice in a gesture of genuine affection which is accepted as the young woman sits down beside her.

'Oh but of course. There will be plenty of things to amuse

us here.'

'And I don't mean more needlework. I get enough of that back at Sheffield,' says Marie. 'I want something different… some music and laughter. Like the old days when I was in France. I used to dance so much when I was young.'

'I am sure we can persuade Lord Shrewsbury to put on an entertainment and furnish us with musicians and singers.' Lettice's eyes are brightening for she too was despairing of what could be done to keep her own spirits up whilst Lord Leicester was away. 'We have enough people I am sure. The Earl of Pembroke, Henry is here. Sir William Mildmay and his wife come soon, along with Sir Thomas Cecil…'

'I hope his father is not with him. That's one person I can do without!'

'…and Elisabeth and Ann, the Earl of Bedford's daughters as well.'

'He's another one who meddled in my affairs, unasked! Is there no one coming who would speak for me?'

'But the two girls are delightful, Your Majesty. They have no interest other than bathing and pleasure whilst here, I am sure.'

'Well, it all sounds wonderful my dear. But I am not sure I am up to dancing. I can watch and sing if necessary and George will lay on a good table. He likes to impress his guests. And *la bonne Comptesse* I am sure will do all she can to shine.'

Lettice misses the sarcasm, not being aware of the antipathy that has grown between Mary and Bess Talbot.

'Just make sure my cousin Elisabeth does not get to find out for she would squash it!'

Cousin Elisabeth is not of a mind for Marie or the Shrewsbury's to enjoy themselves. She frets and stamps at the thought of Marie at Buckstones. It had been her intention to come up to Buckstones herself; a meeting with Marie was discussed with Burghley, Leicester and Walsingham and then discarded. Walsingham, the zealous puritan, will never countenance a meeting with the enemy for fear that his Queen might weaken. Leicester is more ambivalent, a man who had secretly championed the marriage of Mary to the Duke of Norfolk.

No, Walsingham and Burghley soon put a stop to any meeting. George Talbot was given strict instructions that Marie was to remain at Sheffield whilst Elisabeth was on her procession in the Midland counties. After Leicester's splendid entertainment for his Queen at Kenilworth, she visited Lettice at Chartley, thirty five miles from Buckstones; it would have been so easy for them to meet.

'We will start the preparations today,' says Lettice who turns to Barbara Mowbray, sitting quietly in a corner, waiting for her mistress to finish.

'Yes, of course. Lord Shrewsbury is out hunting but I know that provisions can be ordered over from Chatsworth. I believe the Countess will arrive tomorrow with her son Gilbert. There will be a fine party!'

'That is settled then,' says Marie. 'And now, to bathe!'

Claude Nau helps her to her feet and bows elegantly. 'Come Lettice, it will do you good too and you can keep me company.'

The two of them, together with Barbara Mowbray and Mary Seton depart and Claude puts away the writing materials. 'I should be in France,' he thinks. 'Not in this God forsaken backwater.'

In a few days the preparations have been made and George Talbot hosts the feast. Singers and musicians have arrived and quite a party has gathered in the long room at the Hall which has been decked out for the occasion. It is not quite the splendour of the French court that Marie remembers; the extravagant displays and entertainments at the Louvre which went on for days. But boughs of willow and beech have been hung for a canopy and the room is brightly festooned in flowers, some locally picked and others from Chatsworth; wild roses, forget-me-not, clove pinks, woodbine and lavender.

Bess Talbot has arrived and despite her fastidious and interfering nature has let the entertainment take its course. She wants little to do with entertaining 'that woman' who has so recently spited her and spread such vicious rumours. Gilbert Talbot, and her daughter Mary, his wife, have accompanied her along with Henry Herbert, the Earl of Pembroke. Edward Manners is expected, and Doctor Bayley who is in attendance on Marie whilst she is here at Buckstones. Together with the party already at the Hall, there are enough people to dance and sing and make it a memorable occasion. Lettice had suggested a modest tableau, but Marie thinks this a little too ambitious. 'Buckstones does not lend itself easily to masques and celebration. Lamentations for a Scottish Queen maybe or give thanks to the healing waters of Buxton.' says Marie, not wanting to dampen her enthusiasm. 'I believe that a small shrine was placed not far from here for just that purpose.'

'It's just a bit of fun, Your Majesty!'

'I am happy enough to watch you take to the floor with the young men and listen to whatever musicians George has found for us.'

Lettice loves dressing up and goes off to plan what she might surprise them with. If only the Earl of Leicester were here to see her!

When all is ready, George Talbot finds Marie surrounded by her ladies, waiting for the announcement of dinner. 'Ah! There you are.' He wipes his forehead which is still perspiring from the heat of the baths, where he had insisted on the fires being built up to keep him warm. 'You look somewhat improved, Your Majesty. I do detect a brightness which bodes well for this evening. It is only a small gathering and the table is not as good as I would wish but we have tried our best, under the circumstances.'

'George, I am very grateful for your efforts. It cannot be easy laying on an entertainment so far from home. I trust we have not put you to too much trouble.'

'Oh no, not at all.' He looks round at the gathering party. 'Is Bess here? Have you seen her?' There is a slight frown as he jerks his head in all directions looking for his wife.

'Not as yet. I have not seen her since my arrival. Busy with Chatsworth business I shouldn't wonder.'

'Quite so. She has much to do there but was insistent that she would be here, on time.'

And as if on cue, Bess Talbot, on the arm of her son, Henry, enters and smiles rigidly round the room and briefly scowls at Marie. She too is not one for over elaboration and wears just enough gilding to show who is the chatelaine of the Hall.

'George, I believe they are waiting to serve. Let us not delay.' And with that she waits for Marie to rise and lead the party into the long room. She waits until most of the guests are in and then enters.

'Sit close to me Henry.' says Bess. 'I will not talk to that woman tonight!'

George beckons his wife. 'Here, my dear. Next to our guest!'

'I will stay down here, with Henry, thank you George.'

There is a momentary embarrassment as the whole party waiting to be seated, watch the stand off between the host and hostess at either end of the room. George is taken aback.

'I will sit next to you George,' says Lettice, breaking the tension.

'Thank you my dear. I should like that.' He throws a last, puzzled look at his wife and then, remembering the company, greets them formally and signals for food to be brought in.

The room has broken into two halves, with one side looking to Marie to carry the conversation and the other attending to Bess. George is left somewhere in the middle, aware that he has a duty to both women, but at a loss as to how to fulfil his obligations without upsetting either.

Marie glances at her adversary and decides not to stab at the corpse that was their friendship; not for tonight at least. This is Lettice's night and she will not be the one to spoil it. She smiles benignly at the company and welcomes the effort that has been made to brighten the proceedings. The men are as brightly coloured as the ladies, with the exception of herself. She has worn nothing but black these past eight years but has made one small concession this evening with silver and scarlet lace trim to her attire. And Mary Seton has braided for her a new peruke which shows off her well shaped ears and the pearl drops she brought out of Scotland with her.

The board is well provided with lamb, pork and chicken, pigeon and beef. There is rainbow trout from the Wye and, if she is still hungry, a rabbit pie is put in front of her. Fruit is also abundant, apples and pears, sugared damsons, raisins in marchpane and oranges in cinnamon which must have travelled some distance to grace this table.

Marie's appetite is generally poor, but does the food justice this evening.

The noise of friendly chatter rises and George, ever attentive, enquires repeatedly if she would like a bit of this or that. She can see that he is not happy; he is blinking constantly and throwing long looks at his wife at the far end of the table who is making a point of ignoring him.

'I see you have softened a little George and let some of the lame and crooked back to drink at the well.'

He looks at her quizzically. 'Crippled? Who? How so?'

'There were a small band of beggars waiting near the well when I had done bathing this morning. Mary Seton and I went for a walk and they were a pitiful sight, I must say.'

George is alarmed. 'They should not have been there. I gave strict instructions that no one was to approach within the town without permission. I will see to it that it does not happen again.'

'But George, what harm? These poor creatures have been using the waters here for longer than we know. Why, the church confirmed it once as a place of miraculous healing.

They do no harm.'

'But, they are not to be given entry! Not whilst you are here anyway!' He forks food into his mouth, spilling some in his haste to avoid further discussion of the subject.

'As you wish George, but I could not help feeling sorry for them. I gave one poor wretch some clothing. She was almost in rags and it would have been uncharitable to pass her by. It was not much.'

But George has already decided that someone will pay for the lapse.

Before long, the musicians file discreetly into the back of the room and begin to play.

More wine and beer is brought to the table and whilst some of the plates and bowls are being removed, tables are re-arranged to allow more room for dancing.

The musicians, brought over from Sheffield in haste, consist of viols and flutes, hautboy and tambourine and have assured the Earl that they can play most new music recently brought to court.

As the music starts, Lettice claps her hands and leads the younger members of the party into a *Gavotte*. Soon everyone, with the exception of Marie, Bess, George and Henry Herbert who is not feeling well, are tripping around the floor, and trying not to bump into one another. Marie looks on, remembering how she had thrilled to the excitement of the dance. During a break in the dancing, Claude Nau approaches her. 'Your Majesty,' he says quietly in French. 'These people are not as good as you. Please, let us show them the *Courant*, as you remember it.'

She is on the point of refusing, when he extends his hand and with an imploring look, has her forgetting the stiffness in her arm. She rises and he escorts her onto the floor amidst clapping and rejoicing from the party. They stand back as Marie Stuart and her secretary, Claude Nau, perform a slow *Courant*. She feels freer than she has felt since first being confined. She tip toes down the room and back again, slowing, turning, as gracefully as her infirmity will allow, touching the fingers of her partner, who matches her steps. Everyone is pleased to see how she thrives on the attention and for a few brief minutes she is transported back to the fantastical court of the Guise. She is alive! As the music drifts to a close, the party, including George Talbot, clap her back to her chair.

'That will probably do you more good than bathing!'

She is a little breathless. 'I do believe you could be right. It is many years since I did that.'

Lettice skips up to her. 'You must show me those steps, Your Majesty. I have not seen them before.'

'They were taught me in France, my dear. Claude knows them too. He can show you.' Lettice asks the musicians to play again whilst she and several others are instructed in the *Courant* by Claude, the dancing master.

Whilst they are all dancing, no one has noticed the absence of Bess who had slipped out of the room on seeing the lime-light shift from her. Her bile has risen and her jealousy will not allow her to spend more time in the presence of that woman. Her absence does not inhibit the gaiety and fun. Even George forgets to worry and finds that his tongue has been loosened by wine.

Lettice insists on singing a song and then insists that others join her. George Talbot looks on and thinks he has not had such a joyous time since he was a young man before the demands of matrimony. In those days he was often at court, a rising star and favourite at the court of Edward VI.

And singing there was by all, helped by the wine. Henry Herbert, more often seen in melancholy, sung lustily of 'nut-brown ale' and Gilbert Talbot roared out a song about 'chopcherry, chopcherry ripe' and 'schoolboys swimming in a stream', accompanied by his father.

To end the evening, Lettice recites the song of Rosalind for the Queen of Scots who sits delighted at the thought that this was being sung for no one else but her.

> *Like to the clear in highest sphere*
> *Where all imperial glory shines,*
> *Of self same colour is her hair*
> *Whether unfolded or in twines:*
> *Heigh ho! Fair Rosalind......* [2]

Marie sits for a moment, tears creasing down her cheeks and then turns to her jailer.

'My Lord Shrewsbury, you have done me great honour this evening. And this company will not be forgotten for a long time. You have ever tried to make my stay with you as easy as is possible. I know you are constrained too, but these small kindnesses will be rewarded.'

George bows solemnly and as on so many occasions feels pity for her. There was a time when her charms did beguile him and he was a little in love with her. Now he is both resentful and protective, contradictions that drive him to distraction especially when he is accused of being too close to her by his wife and not close enough by his Queen.

The entertainment breaks up shortly after and Marie is escorted by her ladies to bed where, for once, she sleeps soundly and without the company of bad dreams.

The following day when Marie has bathed and is feeling lighter than she has done in an age, she encounters Bess who is giving instructions to a servant and preparing to leave.

'You are leaving us, Bess?' Marie had resolved to speak with the intention of cutting through the atmosphere of mistrust and spite that had grown between them.

'I am. I am back to Sheffield to clean the place before your return' she says bitterly.

'Please. Stop awhile and tell me of news of your grandchild. Let us sit before you go.'

---

[2] Rosalind by Thomas Lodge

'Which one?'

'Arabella, my niece. I hear that she sucks well and is growing. I would so love to see her when we return to Sheffield.'

'She is too young as yet.' Bess sits down uncomfortably on the edge of the chair. She wants to be gone but, despite her antipathy, feels duty bound to treat with Marie in accordance with her status. Besides, she has been her constant companion these past seven years and will continue to be so into the undefined future.

'Bess, I know there have been words spoken out of turn for which I am sorry. We are too closely confined together to be at war with one another.'

'You might be closely confined with my husband,' she snaps.

'You know that is not so! These spiteful rumours that I might be improperly close are unfounded and do none of us any good. How can you suspect anything, when you know my dearest wish is to be free of you and George to live my own life. I want nothing from either of you!' Marie is close to tears; tears of frustration for she has no opportunity to confront scandal and rumour directly. All she hears is second hand and has no means to fight back. The evenings when the two of them would sit for hours embroidering and gossiping seem an age ago. But now, things are different. Rash words have been spoken on both sides; slanders and back biting, suspicion and jealousy have clouded their relationship.

'I was angry and upset that you could have harboured suspicions about George and I. Your husband is a man of honour. He hates being my captor as much as I hate being held and you should have no cause to doubt him.'

Bess too is frustrated at being held in check, guarding a queen who will never succeed in winning her freedom and thereby keeping her and George in confinement as well.

'For the sake of Arabella?' implores Marie. 'Can we not find common cause? She now is the future of both of us. I have asked in my will that she be awarded the Lennox entitlements. And she stands in line to the throne of England. That is our common bond.'

Bess is not easily placated but recognises the importance of what she says. 'Perhaps it is best if we are not so often in each other's company. I cannot be privy to what you engage upon with others for your release...'

'But your grandchildren; little George and Bessie. You were agreeable to me being George's godmother. And I love to play with these children so. They give me hope. I cannot see my own son who is being turned from me. What else can I do but find solace in those who might one day carry forward our names?'

Bess rises and looks out of the window. It is raining and the day is cool. She stares at the enclosing wall of the Hall and feels as closed in as Marie. At least she has the option to return to her beloved Chatsworth which is nearing completion.

Just then George Talbot strides into the room. His composure of the previous evening has evaporated and he is in a black humour. 'Ah! Here is my darling wife who will order *my* people at her will!'

Bess stiffens. These arguments are becoming the norm. 'What now, George. I go to Chatsworth...'

'And would instruct my man to take what is mine to your new palace! Without my leave!'

'That man of yours should be whipped for he was grossly discourteous. A simple request is beyond him. I have dismissed him...'

'Dismissed him! How dare you! He was on my instruction not to follow your request as I strictly forbid you to take any more hangings and furniture out of Sheffield.'

'And I will do what is my right to do. A servant is a servant...'

'Not when he is my man!'

Marie has heard George and Bess in full screaming temper

but never stood between them. He catches her eye and turns on her without warning.

'And I am not paying any more for you either!' You will have to release some of your staff.'

'I will do no such thing,' says Marie affronted. 'You seem to forget that I am held illegally. Any legitimate costs for the upkeep of my staff, is borne by me. What arrangements you have to make to keep me captive is your affair.'

All three of them are reddened with emotion. The Hall staff keep out of their way and surreptitiously listen to the rage, storing up gossip that will soon get round the county.

George has been hopping from one foot to the other, as if his feet were on fire. Of late, everyone has noticed that he is waspish, finding fault and generally out of sorts with the world.

'These are private matters, George and not for open discussion, especially in front of our guest...' says Bess

'I will discuss what I like with whom I like in front of any-one I like! And just now I want you to know that you will not have a penny more of my money for your wretched palace!'

Marie has rarely heard George shout in quite such strident terms before. Her heart sinks for she believes she is the cause of his uncharacteristic moods. George strokes his beard and mumbles something neither of them catch. He turns abruptly on his heel and walks out, shouting over his shoulder. 'I will not have it! I am master in this house!'

Bess stares at Marie accusingly. She does not have to say anything.

The day is wet. Rain comes in across the town horizontally in a thin drizzle and does not let up. No one at the Hall ventures out unless they have to and Marie, who has been sitting sewing with some of her ladies, feels the need to stretch her legs. She walks up and down the gallery.

'Have you seen the writings on the windows Your Majesty.

There are some new ones,' says Mary Seton.

'Oh? I saw those left some time past by the Countess of Sussex and that strange message by that awful man, Richard Topcliffe who would burn every catholic he can find. And the poems I scratched when last I was here are still readable.'

'Claude Nau has written as well. And the Countess of Essex.'

'I must go and have a look. Will you come with me Mary? I might feel tempted to write something myself.'

The two women leave the room and walk along the corridor to the window near the entrance to the baths. She bends to the glass, the better to see and runs her finger over the most recent scratchings. 'What does it say?'

Mary Seton bends closer and reads the inscription.

"*Buxtonicus thermas quad tantum numen adivit*
Si cupias lector descere nomen habe
Haec decimal est Pieris, Venus altera gratia quarta
Stewarta una tribus addita Diva choris"[3]

'And Claude has written that?'

'Yes Your Majesty. He has signed it *Jac. Nau.*'

'Jacques, yes. That is his name but he prefers Claude. The sentiment is a very kind one although I am not sure that Buckstones merits quite the epithet that he bestows on it. As I remember, Piera is the spring in which the Olympians would bathe. And Venus!' She smiles thinking that Buckstones must be as far from Greece as it is possible to get, but is secretly enchanted by Claude's praise. And she knows that whatever George Talbot thinks of her, she has had a beneficial effect on the popularity of the wells here. Would the Earl of Leicester himself have travelled this far if it were not to catch a glimpse of her?

---

[3] If you are looking at the fame of these springs
one part is as Piera, another is Venus
a third is one of the Graces and the fourth is Mary Queen of Scots.

And what is this line?' asks Marie, pointing to another scratching below.

'"*By chance, not by mind*" It is written by the Earl of Pembroke Your Majesty.'

She repeats the line. 'It is not clear in meaning. Henry is still in mourning for his wife Catherine, poor man. It may be something to do with that?'

'Or he may have read the poems you left on your last visit and is responding to those. I think he says that whatever has happened to you, it is not of your making.'

'Oh Mary, I do love you so, for you never find any wrong in me and yet I am the most sinful person that ever lived.'

'No, Your Majesty. The Earl is right. Yours is a life of misfortune and not by design.'

Marie smiles benignly. 'Thank you,' she says quietly. 'You will have me weeping again if you are not careful.'

They re-read Marie's poems from her previous visit.

'Oh, I was so strong in my anger and pity then. My contempt for the world was so much stronger than now.' Her look darkens as if a cloud has suddenly passed over the sun.

'I weary so. It is only for James that I still live in hope.' She touches the window writings once more. 'I will write something.' And she sets about scratching lines with a diamond ring.

> *Durum sed leve fit patientia*
> *Quicquid corrigere est nefas...*[4]

She stops, pondering what else to write. It is a slow process, thinking.

'I will finish it later. My mind has gone blank'

Mary Seton looks at her mistress and sees the lines in her face tell of the suffering. That a Sovereign Queen should be

---

[4] But what is hard becomes bearable through the ability to suffer
It is a crime to set anything straight....

treated as a prisoner by her own cousin… 'If I could kill Elisabeth I would!' she thinks.

'I must find the Earl of Pembroke and sit with him awhile. I know what it is like to loose a loved one and perhaps I can offer some solace.'

The two of them make their way back into the gallery and Marie asks a servant to let the Earl of Pembroke know she is down.

The weather stays wet and windy for the last days of her visit and Marie has not the opportunity to step too far from the Hall. She walks the small gardens along the river Wye with the Earl of Pembroke, but his health is not good and he soon requests that they return to the warmth of the Hall.

Bess has returned to Chatsworth and George Talbot is left to supervise Marie, fussing about her and constantly telling the guard to keep people away from the bounds of the town. Word has got back to the Queen (how, he knows not) that Marie has been consorting with poor people and has condemned his ineptitude once more. Lord Burghley takes a vicarious pleasure in letting him know of Elisabeth's displeasure which makes him even more jumpy.

'The Queen will have you return to Tutbury,' he tells Marie a couple of days before they are due to end their sojourn at Buxton.

'Tutbury! I refuse. I will not return to that stinking midden!'

'I have told the Queen that the place is not fit; that it would make you ill.'

They are sitting at dinner; a private affair with just Marie, Mary Seton and himself. It is the kind of arrangement which has given Bess the jealous vapours and she has placed one of her servants to wait on them and report back exactly what is said at the table.

'I have given instruction that Sheffield is to be readied for you.'

'And visitors? Will I be able to receive whom I want or has my cousin told you who I can see as well.'

George coughs to give himself time to phrase the answer.

'You know she is ever concerned about the state of our country.' He laughs sardonically. 'Who would think that the state of all Europe could be affected by one person, living a secluded life up here in wild country away from everywhere? Everyone you meet has some importance, some influence on events and our Queen is concerned that the fate of nations may hang on who you meet and don't meet.'

'Thank you for the lesson, George. I am well aware of what my cousin's suspicions and prejudices are.' She wearily puts down her fork. 'I tire of politics. I tire of the constant indecision. I tire of the obduracy of men like Burghley and Sussex. And most of all I tire of myself; the endless thoughts that go nowhere but round in my head. I would like to live peacefully, to come and go as I wish and to see my son in his rightful place. That is all I ask. But what chance of that?'

'If I may say so, Your Majesty, there has been a certain obduracy on your part as well. People still see you as the flame of the old religion and you have done little to renounce the Catholic faith; little to douse the flame….'

'And I never will! It is all I have left to comfort me. And besides, am I to be held responsible for the actions of people I have never encountered? I have never been given the chance to face any of my accusers.'

George has always admired Marie's strength of will. She has been impetuous and has made many silly and dangerous mistakes. But he cannot condemn her character and is still swayed by her charm, even if on occasions it is a little artful.

'Well, visitors will always want to see you. Leicester is jealous that Burghley has access to you in a way denied him by the queen, although I daresay he will find a way to visit. As you know he is up in these parts quite often.'

'Well, at least let me have access to the children. They have no ulterior motives for wanting to see me. Arabella and little George and Bessie. Surely Bess will not deny me the chance to play with them?'

'No, we will ensure that you have that pleasure, although Arabella may be an added concern for her Majesty. She has not forgiven your step mother, Lady Lennox and Bess conniving, as she sees it, to Charles and Elisabeth marrying and producing an heir to the throne! Arabella is *persona non grata* and will never be recognised.'

'She is a sweet little child. My step mother, Lennox may not wish for me to see her either for she still accuses me of being responsible for the death of her precious son.'

George grunts. He does not want to go over old ground as he too harbours the suspicion that Marie might have known more about the killing of Lord Darnley, her useless husband, than she ever let on.

They finish their meal. A servant has made a careful note of all that has transpired and will debrief Bess on her return to Sheffield.

'Well, we will be on our way tomorrow. Do you wish to bathe before we set off?'

'Yes. Yes I will, one last time. Who knows when I will get another chance?' As she leaves the table she looks down at him. 'I am grateful, you know. It cannot be easy for you George.'

Was ever known a fate more sad than mine?[1]
1580 Arrived 28th July.

The journey is slow and bumpy and every movement jolts her spine and adds to her misery. This is not the way Marie had intended to arrive in Buxton. But just as they were leaving Sheffield Manor, her horse shied and she was thrown, landing painfully on her back, which now screams out every time they bump over a stone or rut in the path. The Earl of Shrewsbury has said many times that he will have the road mended between Sheffield, Chatsworth and Buxton. But it is no better than when she first came across in 1573.

And now, here she lies on a litter, a hastily assembled cart, pulled by two large horses, on which is erected a crude canopy, straw for the base and a down mattress upon which she is jolted around like the vegetables that were its last occupants. She can still smell over ripened produce that has not been properly washed from the cart.

The Shrewsbury coach which George had built the previous year, is being used by Bess as she tours their estates. Word has it that she has gone to Wingfield and will go on to Hardwick, where she is already making plans to rebuild the place, just as she has done with Chatsworth.

As Marie lies propped up on cushions with no one but Mary Seton and Jane Kennedy for company inside and twenty riders outside to guard her, she reminisces. Since her last visit to Buxton, much has happened. Her despised mother in law, the Countess of Lennox has died as has her younger son,

---

[1] Book of Hours 1579

Charles Stuart, little Arabella's father. 'The old witch,' she thinks. 'Never did like me and nor I, her. Huh! Writing me those sweet letters absolving me of her son's murder. A cat doesn't loose its claws that easily. Always had ideas way above her station and never could accept that her other precious son, my husband, was a pox ridden drunk bent on nothing but his own pleasure, who deceived me and deserved what he got! Oh, Henry Stuart, you were nothing but a preening fool with little brain and I loved you and made you a king. What was it I loved in you? You were beautiful, which was something novel for a Scotchman. And you could stand head and shoulders along side me. You charmed me with your little poems…. Was that all you were? A pretty face on long legs? I was all you had at the end. You had too many enemies and they were always going to kill you.'

'Are you comfortable Madam?' asks Mary seeing Marie looking wistfully out at the side curtains. Because of her injury, they are having to take a longer route and will stop off for the night to save her too much discomfort.

'Yes… yes I am as comfortable as I can be thank you Mary. I was just thinking of what has happened to us. How long is it now since we came into England?'

'Eleven years Your Majesty.' Mary keeps a mind of every minute of every day that her Queen has been held prisoner.

'And so much has happened. I was thinking of my husbands…' she stops suddenly. 'Oh Mary, I am thoughtless. Forgive me,' she puts a hand out and touches her arm, remembering that Mary Seton's last hope of marriage has gone.

'I am getting over it.'

But Marie knows that it is not so for Mary Seton has shrivelled since the only man she could ever love died in pursuit of her. Andrew Beaton, the man who waited and waited to be her husband, had travelled to Rome to seek an annulment of the vow of chastity that Mary had taken and been drowned on his way back to her. There had been a fleeting moment when Mary had blamed her mistress. She had taken a vow of celibacy to bind herself to the service of Marie Stuart and cut herself off from any thought of marriage or motherhood. Andrew Beaton, Maria's loyal master of the household, was loved by Mary as much as she loved her Queen. And now she grieves for him and will do so unto her death.

There seem to be nothing but agonies for Marie to endure. Every year brings some new reason for her captivity to be extended. James, her son who refuses to talk to her, has been proclaimed King of Scotland without her agreement; suitors for her hand have come and gone, usually in death. And the countries in which she was held in high estate no longer need her. A tear springs from her eye. She listens to the creaking of the cart wheels and the voices of rough soldiers over the clop of their horse's hooves. They see her as no more than what she is; a prisoner, a nuisance who keeps them from the real sport of warfare in the Netherlands, where there is money to be made. She is nothing but a dangerous catholic who should be burned, like the priests who slip in from France.

Even the children are leaving her. Little grandson George, the pride of George Talbot and Bess, is dead two years since. It has made George morose and Bess even more antagonistic towards her. The three of them circle round each other, playing deadly games of blame, each of them accuser or victim as the game demands. The three of them trapped in a cage, being prodded and spied upon by Burghley and Walsingham and Huntingdon on the orders of their mistress, Queen Elisabeth. Marie sits between the two of them, knowing she is the cause of their failing marriage and she can do nothing about it.

But there is always Buckstones. Marie has not been for three and a half years but she looks upon the place as her own little oasis of tranquillity where she can soak away some of the grinding boredom of captivity and find comfort for her painful bones. In the time she has been away from the place she has grown stout. She has become pinched of face and full chinned; the bright look that turned heads in her youth has gone. Lord Leicester, once a suitor for her hand, was polite when they met last year at Chatsworth, but she could tell he was no longer charmed. And Lettice, who had so delighted her on their last visit, is now his wife. There is no reason that either of them should be concerned for her any longer.

'I think we will be stopping soon Your Majesty,' says Jane Kennedy.

The journey is broken at Haddon Hall, the home of young Sir John Manners and his wife Dorothy, who were both the subject of much scandal themselves not so long ago. 'A good bed is what I crave. And hot stones against my back.'

I'm sure that can be arranged,' says Jane, ready to jump down and help her mistress.

The following day the party arrive at Buckstones in the afternoon in fine weather and Marie has recovered some of her spirit. George Talbot is already there having arrived the previous day and has spent much of his time nervously walking the bounds of the town, making sure no one without notice is found anywhere near the place.

'I will not have pilgrims and recusants taking advantage of her presence here! This place will become a shrine to her if we do not take care!'

He greets her graciously as usual, if a little wearily. They know each other too well, but he always accords her a greeting befitting a queen. Wherever she is housed she hangs her cloth of state above her chair, but not in Buckstones where she conducts no formal business. Her entourage on this occasion is small; no Claude Nau. Just Mary Seton, Jane Kennedy and a few servants to wait on her, including Robert Tunsted, her gentleman in waiting and Bastian Pages, her ever faithful valet and general factotum.

'How is your back? I see you can walk, albeit with some difficulty,' asks George Talbot solicitously.

She is leaning on the arm of Richard Tunsted. 'In all my riding I cannot recall a fall which has caused me so much pain, George. Either that or the state of the roads.'

'Yes. I must get something done about them.'

'You said that ten years ago.'

'Did I? Well, I have had other things to worry about.'

She lets it go, having acquired a tolerance with her guardians after such a long time. She no longer lashes out intemperately, no longer berates anyone who says "no". She has been worn down by her captivity and now finds that she is drifting beyond the corporeal; looking back on the events and people with a serenity born of her weariness and her faith. Now God is the only person she believes will listen and comfort her.

She has not lost her sharp wit however; her intelligence is not dulled and she has a perspicacity which can catch people unawares; she is still nobody's fool.

'Is Bess joining us?'

'No,' he says sharply.

'And are you staying?'

'Of course.' He rubs his hands consciously. 'My hands are stiff. I will bathe and drink some water.'

'And is anyone else coming to stare at me?'

' My children, Francis and Ann will come tomorrow, but I am not aware of anyone else.'

'Good. I like being on my own.' She says sarcastically.

'You know she forbids it...'

'I know George, I know. But I cannot think of a single person whom I have met here who would make off with me. On the contrary, most of them just want to stare at me, like some caged animal; want to boast to their friends about how they took dinner with that dangerous woman!'

But there have been other visitors with more than idle

curiosity. Francis Rolleston and Sir Thomas Gerrard for instance, two die hard recusants came to Buckstones and plotted her escape some years previously. The young man holding her arm is of a Catholic family who, given the chance, would do anything to aid her freedom.

'We cannot stay long,' says George.

'I trust sufficient time for both of us to feel the benefit.'

'Oh yes. But time is ever at my heels and I have much to do'

'And time is ever in front of me and I have so little to do.'

They fall silent for a while. They find it is best to say nothing at awkward moments. After a while she says 'We have both suffered since last we were here, George.'

George smiles limply. He has lost not only his favourite grandson but his eldest daughter, Catherine, the Countess of Pembroke who has died recently. 'Your losses have been as great as mine. Your wife should be here by your side.'

'Huh! She would merely add salt to the wounds. She never thinks to die and leave me in peace!'

'I feel sorry for you George. You need someone who will comfort you. She must have loved you once.'

The two of them are sat near a window in the long room. He takes some wine and laughs. 'My wife, the good Countess, Lady Cavendish would rather make love to the bricks and mortar of Chatsworth than be in my bed! And lie there with my money as well.'

'She has not been at Sheffield for some time,' says Marie, quietly adjusting a cushion behind her to ease the pain in her back. 'I miss her. Our sewing together. She is very good at that. She can be hard but she is shrewd. And single minded. Her family is all to her. You must have known that when you married her.'

George strokes his beard and blinks, a habit Marie has noticed when he is agitated. 'She has no compassion or understanding of my feelings. She can be very cruel when she wants to be. Not like my first wife, Gertrude. She understood me better.'

'Under his thumb', thinks Maria. 'A mouse, by all accounts, who was quite terrified of him.'

'Bess does not treat with you well. She should allow you some discretion in the discharge of your duty to your office.... and to me.'

'Huh! She thinks only of her precious houses and her precious children who will inherit the earth. And she also has the good opinion of the Queen; Lord knows what foul slanders she has spread about me when she was at court!' George stands up abruptly, his agitation gets the better of him and he paces the room. 'I am sick of it! She is bleeding me dry. And now the Queen has reduced the allowance for keeping you and all your people! I am given a paltry thirty two pounds per week to keep you!'

'George, please do not distress yourself. Please, sit awhile.' She gestures the chair and he dutifully sits, crossing his legs and snorting his displeasure.

'I have nothing to offer you but sympathy and prayer. You know that if it were in my gift you would not have to pay anything towards my keep. But it seems that a Dowager Queen in France does not carry the same weight if she is unable to collect what is her due in person. My emissary, Beaton, does nothing and Claude Nau does what he can. It is many years since I was in France and I believe my family have quite forgotten me. Whatever money comes to me, I spend on my household.'

'Do you know how much it costs me?' he shouts on, as if has not been listening to her. 'I spent a thousand pounds on food last year. The guard at Sheffield alone costs me one hundred and fifty pounds each week. Plus other sundry expenses! And then my wife comes asking me to support yet more building at Chatsworth! Gilbert will start his own household and come running to us for furnishings soon for his own place. It is never ending!'

'But I no longer have as big a household as I need or am entitled to. Elisabeth has seen to it that my household can barely keep me. My needs are now few.'

'Huh! You don't know the half of it! You don't see what hoops I have to jump through to keep you in the manner to which the Queen has instructed! To bring you here to Buckstones costs me extra in food, guards, servants, servants to servants, jaggers, animals and their feed… Need I go on?'

Marie sits quietly, whilst he blows himself out. He is red in the face and breathing heavily and wrings his hands.

'Do they ache?' she says quietly.

'What ache?'

'Your hands. You have wrung them constantly since you arrived.'

'Yes. And my rheumatics are no better.'

'May I suggest you go to the baths now and take a good long soak and forget, just for a short while, all your tribulations, George. It will do you good.'

'But you were intending to bathe….'

'It will wait. I will drink some water and bathe tomorrow morning.'

He slaps his thighs, and rises. 'I'll do that! Yes that's a good idea.' He spins round before leaving and looks at her with an expression of regret.

'Thank you,' he says.

Marie smiles ruefully. 'Silly man', she thinks. 'But I do need him to be on my side. I cannot let him go for who knows who may be put in his place?'

Outside the pleasant start to the day has turned cloudy and cool. She had thought to try and walk a little if her back would allow. She stands and stretches and with a hand on the heavy oak table, walks its length and back again, her fingers running along the smooth surface. In the other hand she has her rosary. The room is quiet, save for the creak of the boards as she steps. She stops near the window and turns to Jane Kennedy, quietly sitting nearby.

'Jane, could you please get my book, my writing book. The one with my poems?'

Jane goes to her room and returns with her leather covered writing book, her 'Book of Hours'[2]

'And some water, please Jane. I will sit here awhile and compose something.'

'I have also packed your essay, Your Majesty, the one you started last week.'

'Ah yes.' She smiles quietly. 'My Essay on Adversity[3]. Perhaps I should dedicate it to the Earl of Shrewsbury, do you not think? The poor man has a terrible adversity of his own'

The following day, after she has been in the baths, she proclaims the stiffness and pain to have abated and that perhaps a short walk would aid the recovery.

'Will I need a shawl, Jane? Is the air clement, or is rain yet waiting over the hills?'

'It is fine at the moment.' Jane looks to Mary Seton for the appropriate words to tell her Queen that the Earl of Shrewsbury has forbidden her to step out of doors.

'Your Majesty, the Earl has been instructed to keep you close quartered.' Mary does not believe in beating about the bush.

'Meaning I cannot step out for fresh air?'

'Yes, I think it does.'

'Is the Earl about? Is he here to see me?'

'I believe he has gone to the baths. Once he knew you had finished there he went in directly.'

'Good. Then we will step outside and if there should be any complaint from one of his guards, we can tell them we have the Earl's permission.'

'But will that not make him angry if he finds out?'

---

[2] 1579
[3] 1580

'Things could not be any worse, Mary. The Earl's temper is something I have come to live with. If Queen Elisabeth finds fault with how he keeps me, that is his problem. It is not I who makes his life terrible.'

The two ladies look at one another and move to help her prepare.

'We will not go far. I do not think I can walk much anyway. We will go to the well, just outside the walls.'

Gingerly, Marie walks out of the Hall, past the guard at the front door and beyond the walls. They stand in front of the small stone built structure which covers the well dedicated to St Ann. The keeper of the well, an old woman, had been told to leave her duties until called back at a more suitable time. She did not know why, and complained bitterly to the Earl's man that she will loose the few pennies she receives from visitors. What will she live on?

'Before Thomas Cromwell had the place knocked over and the statue of St Ann removed it was a place of pilgrimage, you know.' Marie speaks quietly to her companions. 'People came from all over England to drink the water and pray for a miraculous cure to their ills. There were hundreds of walking crooks and sticks left behind by the poor souls who found comfort. They were all taken away and destroyed.'

'The Protestant way has much to answer for, Your Majesty.'

'It does but not all are devils. Only those who would break things, like King Henry, my great uncle, who believed the only way to change man's faith was to knock down their houses. How wrong he was. You cannot force a man to worship what is not natural to him; what he has been born with. Faith is enduring.'

'But they try Your Majesty and they would turn us all with their new prayer books and bibles.'

'Do you know John Knox called me Satan's whore once? Called for me to be put to death.'

'He was not a man who cared for women. He had no kindness about him. I did not like him,' says Mary.

'But he had the orators skill and turned heads; A Cato of Scotland who could persuade my council that red was black. And he had the ear of Elisabeth. When I first came back to Scotland, he and I debated long and hard. He was surprised that a mere woman knew so much of moral and religious philosophy. But, like all men, he got his way by denouncing me for being a woman.'

'Would you like to sit Your Majesty?'

'No thank you Jane. But I will rest on your arm, if it does not discomfort you.'

The three women stand, quietly with Marie still tall and up-right, a stark figure in her black dress, flanked either side by her most loyal waiting women. They too are dressed sombrely. There is no sound other than the rustle of leaves in trees above the cliffs. The three of them form a melancholy tableau in grey light, for the clouds are low and threatening.

'I would like to pray.' She looks at her companions. 'St Ann can be our chapel.'

The three ladies bend their heads as Marie intones:

> *'O Lord our saviour, give me perfect patience under my*
> *suffering*
> *And the grace to amend my life,*
> *That I may be worthy to be named with those sufferers*
> *Who have willingly carried their crosses in the world.'*[4]

She squeezes the hands of her friends. 'I owe both of you so much which can never be repaid on this earth,' she says, with tears in her eyes.

When George Talbot is told of Marie's excursion, he is more agitated than ever.

-----

[4] From the Essay on Adversity

'Your Majesty, you jeopardise the chance of ever returning to Buckstones if it be made known that you strayed outside the walls.'

'Did my cousin tell you that, George? Is she now so terrified of me, a crippled woman with no country, no force and no persuasion left to unseat her, that she would box me up and throw away the key?'

'Your Majesty, you know that Our Sovereign has the interests of the whole nation…'

'I have heard enough of what my cousin does for the nation. And I know what she does *not* do for me. Don't worry George, I will not be your responsibility much longer. I sense that my time on this earth will be drawing to a close.'

'But whilst you are under my roof, I must account for you and your safety.'

She laughs quietly, 'My safety is now the responsibility of my Lord and Saviour. My contentment now lies with God.'

He says nothing, but pulls at his beard and blinks wildly. There is nothing he can say.

She moves towards the door. 'I will lie down before dinner. Are we many tonight?'

'No, just the family and one guest and his wife. Sir Robert Stapleton.'

'I hope they have been vetted by Walsingham. They may have come with an army to release me.'

In the days she spends at Buckstones, George Talbot stalks the rooms, ever watchful that she does not venture out. But she spends her time bathing, writing her essay and letters. One of these is to the Earl of Leicester, whom she met the previous month at Chatsworth. It was a happy meeting at which two minds were able to discourse on a wide range of philosophical subjects, which annoyed Bess who is not as acute as they. The Earl left Chatsworth sorry that such a mind was not allowed an audience with Elisabeth. Any question of a meeting between the two queens is well past reality, now that the threat of the Catholic menace had increased.

My Lord,

I had not time to say my goodbyes at Chatsworth as I found myself being escorted back to Sheffield on the same day that you were hunting with the Earl of Shrewsbury. But I do thank you most sincerely for your conversation and kind words; it is unusual and gratifying for someone as close to my cousin Elisabeth as you are, not to be tainted with the ignorance or prejudice of so many at court. Huntingdon treats me with disdain and those who would curry favour with her, in expectation of advancement through denigrating my position, are no better. Humility and forgiveness are not the virtues of the ambitious.

I have written so often to the Queen and received such a paucity of answers that I am loathe to ask anything more. But positioned as you are, I would deem it a great service if you would write and tell me of her temper. His Holiness the Pope has sanctioned my right to sit in joint reign with James, my son, in Scotland. James' mind has been so poisoned with un-truths about me that he is even prevented from writing to me. Argyll and Atholl make sure that he refuses to acknowledge such an arrangement and I know not what Elisabeth thinks. Perhaps she is too taken up with marriage plans with the Duke of Anjou. But I can do nothing but repeat what we discussed at Chatsworth. My soul purpose in life now is to ensure that the ordained and legal order of Kings is established for both our countries. I trust by now you have uncovered the truth about Huntingdon being favoured over my rightful claim in the succession to Elisabeth and acquainted her with this duplicitous move. I want nothing of Catholic restitution in England, but only to let those who will, practice the true faith. I am no dissembler, no diplomat and no plotter. Surely you of all people can see that I pose no threat to anyone and want only that which has been decreed by God.

My captivity has taught me both humility and patience. I am given to reflecting on the diversity of human afflictions and the accidents of this mortal life. We are all sinners and the worst sins of all are those committed not against others but against ourselves. There is but one way to cleanse our worst thoughts and that is in prayer and forgiveness which I practice every day.

You were kind to me and I shall treasure your words of sympathy. My Lord Shrewsbury too speaks well of me, but is constrained by his position. I know the purpose of your visit was to reconcile the differences between the Earl and Countess which have grown wider. I am not a fool and know that I am the cause of this discord between them. Surely it is in all our interests that I am set free? I would go to France and live quietly in prayer and contemplation if allowed to do so. I believe that Elisabeth would not be averse to this but listens too much to those who wish me dead.

I have read the lines you left on the big window. 'Times change and we change with them' I like to think those sentiments were written in reply to the lines I wrote on the difficulty to persuade those who are otherwise so determined to rob me of my rightful place in this world.

Before I forget, how is my dear friend Lettice, your wife? You will remind her of the time she entertained us here at Buckstones and I hope we shall meet again.

And to you I hope your stay here at Buckstones proved efficacious and that your leg no longer troubles you.

Please write when you have had opportunity to discuss my position with the Queen. I look forward to meeting you again.

Yours in hope

Marie Scotorum Reginae

No sooner has Marie finished and chalked the letter than a stabbing pain runs down the side of her body which makes her cry out. Jane Kennedy comes quickly, for she has been with her on many occasions when the pains arrive and knows that there is little they can do, other than help her to bed and keep her warm. When informed, George Talbot feels little sympathy. 'Again! Its not two months since the last time she was in bed. How long will it be this time?'

Fortunately, it is not a severe disposition and Marie is up and about within two days. Her back no longer hurts as much either. But she is very down and sits in her room looking out over the river and cries very often. Slowly her captivity is sucking the life blood from her and her resolve is weakening. How much longer will she endure?

It is late August and the weather generally has been unkind to Buckstones which has frustrated all; George because his hunting has been curtailed and Marie because she has no routine other than of rising, bathing, writing, bathing, dinner and bed. Although others have continued to write lines and messages on the big window this year, she has lost her desire. She reads what has been written and is grateful for the many homilies, most of which are in response to her situation.

There are some lines written which she has not seen and Mary Seton teases her for they appear to be amorous lines addressed to her.

"*Sweetest is that which gives me life*'. What can it mean, Mary? And look, here is another. '*Think about me*'. It is many years since anyone sent me a love note. And with flowers, for there is a drawing of.... What is it?'

'Marigolds, the flower of love. And here is a rose. *I live for the scent of the flower*. He is a very ardent man, Your Majesty.'

'Who is it?'

'I believe it is Sir Thomas Gerard.'

'Oh,' says Marie a little disconsolately. 'Poor Sir Thomas. He tried to rescue me once. I did not know he was hereabouts.'

'And here is the last one he did and drew a pierced heart. Your Majesty, you have a secret admirer,' says Mary teasing.

'Not so secret that he displays his thoughts for all to see. And besides, they might just as well be for the serving maid as for me. Unless Sir Thomas has an army about him and will carry me off to France, I must turn down his advances.'

A few days later, Jane Kennedy and two servants are packing her things, ready for the journey back to Sheffield. Marie sits quietly in the long room, reading from her book of poems, when she is conscious of someone standing in front of her. She looks up and recognises a young man, recently come into the service of the Earl of Shrewsbury as a page. He has come over from Sheffield to help with any last minute arrangements and is favoured by her.

'Anthony, I am so pleased you have come to help. I am still not able to do all I want. Is there any news, anything you have heard on your journey over here?'

'No Your Majesty, nothing that would affect you.'

'I hear you are recently married. Am I known to your young wife?'

'Margery Draycott, Your Majesty. She is the daughter of my guardian, Phillip Draycott, of Staffordshire.'

Marie thinks he is very young and knows him to be impetuous. A little like herself, maybe?

'Your Majesty, I have news of myself, for I will be going to Paris to further my education.'

'So soon? And just married?'

He smiles in embarrassment for it is exactly what his mother has said.

'It is important. I could also be of use to you. And your cause, Your Majesty.'

'My cause?'

He relaxes a little now that he has her full attention

'I know there are many people in France waiting to be of assistance. I too wish to see you restored as our rightful Queen and will do all I can to that end. Elisabeth would have us all killed if we do not recant. There are many already who are dispossessed and flailed for not attending the Protestant service. I will never recant! I will serve you!' He is breathless with the boldness of his words. Marie is taken aback and placates him with a smile.

'Anthony, I must remind you that whatever you may think, Queen Elisabeth is a sovereign queen. You would be wise to keep your own counsel.'

'I do! There are those about me that are nothing but church papists, but I will not bend to the decree of a cast out queen. She is not the true Queen! Why, even her own father did not recognise her. She was the bastard of his whore, Ann Boleyn...'

'Anthony, I would ask you to be more moderate in your opinions, for as much as you champion me I cannot countenance these slurs against my cousin.'

'But you are my Queen! My allegiance is to Rome and to you, Your Majesty.'

Marie falls silent. She has heard that this young man has made indiscreet comments in front of her servants on other occasions.

'Who do you go to see in France, Anthony?'

'Thomas Morgan, amongst others who work for the restitution of the faith in England. But I would be happy to meet any others on your recommendation.'

She ponders. Is he just hot headed? A dreamer, or has he influence. Can he be secretive, or is he just loud mouthed and boastful? She will be cautious.

'I am grateful to you. Let us talk again when we reach Sheffield and I may have messages for you to take to my ambassador and members of my family.'

He has a wide, open face which appears guileless, but she does not know how astute he is. Can she trust him with matters that will put him and her in danger? Can she be held responsible for what he might or might not do?

When she is alone once more with Mary Seton she asks if

he is known to her.

'Master Babington is very energetic, Your Majesty and speaks with great reverence for you. He speaks of you as his Queen.'

'I know. Would you trust him, Mary?'

'Is there anyone you can trust Your Majesty?'

'Only you. And Jane. All others are now unknown to me.' Once more tears start from her and Mary takes her hand and kisses it.

'I will pray for you tonight.'

'Thank you. And I will pray for you. You deserve better than this, Mary.'

The two women make their way outside where a carriage is waiting. 'I hope it is cleaned and fresh straw laid,' she says, remembering the conveyance she came in. 'Which way are we to go?'

'Tideswell and Brough, Your Majesty.'

'No Chatsworth then. *La bon Comptesse* must have returned home.'

*T'Wards me they all change their nature and
their mien'*
1582
First visit in May, of two weeks.

In November 1581, Marie suffers what some think is a 'life threatening' turn in her condition whilst others are convinced it is contrived. At Sheffield she lies in a darkened room, lit by a few candles, windows shuttered, attended by no one but her closest ladies. The news is conveyed to London and Walsingham sends up Robert Beale, clerk to the Privy Council, to assess the situation. George Talbot is panicked. The death of Marie whilst in his charge might not go down well with the Queen of England.

Robert Beale is confounded. Unable to adjudge how serious the situation is, he asks Bess to see her. 'I have seen her worse' is the unsympathetic diagnosis but as a result, Marie is given a little more leeway to exercise beyond the immediate confines of the Manor at Sheffield. She is also given permission to make another visit to Buckstones.

The following May George and Marie travel across the Derbyshire moors in a new coach, paid for by Marie who has received one of her erratic dower payments from the Duc de Guise. The wind is cold as it bangs against the coach but the passengers are well wrapped. Marie has been helped into the coach as rheumatism and weight are taking their toll and it is some time since she has mounted a horse. But despite her physical state, she is looking forward to her visit, brief as it must be. George Talbot too is looking forward to leaving the dolorous cloud which hangs over the family after the death of Bess's daughter, young Elisabeth Cavendish in January. Bess is distraught and he is unable to get close enough to her to offer any kind of comfort. And besides, their marriage is an impasse over money and their royal guest.

He looks at the pale face, now lined with concern. There has been little progress on her dreams of an association with her son and even less progress on reconciliation with her cousin Elisabeth. Hope has faded. He feels pity for her. He feels pity and remorse for himself as well, saddled as he is with three women who dictate his every move. Elisabeth, through Lord Burghley, is ever spying on him, belittling him at court; his wife Bess is draining him of his money and Marie holds him in check, preventing him from leaving his duty as jailor to attend the Privy Council or present himself at Court. Misery hangs over him like a cloud, not lifted by the thought of any of his children who are forever squabbling and demanding of him things he is reluctant to give away, particularly money.

'Tell me George, will our aching bodies ever be eased by the healing waters at Buckstones?'

'Why do you ask?'

'Because this is my fourth time of bathing and drinking at the baths and each year I have some new ailment.'

'But you say that it does you good. Many people testify to it's properties. Perhaps you are not following Dr Jones' advice.'

'Oh, I do, and when I am in Buckstones I do recover some of my spirit. But it is more than the water that makes me feel better. It is being out here, George, away from my little dungeon.'

She looks out at the stark countryside as the coach winds its way slowly along the Causeway and down to Batham Gate. George Talbot has taken a wide sweep away from Chatsworth and over Hallam Head on the old road through Brough. He does not want to set eyes on the monument to his wife's vanity.

'I have not that luxury, Your Majesty for I am ever stationed outside your locked dungeon door.'

'Poor George. Well at least you will go hunting whilst we are there, which is something I am not able to do, whether I can or no.'

'I do not think I will have time for hunting, Your Majesty. Things press upon me and I am here for the water, as you are. Ours must be a short visit.'

'If the weather is anything to go by, we may not even get to Buckstones. It rains again. The month of May is too early for this, George.'

'But you were desperate to come. Her Majesty was told of your condition and sanctioned it.'

'Yes, yes, but I will not be able to set foot outside the Hall.'

'No you will not! There are spies everywhere only too happy to undermine me. Look what happened that time you decided to give some beggars a dress or some such. I never heard the end of it.'

The procession of coach, guards and servants is now strung out, squelching its way along the muddy road, desperate to get out of the cold and wet. There is an absentee amongst Marie's entourage, for Mary Seton is not well and declined the opportunity to travel with her mistress. Mary has been growing weaker and less able to look after her mistress for some time and Marie knows she will have to leave her employ soon to seek a quieter refuge. She might see if she can be sent to a nunnery in France, where she will be well cared for.

Buckstones has grown since her first visit some nine years ago. Sturdy lodgings have been built in close proximity to the Hall to cater for the growing number of visitors. It makes the Earl of Shrewsbury's job of keeping Marie close confined all the more difficult as most of the visitors are well connected to the Court of Elisabeth in some way. He can hardly prevent them from visiting on the grounds that they pose a threat. It is her servants and to some extent, his own that worry him most for he has trouble in identifying who is a true servant and who an intriguer. She is demanding and as a sovereign queen, albeit one who has been dethroned by her own people, she has the right to be treated as a queen.

In the cold blasts of May the numbers of people visiting are few for which he is grateful. She has no more than four or five serving women and an usher and as she is weakened, it is unlikely that she will be disturbed. She keeps to her room for much of the day and ventures down to the baths in the morning and evening with Jane Kennedy and two serving women in attendance.

She had read Dr John Jones' book on the benefits of the waters and now follows his suggested regime. She walks along the passage of the Hall and goes into the principle warm bath, the largest of the three which has the benefit of seating and a fire which is kept constantly lit. She is helped into the bath and sighs with delight as the water closes around her. 'I could just sink down and stay under and all my troubles would be over,' she muses. But her ladies, holding her suspended make sure she is in no danger.

When she has had enough, she is towelled down and sits in front of the fire, warming herself. She looks at her feet. The ankles are swollen and she thinks her pretty feet will never dance again. Her thinning hair, cut short, is rubbed dry and the peruke placed neatly back on her head by Jane, her most expert of hairdressers.

'I must send to my wig maker, Jane. This one is not wearing well.'

'You look as well as ever in it Your Majesty. But if you wish I can send to London for some new ones.'

'Please do so. And give instruction that I do not want it set back as far as the last ones. I have no forehead to show off and frowns are not in fashion. I will leave those to my cousin who I hear, has set her forehead so far back as to be behind her ears!'

Jane laughs at the jest. It is a sign that she is relaxed.

When she is in a dry shift and woollen cloak she is helped back to her rooms. Visitors and servants are hurriedly shoo'd out of sight as she makes her way back along the corridor and up the stairs. She will not have anyone but her ladies see her 'looking like a common washerwoman'.

The room is quite dark but comfortable with hangings on the wall and a fire in the grate. She is dressed and pomaded and sits warming her feet. She wears little makeup, unlike her cousin who she understands wears leaded creams so thickly applied as to make a mask of her face. 'At least, thinks Marie, I still have my looks.'

Next to her on a small table are a jug of spring water and glass which Jane fills and hands to her.

'Your Majesty?' Marie is in a reverie and does not notice the proffered glass.

'What? Oh, yes. Thank you. How much shall I have?'

'Twelve glasses full today and ten tomorrow.'

She drinks slowly and carefully puts the half full glass back on the table. 'I am filled already. My stomach will not take anymore.'

'There is time, Your Majesty. Dr Jones does not specify how long you should take to drink the water. But I am sure it is having an effect for you look better today.'

'I do not feel it. Oh, the gripe has dissipated but I feel… out of myself; unreal, as if I no longer inhabit this place. Who am I, Jane?' She looks beseechingly at her favourite serving woman and tears once more spring from her eyes. 'If this is purgatory, then let me pass on through, for I am certainly not wanted here.'

'Your Majesty, there is always hope. The Lord will provide. He is looking down on you and you will vanquish your enemies. You are his representative and as a sovereign Queen there is no earthly authority who can judge you. It would be a heresy to remove you.'

'Heresies are already committed Jane. Elisabeth is a

walking heresy who should be cut down. But who is there? Norfolk was my last hope. Phillip in Spain is willing as is my uncle Guise but they stall for want of guidance here in England.'

She wipes her tears and finishes the glass of water and sighs deeply. 'Is there word from Beaton in Paris since we arrived?' she says wearily.

'No, but the priest, Samerie is here and he will hear Mass with you.'

'Samerie? Here? I have not seen him.'

'He arrived yesterday with clothing for you and tells the guard that he is a valet whom you have sent for. He has letters.'

Marie brightens. She enjoys a little intrigue, particularly if it outwits her jailor.

'I will see him when the Earl of Shrewsbury is out of the Hall. Please find out what he is doing today and then arrange for the priest to come to my room. I will also have him hear my confession.'

Jane finishes tidying up, removes the towels and garments to be cleaned and leaves. Marie picks up her bible and opens it at random.

'*And the Lord sent an Angel, which cut off all the mighty men of valour, and the leaders and captains in the camp of the king of Assyria.*'[1]

She reads on and smiles when she sees that Hezekiah and the inhabitants of Jerusalem are saved.

Marie and George Talbot stay only three weeks and then make the soggy way back to Sheffield, where once more she takes up her position as lonely captive. Not even the grand-children of the Talbots are brought to her and she misses playing with them. She harries George constantly and begs him to take her back to Buckstones as her side once more

---

[1] II Chronicles 21 (Authorised)

troubles her. He relents and a second visit is made.

Second visit, August, 1582

The Hall is full this summer. The popularity of the baths among those with the money and means to make the journey across forbidding moors is growing and George Talbot, who is not averse to making money from the place, looks on contentedly. He has little else to be cheerful about, as the sight of Bess constantly reminds him.

This evening the party at dinner consists of Marie, the Earl and Countess of Sussex, the Shrewsbury's, Thomas and John Manners and their wives and Sir Robert Constable. There are other visitors who are housed in lodgings near the Hall who have not been invited to dine. Amongst them are Sir Thomas Gerard and the Earl of Sussex' physician, Edward Atslowe. These are men who have attracted the attention of Burghley and Walsingham for their unashamed support for the Scottish Queen. George thinks it safer to keep them at arms length.

Marie has insisted that Barbara Mowbray, newly arrived back into her service from Scotland, accompanies her, together with one of her secretaries, Gilbert Curle.

Thomas Radcliffe, Earl of Sussex is not a young man. He is gouty and his wife, Frances, helps him to the table, next to the Queen. He and Marie have never met, but she is only too well aware of the part he has played in her tragedy over the years and this is an opportunity to see how well he favours her now.

Frances Radcliffe places herself next to Bess the better to hear the latest gossip about their illustrious prisoner.

Barbara Mowbray helps Marie into her seat and props a pillow behind her back. 'Sit close by, Barbara. I do not know how long I wish to be in company.'

Thomas Radcliffe leans into the Queen and welcomes her in French. 'I came to Buckstones first in 1575. Not sure what good it did me. Frances insisted we come back. Thinks it will cure my various ailments. I tell her you can't cure age, but she thinks differently.'

'It depends on whether you believe or not. Dr Jones says that in order to feel the cure, one must pray to the Queen of England, the Earl and Countess of Shrewsbury and all their offspring. Personally, I prefer to pray to God and let the waters do what they will.' She takes a sip of wine which has been poured into her glass. 'I drink a lot of water whilst I am here too. Water by day and wine by night.'

From down the table, George is eyeing his two senior guests with apprehension. He does not want Marie dripping slanders into the Earl's ear about how badly she is treated. He is not sure where Sussex stands on the Queens' rights and does not want any intriguing conversations between them. Bess knows what Sussex' views are. She has made it her job to find out from Frances Radcliffe and has little worry that the Earl will spirit her away.

Marie has been in Buckstones for the past week and has welcomed the change from her claustrophobic quarters at Sheffield. The weather has been kind and she has taken advantage of the warmth to insist that she is better served by being in the sunshine, than cooped up in the Hall. George relents and a canopy is erected near the river under which table and chairs are placed where she writes her letters and reads her bible. Her eyes of late have begun to let her down which means she finds needlework does not satisfy as it once did although she has brought some small pieces to finish.

'What news of my cousin, my Lord? Does she send you here with news of my release or to spy on me?' She asks whilst being served a thick slice of beef.

'Neither, Your Majesty. I am here for my health and that alone.' He does not tell her that he has agreed to appraise his great ally, Lord Burghley, of his visit.

'And what of her marriage plans? You were always her emissary to the various princes and kings of Europe? Will she ever marry?'

'Events in France have precluded any further matrimonial developments. Her heart, as you know was given to the Due d'Alencon, her little 'Frog', but the Council was lukewarm...'

'Her heart belonged to Robert Dudley, until Lettice captured him.'

The concern is now the Netherlands, Your Highness' He is guarded in his replies, knowing the reputation of Marie as a skilful manipulator of words. He only has to look at George Talbot to see how well she has played him. Even now George is blinking furiously and paying little heed to Sir Robert Constable sat next to him, whilst glancing in their direction.

'It would be well for you that she finds a match soon, else she be beyond carrying a child,' says Marie. 'With the birth of an heir, my rightful claim would be set back. You could release me then.'

Thomas Radcliffe sucks noisily at a piece of fish before answering. 'I fear Her Majesty is irrevocably wedded to the people of England and her only desire is to see them safe and happy. It is unlikely that they would countenance a divorce in favour of a foreign match with its attendant risks and upsets.'

'But she signed a marriage contract...'

'For strategic purposes only Your Majesty,' he says with the authority of one who sits on the inside of the Privy Council and knows about these things. 'The people need to be guarded from the predations of Spain and the Catholic French. Closer ties with the house of Valois would have served a purpose but now we prefer to be on our own.'

'She has been negotiating marriage treaties for ten years. The whole of Europe wonders if she will ever be brought to bed.'

'Her Majesty is cautious. Marriage is not something to be rushed.'

Marie looks at him sideways and smiles. 'Unlike me, I suppose who was ever reckless in that regard.'

'We all follow our hearts and put our trust in God in such

matters. Your Highness.'

'You once championed my suit with my Lord Norfolk...'

'I was a dear friend of his, yes but cautioned him to think long and hard about such a match. The people of England do not wish to be turned upside down, as was the case with the last Queen. There was already a stirring of discontent in the North as you well know and a Catholic marriage would have set malcontents against good order. Civil war is for France. Not England.'

'You underestimate how many of Elisabeth's people still cling to the old faith my Lord. No matter how many Acts are passed and how many people are tortured, she can never turn those of true faith. No Act of Persuasions will deny us our right to the liturgy of the true church.'

'I fear you may have been too long away to hear or understand the public mood. The tide has retreated from the Roman church. Why, even most Catholics are loyal to the Queen.'

'Out of expediency, my Lord. No man is willing to profess his true faith in the knowledge that he may be racked or branded for not attending your church.'

I abhor such fanatical practices Your Majesty. Far better to change a man by persuasion than by force...'

'That's not what I heard about you in Ireland, my Lord.'

He smiles wryly. 'Age mellows one. And besides, the Irish are a barbarous people...'

'And the Scots?'

'Now our allies, Your Majesty.'

'And my son James the rightful heir to the throne of England.' She finishes her meal and the plate is removed, to be replaced with another for her to sample the chicken or other small birds that have been placed before her. She declines and insists that the Earl take something more than the meagre helping he has picked his way through. He too declines.

'And where stand you on my association with James in ruling our people in Scotland? '

Thomas Radcliffe mulls over his answer, for he knows that an association with James on the throne and Marie as regent Queen is a chimera. The English Council would never have it and the Scottish Council has vowed never to have her back again. Besides he knows that Elisabeth has sanctioned much closer ties with her son James and Marie has not been included in the bargain.

Your son…. have you had word?'

'Little that is of consequence. I suspect his letters are kept from me. Burghley, no doubt.'

The Earl chooses not to reply for he knows that Marie is no longer of much importance in the merry go round of diplomatic negotiation. And she has been so long out of society she has lost touch with what people are really thinking and doing on her behalf.

Thomas Radcliffe is finding the room hot and stuffy and calls for a window to be opened.

'And my god daughter, Arabella Stuart? Do you favour her right to succession?'

'Your Majesty, Queen Elisabeth recognises the rights of all contenders to the throne. The strength of the case lies in what is best for the country….'

'But I have already given my blessing to Arabella. The Countess of Shrewsbury is now her guardian and will bring her up to be a queen if God so pleases. Elisabeth cannot deny her divine right.'

'Indeed,' he says warily.

As the two talk, food and drink is delivered in an endless procession of plates and tureens by softly shod servants. Bess is keen to impress the Earl and Countess of Sussex with a lavish table. But the Earl is off his food and the salvers of meat and fish pass him by without stopping. His illness, which he swears he caught in the Irish colonies, takes its toll and his wife looks at him anxiously. Marie is conscious of his flagging spirit but is equally anxious to leave him with a good account of herself. 'Perhaps tomorrow we may continue our talk, my Lord. There is much I would have you convey to the Council and my cousin. If you will take some letters to her…'

'I will do what I can. But now I will retire, with your leave, Your Majesty. I do not feel up to any more. It is too warm and stuffy.'

The Earl of Sussex is helped out by his attendants and his wife follows. Marie now senses the interest has turned once more towards her.

'I must congratulate you Bess, on a splendid board. It cannot be easy to produce such food out here in the middle of nowhere.'

Bess is not quite sure if this is a compliment or not.

'Your Highness is too kind and I notice that you have paid me the ultimate compliment by clearing your plate.'

Marie bows her head and smiles. 'I too will retire. This new bathing regime tires me a little.' Barbara Mowbray moves to assist her mistress and together they leave the long room.

'George, I will bathe early tomorrow and if the weather is as fine, I will sit near the river, as today.' She walks slowly to the door, her feet and ankles swollen but she will not show the pain. George Talbot follows her with his blinking eyes and then turns his attention to the rest of the party.

There is only one other inn within the confines of Buckstones, worthy of the name. It is sparsely furnished but serves an adequate meal and indifferent ale. Dr Edward Atslowe and Sir Thomas Gerard are found in a private room, finishing their meal. The two men are known to one another, although they have not met up for some years. Both men have suffered for the cause of the Scottish Queen and Edward Atslowe is watched, even here in Buckstones. It was on his suggestion that the Earl of Sussex attend the baths which gave him an opportunity to visit the north where men sympathetic to Marie are to be found.

'Your health, Thomas.'

'And to the true Queen, Edward.'

'To Queen Marie of Scotland….. and England.'

They drink and call for the plates to be cleared. A bottle of brandy is produced and they set to discussing the state of the Catholic cause in England.

'You know that plans are being laid,' says Atslowe cautiously. 'I have recently received letters from Morgan in France that people are making arrangements for her release and …other things.' Atslowe must be careful about what he says and to whom. He trusts few people and although Sir Thomas was imprisoned in the Tower ten years previously for plotting to kidnap the Queen, he has remained silent since then. Has he been turned? Can he be trusted with news that might take them all off to the executioner?

Sir Thomas pauses. 'Marie Stuart is very dear to me. I would see the people of England welcomed back into the Church of Rome with her sitting in her rightful place. The terrors and persecutions grow worse.'

'And how have you found her?'

'As you see her. Melancholic, often ill, lonely, but still proud.'

'Does she give way? Is she still resolute?'

'She still talks of freedom but it is difficult to know what is in her mind. She has placed herself in the hands of God,' Sir Thomas Gerard is a passionate man. As he pours water into his brandy he says, 'It is clear that the Devil's Bitch will never release her and Burghley will have her head from her shoulders as soon as he can manufacture a reason.'

'You are right. But there is hope.' Atslowe leans forward. 'Thomas, there are great movements taking place which if they can be fashioned, will see Marie Stuart on the throne of England. Phillip of Spain and her uncle, the Duc de Guise, are willing to support a rising and send troops.'

'How so? We tried before. What is different?'

'There are men of substance here in England, willing to take up arms; willing to lay the foundation for a force to land. There are thousands who will rise once the flame is lit.'

'And these thousands? They are ready and waiting, for I have no intelligence of such a mighty movement.'

'I am but a cipher in the scheme of things. What is told to me is but a small piece and I know that people are working for her freedom in Spain, in France and here in England.'

Sir Thomas is not convinced. 'Edward, you know that my heart lies with her, but the forces against us have strengthened too. When I and the Stanley's were prepared to snatch her from her captivity she was allowed some measure of freedom outside the confines of her prison; riding and hawking on the moors. But that is no more. Shrewsbury keeps her much more confined under the instruction of Burghley. Besides, she has not the strength now.'

'We are not in the forefront Thomas but we can play our part; some letters and communications. We are trusted by the Queen and can keep her informed.'

Again Sir Thomas pauses. 'Do you know why the last attempt failed; that impossible scheme to snatch her off the moors whilst out riding? Because she was not for it! She believed that the Duke of Norfolk would raise the North and carry her off as his bride! Well, we all know the outcome of that. The richest man in England together with the cream of the nobility could not defeat Elisabeth. We were as nothing and too few in numbers.'

'This time, men stand ready...'

Where? Where do they stand, Edward? Here on English soil or in France and Spain?'

'Spain fights in the Netherlands, just across the water. The Duke of Alva has an army which will be sent over. Elisabeth has nothing to match that.'

'The Duke of Alva is too busy fighting there. He has no troops to spare. And besides, Elisabeth is sending aid against him, so that he is kept there.' Again he pauses. 'Who stokes these embers, Edward?'

Edward Atslowe bends his head lower. Names are the passport to the block. Names, racked and manacled out of screaming lungs can break a whole carefully laid plan and condemn even the innocent to death. 'The Spanish Ambassador, Mendoza. Henry Howard. Francis Throckmorton and others.'

Sir Thomas laughs lightly. 'Mendoza, a Spaniard with no more than his King's interests of invasion at heart. In my plan back then, it was Ridolfi, an Italian who had the ear of the King of Spain and the Pope. He was a dreamer too. Henry Howard? Revenging his brother's execution. And this Throckmorton, is he of any substance?'

'He has been with the Queen's ambassador in Paris and returns with great enthusiasm. There are still others. Paget who is in the employ of Queen Marie with James Beaton, her ambassador. And Anthony Babington who is in Paris as well and known to her. These are all good men, Thomas.'

Thomas Gerard sits quietly for some time. 'I spent two years in the Tower for our Queen. Two years in which to reflect upon what had gone wrong. I was betrayed, you know; by that rat Rolleston, God rot him. But there is one thing you may not know. Had we succeeded in kidnapping Marie Stuart, I would not be sitting here now. They would have hung four parts of my body around the country and put my head on a spike on London Bridge! Why? Because we had no idea what to do with her after we sprung her. And more importantly, when we looked behind us there was no one there! The people of England do not want a war, Edward. They want peace and most of them will pay the price of silence to keep it that way.' He drinks down his brandy and wipes his mouth. 'And whatever you do, do not tell anyone else what you have just told me. It will be your death warrant too.'

Edward Atslowe is surprised and upset at the vehemence of

his friend. He had hoped that Thomas Gerard could be relied upon to help influence an uprising in his home county. 'I fear you have turned, Thomas. Those are not the words I expected of you…'

'I am no coward if that is what you think. I will carry letters to her whilst she is here in Buckstones but I will not join this band of dreamers. Unless I can see an army of fifty thousand marching down the North road, you will have to do without my service in arms, Edward.'

The two men remain silent, thinking about the others motives. The youthful exuberance which saw Sir Thomas involved in the reckless scheme to save Marie ten years ago has been damped, although his faith burns as brightly as it ever did. His son John has picked up his mantle of Catholic zeal and is even now in France with the Jesuits, preparing to return and proselytise.

'Does the Earl of Sussex provide you with intelligence that may be useful to the cause?' he asks.

'Not much. He is ill and speaks of little but his ailments; asking my advice on how much water to drink and what foods to eat. The Buckstones wells will bring him some relief, but I do not see him living long.'

'And our Queen? Have you had chance to talk with her?'

'A little. She has been out of doors but Shrewsbury keeps a guard around her and prevents anyone from approaching. Otherwise, she keeps to her room and ventures out only when going to and from the baths and then not even a doctor is with her.'

'So we do not know of her health?'

'Oh yes. Gilbert Curle has furnished me with some details. She suffers with a pain in her side, and last year had violent pains in the stomach which caused her to vomit blood. Her rheumatics are stiffening her joints which is why she is here. Dr Bayley has visited her at Chatsworth and we consulted and agreed upon a cure. But the only real cure is to be found in her release.'

'I will try to see her as well. Are there messages that need to be taken? I go back to my estate in Lancashire if that helps.'

'Curle has prepared a bundle for me and I will take them on my return with the Earl of Sussex. At least I will not be suspected whilst in his company.'

I wish you luck, Edward. I will pray for you and all those who work for the true church.'

'Thank you Thomas. Let us meet in happier times.'

Marie is made aware that Sir Thomas Gerard is in Buckstones and with Gilbert Curle's assistance, gets a message to him that she will take her bath the following morning at nine thirty. If he happens to be walking through the Hall, she may bump into him.

As Sir Thomas lingers in the gallery the following morning, there is a rustle of movement and Marie and her entourage appear on their way to the baths.

'Sir Thomas Gerard.'

'Your Majesty.' He drops to one knee and kisses her proffered hand.

'It is such a long time but I never forget the kindnesses of those who have helped me.'

'Your Majesty, my heart breaks for you....'

'Now that is something I would not wish. Too much has been broken already. You are in good health and must remain so. With God's help we will all meet in a happier place. It is people like you, Sir Thomas, who keep me alive. I have read the words you left on the big window when last you were here. They are a balm to me. Why, they are the words of a suitor...'

'I mean no disrespect, Your Majesty.'

She is smiling. 'No, no, they make me feel young again. You have chosen to put them in both French and Italian, my favourite languages; the languages of my youth. And marigolds. In France as a young girl, marigolds were every-where.'

'I am glad. There is so little I can do.'

'You must pray. God will divine our future. Here, take this as a memento; for everything you have done for me.' Marie takes from her finger the ring which he kissed and presses it into his hand. 'I have so little to give. So much has been taken...'

Once more Sir Thomas drops to one knee. 'Your Majesty... a blessing.'

'Let us both pray. You will forgive me if I do not kneel.' She turns to Barbara Mowbray. 'A chair please Barbara. And please join us.'

Jane Kennedy too is in the party and the four of them bow their heads, whilst Marie intones softly, the Act of Hope.

Almighty God, with Thy power and infinite mercy, grant us pardon for our sins with the help of thy Grace and life ever-lasting, through Jesus Christ, our Lord and Redeemer, Amen.

They rise 'We must all be strong. Hope is all we have left.'

'Your Majesty, hope will be rewarded. There are many who stand ready to serve.'

'Thank you. And now I must hope that the waters will ease the stiffness in my bones. Prayer alone is not enough'

She walks slowly away with Sir Thomas looking after her with tears in his eyes.

Before he leaves, the Earl of Sussex, in a spidery hand, writes to Lord Burghley, about his stay at Buckstones. He relates how his conversations with Marie yielded nothing that his Lordship would not know already and that she was 'becalmed.' Whether this was in anticipation of some further attempt to release her, or an acceptance that she would spend the rest of her life in confinement, he could not say. She was still in great hope of reconciliation with her son and seemed unaware that he was playing her false.

It was also noted that both Sir Thomas Gerard and his own doctor, Edward Atslowe, were in close conversation on numerous occasions but he could not say what about. The Scottish Queen dictated many letters to her secretary Curle, and he presumed they were smuggled out, possibly by Gerard or Atslowe, or both.

He hoped that Lord Burghley would be able to avail himself of the healing waters some time soon which would give him the opportunity to see the Scottish Queen himself and come to his own conclusions about her state of mind. He also remarked that the rift between the Earl and Countess of Shrewsbury had widened and that they were hardly on speaking terms which made for an unpleasant atmosphere.

'Alas, what am I? What use has my life?'

1584
June and July

George Talbot looks dreadful. He has been brought to Buckstones in a litter on account of his weakened state, brought on by worry, anxiety and a general malaise which has debilitated him to the point of exhaustion. The war between he and Bess has spiralled downwards and the less he is in the company of his wife, the better. Marie has taken the opportunity to come over with him because she too had not been well again that winter. Permission was sought and grudgingly given by Elisabeth who is being increasingly urged by her Council and Parliament to agree to a 'final solution.' Elisabeth is more cautious. The whole of Europe stands watching and she will not commit an illegal act. She will not have her cousin dying unnecessarily either. George has asked Robert Dudley, the Earl of Leicester, to meet him in Buckstones, where he can seek his advice (or is it sympathy) over the rupture of his marriage. Leicester has already been a confidante on a number of occasions, first with Bess then with George and has found both to be intractable. What good this meeting will do, he knows not. But it will afford him the opportunity to see Marie, for whom he has sympathy. Besides, his leg is playing him up again and the waters might offer him some ease as well.

There are few visitors other than Dr Bayley, there to supervise the treatment of all three invalids, Jane Kennedy, Gilbert Curle and Barbara Mowbray. George and Robert Dudley have their own entourage, but not as numerous as on previous occasions. A strong guard is placed around the Hall, and strangers are kept well away from the town. This is a private visit, made with as little fuss as possible.

On their arrival, Marie is upset to find that she has not been given her usual rooms. They have been allocated to Robert Dudley. George may be out of sorts but he knows that Dudley is an important ally. Elisabeth is forever chastising him for some indiscretion and Robert Dudley will speak up for him at court. She has not forgiven him his unauthorised second visit to Buckstones in 1582 when the Earl of Sussex was there. She is losing his confidence and has talked of removing George from his post of royal jailor, in favour of someone more robust.

The rooms she is allocated are smaller and have less light, as they face the cliff side overlooking the well. She slumps down in the chair and puts her head in her hands. 'This cannot go on,' she thinks. 'One insult after another. I did at least think that here, away from any intrusion, I might have been treated better by George. I ask for so little.'

Her clothes are unpacked and she asks for her books and bible to be placed close.

'Are the Lords Shrewsbury and Leicester downstairs, Barbara?'

'Yes Your Majesty. I heard them coming in shortly.'

'And what is the mood?'

'That I could not tell. The Earl of Shrewsbury is animated and flinging his arms around and my Lord Leicester limps.'

Maria smiles. Her ladies are ever attempting to keep her spirits up with small anecdotes of who is doing what to whom.

'I am accused by Bess of having carnal relations with that silly little man you know? Supposed to have lots of bastards by him. He does nothing but bleat to anyone who will listen that *la bon Comptesse* is bleeding him dry. He thinks nothing for my reputation!' Marie fiddles with the books on the table, straightening them. 'Did you bring my embroidery?'

'Yes Your Majesty. Would you like it now?'

'No. The light is not good enough.' She sighs heavily. 'You know I have written to my cousin, telling her about all the lies that Bess has been spreading about her. Two can play at that game.'

'No Your Majesty, you did not say.'

'What else can I do when my enemies will not confront me? That stupid woman made me so angry with her lies and jealousies that I could hold back no longer. If I continue to be held against my will, illegally, then what recourse do I have when my reputation is so besmirched? I asked to come to court to clear my name, but oh no! The council would not have it. So I wrote to Elisabeth, telling her all the stories Bess related about how Elisabeth herself plays the bawd with my Lord Essex; how the Court mocks her, laughs behind her back.'

'Was that wise Your Majesty?'

'Wise? Probably not. But I have little left with which to fight other than to cry out, to howl and keep howling until someone takes pity.' She pauses. 'What time is it?'Barbara looks through the window. It is not easy to tell, the sky is so overcast but she guesses it to be late in the afternoon.

'I shall eat here in this room this evening. I do not feel in the mood to talk with the men.'

'Yes Your Majesty. Shall you go bathing before eating?'

'Yes. Yes that would be lovely. I can float my cares away.'

'I will arrange it at once.'

Downstairs in the long gallery, George Talbot and the Earl of Leicester are seated either side of a flagon of wine and some food that were prepared for their arrival. Serving staff keep to the shadows. Of late, George Talbot has been terrorising the staff; accusing them of betrayal and spying on him. Recently he impetuously sacked two members at Sheffield who had been in his pay for twenty years. Times for all are turbulent.

The Earl of Leicester listens patiently. He has heard most of it before but owes it to both George and Bess to seek some kind of reconciliation. He has recently concluded a marriage agreement between his two year old son and little Arabella Stuart which makes he and Bess allies. George Talbot will speak in his favour against his rivals, particularly the Earl of Sussex with whom he has recently fallen out again.

'George, you know things cannot go on like this. Have you not enough worries and concerns with the Scottish Queen? She needs to be more closely kept if poisonous plots like the episode last year with that ridiculous Throckmorton are to be prevented. He's just been executed by the way, did you know?'

'Yes I had heard,' he says with little surprise.

'You have too big a responsibility than to be fighting with your family.'

'Her family! She has only one thought in mind and that is to better the Cavendish name in favour of the Talbots! She would deny me everything if she could.'

'But you have both suffered more than most. First Francis, your eldest and then Margaret dying. And Bess losing Elisabeth and having little Arabella without her mother. It is more than any family can stand. And now your heir, Gilbert also at dispute with you.'

'Its that fucking wife of his! In cahoots with her mother to rob me of everything I possess!'

'But such turmoil, George….'

'That ridiculous son of hers, William, actually denied me entry to Chatsworth! My own house! And the whelp swore at me, called me a disgrace who was not fit to be in the shoes of his own father! I will see him swing for it!'

George Talbot rises and knocks over his glass of wine in his anger. He paces the room, blinking madly and banging his fists together. A servant ventures to clean up the spilled wine.

'Get out you cretin!' He aims a kick at the man, who backs

off hurriedly.

'George, George, calm yourself! Please. Sit again and let us be rational.' But George is not listening.

'Actually barred me entrance! That bitch has no right any longer to any of the properties and lands that came with her to this marriage. Nothing! Any trust set up in her favour by that Cavendish husband of hers is forfeit after what she has done to me!' Leicester says nothing, hoping that George will burn himself out. Once more he paces the room. He is red in the face and any malaise he suffered on the journey over is being burned up in his fury.

'Let her bugger off to Hardwick. Stole that from her brother anyway! He turns once more on Leicester. 'Took all the best plate from Chatsworth with her too. But I sent my men in to teach that ungrateful, lying, pox ridden family a lesson! Laid about them! I am master in my own house and will remain so!' He wipes his face and paces even faster up and down the room.

Robert Dudley sets his glass up and pours some wine. 'Drink this and let us talk no more of these things awhile. We are both well away from our respective troubles so let us just enjoy the interlude whilst we can. No one to worry us. No one to make demands whilst we are here. And in time, we can work out a solution.'

George twitches and scratches and sighs. His breathing is heavy as he slurps mouthfuls of wine.

'One solution would be to rid me of that woman upstairs! I have asked the Queen if she can relieve me of the duty, but she says nothing. She gives me no money and expects me to pay for keeping her, out of a sense of duty! Well, Robert, I am tired. I have been her guard for fourteen years. Fourteen years, without any thanks from our Queen or the council or Parliament for that matter. Instead, I have received nothing but brickbats and false accusations and demands and never any let to attend my duties at court. Is that the way to treat with me, elected to the Garter these twenty years; the Lord Lieutenant of most of the north of England?'

Again Robert Dudley remains quiet whilst he thinks on what to do. He is disturbed by this volcanic change in George's temper. He recognises a man under immense pressure, most of which, he concludes, he has brought on himself.

'Well George, I will do what I can to help both you and Bess. Elisabeth is rightly concerned by this terrible rift between the two of you. That is why she sends me, but I am also here to relieve the pain in my leg,' he says more jovially. 'Her Majesty has desired that I seek some relief and also adjured me to be modest in my appetites.' He taps his stomach which has grown round with too much good living. 'So, you will not need to be lavish as on previous occasions. Heavens, the last time I was here I believe we did our constitutions more harm than good. Do you remember, George? That was some feasting!'

George smiles wanly. 'I remember. They were happier times.'

'Now! I am for changing out of these riding clothes and then a rest before dinner. I presume the Queen will join us?'

'I know not. *She* orders me about too.'

The following day George is approached by his keeper of the house to say that some men are just outside the boundary of the town seeking an audience with him.

'About what?'

'They are aggrieved My Lord that they are prevented from meeting for prayer and other gatherings.'

'Where are they from?'

'Here, My Lord, within the parish and around. Freemen all, farmers and the such. They say they are much inconvenienced as they have no market this month past and no liberty to worship as a body.'

George sighs. One more problem caused by the Scottish Queen. It is because of her presence that these people have been prevented from assembling on Elisabeth's orders. Backward people she calls them; superstitious and susceptible to the false teaching of secret priests. She will have them nowhere near. 'Tell them that they will be at liberty to go about their usual business next month. I will give you notice of the date. But in the meantime, they will have to stay without the town and no assemblies, on pain of imprisonment. Understood?'

'Yes My Lord.'

He turns back into the Hall and heads towards the baths.

'Has the Queen finished her bathing?'

'No My Lord. She has given orders that she will remain there all morning. And possibly this afternoon as well.'

George opens his mouth, ready to swear at the servant and thinks better of it. 'I will go… out. Out! By myself. Tell them!' He walks slowly away, mumbling.

'Yes My Lord. I will tell the sergeant to look out…'

'Tell no one! Alone is what I said! Away from all of you… All your backstabbing and laughing. Tell no one!'

Towards midday, the Earl of Leicester comes into the Hall and enquires after George.

'He is out, My Lord.'

'Out? Where?'

'Just…out. He did not say where.'

Robert Dudley senses the man's unease and presses him no further. 'And Her Majesty?'

'In her rooms. She has recently returned from the baths, My Lord.'

He goes up to her rooms, walking gingerly on account of his leg and knocks on her door and enters on being summoned.

'Your Majesty.' He bows. Marie is grateful for the small courtesy, for few in the Shrewsbury household bother to pay her such due now. She smiles her approval.

'How do I find you this morning?'

'Stiff. The waters have helped a little but as you see I am unable to walk much. I drink the water, as prescribed, though I am never sure what good that does. Are you following a regime?'

'Like you, I drink as much as I can and eat as little as I am able without falling into a faint. As for the baths, I will go in when you have finished for the day, although I do not care for the cold bath. I am too hot blooded,' he says with a smile.

Marie cocks her head on one side and looks at his fine bold face, now sagging, like hers, at the chin. 'You always were on my side Robert. I wonder what would have happened if we had been wed, all those years ago? Would we be on the throne of England now?'

'You are being mischievous, Your Majesty. That was a long, long time ago and Elisabeth would have had our heads off had it been so.' He sits near her and picks up a strawberry. 'Do these grow up here in this cold forbidding land?'

'They were sent me by the French Ambassador. He pities me and sends small presents. Some people still remember me.'

'Indeed, we all do.' He takes another strawberry and wipes his hands on a laced 'kerchief which he draws from his sleeve.

'I have recently heard from my son, who at long last writes that he is in agreement with my proposal that we should rule Scotland, in association.'

'That must please you, Your Majesty. I know you have not seen him for many years.'

'Too many, and what letters I receive are too few. But this could be my freedom.' She straightens, and the old regal look returns. Robert remembers what a beauty she was; tall, handsome and coquettish when the mood took her. 'I have asked James to ensure that any negotiation on the proposal must include my freedom. Lord Gray, my emissary, is in London now, making that very point to Elisabeth.'

'And he will be well received, I am sure,' he says diplomatically.

'And what do you think, Robert. Will my cousin receive the proposal as well as she receives Lord Gray?'

'I cannot say, having not been privy to the proposal, but if anything is to work after such a long time, it is the assurance that you are no threat to Her Majesty…'

'Indeed I am not. My secretary Nau is busy drawing up the heads of proposal. I am giving much away to secure this Association, Robert. I am prepared to give all those who have wronged me in Scotland and those who have held me illegally, an amnesty. I do not want to bear grudge. I look to the Lord to guide me in such forgiveness.'

Robert looks at Marie, and sees the spark in her eye. She really believes that this plan will meet the approval of Elisabeth and the Council. His heart goes out to her, for he knows it is a chimera. The Council and Parliament are busy making alternative plans that will send her to the block, if anyone so much as whispers the word 'insurrection'. She will be condemned as a beneficiary in lieu of any malfeasance committed by anyone and forfeit her life.

'I am prepared to abandon any claim to the throne of England over my cousin. Is that not a generous, forgiving act, Robert?'

'You would give up much Your Majesty. And where would you go?'

'I had not thought. France, probably, where my memories are fondest. But I would be happy to stay here. My only demand is that I be set free immediately.'

'I am sure we would all be pleased with an outcome that satisfies everyone. Our two countries have too much in common now for there to be any further discord…'

'There is no further discord now that James is to succeed to the throne if my cousin has no male heir. No, we still need religious toleration and I have agreed there will be no change to the religion of Scotland. My old tormentor John Knox will prevail over me at last but I demand the freedom for people to worship as they will.'

Robert Dudley sits quietly, mulling over her words and looking into her eyes. There is much pain behind the spark of defiance and he feels he is in some way betraying her, by not alerting her to the impossibility of what she desires. Has she not suffered enough? He knows that James, that "devious little bent son" as Lord Burghley calls him, is not to be trusted. Even now he is polishing up his English and sees no profit in helping his mother.

'And you Robert? Where do you stand? Will you speak for me? I hear that you wish your son to be wed to Arabella. I do not favour that marriage, even if she is my god daughter. I am sure my cousin will like it even less. Is she told yet?'

'No. But I will acquaint her when I return.'

'You must have grown a very thick skin, for she will let fly at you,' Marie says mischievously. 'But I was very pleased when you and Lettice had a boy. I prayed for you both. Lettice was very kind to me when we were both here at Buckstones...'

Just then there is the sound of a commotion under the window. 'Jane, please see what is happening.'

Jane Kennedy leans out and is surprised to see the Earl of Shrewsbury belabouring one of his stewards and shouting obscenities.

'George will be pleased to see me go as well,' she says. 'The poor man is tormented on all sides. I do what I can to help, but as his prisoner, what can I do? Bess is to blame.'

'I had best go down and see what is wrong. I try to help both of them, but...' He shrugs his shoulders and prepares to leave.

He hesitates. 'Marie... Your Majesty...'

'Go on. It is a long time since anyone was informal in my presence.' He steps back into the room and puts a finger to his lip, as if trying to stop himself from speaking. 'You wrote on the big window "*I hate the one who speaks falsely, and who flatters me*" I will never do that. Marie, there are still dark clouds about you. There are still men who use your name to ferment insurrection. They are false friends, the very people to whom you have written. Beware of them. Do not let them use you.'

It is Marie's turn to pause. 'Thank you Robert. I am well aware of what you say. There are many who would use me but a desperate woman will sometimes need to take risks if she is to gain her freedom.'

'Put your trust in God, Marie, for you are on your own.'

'I know. He is now my only friend. I too have read what you have scratched on the windows – "*All in good time*" But I don't know how much good time I have left.'

That night, she cannot sleep for thinking about what the Earl of Leicester had said. Was it a warning? She feels the shadows of death, like the night, creeping up on her.

The following morning, Marie asks that a canopy be set up near the river where she may sit and sew. This is refused. She goes down to the baths, where Jane Kennedy and Barbara Mowbray have to help her into the water because her legs and hip hurts too much. They hold her in a cloth sheet while she floats. She is heavy and the ladies struggle to keep her horizontal. A chair has been lowered into the water and Jane asks if they may place her there for a while, to get their strength back.

'I am sorry Jane. I did not realise that it was becoming heavy.'

They seat her and Jane lifts her legs under the water. Marie lets out a cry of pain. 'It is no good, Jane. My hip hurts so. Perhaps I will leave it for today.'

They help her out with some difficulty and sit her down near the hearth where the fire has been stoked up. 'It is a bit too warm, Jane. Could you move me away, else I will singe. I may be a Martyr but I do not want to suffer the fate of one just yet.'

The two ladies towel her down and Jane carefully dries her hair. It is now thin and quite grey. At nearly forty two years worry, illness and despair have aged her prematurely. The lack of exercise has made her body heavy and leaden. She now stoops a little which means she no longer stands above most people, although when the occasion demands, she can still raise herself up to look down upon others. Her face is now full and whilst her eyes are still amber bright, her lips are drawn into thin anguish.

'Would you rub my feet and ankles, please Jane. They have no feeling.'

They finish at the bath and covered in a large cloak and wearing a tight bonnet, she is helped upstairs where she is dressed; long black dress, short lace collar and cuffs, but no rings which now hurt her small plump fingers. Small pearl earrings are fitted and the gold crucifix placed round her neck. Her peruke is brushed and combed and set on her head with a French cap placed neatly to show some light brown curls at the side. She is once more Marie, Queen of Scotland and one time Queen of France. Before long she is visited by George Talbot.

'So, I am prevented from going outside this building now, George. Are you afraid that I will inflame the religious sensibilities of the birds and small creatures by the river; that they may rise up and slay you in your bed?'

'Your Majesty, there is too much ill feeling towards you for us to take chances.'

'Nonsense! If there are any poor creatures within miles of this place who bear me ill will, it is most unlikely they will get past the guards you have ringed. The servants here bare me no ill will. I wish merely to sit in the sunlight and pass the time in quiet contemplation of a life misused.'

'I…I have the consideration of others to think of….'

'Elisabeth's wrath and your reputation you mean!'

'There are desperate people, who would try desperate measures to kidnap you. Why I thought to bring you here again, I don't know.'

'Yes you do George. To get away from that wife of yours and to bleat into Robert Dudley's ear. You are so easy to read.'

He looks crestfallen. The fight has gone out of him and he had thought Marie might be a little more sympathetic.

'Like you I am no longer master of my own house. Even my own children attack me.'

'Please George, you sound pathetic. If Bess is seeking to overthrow you, you will go down in history as the fourth husband she has got rid of and each time made herself richer by their going. You came into this world with a fortune and she none. And now she will reverse the ordering of things, with her going out with a Cavendish dynasty after her and the Talbot's being but a footnote in history.'

'But I am not to be made fool of! I reserve my right to take all that she brought into this marriage and that includes that monstrosity of a house at Chatsworth. The law of this land says that what is hers is mine!'

'Oh George, you are a fool. She has used the law more wisely than you. Much of her land is tied to her family so that you may not get your hands on it. She is clever. She is at Court when she will and has the ear of your Queen and you... left up here to guard me; banished to the wilderness.'

George is slumped in a chair. His face is mottled and he has developed a tic which causes the servants to mock him behind his back. He looks at Marie with the pathos of an old dog, hoping its master will pat it on the head.

'Well, I cannot help you George. I have fights of my own. I will not forgive Bess for the harm she has done to both of us. I will not grant her audience again.'

'You will not see the children again either, she has made that plain.'

'So be it. I hope that my own son will make amends for that.'

106

George suddenly leaps up and with a roar shouts 'Damn the lot of you! I hate all you women who have caused me this… this wretchedness! A pox on the lot of you!' With that, he stomps off to his rooms.

On the following day a young man approaches Buckstones from the east and enquires if the Queen of Scotland is in residence. The young man is dressed like a gentleman and has two servants and sits a handsome horse. He has a sharp, darting eye and an arrogant air.

The keeper of the Hall is suspicious. 'I will enquire if the Queen will receive you sir, but I know she is often busy at the baths at this time of day. Perhaps you would like to see His Lordship?'

'Not particularly, although I was in his service some little while ago. I doubt he would remember me.'

'The Earl of Leicester is here as well, sir. But he is out hunting and is not expected back till this evening.'

'I can wait until Her Majesty is ready. A meal for me and my servants would be welcome.' He slips from his horse and hands the man the reins and walks through the entrance.

'Who can I say wishes to see her majesty?'

'Babington. Anthony Babington. She knows me.'

Marie has finished her bathing for the day and is surprised but cheered by the news that young Master Babington is paying her a visit. When she has finished dressing she invites him up.

Anthony Babington has brought with him John Ballard the priest, disguised as a servant. Both men kneel before her and she asks them to be seated.

'Jane, could you please give our guests some wine. It is some time since we last met and we have much to discuss.'

Whilst Jane goes to order wine, Babington hastily informs her of the purpose of their visit.

'We have recently been in France and have letters for Your

Majesty. We have been in contact with many people who are for the cause…'

'The cause? What cause is this Master Babington. The only cause of which I am aware was snuffed out last year when poor Mr Thockmorton was caught with some ridiculous idea that my uncle and the King of Spain were on their way to rescue me.'

'No Your Majesty, we are aware of the misfortunes that accompanied that plan but I have been sent to acquaint you with ideas of a stronger sense. Our good friend John here, is on his way to Rome shortly, where the English faction still keep your name alive. The Pope is still mindful to support us in overturning Satan in England. And I have recently been with your ambassador Beaton and Morgan in Paris, where much purposeful discussion is taking place.'

Jane returns with a house servant who places wine on the table. Marie asks him if the Earl of Shrewsbury is about.

'No, Your Majesty. He has taken to his bed. He is not well.'

'Please keep Jane here informed should the Earl make a recovery and inform us immediately.' The servant leaves. 'Pray, continue Master Babington.'

'The letters I bring are from the Duc de Guise and Mayenne. John has letters from the Spanish Ambassador Mendoza.'

Marie sniffs derisorily. 'Mendoza was behind the last plan which failed. Is he any better informed?'

'He is, Your Majesty,' says John Ballard. 'He has been in regular contact with King Phillip in Spain and we are informed that the King grows more determined to overthrow the Queen here in England. He thinks the time is ripening, now that the Dutch are weak and Elisabeth will send troops to support them.'

Marie looks at the two men. Babington still looks so young. 'How is your wife master Babington? Have you children?'

'I have a daughter, Your Majesty.'

'Good. You must look after them.'

Babington is momentarily thrown. 'I will Your Majesty. They are well provided for whilst I have this important work to do.'

'How far are you in these plans?'

'We gather people around us Your Majesty. There is still much to do, but God willing, we will overcome.'

'And you, Father John? You have lost many good fellow priests here. Walsingham and his priest takers grow bolder. Why, Richard Topcliffe has been in this very building looking for priests. He even wrote something on the big window, which you must see, for it tells me to jump into a volcano! You too must be in constant fear of your life.'

'My life is of little consequence if it means I can bring the true liturgy to the people. The word of God is carried by many lips beside mine and I have no fear,' says John Ballard.

'You should know that I am putting much faith in the Association with my son, James to rule in Scotland. I have made certain concessions towards that end and I do not want any foolishness to upset these plans of mine.'

'Indeed not, Your Majesty, but you must have some concern that your son has refused Catholic worship and is in the pay of Elisabeth herself. We would not wish for him to succeed Elisabeth without fulfilling his duty to Rome.'

Marie stiffens. 'The conduct of my son is my business, Master Babington. This agreement being drawn up will provide for the people of Scotland. He will succeed my cousin on her death and will be well advised on that occasion.'

'You should know that we intend to kill this queen and will see Spanish forces in this land, Your Majesty. You will be placed on the throne.'

'Master Babington, I know not how far these plans and plots run, but I will not countenance anything that brings my son's claim to the English throne into doubt.'

'No Your Majesty, it is you we wish to bring to freedom and your just place in the world.'

'And that is something I am happy to countenance. Twelve years I have been held illegally by my cousin and my time is getting short. But I will await the response of Elisabeth to my proposal for Association with James. Until then I will sanction nothing on my behalf.'

'But Your Majesty, you must know that your son James has no intention of agreeing to any such arrangement. Your emissary, Lord Gray is playing you false. Why, half the court laughs at such a suggestion and he speaks only for James. The Association is dead before it is born.'

There is a chilled silence in the room and the look on Marie's face tells the two men that she is unaware of developments in London. She says, haltingly, 'You can be very impetuous in your speech Master Babington and with impetuosity comes cruelty. If what you say is false, then I will have nothing to do with you. Indeed, I will expose you for a traitor.'

'And if I speak the truth?'

'Then I would ask you not to be so arrogant and foolish. My captivity is a great burden to me and I have nothing left but prayer and the shreds of hope that one day I will be free. Whatever you and those who still profess allegiance to me do for my freedom, I will heartily endorse. But do not come to me with lies and half truths for I have not the means to test your veracity.'

'I humbly apologize, Your Majesty. But I must speak the truth. The only means of your release will be through the efforts of those who still love you; who are ready to raise arms against your enemies.'

Marie sits quietly, saying nothing, her brow furrowed. 'How long are you here?'

'Not long Your Majesty. Father John will preach where he can and we will stay at my estate at Dethick.'

'Stay long enough for me to write some letters which I will ask you to take with you.'

'Of course, Your Majesty.'

'Father John, will you hear my confession?'

That evening, when Robert Dudley returns from his hunting, he has supper with Marie in her room. George stays in his bed.

'Robert, why did you not tell me that my plan for an Association with James is still born?'

Robert Dudley puts down his knife and wipes his mouth and says quietly 'Because I am your friend.'

She pushes away her plate and he watches as tears roll slowly down her cheeks.

The final few days are spent in the usual way, with bathing and writing. Gilbert Curle is kept busy writing begging letters to her uncle, asking for money. But some of the more intimate letters she writes herself; those to the King of Spain and Thomas Morgan, touching upon what Babington has told her. She is depressed by the turn of events and keeps to her room.

'Buxton has been unkind to me on this visit, Jane. I do not think I will be back.'

On the penultimate day, there is much commotion as horsemen ride in who do not wear the Shrewsbury livery. Marie looks out and is alarmed to see that these men are fully armed. Have they arrested Babington and John Ballard?

When she goes downstairs, she is met by Sir Ralph Sadler, a man who had dogged her footsteps since her reign in Scotland and her flight to England.

'Sir Ralph, we were not expecting company. Are you here for your health?'

He bows low. 'Your Majesty, I wish it were so, but I am here to escort you.'

'And the Earl of Shrewsbury? I am honoured. You have missed the Earl of Leicester who left for Kenilworth yesterday.'

'I know. We passed en route.' Sir Ralph, with a lifetime of

military service behind him and despite being one of Burghley's chief advisors, is not an unkind man. His experience has taught him that an amenable approach produces easier results.

Despite his easy manner, a sudden chill goes through Marie. There has never been any cause for her guard to be changed and she suspects this sudden change is not to her advantage. 'Where is the Earl of Shrewsbury?' she asks of no one in particular.

He had hoped not to see her before she leaves, but she sees him in the long room.

'George, you did not tell me that we had company on our way back to Sheffield.'

'I don't Your Majesty. Sir Ralph alone will escort you. I have been summoned to London.' The twitch has gone and there is a lightness about him which comes from the break in his routine. 'I go to attend Council business. The first time in twelve years.'

'And you would leave me so suddenly. I am disappointed George.'

'I will not be gone long, Your Majesty, then we can resume our happy bond.'

'Do you know why you go? Is it on my account?'

'No. There are other things happening in the world besides looking after you.'

'But you will enquire as to the progress of the proposals Lord Gray is presenting. We have had no word and it is some time since he went down.'

'I will, Your Majesty.'

'And you will talk to Elisabeth. She will want to know how I fare and you above all are in the best position to tell her that I bear her no malice. Speak for my freedom, George.'

'I will do what I can, Your Majesty, I can promise no more than that.'

George Talbot leaves before Marie's entourage is saddled

up and ready. She spends the rest of the day preparing for the journey back to Sheffield. Sir Ralph keeps himself to himself but late in the day, she asks him which route he intends to take. Her coach has been brought up and she thinks that the route through to Chatsworth, along the river Wye and up the Derwent would be pleasant.

'We don't go to Sheffield,' is his curt reply.

She thinks then it must be Chatsworth.

'We go to Tutbury, Your Majesty.'

With those words her heart sinks. 'Tutbury! I cannot go to that place. It is not fit!'

'Her Majesty will have you go to Tutbury and I am to escort you.'

The thought of the stinking midden that is Tutbury fills her with horror. 'I will not go! My Lord Shrewsbury will not allow it!'

'The Earl of Shrewsbury is no longer your keeper, Your Majesty. I am to hand you into the keeping of Sir Amyus Paulet.'

Marie drops into a chair and stares at the floor trying to understand. 'But why?'

'Catholics, recusants, Your Majesty. There is a stirring in these parts which make it unsafe for you to be held at Sheffield. The Queen will have you quartered somewhere safer.'

'And Paulet! The man has no soul. He hates me! Why is my cousin being so cruel! This will kill me!'

Sir Ralph says nothing. The proud woman who he first escorted from her flight from Scotland twelve years previously is now broken. She sniffs away tears and looks at him with contempt. 'May God forgive you, Sir Ralph for I surely will not.'

Her ladies, Jane Kennedy and Barbara Mowbray are with her as they spend their last night at the little town.

'I have been as content in this place as anywhere in

England, Jane. It is not a pretty place, but it has afforded me some freedom. Now it seems even that small break in the clouds is to close. Rain falls.' She sighs. 'Will we ever return?'

Jane hangs her head. She does not need to say anything.

'No, I think not either.'

Before it gets dark, Marie goes down to the big window, now almost completely covered in scratchings and little drawings, left by so many people over the years; comments and messages to a queen in captivity. She takes off a diamond brooch and with tears in her eyes, writes the lines that will ever be associated with her visits to Buckstones.

Buxtona quae calidae celebrabere nominee lympae
Forte mihi postac non aduenda, vale.[1]

---

1 Buxton, whose fame thy milk warm waters tell
   Whom I perhaps shall see no more, farewell.

Appendix
MAJOR CHARACTERS

Marie Stuart, Queen of Scotland

Born 8th December 1542 at Linlithgow Palace, beheaded at Fotheringhay, 8th February, 1587. Held captive in England from May 1568 until her death. Mother of James VI of Scotland and 1st of England.

Mary Livingston

One of Marie's 'four Maries', maids of honour, who accompanied the Queen to France at the age of five. Married Robert, later Lord Sempill.

George Talbot, Sixth earl of Shrewsbury

c.1522 – 1590. Married three times, lastly to Elisabeth, Lady St Loe (Bess of Hardwick). Custodian of Marie from February 1569 to September 1584.

Elisabeth Talbot, nee Cavendish, Countess of Shrewsbury (Bess of Hardwick)

1527 – 1608. Married four times, lastly to George Talbot. Formidable builder of fortunes and families who built Chatsworth House and the new Hardwick Hall.

William Cecil, First Baron Burghley

1521 – 1598. Lawyer who rose to be Lord Treasurer and close advisor to Queen Elisabeth 1st.

Thomas Howard, 4th Duke of Norfolk

1536 – 1572. Earl Marshall of England. Attempted restoration of Catholicism and marriage to Marie resulted in his execution for treason.

Henry Stuart, Lord Darnley and 1st Duke of Albany

1545 – 1567. King consort to Marie and father of James 1st. Divisive member of the Scottish nobility and unreliable husband. Murdered with the connivance of members of the Scottish council and, possibly, Marie herself.

Queen Elisabeth 1st of England

1533 – 1603. First cousin, once removed to Marie. Finally persuaded by her council to execute Marie for treason. (The Throckmorton and Babbington plots.)

King Phillip of Spain

1527 – 1598. One time husband to Mary 1st of England. Provider of money and support to Marie and Catholics in Europe who desired the overthrow of Elisabeth.

John Lesley, Bishop of Ross

1527 – 1596 Advisor to Marie and negotiator on her behalf. Scottish historian.

James Hepburn, 4th earl of Bothwell

1534 – 1578. Close confident and third husband of Marie whom he married by 'force'. Implicated in the murder of Darnley.

Mary Seton

1541 – c1615. Marie's most loyal lady in waiting who followed her throughout her captivity.

Andrew Beaton

Master of the household. Suitor of Mary Seaton who dies tragically at sea.

Claude Nau

1574 – 1605. Ambitious secretary to Marie and author of a long defence of her life and actions.

Lettice, countess of Essex and then Leicester

1543 – 1634. Visitor to Buxton and lover of the Earl of Leicester, whom she marries on the death of Essex.

Sir Walter Mildmay

1520 – 1589 Chancellor of the Exchequer. With Burghley, tried to negotiate Mary's release back to Scotland, without success.

Sir Francis Walsingham

1532 – 1590. Principle Secretary and Privy Councillor. Chief spy master and instigator of the Babington plot.

Charles Stuart

1555-1576 Brother of Lord Darnley and brother in law to Marie.

Elisabeth Cavendish

1555 – 1582 The daughter of Bess, married to Charles Stuart. Their daughter, Arabella Stuart, was a claimant to the throne of England.

Lady Arabella Stuart

1575 – 1615. Daughter of Charles Stuart and Elisabeth, claimant to the throne of England. Brought up by Bess after the death of her parents.

Jane Kennedy
Maria's favourite lady of the bedchamber.

Anthony Babington
1561 – 1586. Young Derbyshire squire who led the plot to assassinate Elisabeth and put Marie on the throne. Had served as a page in the Shrewsbury household.

Dr John Jones
Published the first medical treatise on the benefits of Buxton water in 1572.

James Beaton, Archbishop of Glasgow
1517 – 1603. Marie's ambassador to the French court.

Thomas Radcliffe, 3rd earl of Sussex.
Lord lieutenant of Ireland and visitor to Buxton.

Barbara Curle, nee Mowbray
Lady in waiting who accompanied Marie to the scaffold. Wife of Gilbert Curle, Maria's cipher secretary.

Dr Edward Atslowe
d. 1594. Ardent Catholic and supporter of Marie. Visitor to Buxton.

Sir Thomas Gerard
d. 1601. Attempted Marie's unsuccessful escape from Chatsworth in 1570. Visitor to Buxton. Father of John Gerard, Jesuit missionary to England.

Gilbert Curle
d.1609. Cipher secretary to Marie.

Robert Dudley, Earl of Leicester
1532 – 1588. Courtier, member of the Privy Council and soldier. Favourite of Queen Elisabeth and visitor to Buxton.

John Ballard, priest
d. 1586. Suspected plotter and visitor to Buxton.

Thomas Morgan
1543 – 1611. A trusted member of the Marie's ambassadorial staff in Paris and double agent of Walsingham.

Sir Amyus Paulet.
Marie's jailer at Tutbury after 1584.

BIBLIOGRAPHY

Alison Weir. *Mary, Queen of Scots and the murder of Lord Darnley*, 2003

Antonia Fraser. *Mary, Queen of Scots*, 1970

Alison Plowden. *Danger to Elisabeth*, 1973

Alison Plowden. *Elizabeth 1*, 2004

Jasper Ridley. *The Tudor Age*, 1998

Ernest Axon. *Historical Notes on Buxton it's inhabitants and visitors*. Buxton Archaeological Society, 1934,1938,1943

Mary Lovell. *Bess of Hardwick*, 2005

E Carleton Williams, *Bess of Hardwick*. 1959

Julian Goodare. *Mary, (1542-1587)*
Oxford National Dictionary of Biography 2004

J Goodacre, *Buxton*, 1928

RG Heape, *Buxton under the Dukes of Devonshire*, 1948

G.O. Storey. *Mary Queen of Scots – A Buxton Patient*, British Society of Rheumatology, 2003

Mike Langham. *Things written on the Glasse windows at Buxtons*. Derbyshire Miscellany, Spring 1998

Thomes, R & JT Leach. *Buxton Hall.*
Derbyshire Archaeological Journal, 1991

JT Leach, *Mary, Queen of Scots, her visits to Buxton.*
Derbyshire Miscellany, 1989

A Jewitt, *History of Buxton.* 1811

Simon Adams, *Robert Dudley, Earl of Leicester.*
Oxford National Dictionary of Biography. 2004

Lee, S & Rachel Davies, *Edward Atslowe.*
Oxford National Dictionary of Biography. 2004

Rosalind Marshall, *Queen's Maries.*
Oxford National Dictionary of Biography. 2004

Peter Holmes, *Claude Nau de la Boisselliere.*
Oxford National Dictionary of Biography. 2004

Wallace MacCaffrey, *William Cecil, first Baron Burghley,*
Oxford National Dictionary of Biography. 2004

Elisabeth Goldring, *George Talbot, sixth earl of Shrewsbury,*
Oxford National Dictionary of Biography. 2004

Alison Plowden, *Francis Throckmorton,*
Oxford National Dictionary of Biography. 2004

P Stewart-Mackenzie ed. *Queen Mary's Book. Poems and Essays,*
1907

Susan Watkins, *Mary Queen of Scots.* 2001

JOHN KANE

Hall Place

1

In which John Kane starts his dinner and recounts his outline for a new play

John Kane steps cautiously towards his dinner. For such a large man he is light on his feet but his kid skin shoes are in danger of being muddied. The rain has been insufferable all day, creating rivulets alongside the footpath making it barely indistinguishable from the road way. The smell of November is of damp, leaf mould and horse dung. The first lamps are lit in the ale houses and shops along the High Street, a flickering glow to light him to his dinner at the Sun Inn.

'No sun here today.' He smiles at the irony.

A cart creaks by, drawn by a horse desperate to drop dead. A head covered shawl squelches past, hanging onto the hand of a yelping child. Two men standing in the lee of a wall, stop their conversation and eye him curiously. 'Good evening gentlemen,' he offers. One touches the brim of his soggy hat. There is little noise in the dusk, save for the bark of a dog, somewhere back towards the Market Place.

His voluminous coat-cape is heavy with rain and he sweeps it from his shoulders before pushing the door to the inn and stepping gingerly across the threshold. Inside, is heard a hum of bodies and the faint crackle of a fire, newly stoked. They greet him warmly, in the way that all popular entertainers are greeted, with an uplift of recognition. He responds to the hallos with a consolatory wave; not dismissive, but as one who knows his worth.

John Kane is an impressive sight; a large head with a mop of greying hair and a face punctured by a snub nose and fleshy lips. His booming voice can hit the back of the gallery in the largest of theatres.

'Mr Kane. Early this evening?'

'Indeed Mrs Mycock, indeed. *He that is of a merry heart, hath a continual feast,....*etc, etc. Is that not so?'

'If you will,' she says and busies past him. 'And your feast will not be long in the making.' She pours ale from a barrel along a wall behind where she stands, into his personal tankard.

'My table…?'

'Your usual Mr Kane. All ready for you.' He is stroking his great coat in the hope that Mrs Mycock will relieve him of it and hang it somewhere to dry.

Mr Kane's tankard is dented and does not sit flat. Beer spills. He stands before her, with the look of a child, his great coat in his arms.

'Give it here,' she tuts.

He laboriously seats himself and turns to the assembly, men all, which is to be found in the Sun Inn on most evenings. This is a place of warmth and rest from the days toils; a place where they can put away the menial and indulge in gossip and warm conversation and there is nothing that John Kane enjoys more.

The drinkers look on approvingly, waiting for him to compose himself. He drinks long. They wait.

'Well, Peter Handyman, what of your day?' They smile and hum once more. He has started with a poser.

'Now't Mr Kane. Weather like…'

'Terrible! Terrible, I know. Reminds me of Cork one year, with an Atlantic gale and enough water dropping from the sky to bathe every man and beast the whole world over. Forty days it rained then and they asked Noah Flaherty to build another Ark!'

The room is now fugged with warm expectation as they laugh politely.

'It was in weather like this that the great Mr Ryley got clean away from the law. In '87 or '88, I can't quite recall. You remember him, of course?'

'Aye,' they murmur. John Kane laughs. 'Yes, clean away with money owing and the sheriff's men in hot pursuit!' He lifts his pot once more and drains the contents.

'But what you may not know, what you may not have heard about our Mr Ryley, is that he is a generous man and did not deserve the shameful treatment at the hands of the officers of the sheriff. Did he not stand me to a good dinner of best Derbyshire trout at the Cheshire Cheese along the way there? And I, as poor as a church mouse, had been in the town but a week as I remember, with not two pence to rub together. Oh yes, a generous man he is.'

Mrs Mycock back in from the kitchen, picks up his empty pot and refills it. She listens over her shoulder to the shuffling feet on the stone slabbed floor, the shuffle of men waiting for something more than a tale of Derbyshire trout.

Peter the handyman asks, 'Is he coming back?'

'Like Will o' the Wisp is our Mr Ryley and I am sure that as we talk here, he is busy arranging a show in Chesterfield or Sheffield. He does not lack enterprise and a debt is not going to hold him back. Indeed, you can put your best breeches on him turning up here with a play in hand that will make his fortune!'

Not that most of his audience are theatre goers. The social niceties of a pit ticket and frock coat do not make up their seasonal routines. Butcher, baker and cabinet maker have other mouths to fill. No money to put into the pockets of Mr John Kane or Mr Ryley, no matter how well they strut upon the Buxton stage.

He loosens the lower button on his waistcoat; stripes constraining an opulent belly. It is worn and the marks of an earlier dinner mar the regimented lines of blue and gold marching down his front.

'Gentlemen,' he addresses them as if it were a private performance. 'Mr Ryley, as you well know was poorly served…'

'But he did owe a debt, Mr Kane.'

'Indeed, but in this profession there are no guarantees as to the security of an income, Mr Hinchcliffe. A man who invests in the theatre has no more guarantee than he who has invested his all in an East Indiaman in the hope that it will return to port with a fortune on board. No sir, patience and a stout heart in our profession, sir.'

Mr Hinchcliffe, a small flint eyed attorney from Macclesfield, is of the 'straight' persuasion although his heart is stout enough. To him, a debt is a debt.

'I beg to differ,' he says in a quiet, legal tone. 'If a man borrows money on the understanding that it will be paid back, with interest, that is not in my book an investment. The money was owing and Mr Ryley was in default.'

The room has gone silent.

'We cannot all be a Sheridan, sir. We cannot all have '*The Rivals*', a roaring success on opening night.' He is growing flustered and looks round at other faces. 'Mr Ryley was ever – is ever – a man of his word sir. I have known him a good many years and a kinder, more considerate and dedicated man you will not find. He is a martyr to the profession. Why, it is not that long since when, faced with one of his principles leaving not hours before a performance in this very theatre, he summoned his wife from Huddersfield, no less, to stand in at short notice. From Huddersfield! Now that's dedication to the thespian cause, sir!'

Mr Hinchcliffe looks unimpressed. 'At her cost no doubt.'

Mr Kane reddens. He finishes his beer and looks round once more for Mrs Mycock. 'Brandy, if you please, Mrs Mycock.'

'But he were a brave man. And a clever one to hop it like he did,' a disembodied voice calls out from the dark side of the fire place. Mr Kane stretches to see who has spoken in his favour.

'And so he was. Was it not a fine thing!'

Just then, Mr Tyrrel, friend and fellow actor, with whom he

has been walking that afternoon, enters the inn together with a rush of soggy air.

'Tyrrel, my good fellow, come and join us. We are debating the merits or otherwise of old Ryley's escape from the law.'

Mr Tyrrel strokes his long chin and drips water from his outer garments as he contemplates the offer.

'Still owes me money,' he says with a jaundiced look. The throng smile, knowingly.

Tyrrel sits and a pewter mug, without dents, is placed in front of him. Mr Kane pours brandy and a little water and toasts the new comer. '*A man hath no better thing in this Sun, than to eat, to drink and to be merry!*'

'In good spirits John. Is this in celebration of the position you have secured in Liverpool for the winter?'

Kane shuffles a little and lifts his glass grandiloquently to his lips. 'It is worth a toast I think, even if it is no more than a Cumberland farce and a pantomime. And a toast to you old friend. You are not easily forgotten.'

Tyrrll bows from the neck. 'Perhaps our Mr Ryley can find room for me in his company. Mr Welch here has packed up for this year and there is no word yet that he will return next year.'

'Mr Welch, I hear will take a season at Chesterfield. But our friend here was reminding us of Mr Ryley, saying that he is not a man to be trusted…'

Tyrrel pauses before answering. 'He's a sharp one, I'll give you that.'

'Did he really stand the sheriff a drink when they got beyond the county line?' The voice has pushed itself a little closer and Kane can see a young man, neatly dressed.

'That is so. And the sheriff's man still with the warrant in his hand.'

'But he went wrong way! He should ha' gone up Goyt Road and across bridge. Only three mile tat' Cheshire boundary there.'

Heads nod sagely at Peter the Handyman.

'There's a drama in this, is there not, Mr Kane? A man dodging the law, hiding in a woman's boudoir, and a chase across the barren hills. That sort of thing.'

'I don't believe we have been introduced, have we?'

'No, sir. I'm newly positioned in the Duke's employ with his agent. Poulter is the name.'

A shrewd observation Mr Poulter. What think you Tyrrel? Is there meat to be had out of the 'Escape of Mr Ryley?'

'Well, you have the title already. Mr Welch might take it for Buxton.'

Mrs Mycock stumps in with a piece of boiled fish in parsley sauce which she puts carefully down in front of John. 'Will you be dining Mr Tyrrel?' she asks.

'I fear not. My wife is preparing something, thank you.'

A small groan of satisfaction escapes from deep within the belly of John Kane as he prepares to eat. He talks at the same time.

'Now, this production, The Flight of Ryley...'

'But is he not with us still? Might he not object to his name being used for such purposes?'

He sits back, masticating slowly. 'Mr Ryley would be happy to sell any part of himself if it will keep him from the doors of penury, Mr Poulter. Is that not so, Tyrrel? Why, I would think he is quite capable of writing the play himself, as he has already written some volumes of his wanderings and mishaps; "*The Itinerant,*" he calls it. You may know it?'

'I doubt he would wish the audience to laugh at his misfortune, John.'

Kane forks food into his mouth. He sips from his brandy glass and wipes his chin. 'But think of it. He could play the lead...'

'I doubt that too. He may be a man who can turn a pretty phrase, but a turn on the stage has often proven to be beyond him,' says Tyrrel, remembering Mr Ryley's inability to remember the simplest lines or stage direction.

Kane puts down his knife and fork with deliberation. 'Let us piece out the plot.' The gathering leans forward expectantly.

'The scene is set outside a public house…'

'It were Shakespeare Inn. Outside,' chips in Nadin the butcher.

'…Mr Ryley is seen chatting to people and seems quite oblivious to the danger that lies in store for him. He is a popular fellow, laughing and cracking jokes with all. In an aside, we see two men talking about how Mr Ryley owes someone money…'

'It was an attorney.' Mr Hinchcliffe reminds him.

'…an attorney. From Macclesfield, I presume.'

'He was. I knew the gentleman in question.'

'Good! May I continue?' says John with some exasperation.

'Now, Mr Ryley has been tricked into meeting the Manager of the theatre at Bath, none less, in the Shakespeare Inn, with a view to transacting a lucrative season. The scene moves inside. The landlady, a woman with whom he is on close acquaintance, hints that all is not as it seems.' His audience, now all attention, let out a low, noise. 'She tells our Mr Ryley that there is a warrant out for his arrest and that he is in danger of loosing his liberty, for an officer is on his way. He pushes her into a cupboard, locks the door and rushes off…'

'Is it to be a comic farce?' a voice asks.

John Kane takes the interruption as an opportunity to swallow his last fork full. 'Should Mr Ryley wish to interpret the events in such a way, it may well be farcical,' he snaps.

'What happens then?'

John coughs, clears his throat and wipes his mouth. 'Mr Ryley had been intending to take the Manchester Coach after his meeting and in great haste, he jumps in and attempts to hide himself. But he is undone, for the sheriffs man spots him, despite his best endeavours…'

'It's a farce alright!' The audience sniggers.

'That is not for me to decide, sir. I am merely the interpreter of the story.'

He is warming to the theme and stands up for better effect. He crouches, as if hiding in the coach and then throws his arms wide and continues. 'Mr Ryley leaps from the carriage and rushes into the inn, where he locks himself in a room. The sheriff's man pleads with him to come out, but he is intransigent. "You will never take me alive," he shouts. "I am a free man, and ever will be!" …or words to that effect.' Mr Kane is now on stage, warming to his audience who sit transfixed.

'Just then, the landlady…'

'Mrs Wheeldon,' reminds Nadin the butcher proudly.

'…Mrs Wheeldon, has escaped from the locked cupboard and rescues our hero by leading him up to her boudoir and locks the door.'

A lascivious hum once more greets the storyline.

"I am unable to pay the debt. My wife and children will starve if they take me!" he pleads.

"I will help. Oh sir, I was ever in love with you. I will save you…"

A cough near his elbow stops him in mid flow. 'John, I do not think Mr Ryley was the sort of man to set ladies' hearts a flutter. As you know he is the most awkward and ungainly man who ever set foot on a stage. He is a pathetic, John, who commands sympathy. Heroic he is not!'

'Poetic licence, Tyrrel. We must pad out the tale to ensure we have the ladies in the audience on his side, surely?'

The thin voiced solicitor says, 'He was still a debtor, sir, however you dress him up.'

'Yes, yes we know that!' shouts John in exasperation, 'but surely such a good man deserves better, sir. He is and continues to be a man of charm and generosity.' Kane stands his ground, hand extended.

'What happens then?' asks Peter the handyman.

'Thank you Peter. At least you have the courtesy to let me

continue with my outline. Well, as we know, Mrs Wheeldon summons a good friend of hers to help him by procuring a horse to effect his escape. Mr Ryley exchanges his coach ticket for the horse with many thanks. He takes Mrs Wheeldon in his arms and with a confession of undying love…'

'But he has a wife and children. I think it goes beyond the bounds of decorum, John.' says Tyrrel, who is a little alarmed at the way the outline is going.

He pauses, caught by his hasty enthusiasm. 'Perhaps you are right. But we will need to spice things up a bit if it is to attract a good audience. The story line will need some work… But now we get to the chase! For our gallant Mr Ryley jumps on the horse, and barely escaping the clutches of the officer, gallops off, up the Manchester Road towards Whaley Bridge…'

'Should ha' gone up Goyt Road…'

'Yes, we have established as much! But he didn't!' John continues with a theatrical flourish. 'He looks behind him and to his great shock, he is being chased by the sheriff's man on a fresh horse!' The audience strain with him as he slaps his thigh for a horse. ' The man continues his chase but before he can stop himself, he careers into a large cart of hay which veers off into a ditch…'

'How you going to get that on t' stage? Them carts is too big. Especially for the theatre here at Buxton.'

Mr Kane glosses over the interruption. 'The technicalities we will work out later. Pray, I am nearly done…'

'The Carter, thinking that the chasing officer is in league with Mr Ryley, pulls him off his horse and begins to horse whip him! He has lost a lot of hay! This altercation allows our hero to escape once more, not twenty yards in front of the pursuing officer and he crosses the county boundary, where the Officer's jurisdiction holds no sway. There, the two men shake hands on a fine chase, as good as either has ever had in a fox hunt. They repair to an inn in Whaley Bridge and drinks are exchanged in good humour!' He ends with a great sweep of his arms to the general acclaim of the throng, sits down heavily in his seat and takes a large measure of brandy and water.

'Still a debtor though', says Mr Hinchcliffe from Macclesfield, who finishes his drink and shuffles out of the door.

John wipes his brow and whispers to his friend. 'You know, Tyrrel, old chap, we are wasted here. We should be in Drury Lane at the very least!'

Tyrrel smiles sympathetically. 'You ever were misunderstood, John. But your heart is in the right place.'

From the entrance to the kitchen Mrs Mycock leans out and shouts 'Your main meal is nearly ready Mr Kane!'

I am all eager anticipation Mrs Mycock, '*They also serve who only stand and wait*. And your feasts are always worth the wait!'

2

June, 1797

*A Grand Ball at the Assembly Room where Miss Butler
causes a stir.*

Tonight, John Kane decides he will go to the dance. It has
come upon him suddenly whilst out walking with Mr and Mrs
Fairbairn, fellow thespians in John Welch's company here at
Buxton. They have walked along the river Wye as far as
Topley Pike which they admire as being a 'frightening work
of nature.' On the way back, passing the great overhanging
cliff known as Lover's Leap, John asks how many young
lovers had leapt. Neither Mr or Mrs Fairbairn know. 'But it
must have been at least one for it to have gained the
appellation and notoriety' proffers Mrs Fairbairn.

It is a fine day and the three of them are content to amble as
best they can along the river bank which, in some parts, is
worn. The men take the arms of Jane Fairbairn and help her
across the more muddy sections, an action which gives cause
for some titillation.

'Young lovers leaping to their death. You couldn't do that on
stage now could you,' says John. 'Juliet, plunging out of the
flies onto the floor below would make an awful mess now
would it not Mrs Fairbairn?'

'John, stop it. Your imagination carries you too far.'

'Only setting the scene. A bit more dramatic than most of the
deaths we play on stage. Unless you count old Spragg last
week. But that was another death entirely. I could hear a shoe
creak in the back row of the pit, poor man.'

'He was unwell I believe and got his lines mixed,' says Jane
sympathetically.

'Lines mixed! You can say that again. Mixed with a pint of

spirits that was.'

'Oh, Mr Kane, you slander the man. Mr Spragg has been a stalwart of the company for ten years and never, to my knowledge, let the Company down. We all have an off night now and again.' She looks sideways at John, hinting with a sly turn of the lip that he himself has been known to forget a line or two.

The day is warm for June up in the hills and the three companions amble along between the brooding cliffs of Ashwood Dale in the company of trilling water as it dances over the stony river bed. The world is greening and there is a sense of expectation. John looks back at the high cliff from which lovers jump in the expectation of seeing a young lady or gentleman standing on top. 'Shame that', he thinks. 'This time of year as well.'

'Now, how about we all get dressed up this evening and take ourselves off to the ball!' exclaims John.

David Fairbairn, never one to make an instant decision at the best of times, hesitates. They, along with the rest of the company have not been paid this month and their rent is due. Ten shillings entry for him and his wife, plus extras is not a sum he would readily shell out spontaneously.

'Oh yes!' cries his wife. 'We haven't been for such along time. I believe Lady Harewood is in attendance.'

'And so shall we be. And a lot more amiable than she! The trouble with that lot is they don't know how to enjoy themselves,' says John, lopping the heads of wild parsley with a whirl of his stick. 'Now if you want a merry evening, the Eagle is the place. Or the Hall. They tell me, for it was before I arrived, that the musical evenings were the best thing in the whole of Derbyshire, led by the landlady herself who had the voice of a linnet.'

'I don't know about that John, but they certainly made a noise with their dancing. Why, it was told to me on one occasion that the whole party were turned out on the order of the local constable for disturbing the peace!'

'How can anyone disturb the peace when there is nothing but merriment to be had! You English are a funny lot when it comes to fun. Why, the men enjoy nothing better than to slaughter birds on an early morning shoot and the women's only delight is to gossip about their neighbours! And then when you do pluck up the courage to kick your knees up, the police throw you out.'

'Now John....'

'Oh, I don't infer that you, Jane are not up for a bit of fun but when it comes to real enjoyment, it takes an Irishman to stoke it up.'

'I would hardly call Mr Tyrrel, your fellow countryman, the life and soul, John. Why with such a choleric disposition, it's a wonder that he finds time to pass the time of day.'

'There are exceptions in all nationalities, I'll grant you but old Tyrrel is a fine actor, you'd agree?'

'To a point,' butts in David, 'A tragedian yes, a sentimentalist, no,' he says pontifically.

'That's because he is no longer of an age to play the swain. Good Lord, we all get to that point in the arc of life when the vigour of youth is overtaken by the sagacity of age. I would hope neither of us would attempt Romeo again.' John Kane is only too well aware that climbing the rose covered bower in pursuit of love is well beyond him now.

'And I, John? What part would suit me now?' says Jane coquettishly.

'Jane, my dear, you are made for ageless parts...a Rosalind would fit you as well as a Mrs Hardcastle...'

'Both of which I have played to much acclaim. I still have the legs to play the young lead.' Jane Fairbairn is still a good looking woman and with a breezy, blithe disposition has often talked herself into parts better suited to a younger person.

'Must we remind ourselves of mortality,' says David

Fairbairn who is ever conscious that his hair is receding and has bags under his eyes. 'If we are to attend the ball tonight, then we should step out if we are to dress for the occasion.'

'Ah!' says John with a discreet cough. 'I meant to ask your advice on that. You see, I find that my best clothes are not quite as fine as they were last year and they are not quite the fit they once were. Either I must wear what I have and hide in a corner, covering up the bald patches of my frock jacket, or must acquire other *accoutrement* that will enable me to stand in the light.'

Jane says. 'Well, you must beg or steal something appropriate. We will not go without you for it would be a dull affair otherwise.'

'I was thinking...' he pauses, finger to his lip. 'I was thinking if there might not be something amongst the props that would do. That last play, *The Soldier's Daughter*, had costumes 'specially made and I rather think the red regimental coat and fine white britches made for the part of Captain Wooley might fit. What do you think?'

They are now at the outskirts of the town and if he is to find his outfit, he must hurry along.

'John, you are incorrigible!' Jane tosses back her head and laughs out loud. 'Mr Welch would not be agreeable I am sure. Not if it is newly bought...'

'I was certainly not about to ask *his* permission. There is no performance 'till Saturday and the Captain's costume is not needed, so it will not be missed. I only intend to borrow it for the evening, and back in its place it will be by tomorrow morning for sure.'

'What about impersonating a soldier of the King? Is there some law against it?' asks David dryly, in the hope that the whole venture might be aborted.

'I hardly think a little gold braid around the cuffs and a tri cornered hat constitutes the full regalia, now David. I merely wish to set myself at some advantage when it comes to stepping out in the *Cotillion*. And it is a dress ball after all. And the white gloves are included in the price of admission, so I don't have to borrow those now do I?'

Both look sceptical. 'Well, if you are set on it, I for one will look forward to the display.' Jane Fairbairn, ever up for larks, thinks it will be great fun. 'It is time Buxton society saw John Kane at his best, don't you think so dear?'

'If you say so my love, if you say so,' says her husband unconvincingly.

Just before the stipulated time of admission of seven o'clock, Mr and Mrs Fairbairn, John Kane and Miss Grace Butler, the principal young female lead in their theatrical company, are lined up at the entrance to the Great Hotel.

'How did you persuade 'the novice' to join us John?' whispers Jane Fairbairn with barely concealed malice. She has never forgiven Miss Butler for stealing the lead in their last production of '*Busy Body*'.

She's a sweet girl, Jane, who harbours no harm to anyone. A little naïve I'll grant you, but a sweet girl who is in want of entertainment in this little town.'

'Oh, how men are so easily fooled!' she snaps and sweeps in front of John Kane to gain admittance.

There is a good crowd. Most of those attending are staying at one of the hotels in the Crescent or the Hall round the corner although there are a few carriages that bring couples from out of town. The evening, although cool, sees some of the ladies brave the exposure of their décolletage but there are, John Kane notices, a fair proportion of people who will not be dancing this night. The lame and infirm, some carried in chairs, are helped up the stairs to the Assembly Room where they are made comfortable. A day spent in one of the baths, seeking the elixir that will make them run and jump again is now to be tested at the Assembly Ball.

John looks splendid in the uniform of Captain Wooley and in the manner of the true old stager, carries himself up the staircase as if he owned all three hotels in the Crescent. With the pretty Miss Butler on his arm, he is causing a stir already.

The party pass into the brightly lit room which is rapidly filling. An orchestra is seated at the far end, tuning up, whilst the Master of the Rooms flits in and out of the Assembly room and the Card rooms, tutting quietly to himself. He is like a dragonfly, buzzing low and looks a bit too important in his purple britches.

John glances round the room and rests on the proud looking woman with the smell under her nose, who must, he surmises, be Lady Harewood. Standing close by is her husband, a little man, balancing backwards and forwards on the balls of his feet, looking for escape. Seated next to the great Lady, in a wheeled chair, sits a young animated woman, aglow with the excitement of it all.

'Where are all the men?' asks Jane Fairbairn. 'There will I fear be young ladies without a dance this evening.'

'Gone soldiering,' says her husband. 'Whilst we are at war with the French, this island must stand ready, Jane. No time for dancing now.'

'And the season is early yet. I am sure the officers will tire of their duties and seek amusement in due course,' says John who is still fascinated by the Harewood tableau. 'Without enough partners for the ladies, I fear we will have much work to ourselves, David. I hope your feet are up to it to my friend.'

David Fairbairn is not a dancing man; not unless he is required to do so in character. 'A cup of coffee before we start?' He ventures rather sourly.

Both the ladies answer in the affirmative. 'Not for me, just yet,' says John who is still intent on viewing his 'audience'. The three of them twist their way through the growing crowd whilst John stands smiling, tapping his toe quite out of tune with the music. An old man, bow legged and wheezy, pushes past him, trailing the scent of cedar. There is a family group nearby; mother looking anxious, father looking protective and two ugly daughters simpering with expectation.

The hum of voices drifts up to the ornately gilded ceiling, the pride of Buxton which some say betters anything at Bath. But to the theatre man, this is mere ornamentation; part of the stage design in which they can all act their parts. And is the performance not like most of the sentimental rubbish that passes for theatre these days? Girls in search of boys, love sick swains, objecting fathers, neurotic mothers, dishonourable suitors and a jester to keep the whole thing passably interesting? It's all here! He smiles to himself as he watches the first of the dances, a gentle minuet to get people in the mood.

The women's colours are bright, some even desperate, whilst the men are a little grey and understated, with the exception of John, who stands out like a barbers pole. They are all playing their parts.

The Fairbairns and Grace Butler return. Miss Butler is certainly one of the prettiest in the room and has a style and bearing learned in the profession which sets her apart from most of the other young ladies. She wears a simple high waisted pearl coloured dress with red sash and ribbons that hang loose down the front whilst her hair is curled and off set with a circle of spring buds. Her cheeks are already aglow and she raises her head, the better to show off her profile. Men glance in her direction.

'Would you step out with an old man in the next dance?' John asks.

'Thank you John.' She is demure but confident. She has been two years on the stage at York and already has a slightly overrated opinion of her worth. Her father, an actor, warned her against the profession but she saw Sarah Siddons at an impressionable age and was smitten.

'Will you join us in a four?' He asks the other two.

David is on the point of declining but his wife takes his hand and leads him determinedly onto the floor.

The orchestra strikes up a lively Bach gigue and they are off. The sound of clumping feet almost drowns out the music but no one minds as they dip and sway and kick their legs along the floor and back again. Despite his girth, John is surprisingly light on his feet and he follows the rotation easily.

It soon becomes obvious that the four of them, particularly Grace Butler, are finer dancers than most of the others. They have done this sort of thing often enough on the stage and attract admiring glances and whispered comments. One or two theatre goers recognise them, but for the rest, they think them to be Italian or dancing teachers or newly arrived from the Court.

'Who is that strange man in the red coat?' asks Lady Harewood of her companion, Miss Greaves.

'I believe he is an actor. I believe them all to be in Mr Welch's company here in Buxton. Isn't she graceful!' gushes Miss Greaves from her wheeled chair. 'I do think she is the finest and most elegant dancer we have here tonight.'

'It is as well we have them to entertain for there are few others here who are capable,' says Lady Harewood sourly.

The music ends and John is about to retire when Grace stays him. 'Do let's dance again. I love it so.' And this time, as they join the line for a gavotte all eyes are on Grace Butler.

Miss Greaves claps here hands in delight and Lady Harewood thinks, 'I could have done that once.'

They swap partners and John takes Jane Fairbairn for the following dance.

'How do you like your audience tonight, Jane?'

'Not as grand as I was led to believe. But then what can one expect in a village up here in the middle of the moors with the season barely started and so few men?'

'Ah, enjoy yourself madam. Give them a show! It will do us

some good and bring a few more in to see us on Saturday. There are one or two young men who will want to see a bit more of Grace, you mark my words.'

And sure enough, Grace Butler spends the whole evening dancing without pause, being called upon by a succession of young and not so young men, all wanting to dance with her.

'A little too forward if you ask me,' says Lady Harewood to no one in particular. Miss Greaves, unable to dance, is living every moment through Grace, imagining the hands of the young men on her back, on her arms, smiling into her face. 'I would so like to meet her!'

After an hour, the orchestra takes a break and the ladies and gentlemen find refreshment, and some step outside for fresh air. It is warm under the candle light and faces are dabbed, and foreheads wiped.

'Will you join me outside, Jane? I need to cool down a bit.' She looks around for her husband who is in conversation with someone she does not recognise and takes his arm. Grace Butler is surrounded by three young men who, in relay, bring her tea and cake.

They walk out and John reaches into his tail pocket to retrieve the small bottle of brandy he has brought with him.

'It's either this or tea. What would you rather have?'

'Tea, please John. I have not reached that point where I am in need of additional stimulation. The dancing is quite sufficient.'

'Oh, I agree. But at my age you need a little something to stiffen the resolve for a go round again. Why, I'm fair danced off my feet already!' He surreptitiously swallows a draft and re-corks the bottle. 'No harm done,' he says with a satisfied wipe of his mouth. Jane Fairbarn smiles. 'A wife is what you need, not to be playing Lothario with 'the novice'. People could mistake your intentions.'

'She is not my Calista and certainly has nothing to be penitent about. Yet. I play the protective uncle and if you could see with that green eye beyond your jealousy, you would notice that she is going places. Too good for the likes of our company. Why, I'll wager she will play *The Fair Penitent* at Covent Garden with a worthy Lothario, come the London season![1]

Just then there is a disturbance behind them. 'Make way! Make way if you will!'

Two men have between them the body of an elderly woman who is being carried down the staircase in a very undignified way. The Master of the Rooms follows behind, panic stricken. 'It's all right. Just fainted. Fresh air! Fresh air!' he shouts, waving a large 'kerchief over the ashen face of the woman who's elaborate wig has slipped.

'Offer her a sip of your brandy, John,' says Jane artfully.

'Not likely! I might find myself in that state by the evenings end and will need all the help I can get!'

The woman regains her composure and stands unsteadily on the arm of the young man who has helped her down.

'There was no need for that.' She admonishes. 'I was quite capable of conducting myself down.'

'But mother…..'

'And look at the state you have put me in!' She attempts to straighten her hair piece and lets out a whimper. 'I need to compose. I need a room.'

Jane feels sorry for her and offers to escort her into one of the private rooms in the hotel. People standing around have the vicarious pleasure of watching the poor woman's predicament.

'Thank you my dear. That stupid son of mine has upset me.'

'But mother, you fainted clean away. On the floor!'

'Never mind. I am quite well now. Go back inside and I will

---

[1] 'The Fair Penitent' by Nicholas Rowe, first performed in1703 was a popular play performed throughout the 18th century in which Calista is seduced by Lothario.

join you later.'

'It's the hair piece that did it, I'll bet. No one wears anything like that now.' He thinks. 'And the dress! I haven't seen a bustle like that since the Duchess of Devonshire declared mourning for the French Court!' John slips the brandy bottle out of his pocket and swigs another draft and then approaches the young man and his companion who had the unenviable task of getting the indisposed woman down the stairs.

'Is there anything more we can do to help?'

'What? No. No thank you,' says the young man in confused hesitation. 'My mother seems fully recovered and I am sure your wife will be able to assist her with her, her a… and things.' He waves a hand in embarrassment.

'I am sure she will. But the lady you allude to is not my wife, merely a companion whose generosity and compassion is ever ready to be brought into service. May I introduce myself? John Kane, a member of Mr Welch's dramatic company currently here for the season. Have you had the fortune to see us perform?'

'No, not yet Mr Kane, but I am sure we will do so. I think I must enquire after my aunt…'

'Of course. May I enquire as to your name, sir? So that I may leave you a pair of tickets at the door of the theatre, should you decide to come this Saturday.'

'Bromley,' blurts out the young man, eager to rid himself of John. 'Algernon Bromley and my friend Sydney D'Abernon. And that is most kind. If we decide to come.'

'Oh, I hope you will. We perform a comedy, *The Dramatist*, a grand production. And I sir, am performing in the after piece, *The Highland Reel*.'

Algernon Bromley is anxious to break free but John is insistent. 'Are you staying in town? Perhaps Jane Fairbairn, the lady with your mother now, could be of further assistance?'

'No, I do not think that will be necessary. We are staying at

The Hall. I am sure she will manage the few steps with our help.'

'Of course. Well, I might see you inside shortly.'

The two young men dash up the stairs and leave John to wait for Jane.

When they rejoin the dancing crowd in the Assembly Room, John sees that Grace Butler has detached herself from the gaggle of beaux and is talking to Miss Greaves.

"The novice' attracts all manner of strange people I see', says Jane Fairbairn waspishly.

'But look at the pleasure she gives to the poor creature. A little charity, please Jane. David, do you not think she has the milk of kindness?' he asks in the hope of soliciting a more positive response.

'I could not say. I have not had the pleasure of working opposite her yet.' David has not had the pleasure of acting opposite many pretty young women these five years past. Jane has seen to that. They can see that Miss Greaves is in animated conversation with Grace and completely in awe of her.

'....and you must come to tea. Can she not, Lady Harewood?'

'Of course,' says Lady Harewood, fanning herself more hurriedly to disguise her misgivings. 'I don't know who she is,' she thinks. 'A dancer! Not quite what I had in mind when I brought poor Anna here.'

'And you can tell me all about being an actress. Do you know Dora Jordan? I saw her at Drury Lane last season. She was magnificent!'

Grace smiles benignly, unable to get a word between the constant rattle of words that keeps Miss Greaves' fluttering heart beating. From the other side of the room stand the knot of young men, including Algernon Bromley, waiting to pounce, once the music starts.

'We are here for the season. Lady Harewood is a great friend of my mother's and when I found she was coming I just begged her to let me come with her. Wasn't that wonderfully kind of her?' Lady Harewood smiles tight lipped. 'And I so love it here. It is my fifth season! Do you like it Miss Butler?'

'I do indeed....'

'Oh, I do hope we can go out for a ride together. Perhaps to Bakewell or you must let me show you Haddon Hall. And Chatsworth of course.'

'I would love to.' Grace looks round and sees that the orchestra is ready to start again. 'I am promised in the next dance Miss Greaves. If you will excuse me, I shall return when I can...'

'Oh do! I shall watch every step!'

Grace rises and Algernon Bromley steps forward to hand her onto the dance floor.

'I see 'the novice' has forsaken you, John.'

'Youth will ever have it's head Jane. But I trust you will not let me down, if David has no objection.'

'Me? No. You two go ahead. I'll stop and watch.'

As they glide into an *allemande* John asks 'Is the Mrs Bromley alright now?'

'Oh yes. There was nothing that a little rouge and powder could not fix. And she's *Lady* Bromley of Hertfordshire'

'Indeed. That's her son taking Grace round the floor. I think we might see a little more of him over the next few days, you mark my words.'

The Ball swoops and glides along, with inhibitions of the first part of the evening evaporating and young and not so young ladies, kicking their legs with abandon. The men tap along as best they can. The old wheezy man who had passed John earlier in the evening has abandoned decorum all together and asked Lady Harewood to dance. She declines.

Before they know it the evening has flown by and the Master of the Rooms has sidled up to the leader of the orchestra and whispered that time is up. At precisely eleven o'clock, the music stops and the musicians start to pack up.

The dancers, red faced and perspiring, gather in clusters, bidding each other farewell, consulting diaries and congratulating each other on their performances. A few are arranging assignations behind the backs of their parents and guardians. The Master hovers nervously near the doors, willing the good people to leave. The show is over and he must have the place emptied.

John Kane wipes the sweat from his brow and concludes in a loud voice that a splendid time has been had by one and all. Grace Butler says her goodbyes to Lady Harewood, Miss Greaves and all the young gentlemen who have had the pleasure of her company. The Fairbairns smile and bow their goodbyes to anyone who looks in their direction and the whole assembly makes its slow progress down the staircase.

The four happy revellers make their way up the hill to the higher part of the town and there they part; Grace Butler to the rooms she shares with the Welch's, the Fairbairns to their meagre rooms at the back of the High Street and John Kane to The Eagle for a nightcap.

3
August, 1798

*In which John Kane and George Fredrick Cooke pick
mushrooms and meet a lonely clergyman.*

Buxton is not a big place. Even with the Crescent – the
magnificent pleasure palace to rival anything that Bath can
throw up – it is a rather mean, insular, cold, wet little place,
nestling among barren moor land and rocks of the western
Pennine hills; a place not easy to get to, which, for those
seeking the elixir of life, makes it all the more miraculous. The
lame and the bronchial, the palsied and the hypochondriacal
come to the baths and drink of the waters in hope and some in
desperation. And romantics come to marvel at the dales and
moors, the rivers and brooding craggy edges that give Buxton
its unique position amongst the watering places of Britain.

The season is short on account of the weather and the state of
the roads. No delicate person would venture up here if it were
not for the reputed efficacy of the waters which cure all ills.

And once here, they need to be entertained.

Mr Welch, the manager who we have already presented, is
doing well this year. The summer is clement, the visitors
numerous, and there is a bustle in the town on account of
continuing building work and refurbishments the Duke of
Devonshire has commissioned. It is not usual for Mr Welch to
do well, but he has had a stroke of luck. He has obtained for
this August, the services (at no small cost) of the great comic
actor, George Fredrick Cooke.[1]

Mr Cooke is a man particularly well known and loved by
audiences in London, Dublin and the provinces but treated

---

[1] George Frederick Cooke, 1756 – 1812, Actor.

with some caution by theatrical managers, on account of his appetites. Women and alcohol make him on occasions, unreliable. His repertoire is extensive, his voice deep and audible and he makes people laugh. And for that, he is bankable.

Mr Welch's band of happy thespians make George Cooke feel at home and he repays them with his tales of great theatres and performances and is not above relaying some of the more scandalous titbits that have not yet reached the provinces. The ladies are not always enamoured of his stories for he can forget himself occasionally, particularly when he has enjoyed a bottle or two. Indeed, Mrs Appleyard vows she will not remain in his company, 'For his language is such that no Christian woman should be confronted with it!' Mrs Appleyard is a reformed Wesleyan and is mindful of the ways of the devil. Strong drink is anathema to her but a blessing to Mr Cooke.

John Kane has taken up with George Frederick in particular, as the two have travelled the same road from Ireland to the mainland, although the latter has travelled in more style and with greater recognition.

It is their custom to join each other after a performance for a 'wind down' at one of the inns in town, although George has made The Angel his favourite watering hole; his *Aqua Arnemetiea* as he calls it, which was the name given to this little village of Buxton by the Romans. 'I have requisitioned the name in honour of the goodness of the waters served in this fine establishment. Why let a name die when it can be put to better use?' Other members of the company join them occasionally but as most of them are married, their opportunity and indeed their ability to match George and John into the small hours of the night is limited by their duty of matrimony.

George Cooke is a man of middle age who dresses for comfort rather than convention. He abjures the wearing of wigs as an affectation which serves no purpose other than to 'set Prince against pauper and an infernal nuisance when a man wants to scratch his head!' To the outer world he is a sanguine man; jovial, hearty, with a ruddy complexion and blood shot eyes to match. Within he is filled with black bile and his thoughts often turn dark and desperate. To ward off the night he sleeps little, and will stay up talking to whoever else is still awake.

At the end of a night, when the Landlord throws them out, they weave their way to whichever lodgings they can remember the location of and there talk till dawn.

On this particular occasion, the two of them have had a particularly late evening in which they played several games of Hazard and then returned to the lodgings of John Kane for further refreshment and talk. They fall asleep and in the morning awake late. The sun slants in through the grimy window and tickles the face of George Fredrick. He rises slowly from a dilapidated settee and looks at the recumbent form of John, lying on his bed, fully clothed.

'John, is that you? Did you leave me here to be kidnapped by Morpheus and left to rot in the dark night?'

There is a groaning sound from the bed.

'A walk, John! That's what we need. I feel the keepers of doom banging at my head!'

'But not before breakfast, George,' says John who is not sure where the voice is coming from. He slowly opens his eyes and lifts his head and surveys what is left of his friend.

George groans. 'Where is that piss pot?'

'Where you tripped over it last night.' He rises from the bed and squints out of the window. 'I think it is lunch we will be having, not breakfast, George.'

'As long as it's edible, I don't care if it's breakfast, lunch or Christs last supper. Did you see my shoe by any chance?'

The two men finally clothe themselves, wash their faces and venture out to find something to eat.

It is not usual for either of them to remain quiet for long but until they have eaten two bowls of soup each and finished a plate of cold mutton, helped down by a mug of beer, neither is capable of rational speech.

'Did I win some money off you last night?' enquires George.

'Not so's you'd notice. Whatever you won went into the pocket of the landlord.'

'That bad was it?'

Their spirits revive and the two men set off on their walk, up onto Fairfield Common where, John informs him the air is fresh and there is a pleasant inn nearby. They walk slowly through town, along Spring Gardens and pass their place of work.

George remarks, 'That's a barn of a place that calls itself a theatre. It is surely the meanest, scruffiest little pit of a place I have ever worked in. Would you not agree?'

'It does not compare with some of the places you work in now, I'll grant you that', says John, who has in the last three years grown fond of its shabby exterior. 'But it is a tolerable place once inside. It is not as bad as some of the places you and I have performed in.'

'True enough, John, true enough. But this Buxton is a place of pretensions and I am surprised that this Duke of yours is not able to augment his fine Crescent building with a place of entertainment of equal stature. Unlike you and me, I'm sure he is not short of the means to do so.'

'In time George, in time he might.' wheezes John Kane, who finds moving his bulk up hill an effort. 'Though they say that wife of his takes some money to maintain.'

'Huh! Wives hey? Were you ever married John?'

'Not me,' he says hastily. 'What woman wants to be dragged around the countryside waiting for her husband to take off his makeup of an evening before they can sit down to dinner? This lot here, the Fairbairns and Martins and Williams, they don't strike me as being blessed with the delights of companionship on the road. Although Jane Fairbairn seems to have worked out her own life and gets by tolerably with her husband.'

'She's a fine woman that. He doesn't know how lucky he is, that's for sure. Why, for two pins I'd...'

'No chance there, George. A fine woman she is and that's how she wants to stay. They all keep themselves busy and interested when they are not on stage. Old Ryley, the one I told you who jumped a horse and escaped the law, now he likes nothing better than a days shooting up in the hills. And William Martin, he's been here some time and has decided that petrification is preferable to acting.'

'Petri what?'

'Petrification. Studying rocks. He's always walking the hills with a bag over his shoulder and a little hammer in his hand.'

'Well if he is not a good actor then he shouldn't act. There's not enough room for those of us that can.'

'He's not bad at what he does; at playing the fop or some other milky part. He was once asked by Tate Wilkinson, over at York, if he would like to join them. Made him a good offer. But he says, 'Why thank you Mr Wilkinson, but you don't have the same kind of rocks in Yorkshire as are found in Derbyshire!' He was writing a book on rocks at the time, as I remember.'

The two men reach the top of the Fairfield road and stop at the church which sits looking over the valley. John wipes his brow and leans on the lychgate to catch his breath. George who is not quite as rotund, sits and waits as his friend composes himself. 'Do you like mushrooms, John?'

'As well as the next man. Why?'

'Because there are early mushrooms all over, do you see? I think we should pick a few for our dinner tonight.'

'Are you sure they are alright. Not poisonous?'

'Sure, you live here, out in the country and can't spot the difference between a toadstool and a mushroom?'

'I was never one for country pursuits, George. A city boy I

was born and will probably die.'

'Well, let's get cracking and then we will have earned a drink. A man's work should be rewarded, do you not agree?'

'Indeed I do. Lead on George.' And the two of them spend a pleasant half hour, searching amongst the shady spots for mushrooms. They talk as they forage.

'What do you think of the little company old Welch has got together here George?' asks John Kane who is keen to find out what the noted actor thinks.

'They are all worthy of their labour, John. Busy, energetic and keen to please. I cannot say that any would light up a London audience, with the possible exception of young Miss Butler.'

'You think she has talent?'

'In the right company and providing too much attention did not go to her head, yes she might.'

John Kane swells with pride at this commendation of his protégé. 'Well, you confirm my judgement and very pleased I am to hear it.' John has secretly appointed himself her guardian and mentor although she is ignorant of the fact. This endorsement will go some way to suggesting that she should seek her fortune with a bigger more renowned company.

'Ah! Will you look at the size of this mushroom? It would fill a plate on its own!' George is on all fours, pulling out mushrooms and scooping them into his hat. 'That should do it, don't you think? We can present our spoils to the landlord and ask that he prepares us a feast. But before our journey back down the hill, let us find refreshment whilst we are here.'

The two of them make their way to an inn not far distant. They call for a tankard of ale each and settle to put the finishing cure to their hangovers.

'Did you ever perform with Anne Catley,[2] John?' asks George when they have seated themselves.

'No, I can't say I did, though I saw her at Covent Garden

---

[2] Ann Catley, actress and singer 1745 - 1789

some years ago.'

'Ah, now there is a beauty. Not only could she out perform Sarah Siddons herself, but could turn men to jelly with a mere glance. Your Miss Butler is a beauty, I'll give you, but for enchantment and wicked seduction, Anne Catley drove men to destruction!'

And in a loud voice he sings her praises to the slight bewilderment of the few other patrons who happened to be at the inn.

> *'Then came Corinna in a long loose gown,*
> *Her white neck hid with tresses hanging down:*
> *Resembling fair Semiramis going to bed*
> *Or Lais of a thousand wooers sped.....'* [3]

'Christopher Marlowe should be alive at this time to paint Anne Catley afresh.'

'You'll be putting us out of business if you go performing for nothing, George.'

'To sing the praises of women should demand no fee. Why, I believe you would do the same for Miss Butler if pricked! Come on', he taunts, 'what praises can you sing to her and I don't want that wretched Shakespeare stuff either.'

'You tax me somewhat.' John pauses, slightly embarrassed, and looks up to the ceiling and at the curious onlookers, attempting to find a suitable line that will do credit to Grace Butler. He begins, arms outstretched....

> *Had we but world enough, and time,*
> *This coyness, Lady, were no crime.*
> *We would sit down and think which way*
> *To walk and pass our long love's day....* [4]

---

[3] *'In Summer's heat.'* Ovid, translated by Christopher Marlowe, *c*.1580's

[4] *'To his Coy Mistress'* Andrew Marvell. *c*.1650

George claps his friend and smiles broadly. ' Bravo! You are misplaced Mr Kane! The lady should be here to hear!'

'I am an uncle to her, no more. And what eye can I catch now. I'm fifty seven years old, no longer capable of clear sight and puff my way up hills. Miss Butler is already besieged by young men but is worthy of far better than the yokels who frequent this place…'

'So you would be happy to see her go?'

'Only to better herself.'

'I hope she does and will not fall foul of perfidious London. There are many who are dazzled by the excitement, the gush and clamour of the stage and many who fall when they get there. Traps and snares, all over London but particularly set for those who would make their living on the stage. You know that as well as I George.'

'Indeed. Why, even Ann Catley whom you praise so rapturously was better known for the number of beds she climbed in and out of.'

'But Miss Butler is no Ann Catley and could easily fall for a pox ridden scoundrel with no money and fewer morals. Lord help her when she gets there!' And he finishes off his beer in one long draft.

'Come on John, time to walk on!' George declaims, rising unsteadily.

The two of them wend their way back down the hill and stop off at two further hostelries before ending up at their favoured watering hole, The Angel. It is a journey that is remembered long after by those who witness it, for they entertain at each stop with bawdy tales of theatre life and the women whom they have known and some they have not.

When they reach The Angel, George is telling of his encounter with Sophia Baddeley a noted actress with whom he had been acquainted some years back. 'She was by then destitute and taking refuge from her creditors in Dublin so the poor woman looked to me to save her! So I did. I saved her for

Saturday nights!' They both roar with laughter as they enter the inn and draw the attention of the patrons who stare at them.

'Gentlemen and ladies, good evening', shouts John, unsteadily holding onto his companion. 'Tonight, my good friend George Cooke and I will be dining in this establishment and trust that you will all give ear, whilst we discourse on the tragic decline of dramatic theatre into the pathetic sentimentalism that we are forced to perform today! And'... he looks round to ensure he has their attention, 'we have brought for the benefit of all, some mushrooms picked this very afternoon.' He looks at George who produces his hat full of fungi. The patrons join in the jest and clap the men to a table, where the landlord places a bottle of wine and two glasses between them and relieves them of the mushrooms.

Before he sits, John turns to the room and with a theatrical flourish declaims in a deep voice:

> *'When night darkens the streets,*
> *then wander forth the sons of Belial,*
> *flown with insolence and wine'.*[5]

He slumps down. 'I think we have found our home for the evening George and if the landlord or his good lady will be good enough to cook some dinner for us, we will be eternally grateful.'

The two of them by now are drunk, but not so far as to be unaware of their surroundings or to converse intelligibly, or nearly so. This is a popular inn and is patronised by people coming and going, waiting for the Manchester coach, or just arrived and the two actors sense the warmth and chatter of the place which suits their mood.

A young man, in well cut style and smooth skin approaches their table and bows. 'Mr Kane. Delighted to make your re-acquaintance, sir.'

---

[5] *Paradise Lost.* John Milton. 1667.

John looks at him with one eye half shut, trying to place him.

'Last year. At the ball at the Assembly Rooms. Your companion, Mrs Fairbairn helped my mother when she was indisposed.'

The light goes on in John's brain. 'Ah yes! Mr…'

'Bromley. Algernon Bromley…'

'Mr Bromley as I live and breathe. How do you do sir?'

'Very well as it happens. I am back here with my mother, Lady Bromley, who found the waters so to her liking last season that she has returned and I with her.'

'As a dutiful son should do, sir. And I trust your mother is fully recovered from the fainting fit she had?'

'Indeed but she has returned to bathe in the hope that her hips will be loosened.'

John has collected what few wits remain to him and refrains from making any injudicious reply. 'Let me introduce the celebrated actor, Mr George Cooke, to you sir.'

George, who has been nodding quietly, suddenly jumps from his seat and grasps Mr Bromley's hand, pumping it vigorously. 'Delighted sir, delighted!'

'And I you, sir. We saw you perform the other evening and are still laughing. We all agreed that your Sir George Thunder was the best we have seen. We saw *Wild Oats* [6] at Bath but this was as funny a performance as I have ever witnessed.'

'You are too kind. Will you sit with us a while and share our mushrooms?'

'Alas, my time is not my own as I have just returned from Manchester and must attend my mother. But another time, assuredly.'

'I will keep you to that, Mr Bromley', says John, who is having trouble focusing on the young man.

'Tell, me Mr Kane, I noticed that Miss Butler was not in the

---

[6] *Wild Oats* by John O'Keeffe, 1791

production. Is she to appear in any others?'

'Oh yes!' says John with a great shout. 'She certainly is. We perform...' he looks at George. 'What is it we do on Saturday George?'

'*The Country Girl* [7]. A good play ruined by Garrick! Lost all Wycherley's fun and sharp wit once the kill joys got hold of it!' George is of strident views when it comes to plays he does not like. 'It's now a part made for prim little virgins being chased all over the stage by the neutered Horner! Probably suit this congregation though, for I see little evidence that any-one in this town is alive!'

People look round curiously at the loud diatribe and Algernon Bromley makes to leave.

'Yes... Well, we will get up a party and certainly make the effort to be there.' He looks anxiously from one to the other and having ascertained that Miss Butler is still in town, makes his exit.

'A bit of a milk sop, hey John? Could you imagine what he would think were your Miss Butler to play the lusty Margery Pinchwife in Wycherley's original? Ha! Then he'd see a real Horner at work!' He is so amused with the thought that he laughs uproariously and attracts the attentions of a gentleman who is slumped in a corner of the room, bottle in front of him and a glum expression.

George notices that he is now staring inquisitively at them and raises his glass in salutation.

The man raises his glass in reply and John notices that he is a clergyman.

'Felicitations sir. Would you be pleased to join us? It is not often that we get the opportunity to converse with a man of God in an ale house.'

The clergyman, Mr Benjamin Truscott, is not sure if John is

---

[7] *The Country Girl*, 1779 by David Garrick was an expurgated version of William Wycherley's *The Country Wife* 1675

admonishing him, or being friendly, for he too is well gone in wine.

He stands, brushes himself down and walks solemnly towards them, accompanied by his bottle and glass. He is a small rounded man, dressed in an old fashioned cut. He sits with a sigh.

'Thank you gentlemen. My name is Benjamin Truscott of the Parish of Fairfield and I do not mind admitting that a little companionship would be a blessing.'

George, who has been studying the clergyman on his way to their table, recognises a toper when he sees one.

'Sir, I do believe you are drunk,' he says in a not altogether friendly way.

The Reverend Truscott is slow to acknowledge the fact but in his defence says with slow deliberation. 'I am a lonely man, sir.'

His look is so melancholic that John feels some pity for him. George on the other hand, is affronted. The memories of a childhood sinned against by the sharp lash of a Jesuit up-bringing has left him with little sympathy for any Christian persuasion.

'Then why, sir, did you take up orders?'

Again the Reverend Truscott deliberates before answering. 'Because I was lonely, sir.'

'I can believe that the responsibilities of a clergyman must be onerous at times,' says John Kane. 'Baptising in the morning and burying in the evening. From the Hallelujah to the Hail Mary. It must be a trial, remembering which face to wear!'

The Reverend Truscott sits quietly in alcoholic fuddlement, not quite grasping the intentions of his new companions. 'I have been ministering to my flocks for twenty six years now and I am still a lonely man.'

'So, reverend sir…, you seek salvation in liquor?' says George with little compassion. '*Give strong drink unto him that is ready to perish, and wine unto those that be of heavy hearts,'* he thunders, causing another stir amongst the drinkers around them. 'Is that not what it says? Proverbs, sir! Is the wine for a heavy heart or to hide from your God?'

'Steady George, we have here a gentleman on the see-saw of life; a man who is more often a comfort to others and who can find little comfort for himself.' John turns back to the clergyman. 'Have you no family, sir?'

'I have a wife. But my stipend is so small that she now lives with her sister in Winchester and I have not seen her for these twelve months past.' He takes up his glass and with a shaking hand drinks.

'And your Bishop? Is he no comfort?'

'My Bishop is in Peterborough,' he sighs, witheringly. 'He visits the parish and then takes the waters to cure his rheumatics. My soul, he says, is in the hands of God.'

'You are pathetic, sir!' cries George, 'I cannot believe that a man who has been schooled in the duties of spiritual care cannot seek his own comfort in prayer and good deeds!'

'I am, like you, mortal. My loneliness is that of other men.'

George is by now exasperated with the maudlin voice of the drunken clergyman.

'Other men, sir, would have stood up to the Devil! I doubt that any of your parishioners has much sympathy for a sot for a priest... you are an anti Christ! Are you not ashamed, sir?'

The clergyman dabs his nose with a large handkerchief which he produces from somewhere under his outer garments. 'My guidance is still valued around here.'

John, who has sat many an evening listening to the mournful history of George Cooke, cannot but notice similarities in the two men's melancholy and thinks his anger is in recognition of his own weaknesses.

'There are callings, sir, in which probity and a strong disposition, not to mention sobriety, are axiomatic and yours is one! Why, there is nothing more shameful than to see a man of the cloth in a state of inebriation!' He tips his glass to his lips with a flourish, wipes his mouth and slumps deeper into his chair, turning his back on the clergyman.

'Even without a glass of wine I would still be lonely. And tomorrow I will still go about my business.'

'*Give strong drink unto him that is ready to perish and wine unto those that be of heavy hearts!*' shouts George into the room where drinkers are once more disturbed. He points to the little clergyman. 'He perishes! We have heavy hearts at the sight!'

The clergyman looks around him in some bewilderment. He had expected some companionship and instead, found bitter words.

The witnesses to this discourse are uncomfortable with the turn of events. Some of them are the very parishioners to whom George alludes and, despite the clergyman's reputation, is one of their own; a man who has performed his duties over many years without complaint. He has baptised their children and buried their dead and given freely of what little money he has to the poor. He may have sunk too often into drink, but he is a man of their community. And so it is that one of the community, a large man who has often helped the Vicar home, intervenes.

'If tha' don't like the company of our vicar, tha' can find another parish to drink in!'

George, is affronted, 'I do not believe that you were invited into our conversation, sir! Please be so kind as to back away! This man is not capable of upholding the word of God or any other word for that matter.'

'And has tha' looked at yourself?' The large man is looming over them, standing, legs apart in an aggressive manner. 'If tha' is so mithered by drink, tha'd best look in a mirror to see the evil in yourselves!'

John suddenly realises that things are getting out of hand. The clergyman is a little too far gone to fully appreciate quite what is happening.

'Gentlemen,' says John, 'I do not believe that we mean any harm in our observations. We merely point out the anomaly that is a man of God and a drunk man.'

That seems to spark the fuse, for another man joins the first.

'I don't believe you heard my friend. Tha'd best find somewhere else to drink'

'And I have no intention of doing so before we have dined!' says George obdurately.

The words are barely out of his mouth before a large hand is laid on George's collar and he is lifted out of his chair. Another large hand is laid on John's collar and the two of them are propelled to the door, with George flailing about him. Both of them are forcefully thrown out and find themselves dumped on the ground with hoots of laughter following.

The landlady emerges with the dinners piled high with mushrooms and squawks in astonishment when she sees her two customers leaving before they have eaten anything.

'I've just made their dinner! They's not paid for it!'

The large man turns to her. 'They'll pay.' He follows George and John who are just picking themselves up out of the dust.

Without a word he thrusts his hand into first one pocket and then another until he finds some coins. 'Tha's not paid for your dinners!' He walks back inside, hands the money to the landlady, sits down at the table in front of one of the plates and proceeds to eat. 'Would you like some vicar?' he asks. 'The two gentlemen ask if you would like dinner, on account of how they think you are a bit lonely and need cheering up!'

John and George hover on the doorstep and are greeted with more shouts and hoots of derision. Quietly they back out. They say nothing and stumble their way to the edge of the road where they sway in indignation at their treatment.

'I shall not eat there again John. Not appreciated.'

'Wretched mushrooms!' says John.

'A drink I think, old friend!'

'The White Heart?'
'The White Heart it is.'

4
August 1798

In which the company perform by desire of the Duchess of Rutland with unexpected results

It is high season and Saturday is usually fixed in the Buxton calendar for theatrical performance. By the desire of the Duchess of Rutland, the company will be doing Mr Goldsmith's *She Stoops to Conquer*, a popular play that will not affront the sensibilities of the audience. Bawdy rhyme and rudery, cuckolded husbands and innuendo have long since left the stage. Audiences want something gentler and besides, as the Duchess herself might have exclaimed, '…they let anyone into the theatre nowadays!'

Mr Welch's company are familiar with the play which will be supplemented with a short offering called *Romp* after the main event, in which John Kane will play the Old Cockney. He will also play the drunken servant in the main offering, a part, some would say, well suited to his talents. He is happy to see that Jane Fairbairn has the part of Mrs Hardcastle, and David Fairbairn, Sir Charles Marlowe. Tony Lumpkin has gone to Mr Robert Elliston[1], a coming man on the stage who's popularity rises in line with his fee. John Kane is particularly happy to see Grace Butler in the starring role of Miss Hardcastle, and hopes Mr Elliston will take shining reports of her back to London, if not taking her in person as well.

The last week has been particularly wet and none of the company is in a good humour. Mrs Nelson has fallen out with Mrs Wentworth and all are complaining about the stock

---

[1] Robert William Elliston, 1774 – 1831 who was to become a famous actor and theatre manager in London

wardrobe which has been used for every production for the last three seasons.

'I'm not getting into that dress any longer, unless it is washed, darned and pressed!' wails Mrs Wentworth. 'It positively smells to high heaven!' Mrs Appleyard, the wardrobe mistress, stands aghast. 'Why, I had that washed only last week! How can she say such a thing, when it took me two hours washing and scrubbing her garments from the last performance. If she is not satisfied, she can wash her own costume!' And with that, Mrs Appleyard storms out of the room and into a puddle just outside the door which discomforts her even more.

'That's done it! We ca-ca-ca-can't have her gi-gi-gi- giving up now,' says Mr Wentworth who has an unfortunate stutter. Whilst he is often caught spluttering his way through a conversation or even rehearsal, he has never, to anyone's certain knowledge, 'lost it' on stage.

'I can't help that Mr Wentworth. Others may lower their standards but I would prefer to keep my reputation and not have half the cast holding their noses at me!'

Other members of the cast know too well that they all hum a little and as long as they are constrained to wear the same wardrobe year in and out, they put up with the offence.

The cast are making final adjustments in the back room that doubles as rehearsal room, wardrobe, theatrical office and on desperate occasions, sleeping quarters for the more impecunious of the troop. It smells damp. Strung across the room are sheets which divide the men from the women and hanging from beams or stuffed into corners are costumes, props of all shapes and sizes, paint pots, musical instruments and scenery. In the far wall there is a small range which offers more smoke than heat, upon which whistles a kettle and one or two pots of food. For the relief of bodily functions, there is a small jakes at the back of the building, whose roof leaks.

A low drone of voices is punctured every now and then by

a cry as someone enquires robustly as to the whereabouts of a vital piece of costume. Two small boys tear around the legs of the stumbling cast as they fit themselves up for the performance. Corsets are tightened, wigs are powdered and brushed, britches are darned, makeup is lost and found.

Suddenly, Mr Nelson, bursts into the chaos, arms waving above his head. 'Where is that wretched stage hand? The scenery is still to be finished! Where is he?'

The half dressed cast pay little regard for they have their own shortcomings to attend to.

'I th-th-th- think he may have gone for some f-f-f-food', says Mr Wentworth, who looks pale with worry as he attempts to foreshorten the sleeves of a frock coat which was made for someone six inches taller than he.

'Well, if he is not here within the half hour, we have a disaster on our hands. There is nothing of the screens up and the stage is bare of all the necessities. Where is Mr Welch? I must report this immediately.'

Mr Welch has not been seen at all that day. 'Would he be at the hotel?' ventures someone.

'Which hotel?' shoots back Mr Nelson who is colouring up alarmingly. 'I cannot go stomping all over Buxton looking for him'

'Try the St Anne's. I know he often drops in there to chat and to take tea.'

Mr Nelson storms out just as a very wet Mrs Appleyard comes back in, dripping.

'Mrs Appleyard, you are back! Thank God for that,' says David Fairbairn.

'I am and I will thank you not to blaspheme. The Lord might be forgiving but he does not take kindly to being abused. And neither do I!'

Justly chastened, he looks away and mumbles an apology. Mrs Appleyard is a reformed woman who turned from drink and the sins of the flesh when her husband left her and John

Wesley came through town. It was a sign that she was saved and her husband damned.

'Please Mrs Appleyard, can you help me with this garment?' pleads Jane, who is loosing patience with her wardrobe. Mrs Appleyard obliges and the cast hasten their preparations with growing anxiety.

Just then the door bursts open and John Kane stands, damp and smiling and from the top of his voice addresses the cast.

> *'A school for scandal! Tell me I beseech you*
> *Needs there a school this modish art to teach you?*
> *No need of lessons now, the knowing think;*
> *We might as well be taught to eat and drink......'*

'Shut the door John!' shouts Jane Fairbairn. 'And you've got the wrong play. It's *She stoops to Conquer* tonight, not *School for Scandal!*'

'Ah! Madam, I stand corrected.'

'You'd best sit corrected, John, before you fall corrected.'

He lowers himself slowly onto a bench and surveys the company through rheumy eyes. 'Did I ever tell you of the time I played Hardcastle opposite Fanny Gough? In Liverpool it was. Terrible hard audience. Jeering and calling as if they had been put up to it. Like Drury Lane, when the Tory claque was called in to shout down anything old Sheridan put on. Well, near the end of the play, we was all ready to see the young lovers happily entwined when this orange comes hurtling across the lip of the stage, out of the dark and poor Fanny has to duck to miss it. She falls on top of me, pushes me over and there we were, rolling about the floor. Ha! Quick as a flash I says, "Fanny me' darling, I didn't know you cared!" "I don't" she says. "I'm just looking to see if you have a knife about you to peel that orange with!" Brought the house down that did.'

'John, I didn't know you had taken up needlework?' says Jane

'Needlework?'

'You embroider a story so beautifully I'm sure your fingers aren't even pricked!'

Ah, ha, Jane! Ever the wit, ever the verbal jouster!' laughs John admiring the riposte. John has been preparing himself with alcoholic stimulants in the Shakespeare Hotel which fortunately is but a short step from the theatre.

'What time is it?' he asks

'Not time enough for you to sit and disrupt us.'

'Ah, plenty of time then! Besides, I'm not required until Act Four and by the time of my entrance most of the audience will be asleep anyway.'

He gets up and stretches. 'Is Grace Butler there, hiding behind the sheets?' he says mischievously, ducking his head round the corner.

Miss Butler has not yet been seen and she is the main reason why many people will come to the performance this evening.

'She'd best put a move on if she wants me to dress her proper,' says Mrs Appleyard who is eyeing John Kane with some distaste.

'Will someone find her?' asks David Fairbairn, 'Or must I venture out?'

But that is not necessary, for at that moment, the door opens and Grace glides in, followed by Mr Elliston and Mr Welch in earnest conversation. She wears a thick shawl and her head is covered by a hood which she now discards and stands, smiling as if there were not a care in her world.

'Ah, Grace my dear, you are here at last!' shouts John with a broad smile.

'Mr Elliston and I have been going through our lines.'

'That is the way of a true professional! And is he pleased with what you do?' enquires John.

'Oh yes, very. We will shine as brightly as Aphrodite and Adonis,' she says, only slimly familiar with the tale of the two lovers and Mr Elliston raises an eyebrow at the prospect.

Grace Butler is ambitious and is determined to outshine any in the company. Although she speaks well, and has a charm supported by a fine dark beauty, she is a little gauche. She is prone to observations unsupported by any intellect and little worldly knowledge. She sings well enough and dances prettily but in short, she is a provincial and as much as John Kane champions her, others know that she is still an *ingénue*.

'Now, Mrs Appleyard, will you dress me please? I want to be at my very best tonight for I hear that the Duchess of Rutland is to have Mr Erskine[2] in her party and others who have travelled up from London.' She slips behind the sheets hanging across the room and members of the company glance at each other, knowingly. John looks on in befuddled adoration 'A star is born,' he whispers.

'Good afternoon dear friends. Everything is in hand I trust?' asks Mr Welch expansively.

'The scenery is n-n-n- not up I believe,' stutters Mr Wentworth.

'I have been into the theatre and everything is now banging along just fine.' Mr Welch is ever the optimist. He has to be for he has no money, only a string of debts. But his heart is in the right place and the theatre is in his soul. And tonight he has a fine cast and a finer audience that will, he hopes, spread word of his accomplishments.

He coughs portentously to attract the company's attention, 'Mr Elliston here has graciously agreed to stay on for another week.' He turns and bows to Mr Elliston who's countenance suggests that the agreement is not fully to his delight. But with every eye on him, he bows again and murmurs his consent.

'We all know of his triumphs at Bath and York and we will ensure that his performances here will be equally glittering.'

'He must be more desperate than we thought,' whispers Jane

---

[2] Henry Erskine 1846 – 1817, lawyer and Whig politician

Fairbairn to Mrs Wentworth in an aside.

'Bravo!' shouts John Kane. 'A noble cause, Mr Elliston. You could not have chosen to join a finer group of players outside of London.'

'Thank you John,' says Mr Welch sardonically, noticing that he is not entirely sober. 'I trust you will be up to your usual standard this evening.'

'Mr Welch, have I ever let you down? Have I ever dropped a stitch? No sir! Not once in the ten seasons I have given this company!'

Mr Welch is a tolerant man but even he has his doubts about John Kane on occasions. 'Well, everybody, this will be a splendid night. A full house, no less!...'

'So we might get paid,' says Jane in another aside to Mrs Wentworth.

'...and such a fine and noble attendance as was not seen anywhere in the North of England this season. Good luck everybody!' and with that, Mr Welch leaves the company to complete their dress and last minute attentions. Mr Elliston looks less than enamoured with his lot, sighs deeply and plunges into the wardrobe to find his costume.

Mr Welch meanwhile makes his way back to St Ann's Hotel in the Crescent, and takes up once more with a gentleman who may or may not be enticed into investing in a theatre in Derby.

Amongst the audience that evening are Lady Harewood, Miss Anna Greaves, Lady Bromley, accompanied by her son Algernon and Mr d'Abernon. The Duchess of Rutland arrives late, escorted by Mr Henry Erskine. Miss Anna Seward and her friend Miss Powys, who have been coming to Buxton for many years, share a box with Sir John and Lady Clarke of Edinburgh.

The theatre at Buxton from the outside is a ramshackle unprepossessing place that is not spoken of kindly. Inside however, effort has been made over the years to render it comfortable for the audience and workable for actors. The pit has benches ranged at a comfortable distance from one another. Along either wall are commodious boxes and above them are the galleries fitted up with rudimentary seating which numbs the backside of any patron after three hours.

The proscenium, now worn and patched, juts out as far as the first boxes and has an arch which is also in need of paint and decoration. The whole is lit by a row of oil footlights, an innovation introduced by the theatre owner two years previously. But the auditorium is still candle lit and will smoke horribly before the show is over.

There is an expectant hum from the growing audience as they make their way into the theatre and people look round expectantly, hoping to catch the eye of someone they know. Surreptitious glances are made towards the most forward boxes when the Duchess and her party arrive. She is all smiles and Mr Erskine is all attention to her and her companions. Lady Harewood and Miss Greaves are in the box next door.

'Oh! I am so excited! I love the theatre better than any entertainment I can think of, don't you Lady Harewood?'

'Indeed my dear', replies her ladyship in the hope that Miss Greaves will not keep up her ceaseless chatter through the performance as well.

'Look! I do believe that is Miss Seward, of whom I told you this afternoon. She is such a sweet soul, although sadly plagued by rheumatism. I do hope we will see her tomorrow. She is so knowledgeable on all things and can discourse on any poet or play you care to mention.'

'Yes my dear', says Lady Harewood only half listening, as she tries to overhear the conversation taking place between the more interesting neighbours.

Lady Bromley meanwhile is fussing over her chair and has sent Algernon to find something more suitable. Algernon is beside himself with the thought of seeing *her* again; the vision who has been driving him to distraction these past few days. 'She will be there, on stage! Oh dear Lord, please may she look in my direction!' he whispers to himself.

He returns with a boy carrying a chair, exactly the same as the one rejected by his mother who now declares it is much better and why could it not have been put here in the first place! Algernon takes up his position next to her and wipes his hands and forehead.

'What is the matter with you dear? You haven't kept still all afternoon. I told you that a bathe would have done you good; settled your nerves.'

'I haven't got nerves mother.'

'Well, I don't know why you fidget so. Do you know Mr D'Abernon?'

'Indeed not Lady Bromley.' Who knows full well that it is his friend's heart that fidgets.

The hum grows louder as the time draws close to the start. Mr Welch is peeping through the curtains and is excited by what he sees. The audience is beginning to seat themselves, the boxes are full and the gallery is quietening down. At the foot of the stage, old Tompkin is trimming the wicks of the footlight lamps. Backstage, the cast is readying themselves with last minute panics.

'Don't w-w-w-worry my dear, no one will notice.'

Mrs Wentworth is ever in a panic about the smallest thing.

'But I will!' She cries. 'My performance will be ruined!'

Mr Welch might be pleased with the size of the audience but is far from happy with proceedings back stage. He hopes no one out there will hear the last minute banging which is taking place. The sets have not been anchored correctly and the backdrops are all wrong. Not that they have a great choice of scenes, the same one's being used for whatever the production.

Mr Welch has chosen to give the Prologue to the play and readies himself. He coughs and hums, to clear his throat. The wicks have been trimmed, the candelabra lit on stage, Jane Fairbairn and Mr Nelson are ready in the wings. And then he sees with alarm a stage hand desperately trying to unfasten the door through which the cast will make their entrances and exits. He goes over to the workman who is wrenching the handle of the door without much success.

'It's stuck!'

'I can see that!' says Mr Welch in an anxious whisper. 'It was working fine in the last production. What could possibly be the matter?'

'Damp!' opines the workman. 'And twisted.'

Mr Welch pushes from one side, the workman pulls from the other and at last, the door opens suddenly and puts Mr Welch on his back.

David Fairbairn picks him up and dusts him down and Mr Welch, formerly composed and waiting to say his piece in front of an expectant audience is now discomposed.

'All right everybody, nothing to worry about,' he says shakily. 'I'm quite all right. Are we now ready?' He eyes the door suspiciously. The stage hand is moving it on its hinges and pronounces it safe.

'Leave it ajar, just in case,' he says and without further ado, steps out in front of the curtains.

The Prologue requires that he be dressed all in black and should carry a handkerchief, which, alas, he dropped in his struggle with the stage door. He pauses and wipes an imaginary tear from his face, which leaves a smudge of grease which causes some early amusement.

He begins

'Excuse me sirs, I pray – I can't yet speak –
I'm crying now – and have been all this week!..'

In the wings, just out of earshot, John Kane stands watching. 'That's because young Mr Elliston has probably got you over a barrel with his contract!'

'Hush John!' says Jane sharply.

He looks round and seeing Mr Elliston, winks exaggeratedl
in his direction. Mr Elliston ignores him. He thinks John i
boorish and does not care for his Irish wit.

The Prologue comes to an end, Mr Welch leaves the stag
and the curtain rises with the entrance of Jane Fairbairn an
Mr Nelson. They are off!

John, who has a very small part in the main production an
is not required for some time, thinks he has time to slip roun
to the Shakespeare for a small brandy and water.

In Lady Harewood's box, Miss Greaves is living ever
minute of the performance in a rapturous smile. When Grac
Butler makes her entrance, she lets out a small squeak c
delight and vigorously fans herself. 'Isn't she beautiful!' Sh
cries to the dismay of her companion who gives her a ster
look. —

Algernon Bromley too swoons at her entrance. She ha
caused him to come out in a rash, which he now scratches a
Lady Bromley smacks him with her fan and shushes him.

Miss Seward makes notes in a small notebook which sh
will later write up in letters to friends. By the end of Act Twc
she has decided that Mr Elliston is very jolly and vibrant, Jan
is 'holding her own', Mr Nelson is too young to play M
Hardcastle and the door to the left of the stage keeps openin
of its own accord.

But it is Miss Butler who she is most concerned for. Sh
will write '...*that Miss Butler played the part of Kat
Hardcastle with underwhelming brio. For all her good look
and fine deportment, she has the voice of a mouse and th
conviction of a dull schoolgirl. It has been suggested that sh
has the makings greatness, but I see nothing that would caus
a stir in Drury Lane.*'

But the audience love it. They laugh and smile their way
through to Act Three in the expectation that this comedy o
errors will play itself out with rousing fun to the end.

Alas, disaster strikes. At that point in the play where Miss

Hardcastle exits and Tony Lumpkin enters, bearing a casket of jewels, the door refuses once more to open. The audience hear his anguished cry from behind the door and believing it to be part of the comedy, laugh at the two performers desperately attempting to enter and exit at the same time.

'I can't get it open! cries Mr Elliston who is now supported in his efforts by the stage hand. Together, they put their shoulder to the door and with a loud creak the scenery, with the door stuck firm, crashes to the stage in a cloud of dust.

There is a hush. Mr Elliston is nothing if not a professional and, as if nothing untoward has happened, continues; '*Ecod! I have got them. Here they are. My Cousin Con's necklaces, bobs and all.......*' But the casket which he is meant to present lies broken on the stage floor, along with his reputation.

The hush in the audience is followed by a shriek of laughter, which ripples and then roars through the pit. Only the boxes, occupied by the more sedate of the patrons is shocked into silence, although Lady Harewood is seen to titter whilst Miss Greaves sits open mouthed in silence for once.

Algenon Bromley rises out of his seat thinking that his beloved Miss Butler may be squashed under the scenery but she is in the wings, hand gripped in horror at her mouth.

The cast is in shock. But John Kane, who has come back from fortifying himself, sees what the audience sees. He is a little unsteady on his feet, but has lost none of his affability. Mr Welch rushes hither and fro, not any the wiser on what to do as the two actors stand uncertainly amongst the debris with the audience braying with laughter.

'There is nothing like a good crisis at someone else's expense that will enliven an audience more. Now, I suggest....'

'Please Mr Kane! I have enough problems and I hardly think in your condition you are in a position to help!' squeaks Mr Welch near to tears.

He is in no frame of mind to trade social observations with his drunken comic. Indeed he is in no frame of mind at all. 'I ask that you remove yourself and let the rest of us get on with repairing the damage.'

John is hurt by these cutting aspersions. It is not for Mr Welch that he stays loyal to the company, but to the many friends he has made. His is a conscience driven by a spirit of communal wellbeing and good cheer. It has to be, for he has never gained the approbation or fortune of solo stardom.

Mr Elliston and Grace Butler make their exit and before any further action takes place, John Kane strides onto the stage unannounced and to the horror of Mr Welch.

He surveys the restive audience for whom the joke has now ended and are wondering what next. The curtain falls behind him.

'Your Grace,' he bows low to The Duchess of Rutland without toppling over. 'Ladies and Gentlemen.' He pauses. The Duchess looks on with wry amusement.

His words are slow and deliberate, 'As you see this is not actually part of the performance. Mr Goldsmith, were he living, would be perturbed. Why, it is said that on his death bed he was asked, "Are you at ease with yourself?" To which he replied, "No I am not!"

The audience are slowly taken away from the collapsed stage.

'This little interlude is not manufactured, for in the original production, there was no falling down of the stage set! And I point out the solecism recited by Tony Lumkin, "Ecod! I have got them! Here they are," which perhaps, for the purposes of this production, should have been "Ecod! Mind your head!" The audience are tickled by John's impromptu performance.

'By their recovery will you know them! "*Piece out our imperfections with your thoughts...*" he says with a dramatic flourish "*...and your humble patience pray, gently to hear, kindly to judge, our play*"³

'Your Grace' – he bows again even more dramatically – 'I can assure you that never before has been assembled a more adept group of thespians who will, within the minute, transport you back to the home of the sorely put upon, Mr Hardcastle.'

He peeps behind the curtain to see if progress is being made in the resurrection of the wall and door. Satisfied, he steps back out.

'Well, I would like to tell you what comes next, but as I have no idea myself, I must leave it to the cast to pick up from where they left off. And I can assure you that in the performance which follows this, in which I will be playing an old cockney gentleman, no such interludes will be necessary.'

And with that, John weaves his way unsteadily across the stage to enthusiastic applause.

In the wings, the cast are ready to resume and all clap and pat him on the back. 'Well done John! Saved the bacon', says Jane and pecks him on the cheek.

'Brandy and water would be a just reward I think.' He looks at a dishevelled, red faced Mr Welch who says humbly 'Thank you John.'

'Ah! Think nothing of it.'

The curtain rises, the play resumes and nothing untoward happens for the remainder of the evening. When John emerges onto the stage as the drunken Jeremy the servant, the audience give him a great cheer and do so every time he makes an entrance in the end piece, '*Romp*' as well. By this time they have taken him so much to their hearts that they hardly notice the growing incoherence of his performance which is being regularly fortified by strong liquor behind the scenes.

After three and a half hours, the members of the gallery rise stiffly, stretch and rub the ache from their bottoms, satisfied

---

[3] From the prologue of Henry V

with the night's entertainment. The Duchess has a few kind words for Mr Welch who comes onto the proscenium next to her box and thanks her most graciously. Miss Seward has completed her note of the play and writes... *'that Mr Kane acted with great verisimilitude in his role as a tipsy servant and the Old Cockney, although it was difficult to understand his delivery on occasions.'*

Miss Greaves, being helped out of the theatre, is still overwhelmed with the gaiety of it all. 'I do think Mr Elliston is such a fine actor; so very handsome and amusing do you not think so Lady Harewod?

'Indeed', says My Lady with a condescending smile.

'And Grace was so enchanting! Especially when she is pretending to trick poor Mr Marlowe, disguised as a serving maid. I'm sure I would have been fooled! Oh I do love her so! I will certainly come and see both of them again next week. Will you come?'

'Certainly', says Lady Harewood with barely disguised exhaustion.

But a week in Buxton can be a long time and did she but know it, Miss Greaves will never see Miss Butler again.

Backstage, the cast is elated that they have been received as well as they have, given the disaster in the third act. It is quite late, but John Kane is all for making a party of what is left of the night. Some decline; those with wives to get home who have not the energy of their youth. But there is a sufficient number for them to persuade the landlord of the Shakespeare to keep them in beverage and food until the small hours. Some of the livelier members of the audience join them and it is only when a complaint is handed down stairs from one of the guests woken by their noise that the party breaks up.

John has, metaphorically, left the party some hours before, but is roused from the chair in which he has fallen asleep and is helped up Hall Bank, to his living quarters off the London Road. He will sleep well on his triumph.

The following morning, John is woken by a loud banging on his door. He opens an eye and confused that a drum is being beaten loudly in his head, shuts it again. The banging continues and now he hears a voice, calling his name. Slowly he comes round and sits up unsteadily. 'Is that St Peter or the other fellow come to claim me?' he calls croakily.

'John, please open the door. It's David Fairbairn. Something dreadful has happened and your attendance is needed.'

He rises and opens the door. 'Now what in the name of the Almighty could be that important that you would disturb a man at this hour?'

'It's eleven o'clock John and I fear you will not like what I have to relate.'

'And what's that?'

'Please dress and then we must go down to the Hall. Mrs Fairbairn is there.'

David Fairbairn stands embarrassed at the door, trying not to look at John's legs protruding from beneath his shirt. 'I would not have burst in had it not been of the utmost importance.' He can see that John is still fuggy from the previous night's celebration and is loathe to say anything until he is in a position to fully comprehend his news.

'I shall wait in the hall whilst you attend to your dress, John. Please be swift, for every moment counts!'

John scratches his head as David leaves the room. 'Well, I never knew a problem solved by a man with his cock in his hand. So, I had better get dressed I suppose.'

The two men are soon striding down the hill to the hotel. John has the sweats and his hands shake a little but other than that he is fully awake and now curious about his part in the hullabaloo.

As they enter the Hall, Jane Fairbairn and Lady Bromley are in conversation. He can see at a distance that the old lady is glowering and distinctly unhappy about something. He sits and waits for the mystery to be revealed.

'John', says Jane quietly, 'would you know where Grace Butler might be?

Grace? No. Why? He wipes perspiration from his face. Lady Bromley puts a handkerchief to her mouth as she catches the smell of stale alcohol seeping from his skin.

'We, that is Lady Bromley, suspects that she has eloped with her son, Algernon.'

'Seduced him into running away with him! A common strumpet, that's what she is!' shouts Lady Bromley

John sits back. Grace? Run off without telling him?

'I can't believe that. Miss Butler is far too intelligent to do anything like that. She is destined for great things. She would never jeopardise her career!'

'I have a letter,' says Lady Bromley. 'Here. Read it if you will!'

He holds the letter at some distance and can just make out the spidery hand.

Dearest mother,
You have often told me that the time must come when I will make my way in the world. I beg to tell you that time has now arrived and I have left for London by the early coach.

I must also tell you that I am accompanied by someone whom I love with all my heart. She is the sweetest most adorable girl I have ever met and as soon as we can, we will marry…

'Why?' cries Lady Bromley, dabbing her eyes and sniffing. 'Why would he wound his mother? It's as if he has plunged a dagger into me. Why has he done this?'

John continues reading.

This will be a great shock, but I know you would never sanction this match. She may not be of our station, but I love her so and with my inheritance due me on my next birthday, I will have enough for us both….

John pauses and looks at the weeping woman. 'There is no mention of Grace Butler here. Are we sure it is she he is with?'

'The probability is great John. I asked Mrs Welch with whom she is staying as you know, and she has confirmed that her bed was not slept in last night.'

'But she was at the party at the Shakespeare. It could be that she took a room there rather than walk home.'

'The landlord at the Eagle says that a party of two, a young man and woman, boarded the early coach this morning. I fear it is so, John.' Jane was solemn in the piecing together of the events for she knew how much he adored his little Grace Butler.

'So, Mr Kane, are *you* a party to this deceit?'

'Your Ladyship, I trust you are not suggesting that I have anything to do with the actions outlined by your son in this letter? I am affronted if so!'

'Oh, Lord knows that the world is a wicked place and I have tried to do the best by my son. He has no father. I have played both mother and father to him and he has always been a most diligent and obedient son.' She sniffs and dries her eyes once more.

'Lady Bromley, if what is said in the letter concerns Miss Butler then I am equally as grieved as you. She is a rising star! She will be on the London stage next season. I will not believe she is the person referred to.'

'She is nothing but a wicked girl who has fanned her feathers in front of my son and seduced him away from me....'

'Now listen here madam! If that ninny of a boy you call a son is fool enough to fall for some brazen harpy the first time she winks at him, I can only say you have failed in your duty as a mother and a father ...'

'Oh! I have never been so insulted...'

'Oh, I can do better than that....'

'John! Lady Bromley! Please!' Jane pleads. 'I hardly think

we will resolve this delicate issue by shouting at one another.'

John turns from Lady Bromley who does likewise in the opposite direction. 'I will not look upon this stinking man. Please ask him to leave before I summon a constable.'

'I'm not going anywhere until I have it for certain that Grace Butler is the girl referred to in this note.'

'And I will find them and have the slattern arrested! Actors! You people are all alike. Immoral!'

'Lady Bromley, I and John Kane will do all we can to find out where they are. That must be the first step, surely? There is nothing to be gained through a shouting match, I'm sure.'

John holds his tongue. He is angry and red faced and upset by the thought that he may have lost the only thing that gives him a reason to get up each day. He is a man without family of his own and Grace fills an important place.

'I will be consulting my attorney as soon as I return home and if there is a hint of your collusion in this elopement, I can assure you, Mr Kane, there will be consequences!' And with that she rises and marches from the room.

John slumps further into the chair in saddened anguish. The three of them remain silent, absorbing the impact of the news.

'Do you think she could be right?' asks John, desperately.

'Yes', says Jane quietly.

Some weeks later John receives a letter, postmarked Holborn, London. It is from Grace who has written blithely to tell him that she is safe and well and has every prospect of getting a part in a new production at Drury Lane through the good offices of a friend of a friend of Algernon Bromley's. She tells him that she is mad in love and that Algernon is the sweetest, dearest, kindest, most attentive man she has ever met. She entreats him not to be too harsh because of her abrupt departure and assures him that she is well and that the name of John Kane will ever be dear to her. She ends,'*Life starts anew!*'

They were the last words he receives directly from her. Word reaches him now and again that she is often seen at Ranelagh Gardens and Vauxhall in the company of the gayest of the *demi monde* and is in popular demand. His friend George Cooke has been right. Her stage career is not a success but she lives quite splendidly on the favours of various gentlemen, some quite aristocratic.

He has no further word from Lady Bromley either and buries the memory of Grace Butler deep in his heart, and never mentions her name again.

10ᵗʰ November 1799

In which John Kane takes a walk to the end.

Poole's Hole, situated just to the south west of the town is one of the main natural attractions for visitors wanting a distraction in between water cures. In his ten years of performing in Buxton, John Kane had never visited this 'Wonder of the Peaks' and resolves to do so. It is late in the season and most of the visitors to the Baths have left town, save for a few of the more desperate invalids or those taking advantage of cheaper rates at the hotels and lodging houses.

John himself has procured an engagement at Liverpool for the Christmas and other members of the company are leaving too. David and Jane Fairbairn are going south, to Bristol but will, they assure him, be back next June. Nathanial Tyrrel has no firm engagement but will try his luck in the Midlands, where he is assured, there is acting work to be had.

Mr Martin, he of the 'petrifications', is remaining in the town, where he will tramp the moors and dales, weather permitting, to find gems, fossils, Blue John and 'Buxton Diamonds' which he will catalogue in his book.

On his last day of the season in Buxton, John has arranged to walk up to the Hole with Nathanial Tyrrel and they set off in unpromising weather after breakfast at the Sun Inn. Mrs Mycock ensures they are well fortified for their excursion with plates of bacon and eggs and beer.

'Mrs Mycock, if I were a marrying man, I would be on bended knee, here and now, to ask for your hand. That was a breakfast fit for royalty itself!'

'And if I said yes but can I leave my pots and pans behind,

would you be quite so keen Mr Kane?'

'Ah, now it would be a shame to leave such useful implements behind you, would you not think?'

'Get on with your blather! You're all the same, you men.'

The two companions rise and put on their heavy coats.

'I'll be in this evening for my supper Mrs Mycock. What will it be?'

'What would you like?'

'Roast beef would be a treat. If I'm leaving you to the tender mercies of this place, I might as well go out with a bang.'

Mrs Mycock smiles a little sadly as she tidies up the dirty plates. She has known this big scruffy Irishman for all the time he has been coming back to perform at Buxton and has grown fond of his harmless banter. She lost her husband some five years previously and the warmth of the inn with its hustle and bustle has long since compensated for the loss. John Kane is her favourite customer and she is secretly saddened when he leaves each November.

'I shall bring you back something pretty from the walk and if I find anything for the pot, I'll bring that too'

As she walks towards the kitchen she shouts over her shoulder, 'You can dig up some horseradish and I'll mix that up for you if you like.'

'Excellent Mrs Mycock. That sounds just grand.'

As they leave the inn, the low slate grey clouds hurry past. 'We are in for a soaking, John, you mark my words.'

'Might be, Nat, might be. There again, the sun might come out. You know what this place is like.'

'I do that.' Nathanial Tyrrel is a man in his late forties who views the world from behind a veil of pessimism. For him it is perpetually raining and if it were not for his friend John Kane, may well have slit his own throat long ago. He is a good actor; not great, but better than most, particularly in dramatic scenes thick with tragedy and pathos. But theatre goers, particularly those outside London, have got used to a diet of something more light hearted. He is a man after his time who accepts his lot with hesitation and scepticism. He is loyal and honest and for that John is willing to forgive him his hang dog face and dire prognostications.

They set off down the hill to the Hall, from where they intend to follow the river west.

'Shall we take a draft of healing water, Nat? It might keep us going for our mighty walk.'

They stop at the gates to St Anne's Well and give the old woman attending a couple of coppers. She gropes her way down the steps to the spring and returns with a jug and two earthenware cups, into which she pours the *aqua vita* without ceremony.

'You know, I can't see what people make such a fuss about. In all my time here, I have not seen anyone throw away their sticks and walk.'

'But people swear by it, John.'

'They have to, after paying such a high price to stay here.'

'You are growing as cynical as me.'

'Well, I have seen the sick and the lame coming here, year after year and they seem to get no better. That Miss Greaves the one always chatting to people, she seems to come not for the curing, but to gossip. And I don't see the poor thing rising from her chair.'

'But perhaps the company is what she comes for John, to be amongst people like herself with a similar disposition. They know they won't get better but it does take a certain constitution to get here. There's a certain achievement in that alone. Bath or Cheltenham are far more equable than this cold wet little place. But unless you have your two legs, a fine face, the right clothes and plenty of money, no one wants to know you at those places.'

They finish their drafts of water and hand back the cups. 'Well, if this stuff is any good we should be able to walk to

Chester. Are you ready Nat?'

'Lead on friend.' He takes John's arm and the two of them set off, past the Hall and along the riverbank.

There is a brisk wind which makes them pull their coats closer and John hangs onto his hat when it threatens to jump from his head. The trees are loosing their leaves which lie soggily as they tramp across them. They look up to the bald hills with a thin misty rain blowing across the landscape.

'Is this a good idea?' asks Nat.

'Oh sure. I'm determined to see this great hole if it's the last thing I do!' They tramp on and talk as they go.

What will you do when you have finished with Liverpool John?

I'm not sure, but weather permitting I may go back to Dublin. I still have family there.'

'Is that so? I never knew that.'

'Oh yes. I have sisters and nephews and nieces and cousins galore. I haven't seen them in an age.'

'And any children yourself?'

'Not that I know of! I was married once, but we had no offspring.'

This is the first that Nat had ever heard of a wife. Open hearted and voluble as he is, John has secrets buried deep and rarely speaks of himself.

He asks tentatively. 'Is she still alive? Your wife?'

'I couldn't say. It's fifteen years since last I saw her.'

Nat looks at his friend. This little piece of information tells him much about John Kane; his love for Grace Butler as the daughter he never had; his drinking; the almost obsessive need for company.

'What happened?'

John pauses, and weighs up his response. Nat might be as good a friend as he had ever had, he and Jane Fairbairn, but he finds it difficult to talk. It is one of his endearing features. Where most actors are only too willing to trumpet their successes with boasts and puffed up rhetoric, John keeps thoughts of himself to himself. Perhaps that is why he has never got on in the theatre; too modest, always quick to praise everyone but himself.

'I'll tell you some time Nat. But it's all we can do to stand upright in this wind. I think we should find shelter and something to warm us.'

They bend themselves against the wind and after a while, they turn from the river and head towards the hamlet of Burbage at the foot of Grin Low. It sits at a crossroads before the roads fork, one climbing towards the moors and on to Macclesfield, the other snaking off into the wilderness, past Axe Edge and on to Leek.

At the crossroads sits an inn and they thankfully push open the door and stand, shaking the rain from their wet things.

A man is sweeping the floor and John approaches him.

'Could we trouble you for something to ward off the rain, sir? Brandy perhaps?'

The man stops sweeping and calls out loudly behind him. 'Customers!'

A woman appears behind the counter, brushing her hair with a dirty hand. She takes down a bottle from a shelf and puts it with two glasses in front of John without a word. The atmosphere is as cold and dank as the weather outside.

'Thank you,' says John with a smile. The glasses are filled, he hands one to Nat and they down them quickly.

'How long will it take to walk to Poole's Hole?' he asks.

She looks across at the man sweeping. 'Within the half hour,' he says without looking at them.

Nat looks outside. The rain has abated.

'I think we should set out again then John, while the rain holds off a while.'

John tilts the bottle and pours two more drinks. 'We'll finish these and be on our way then. Don't want to overstay or welcome,' he says dryly.

They pay the woman who looks disdainfully at them and they leave without further word.

'Well I never! Did we say something to break up a happy marriage do you think? No wonder the place was short of custom.'

'I'll know where to come if I need someone to clear a bar-room, that's for sure,' says Nat.

The two men start to walk along a track towards Poole's Hole. It is not steep but John is slowed by his bulk. His breathing comes short and he stops every now and then, on the pretence of looking out across the valley in which sits the town. The rain holds off long enough for them to make out the Crescent and the Stables and the few houses clustered round.

'Can you imagine what those Roman soldiers must have thought when they tramped over the moors and ended up here Nat? I'll bet they were delighted. Not an olive tree in sight or a cup of their favourite grape!'

A thin smile cuts into the mouth of his friend. 'I sometimes think you are too hard on the place. You have made a living of sorts out of it. The Duke obviously likes the place...'

'Huh! Have you seen him sipping the waters round here lately? I have never made his acquaintance in all the time I have been here. But I believe he likes the shooting and fishing. Plenty of that. Old Ryley took me fishing once. You remember him? Fine manager, but a bit loose in the paying department, when it came to our meagre wages.'

'The country side is fine, I'll grant you that, John. A pretty place to paint and write poetry about. Although I hear that most of those with a poem inside them go up to Cumberland; Windermere and such like, and pass by on the other side of glorious Derbyshire.'

'Well, at least they don't have a big hole like this one. We must be nearly there, surely.'

They walked on in silence and as they breast a brow in the

190

road, see a cluster of small cottages near the Hole.

As they approach the brooding dark scar in the side of the hill, an old woman comes bustling out of the nearest cottage.

'Come f't 'ole?' She is bow legged and even in the stiff breeze they can smell that she and the magic of soap and water are not acquainted.

'Yes, madam that is so,' says John pleasantly.

'I'll get guide. It'll be six pence each.'

The two men look at each other, slightly taken aback at the brevity of the welcome. As they wait they look up at the barren hillside dotted with lime heaps.

'We should go and look at those Nat. Meet the people who live there.'

'Why's that John?'

'Curiosity, that's all. I've never met anyone who lives in a hole in the ground, have you?'

A man of indeterminate age appears from the back of the cottage. He wears a stiffly brimmed hat with a candle attached to the front and holds two lanterns, one for each of the visitors.

'No one else is there?' he asked the old woman, who grunts and disappears into the cottage.

'Right gentlemen, if you would follow me. Best keep your hats on. Some parts is very low.' It appears that like his ancient relative, explanations are in short supply.

John has a little trouble stooping to enter the hole and Nat takes his arm. 'Don't worry,' says their guide. 'It gets wider just inside.'

They hear water and after a while, find themselves descending into a large cavern through which runs the stream.

'Well I never!' cries John who is amazed by the natural cathedral of colours and columns, formed by millions of years of water, drip dripping from the ceiling.

The guide points out formations which over time have been given strange names. 'That there is the Bacon flitch, hanging down,' says their guide proudly pointing to a large formation which, from a certain angle does resemble a side of bacon.

The light from their lamps dances across the smoothed lime-stone forms which, with the echo of their voices, gives the spectacle a haunted appearance. The stalactites drip with eerie plips as they feel their way further into the cave, slithering and sliding along as they hang on to one another.

'And Mr Poole?' asks John. 'Is there any remnant of him?'

'No', says the guide. 'Don't think there ever was anyone of that name who stayed here.'

'But the common understanding is that he was a famous highway man or robber who hid himself and his booty here?' says Nat.

'Nothing found of him here and I should know. I've been as far as anyone has been, and there's nowt, save a few animal bones.'

They have reached the end of the cave and are confronted by a large limestone pillar

'Queen Mary, God bless her, came here. That's her stone yonder.' The guide points to the pillar about which, if they had not been told, they would be ignorant of its royal association. The guide gives it light as best he can and they marvel at it's size and the abundance of hanging rocks and limestone shapes surrounding it.

As they turn for the entrance, John concedes that the trip has been worth while. 'This then is a wonder of the Peaks and I waited a long time to see it. They say many a worthy person has been before us Nat, Ben Jonson himself included.'

'Yes it is a wonder, John. Millions of year's worth of wonder. And the water running through here is what the good people drink and bathe in once it gets to Buxton.'

'Is that so? I just hope no one has pissed in it then.' And his cackling laugh echoes round the chamber.

The guide helps them along the uneven path, back towards the light. They emerge blinking and are surprised that they have been underground for a good hour. They hand back their lanterns and tip the guide. '...and keep looking for any treasure that Poole fellow might have left. You never know.' John suggests but his advice is met with mute indifference.

'Let's visit the lime people Nat. I would dearly like to see inside one of these places they call home.'

Behind Poole's Hole are a number of lime kilns, alongside which are dumped mounds of waste which have been hollowed out into serviceable dwellings, complete with windows and doors.

The two men climb up the slope behind Poole's Hole to find a rather forlorn family group, outside one of these strange cottages.

'Hello there! Would you mind if I rest awhile?' wheezes John who sits on a rough hewn chair placed just outside the door. The group stare in bewilderment. Nat looks nervous. The sorry group are suspicious and nervously edge away.

'Now, I have lived in Ireland and seen some strange looking houses, but I can't say I have ever seen anything quite like this. How comfortable is it to live in?' asks John. The bedraggled woman of the house looks barely out of her teens with a baby on her hip and two young children clutching at her dress. 'They look cosy enough,' he says with a broad grin.

'Are you from the Estate?' ventures a man who emerges on the sound of John's voice.

John looks puzzled. 'Estate?'

'Aye. Dukes agent.'

Oh! No, certainly not. Allow me to introduce us. I am John Kane and this is my friend, Nathanial Tyrrel; both of us practiced performers, comedians, actors, but no Opera. We have not the voices. We are lately with Mr Welch's company but the season is now over. But we will return to Buxton, make no mistake. We like the bracing air.'

The group continue to stare. 'May we have a peep inside? As we have come all this way to visit Poole's Hole we would deem it an honour to be shown inside your home.'

An elderly man who has also appeared nods in the direction of the young woman who pushes the door open, inviting them to look in.

John turns on the stool to look inside while Nat bends his head and enters. It has been divided up into separate compartments and although small and dark, the place has warmth and seems dry. The walls are of clinker crust and slag gone hard in the baking of the lime which makes it strong and impermeable.

After satisfying their curiosity, they make ready to leave and Nat gives them some coppers for being so obliging.

'Most grateful, we truly are.' John lifts his hat to the small crowd that has now gathered around them.

As they prepare to leave, an old woman emerges from another dwelling close by. Her ugliness is matched only by her untidy appearance and a thatch of white hair hanging in tails, matted and dirty. She is small and bent and breaks open a toothless smile.

She sidles up and looks inquisitively at John, who is adjusting his hat and straightening his great coat, ready for the walk down the hill and suddenly puts a hand on his arm. John flinches. She looks up at him and says, 'Tha wants to be careful what tha eats sir! Tha's too fat!' and she cackles in a high pitched disturbing rasp.

John, uneasy, attempts a joke. 'Have you ever played Macbeth, madam?'

She merely cackles again. 'Tha should be wary of what tha eats.'

The man hustles the old woman back inside the lime house and apologises for her strange behaviour. 'She is a cunning woman sir, always free with strange words, sir. She means no harm.'

'No harm done,' says John relieved that she has gone. 'A seer is she?'

'Not so much seer, sir, as healer.'

'Well, thank her for the advice will you. Good day.' And with that he takes Nat's arm and they proceed off down the hill, a little disconcerted.

'What, pray was that Nat? Telling me I'm too fat indeed. I'm as sound as I have ever been and ever likely to be.'

'Perhaps it was a warning of some kind.'

'Some of these old witches have been burned for less,' says John, who seems still discomforted by the old woman's pronouncement.

'Are you good to walk a bit further?' asks Nat in an attempt to distract his thoughts.

'As ready as any man.'

'Good. Lets walk over to that farm and then round to the London Road and back in time for a rest before you have your dinner.'

'Will you not be joining me this evening?'

'No. Mrs Tyrrel was most specific on the point that I dine with her this evening.'

'Thinks I will lead you astray, does she?'

'Something like that, yes. She knows your persuasive tongue, as well as I do.'

They walk for a while in silence save for the slight wheezing from John and the fading shouts of children playing amongst the lime kilns.

'You know, I sometimes look at you and Mrs Tyrrel and the Fairbairns and wonder, – no genuinely marvel – at the way you keep to your marriage. An actors life is a marriage breaker. There's not many that stay the course in our profession. I envy you, Nat!'

'So, what happened to you then?'

The day seems to suit the mood of reflection. It is dark and elementally powerful with the low clouds seeming to envelop them; the wind whipping them as they trudge along.

'If you don't want to talk about…'

'No, no. Perhaps it is time I let some of it out. Besides, if I don't share some of my secrets with anyone, there might be nothing for a eulogy at my funeral!'

'John, please, I'm not taking confession here.'

John looks at his friend with a broad smile. 'Did anyone tell you would have made a fine priest with that look of doom upon you.' He laughs and slaps him on the back. 'Come on Father, I'll tell you everything on one condition.'

'What's that?'

'You buy me a drink when we get back into town. Anyway, I follow no religion. Why, I'm from Dublin, the city of sin! My father was a printer in a small way and if I had not made a nuisance of myself at the old Theatre Royal just around the corner from his shop, I too would probably be a printer this very day. When I was a boy, I would wait outside the stage door, waiting to run errands for whoever poked their nose outside. John O'Keeffe, Jane Daly, Dora Jordan; I ran errands for them all. I remember having to take a note from Anne Catley and sworn to secrecy, had to deliver it to a gentleman friend. She was beautiful. Smiled at me and my little heart melted. She had many gentlemen friends in those days.'

'I remember the lady,' says Nat. 'I saw her as Polly in the *Beggar's Opera*. The audience wouldn't let her go. My father was in the profession. He was a juggler and puppeteer you know.'

'I didn't know that. Would I have known him?'

'No, he died some while ago.'

'Isn't that the way, though. My father did not last beyond my fifteenth birthday, which left us in a pretty pickle, although my mother managed to sell the printing shop for a sum which kept her going. But I had to leave; came to London and headed straight for Drury Lane.'

'Started young, did you?'

'Oh no. No one wanted a snotty nosed Irish boy with not a penny in his pocket. I got a job with a printer. My father at least left me with the rudiments of the trade and as luck would have it, the man was a printer of plays amongst other things. He provided most of the playhouses in London with scripts and re-issues, new plays and old. Which meant that I got to deliver them all round town. I read them all and would often find an excuse to go to the theatre just before curtain and tell the man on the door that I had been sent with a script. I'd get in, and put myself somewhere quiet and watch from the wings.'

'You must have seen some fine performances then John.'

'Oh yes. I saw them all. And that's how I first saw Kate, my wife.'

'Oh? Was she in the profession?'

'You might say that,' he says caustically. 'Chorus work, dancing, walk on's, fill in's. We were both young. I was about nineteen and she the same.'

Nat slows his pace. John is already puffing a little and he is anxious to hear more.

'By then I had got some parts too. Light stuff mainly. It seems that I could make an audience laugh, so work came my way.'

'And your wife?'

'When we married we found a place to live, but things went sour right from the start.'

'What happened?'

John stops and looks at his friend before answering.

'What happened? The arrogance of youth. Chasing rainbows. I can't say for sure but I was mad in love with her. She was untamed; a beautiful wild animal with all the grace and claws of a cat who could never be caged.'

There is bitterness and sorrow in his words. He looks deep into the eyes of his friend.

'And I killed her.'

Nat's long jaw falls open and words fail him.

The rain starts again, sleeting in horizontally across the hills. John suddenly looks broken, as if something has come detached.

'You killed her?' Nat too feels as thought the world has suddenly jolted on its axis.

'I was to blame, yes,' he says in a voice Nat has never heard before; deep and shaken. Rain drips from the brim of his hat.

'Perhaps we should get on John. You look as if you could rest awhile.'

'No!' He puts his face up to the rain, and like Lear, defies the elements.

The two men stand against the wind, stark against the sky-line.

'I have never told anyone about that terrible night. We were young and in love and we swore to keep faith with one another. But we were both wildly impetuous. You couldn't help it, drinking and carousing with fast friends and strangers. London is so full of lust and depravity and we took what we wanted but Oh Lord, what a pustulous whore the place is.'

'I don't think things have changed much,' says Nat who has taken his friend by the arm and is slowly guiding him back down the slope.

'No, I suppose not. Kate, my beautiful Kate was a good dancer and found work easily. Me, I had to take to the road sometimes; a stroller, finding work out of London, Oxford, Reading, Brighton.

He wipes the rain from his face. 'It was not long before she had our first child; a boy. Patrick I called him. The little fellow lived for three weeks. Kate did not weep like I did. She just accepted it as part of God's will and went back to dancing. There was a hardness about her, a grim fatalism that I could never understand, Nat. She fell pregnant again and I hoped that this time we might hang on to the little creature. A girl this time, the poor little thing lived for six weeks.'

The rain eases and John's words take on a hard edge.

'Well, by now, Kate had decided that she was not destined for motherhood. Not that she seemed keen on the idea in the first place. But it also broke us. When I was working out of town she would take up with anyone prepared to buy her a drink. Every time I came back, the threads that bound us seemed to get thinner. But she could never let me go. No matter how hard we fought, and by God we had some fights, she wanted me. You see, Nat I was so in love with her, I would have done anything! I was her harbour, the place where she knew she could always find me; I would always look her in the eye and tell her I loved her; not someone who would just indulge himself and throw her away. There was little I could do to slow her down, mind. She had this…. this wish…., I can't say the word, but you know what I'm saying!'

John's face is screwed up with tension.

'I don't know why some people are like that but she found no ease unless she had a drink in her hand, a song on her lips and a pack of pox ridden revellers to be entertained. Perhaps it was the loss of our babies. I remember after we lost the little girl, she just stayed in bed for ages. Would not talk to anyone, not even me. Ate nothing. Just lay there with her face to the wall. And then one day, up she jumps, out she goes, saying there is a part waiting for her and she did not come back for a month.'

'How long were you married John?'

'Oh, on and off seven years or thereabouts. Towards the end, I could stand it no longer. She became resentful; she would flaunt her men in my presence and I would loose my temper. Got into terrible fights because of that. Ripped a man's ear off once and she screamed at me as if I had killed him. Swore she would see me in jail.

And then, the next morning she would come round crying her eyes out, swearing she would change, stop her drinking and be a good wife.

That would last all of a week. And, do you know, Nat, in that week we would be the happiest, most carefree couple, laughing and joking with each other as if nothing had ever come between us. Her Dionysos, she called me, to her Ariadne. I think deep down she really did love me.

But it never lasted. As soon as we got back to the boards, and we hardly ever worked at the same theatres, she would be up to her old tricks.

So, came the day when I could stand it no longer and decided to go back to Dublin on my own. Of course she could not have that. I was deserting her! How was she to live without me; why was I being so cruel! It was terrible Nat. I didn't want to leave her but we could not live together like this.

We had a terrible fight, throwing things and hitting out. I hate the memory of it but I can remember every detail.'

John is almost whispering. They stop near the outskirts of the town and he looks beseechingly at his friend, seeking absolution.

'We were both drunk, but she worse than I. It was so easy. One minute she was standing at the top of the stairs, swearing like a fish porter at me; swearing vengeance and the next she was at the foot of the stairs with her neck broken.'

There is a silence between them. 'Oh, John. I never knew of your pain. You hide it well.'

John is silent, a distant look on his face. 'And why not? It happened a long time ago. No sense in telling the world; no sense in having others carry my burden.'

'But you still hurt, I can see that.'

'At times, yes, at times. But not so often.' Nat looked at his friend who's eyes are filled with tears.

'My dear friend…'

'I'm getting too old for this life Nat. I look at the younger ones and think it all belongs to them now. I'll do what I can to help some of them; show them where the pit falls are. Some listen…… others…… well.'

'Young Grace Butler?'

Again he takes his time in answering. 'Yes.'

John takes a deep breath, wipes the tears and looks up.

'Sky's clearing Nat. I'm not sure I feel any better, but its good to have a friend like you and a drink will see me good as new.'

And as if the sun has emerged from the gloomy sky, his face suddenly changes. He shakes his coat, sighs deeply and puts his memories away.

'Well, that's that! I said what I have to say to my confessor and soon we will both be gone from this place.' He looks around him and then remembers. 'Come on now I promised Mrs Mycock I would dig up some horseradish for my supper. Will you help me?'

Can you answer me one question John?' asks Nat sombrely. 'Did you push her...?'

John pauses and his face has a curiously intense twist. 'Do you know, I really can't remember. Now lets find this horse-radish, else Mrs Mycock won't marry me!'

They get back into the town and Nat leaves John to go and get out of his wet things. John stops off at the Wheatsheaf first. He stands at one end of the bar, not wishing to engage anyone; thoughtful, brooding. 'Well', he thinks, I'll be in Liverpool in a few days. Another day, another adventure no doubt.'

The afternoon is spent in his rooms. He changes his wet clothes and reads for an hour. Then he writes a letter.

My dear Jane,

I think I will not be back in Buxton next year. Ten years is an awful long time to be coming back to annoy the good people in this town and I believe I have outstayed my welcome.

I will miss much in this place, for I cannot deny that there is an honesty bred of people who have to live amongst these barren hills. Above all I will miss you and David and Nat Tyrrel my dearest friends.

I have no firm thoughts after the Christmas season in Liverpool, but will try my luck back in Dublin.

"Such is the Patriot's boast, where'ere we roam

His first best country ever, is at home"

I knew Oliver Goldsmith shortly before he died. I think you would have liked him and he would have laughed with us that night two years ago when the stage sets fell down on poor Elliston.

Remember me in your thoughts and who knows, we might get to act opposite one another again.

Your ever thoughtful and attentive friend.

> *John Kane.*

He seals the letter and leaves it for his landlady to deliver.

'Well, I'll be off tomorrow.' He looks around the small untidy room. Most of his belongings can be fitted into one bag; a strolling player needs very little.

At The Sun Inn, he has just related the tale of Ryley's escape from the Sheriff's man and finished the first course of his dinner, a river trout in parsley sauce. He smiles, as his plate with nothing more than the well plucked bones is removed 'Wasted here, am I not Mrs Mycock? Old Ryley can make a fine play with my help.'

'I don't know about that Mr Kane. Certainly no waste left on your plate, that's for sure.'

People move in and out of the cosy inn and there is still the air of expectation that John Kane will entertain them further. It is warm and jolly with cheerful laughter.

Nat Tyrrel finishes his drink and rises. 'Well, that's it for another season John. I'll wish you the best of luck and hope to see you next year.'

John rises to shake his friend's hand. 'And the same to you old friend. My very best regards to Mrs Tyrrel, and may Saint Genesius who looks down on all actors grant you the success you deserve. You're a good friend, Nat. I won't forget you.'

They embrace, patting one another on the back. 'See you next year then.'

'I hope so Nat, I hope so. Who knows.'

The assembled group of drinkers witnesses this scene with satisfaction.

'He's a fair man that Nat Tyrrel,' says Nadin the butcher. 'Wife always pays me regular.' There is a murmur of assent around the room.

'None fairer,' says John. 'A true friend to me, that's for sure. He looks towards the kitchen, where he can see Mrs Mycock preparing his main course. 'Will you bring in a bottle of claret please Mrs Mycock and stand these good people a drink of their choice as well.'

They all mumble their thanks. 'I'll be leaving you by tomorrow, so it's only fair that I leave some memory of myself, else, knowing you lot, I'll be getting nothing but paltry comments behind my back.'

'No! no.' they call, 'Not you Mr Kane. says Peter the handyman. 'Tha's a gentleman, even if tha is an actor!'

John laughs along with the rest of them. 'I've never been called a gentleman before, Peter! I've always settled for actor or scoundrel but I like the epithet. Gentleman actor! It suits, don't you think?'

Mrs Mycock comes back in and puts a bottle of wine on his table. By now John is feeling quite merry, but thinks that for his last night in town, it is his right to be merry.

'Your food is just coming,' she says cheerfully. 'I've found a really nice piece of best rump, courtesy of Mr Nadin'

'Thank you my dear, and here's thanks to you Nadin.' And he holds his glass up to the butcher in salutation.

She bustles back in with a large plate on which lie two thick slices of beef. Alongside she places a pot of gravy and a second plate piled high with potatoes, carrots and greens. 'There we go Mr Kane. You won't go hungry on your journey tomorrow now, will you?'

He licks his lips in anticipation, picks up his knife and fork and is about to begin.

'Just a minute Mrs Mycock. The horseradish? Where's the horseradish which I so laboriously dug out for you this morning in all that wind and rain?'

'Oh, I nearly forgot. I'll just get it. I've made it up to my own recipe Mr Kane.'

The group watch him with some envy as he begins his meal. Most of them will leave soon to find a more modest fare set by wives or mothers on their own tables.

She puts a small bowl of creamy sauce next to him which he spoons liberally onto his beef. The meal is now complete. He picks up the knife and slices off a large piece of the rich dark red meat, smears on the sauce and groans with contentment. The first slice soon disappears.

Mr Poulter spots it first. John's fork falls from his hand and he grips his throat as if he has swallowed a fish bone. 'Are you alright Mr Kane?' he shouts across but John is far from alright. He coughs. 'My throat!' he gurgles. 'My throat is on fire!'

Mr Poulter, together with one or two others, moves towards him. John tears at the buttons of his waistcoat. 'I'm burning!' he screams and before anyone can reach out, he vomits up the contents of his stomach. Mrs Mycock enters and screams at the sight of John who is now writhing in his seat, in great torment. 'Lie him down!' She shouts. 'Lie him on the floor!'

John Kane is a big man and it takes four of them to help him out of his chair. In doing so, the plate of beef and horseradish are sent crashing to the stone floor, just where they intend putting his head. His breathing is shallow and laboured. Mrs Mycock is too upset to do anything but run to the kitchen where she breaks down, wailing uncontrollably. Mr Poulter feels his pulse and wipes his forehead and is surprised by how clammy his skin feels. John by now is jibbering incoherently. Panic has set in with most of the drinkers. Some leave quickly whilst others look on ghoulishly. Only Mr Poulter and Nadin the butcher maintain sufficient reason to help.

'Is there a doctor anywhere?'

They all look at each other, no one quite sure.

'I think there is one down at the Hall, if he has not gone. They only come in the season, when there are bath patients.'

'Run on down and see if he is still here,' says Poulter. 'Mrs Mycock! Mrs Mycock, water if you please!'

She hurries back in and together they hold his head up and get a few sips of water into him which he accepts gratefully.

'Thank you,' he whispers and then lets out a howl of agony. 'The pain! I can't stand it!' He shakes and mumbles. 'Mrs Mycock', he whispers. 'Mrs Mycock, it wasn't the beef!'

'Oh Mr Kane, what have I done! Mr Kane…' but she gives way to more tears, devastated that she is the cause of this calamity.

For some time, he lies shivering but conscious, taking sips of water and then letting the water dribble back out. It is too painful. His gut is a screaming hell fire which he has no control over and his breathing is getting weaker. He sees nothing but white lights and fearful colours and hears little.

If he were audible, they would hear him mumbling, '*I believe in God the father almighty, creator of heaven and earth; and in Jesus Christ his only son our Lord; who was conceived by the holy spirit, born of the Virgin Mary…*'

John had not recited the creed since he was a boy but he is terrified and can think of nothing else….he is desperate.

A doctor is found but by the time he gets up the hill it is too late.

John Kane dies on the stone floor of the inn, with strangers about him. His last sight is of Peter the handyman, simple Peter, who has tears running down his cheeks.

The whole town is shocked for there are few who did not laugh along with the big man. He was generous and kind, although he had little to show for his years on the stage. But a man who smiles as much as he did is rich in friendship and they all come to bury him in the little church across the road from the place where he breathed his last.

Nat Tyrrel, Jane and David Fairbairn delay there departure to say their farewells to John. She received the letter he had written just before he made his way to the inn and has not stopped weeping since. She vows never to return to Buxton.

Nat Tyrrel too is changed by the death of his friend and his story. He knows his acting days are over and, in the years following, you will find him working for a charitable institution that cares for distressed actors and actresses in London.

John Kane is fifty eight years old. He bequeaths nothing to anyone but his memory and for years after, people swear they hear the clink of a glass and his laughter in the tap room of the Sun Inn. Mrs Mycock keeps his bent beer mug on a ledge for all to see and often looks at it in fond memory, and smiles.

EPILOGUE

John Kane died a painful death on the 10th November 1799 aged fifty eight, poisoned accidentally by his own hand. The commonly held view is that whilst out walking he mistakenly dug up hemlock instead of the horseradish he wanted for his beef dinner.

Horseradish is a member of the Brassica family which includes broccoli and cabbage. The root is used as a condiment after being grated and mixed with vinegar. As such it would have been commonly used in the late 18th Century with a range of cooked meats and fish.

It is found in relatively shaded, drained areas. November, the month in which John Kane died, would have been the right time to go digging for horseradish roots after the plant leaves had died back and the root has reached maturity.

Hemlock is found as two different strains; Poison Hemlock and Water Hemlock (Musquash Root). Both are equally as poisonous.

Poison Hemlock is a tall plant with small white clustered flowers, which gives off a foul odour and found most prolifically in the spring. It is quite often mistaken for cow parsley or wild parsnip.

Water Hemlock although botanically the same as Poison Hemlock, is toxicologically different with the root clusters being highly poisonous.

Both plants are found in damp wet areas near streams and swampy ground and it is quite plausible that it would have grown along the River Wye and other damp areas around

Buxton.

There is however another plant with highly poisonous properties that John Kane might have dug up rather than Hemlock.

Aconite, otherwise known as Wolfsbane or Monkshood belongs to the buttercup family. It grows in well drained soils in hilly areas and whilst its flowers are colourful and distinctive, it is the root which carries the sting. Unlike hemlock, the root looks similar to the horseradish root. It has been used for generations for medical purposes and as a fast acting poison.

So, it is possible that whilst walking down from the plantations above Poole's Cavern, he found aconite, the stems and flowers of which had died back and the root mistaken for horseradish.

The symptoms shown by John Kane would have been very similar had it been aconite or hemlock which he put on his beef. Nausea, vomiting, gastric pain, numbing of the skin and sensitive areas, convulsions, and slow asphyxiation leading to heart failure and death.

He was not the only one however to be poisoned by either of these toxic killers.

Socrates was the most famous victim of hemlock poisoning and the Witches in Hamlet used it in their stinking brew.

Aconite has been used most recently by Lakhvir Kaur Singh who was convicted of attempted murder of her lover in 2009 when she mixed some in his curry. There have been other more successful attempted murders ending in death, both real and fictional, throughout history and accidental deaths have also been recorded.

Either of these poisons might have been responsible but we know he died a painful death. Of John Kane himself, we know little, but as a possible testament to his popularity, he was buried in St Anne's churchyard, with his head facing towards all the other gravestones, as if they were his audience. His grave can be seen there to this day.

BIBLIOGRAPHY

Ros McCoola, *Theatre in the Hills* 1984

Ivan Hall, *Georgian Buxton* 1984

William Adam, *Gem of the Peak* 1851

Mike Langham, *A People's History* 2001

Allardyce Nicoll, *British Drama* 1925

Earnest Axon, Buxton Archaeological Society 1932 -1941

Anna Seward *The letters of Anna Seward* Published 1811

J Black, Buxton in 1787, *Derbyshire Miscellany*, Vol X, 1985

H Heslop, *Buxton Old and New*, Vol 1, 1931

E Burton, *Coaches and Carriers*, Derbyshire Life and Countryside, Vol.43, 1978

Phyllis Hembry, *The English Spa, 1560 – 1815*, 1990

Oliver Goldsmith, *She Stoops to Conquer*, first performed 1773

Miscellaneous items at the Derbyshire County Records Office

Miscellaneous items at the Buxton Museum.

PRO PATRIA

Soldiers at the Pavilion

ALBERT
June 1922

Albert George Gibson stepped off the train at Buxton Station and looked around. 'Not changed much,' he thought. There was little joy in him as he picked up his cardboard suitcase and proceeded out of the waiting room and down into Spring Gardens. It was mid day and he was ready for something to eat and drink. His breakfast at six o'clock that morning had consisted of a warm cup of tea and crust of bread left over from the previous evening. He had left his home in South Yorkshire without anyone noticing.

Albert was small and wiry and looked even smaller in his second hand suit, a size too large for him. He wore his cap at a slight angle, an affectation he had once thought might be attractive to women.

Albert walked slowly along the bustling road, looking for a suitable tea room that would not stretch his meagre budget. He would have to find somewhere to sleep for a few nights and he did not have enough money to splash out on silver service.

The door bell clanged as he pushed open the door of a small café and the diners looked up, silently urging him to close the door against the chill wind that had entered with him. He sat at a table near the door and glanced at the menu.

A young girl approached. 'Can I get you anything sir?'

'Yes. Please. I'll have the mutton stew. And a round of bread and butter. And a cup of tea. Thank you.'

She sniffed and hurried away to deliver his order through a curtained door. Albert glanced around at the other diners. They looked like tourists or out of towners like himself. He removed his cap and brushed specks of soot from the arm of his jacket, the result of him leaning out of the train as they entered the station. Despite his twenty six years, he looked worn. His shoulders sagged a little as if he carried the woes of the world. A young woman listening disinterestedly to her companion, glanced in his direction and thought he was not bad looking, but could certainly do with smartening himself up a bit.

He pushed back the flop of hair that fell across his forehead and ran his fingers through his thick dark mane. He sighed inwardly and momentarily thought about what might be happening back home in Yorkshire. No one knew where he was. They would not start worrying until he failed to return home.

The waitress came back with his cup of tea and clumsily placed it in front of him, spilling some into the saucer.

'Stew's just coming,' she said unenthusiastically. Alfred poured the spillage back into his cup and briefly caught the eye of the young woman. He smiled and she turned away abruptly. 'I must look a right state,' he thought. He ran his hand over his chin which had not been shaved that morning in his haste to leave. His shirt collar and cuffs were un-ironed. He felt shabby.

His food arrived and despite his hunger, he took his time about spooning the first mouthful and chewed the tough gristly meat slowly. It was something he had taught his young daughters, Clementine and Beatrice. 'Eat slowly and politely and people will think you are proper brought up,' he had told them.

He finished the stew and wiped round the plate with the remaining piece of bread.

As he looked around, he suddenly felt lost. The early morning flight, whilst not spontaneous, was done in haste and now he wondered what to do with his day. He might go up into the plantation, past Poole's Cavern, if the rain kept off. And he had to find lodgings as well.

People came and went, including the young woman who glanced once more in his direction before she and her companion left.

He finished up and paid a man who sat near the entrance to the café.

'Can you tell me of a decent place to sleep this night. Nothing too expensive like.'

'What, a hotel or something?'

Well, I was thinking more of lodgings. A room or summat. Somewhere I can lay me 'ead for a couple of nights.'

The man scratched himself and grimaced. 'Not sure. There's plenty hotels of course and there's guest houses along by the Gardens. They's a bit dear.' He paused. 'I tell thee what, why not pop into one at' public houses and ask there. Bound to be someone who knows of a room you could have.' The man smiled broadly. 'Ye come far, have you?'

Alfred said 'No, not really. I were billeted here for a spell during the war and I'm just visiting old haunts.'

Oh? 'Who were you with?'

'Sherwood Foresters.' Alfred said proudly and momentarily his shoulders straightened.

'You saw some action then?' The man said.

'Yes, you could say that. But I liked me time here. That's why I come back for a look round. See what's changed.'

'Oh, not much! Still same dreary wet place as ever was.'

Alfred picked up his suitcase. 'Well, ta fort' advice, like.' He was about to leave and turned. 'How long do you stay open?'

'Till about six.'

'Can I leave me case with you? I don't want to drag it all over t' town. I'll be back before then.'

'Aye,' the man said expansively. 'Just drop it down here by me. I'll look after it for you.'

'Thanks. I'll be back for me dinner an' all tomorrow,' he said as recompense for the small kindness.

He walked out and for once the rain let up. 'Well, I'm here,' he said forcefully and turned in the direction of the Pleasure Gardens. He walked past the looming Crescent with a thin trickle of people milling around the entrances to the Baths. Men leaned against bath chairs, waiting for their passengers and looked guardedly at Albert as he sauntered by. In the gardens the trees were in full leaf and flowers beginning to bud. The shouts of children echoed off the buildings and the ducks quacked a greeting. Memories flooded back and lifted his dark humour; a brief shaft of sunlight which reminded him of happier times.

2
June 1916

'It's come'

'What's come?'

'Me call up.'

Alfred's mother turned pale. 'Oh Jesus!' she said quietly and sat down at the kitchen table.

'We all knew it were going to happen.'

'I know, but I hoped not yet. You're only just nineteen. You should 'a followed your Da down pit. Least wise you would have been in reserved occupation.'

'I could die just as same. Same as me Da.'

'That were different. He were here. I'd rather have you stop 'ere, with me an your brother an sister. I'd know where you are.'

'Mam, I have to go. You won't be alone. There's Uncle Jack and Aunty Ilene round corner. They can look out for you.'

His mother had been expecting the news and now her face was contorted with concern. He was the man of the house since her husband had died and she relied on him.

'Well there's now't I can do,' he said as gently as possible and threw the letter on the table in front of her.

'I have to report to recruiting office tomorrow.'

He wasn't the only one in the town. All his pals had the letter.

A little later, he went in to work and told his supervisor who, whilst sympathetic, could not promise to keep his job open until he came back.

Albert was a sign writer. He had been apprenticed to the Council since the age of sixteen and was good at his job. It also got him round town and into villages nearby where he could escape the smell of the coal pits and the coking plant. He was a country man at heart and the thought of working down a mine, in the dark, sent shivers through him.

'I'll do what I can, lad. To give you your job back when you return. But no promises.'

'Thanks,' said Albert. 'I'll make sure I get back in one piece.' It was the most he could hope for.

The following day he went down to the recruiting office along with a number of his friends. There were quite a few of them milling around, joshing one another.

'You're too bloody small you, Babcock! They'll never have you!' shouted Joe Mason. 'And as for you Jones, ya's sken eyed! Tha'll see t' enemy coming from two different directions!'

They all laughed and joked nervously, pushing and shoving each other as they waited for the doors to open. Albert joined in and forgot the tears his mother shed when he left the house. Cigarettes were passed round and they lounged against the wall, trying to look older and more confident than they really felt.

All the recruits filed into the hall where, in front of two desks, sat two recruiting sergeants, caps placed on the corner of the table, ready to complete the preliminaries. They didn't smile but sat stiffly filling in the necessary paperwork for each man who presented himself. They were then all directed to a large room where they completed their attestation. After that they were told to go home and await further instructions.

'Do we get the King's shilling now?' asked Joe and was met with an icy stare.

'Now don't go upsetting me, son.' said the elderly sergeant. 'Tha's only just arrived and I don't tek to a smart arse.'

'So, that's that!' said Joe as he and Albert walked back down the street. 'We're now the property of His Majesty who can do what he likes wir us and we can do nowt about it.'

'Are you excited?' asked Albert.

'Oh aye, too bloody right! Gets us out of this shit hole for a start,' he said sardonically

'And what about your family. Will they miss you?'

'Can't wait to get rid of me, me dad says. One less mouth to feed, he says.'

Albert too was excited at the thought of getting away and exploring a new world but would not readily admit to the ache in the pit of his stomach when he thought about leaving them all and he hoped Joe felt the same. He did not want to be any less courageous.

'Well, I'll see you around then Joe. Lets hope we get sent to the same place for us training.'

Albert did not go home directly, but walked round the corner at the end of his street and back tracked through town and into the woods that lay to the west. He often walked out here by himself. He would listen for bird song and spot small animals as they scurried through the undergrowth. But now, his mind was elsewhere and he sat under a large tree and imagined what life might be like in the trenches.

'I wish you were here Dad,' he whispered. 'I don't like leaving me Mam.'

A lump rose in his throat. 'Can you look out for her. I don't want her worrying about me.'

He looked up through the trees. There was no noise other than branches swaying and leaves swishing in the early summer breeze.

'I wonder what it's *really* like over there?'

3

Albert had never been further than Leeds. When he got his instructions and rail warrant for Clipstone in Nottinghamshire, his excitement grew. At last, after six weeks of waiting, he was off. This was something new. Most of those who had signed up at the recruiting office had been earmarked for the infantry and also found themselves heading into the vast battalion of reservists, ready to be trained.

The family gathered to say their good bye's and his mother pressed a small, silver plated St Christopher into his hand. 'To look after you,' she said with tears trickling down her cheeks.

It was at Clipstone that Albert got his first sight of what war was capable of. One of the barracks housed wounded men returning from the trenches who would be going back to their regiments, once they were mended and fit.

He approached a man one morning at breakfast and asked, in a friendly way, how he found things at the front. The man, who looked a lot older than his years, turned slowly to Albert.

'Where are you from?'

'Village near Barnsley.'

'Mining country,' he said enigmatically. 'Well, you should be fairly used to injury then.'

Albert thought of the day they brought his father out of the pit, along with four others. His Da had been crushed by a fall and although Albert had been prevented from seeing the remains, he remembered all too vividly the blood soaked canvas that had been thrown over him. The experience had numbed him and for weeks afterwards he was woken by the nightmare of his father's bloodied corpse.

'Ay, I am.'

'Well, double what you've seen. Nay, triple it. I was lucky.' He lifted his shirt to display a long scimitar of a scar running down the side of his chest and stomach. 'Just a scratch for me. Shrapnel never went very deep.'

'And they're sending you back?'

'Aye. No option. Besides, I can't let my pals down.'

The man stood up and turned to Albert before moving off. He had an intense look.

'A word of advice. Don't get to close to anyone; don't make any friends. You'll regret it.'

The months at Clipstone were spent in drilling and marching and field craft. Many of the young men, particularly those from cities and large towns, needed fattening up and Albert himself needed to be stronger for the rigours of trench life.

When he got home on leave, his mother looked at him dressed up in his khaki uniform and smiled. 'You've put on a bit of weight.'

'They feed us well.'

'Will you come down to the photographer and get your photo taken?'

'Why?'

''Cause you look like a proper man, Albert. Your Dad would be proud. And I want you standing on t'mantle piece, so's I can look at you.'

That evening, he went down to the pub on the corner of his street. Some of his friends were there, along with others on leave from the Training Reserve. He felt proud to be in uniform and puffed out his chest as he marched down the street. He was greeted warmly and as he settled in for an evening of beer and banter, he wondered how best he could ask John Bairstow how his sister was faring.

'Aye up Albert lad! Yer look proper smart in that uniform.' It was his uncle Peter who could usually be found in the pub most evenings. He was a kindly man with a purple nose and the dark grey and coal flecked skin of the miner. He had been good to the family when Albert's father had been killed and Albert always had a soft spot for him.

'Hello Uncle Peter. I'm not home long. I'll be joining a proper regiment soon and then more than like going to France.'

'Oh, good lad. Good lad!' and he slapped Albert on the back in a friendly drunken show of affection. 'We can count on you, lad. You stick it to 'em!"

On the other side of the pub sat his other uncle, Peter's brother, Robert who wasn't so kindly and even less so when he saw Albert in uniform. The brothers had not spoken since the outbreak of the war. Uncle Peter was all for giving the Hun a good kicking whilst uncle Robert, the Marxist, wanted revolution in his own country before killing Germans. Nothing short of the overthrow of the King and the capitalists would do and he spent many hours fermenting revolution at the local Labour party and Union club. If the Russians could rise up and start fighting the real enemy, so could the working people of Britain.

Albert acknowledged him with a frown. 'Uncle Robert,' he said, gesturing a half hearted hello towards him with his pint in hand.

'How do.' Uncle Robert sucked hard on his pipe and said in a loud voice. 'More cannon fodder. I'll not congratulate you, but I will wish you well. It's men like you we need at home, not over there.'

'Aye, I'll bear that in mind,' Albert said ungraciously and turned to find Johnny Bairstow.

He was sat in a corner with a couple of other young men. 'Room for another?' Albert asked, pulling up a stool.

'How are you?' asked Johnny. 'You look right proud of the

'sen. Do you know when you're going?'

'No not really. There's a rumour that the Sherwood Foresters need more men, but nothing confirmed. Probably end up doing guard duty at a depot in England somewhere.'

Johnny was not in uniform. He had been down the pit for the last year now as were a couple of other friends sitting at the table.

'Hey, you remember that Eamon Capstick who were in same class as us?' said Johnny. 'Well, he's only skiddadled. He got his call up papers, same as you but then he buggered off! No one's seen him for weeks. Big sergeant come round his house, knocking ont' door asking where he was.'

'Where's he gone then?'

'Fook knows. Just didn't fancy having his balls shot off.' Johnny immediately regretted what he said in front of his friend who might find himself emasculated before long.

'Sorry Albert, I didn't mean...'

'That's OK. I think I know the score. How's your mum and dad?' he asked, weaving his way unsubtly towards finding out about his sister.

'OK 'spose.'

'And Jeanie?'

'Got a job in Jackson's. You need to move a bit sharp in that direction though Albert. She's got that Harry Jackson sniffing round her.'

'Oh?' said Albert and his stomach leapt into his mouth on hearing the news. 'I was only asking, like.'

'Yeah? We all know you have an eye for my little sister, but I reckon that slimy twerp might be coming on the inside rail.'

Albert felt his cheeks redden. Harry bloody Jackson! Jumped up little toss pot, if ever there was one. Just because his father owned the drapers shop in the High Street, he thought he was better than all else! 'I'll knock the little fooker's head off!' he thought.

'I might come round your place and say hello then.'

'She'll be there,' said Johnny with a wink. 'Though I'm not sure she'll want to see you now she might be in the money!'

They all laughed at Albert's discomfort and ragged him some more before turning to the serious matter of getting drunk. If Albert was only on a forty eight hour pass, his friends wanted to make sure he did it in style.

He awoke the next morning with a head like a ringing anvil. His mother let him stay in bed longer than she would normally and then called him down for a bit of breakfast.

'What you got on?' she asked.

'Oh nowt much. Not much I can do with the time I got left. Think I might go out and see if anyone's about.'

He helped her tidy up, got the coal in and waited impatiently until mid day, with his stomach doing summersaults all the while.

'Think I'll just pop out for a bit.'

'Where you going? Don't forget that we're going down to Frith's this afternoon to get your photo done.'

As the clock struck twelve by the church bell, Albert was waiting on the opposite side of the road to Jackson's the drapers, hopping impatiently from one foot to the other. He could see Jeanie scurrying about, glancing to see if he had arrived. At last, she came out, clutching her sandwiches in a paper bag. Nervously she said, 'Hello. I can't stay long'

'Me neither,' he said and together they walked slowly up the High Street, with one or two knowing glances from neighbours thrown in their direction.

4
1922

It started to rain again. He remembered the last time he had been here it seemed to rain most of the time. The Battalion had been billeted in rows of tents just outside the town but some had been lucky enough to be billeted in large houses and hotels which made things a lot more bearable. But every time they stepped outside, the rain came on the westerly wind. The endless marching and parade manoeuvres with rain water trickling down the backs of their necks made them all tetchy. No matter how much it rained, he delighted in the place; the way it closed itself round with woods, the town nestling in a bowl; the fine buildings, the clean air, the smell of the place. All, so different from his own village. He had never slept in a large house before. He told his uncle Arthur that he felt 'right grand', opening the double doors and stepping out onto the gravel path that ran round the neatly kept garden.

And he remembered the Canadian troops. Hundreds of big men who had the glamour of being from a far off land, with accents which sat liltingly on the ear. Men of the wide world, of forests and mountains. He vowed that Canada would be his destination after the war.

He walked down the busy main street and found a pub where he hoped someone might tell him where he could put up for a few nights. He wanted somewhere quiet and out of the way, somewhere he could not be disturbed.

The pub was already full of men sat at wooden tables and the atmosphere was stale and smoky and they all looked at the stranger in his thin suit which made him a little self conscious.

He ordered a beer and stood at the bar, sipping slowly. When the landlord had a moment, Albert asked if he knew of any- where he might stay.

He eyed Albert suspiciously.

'We don't have rooms. Try one of the hotels along the street.'

'I was looking for a room really. For a couple of nights. Somewhere quiet like.'

'Not sure.' He started serving another customer. 'You know

of anywhere Bob? This here bloke's looking for a bed for the night.'

The customer weighed up Albert. 'I might. You just passing through? You got business here?'

'Aye,' said Albert. 'Aye, I have a bit of business but I also just wanted to have a look around. I were here a few year ago and liked the place. Always wanted to come back.'

The customer said, 'Well, old Jack Mycock has the cottages up the back there which he lets out. He might help.'

The landlord sniffed. 'He might. But he's a fussy bugger.'

'Where can I find him?'

'Try the White Lion further down the street. He usually sups in there.'

'Thanks, I will. And can I get something to eat round here?'

'Grove Hotel,' said the landlord without much enthusiasm. All he seemed to do was direct Albert and his money to other establishments.

Albert found Jack Mycock. He seemed to be a local property owner and builder in a small sort of way and showed Albert a room in a grim little row of cottages at the back of the main road.

'This is all I have at the moment. You can have it for seven and six a night. How long you intend staying?'

'Not sure. Two nights at least. This will do.'

Albert gave him fifteen shillings and thanked him.

'There's a pump outside and you can use the bucket over there. No disturbing the other occupants and no getting drunk. OK?'

Jack Mycock left him and Albert slumped down onto the thin bed which looked as if it had been made from a few wooden planks nailed together with a thin horse hair pallet tucked into the frame. There was a basin on a small rickety table in one corner, a couple of chairs and rather incongruously, a large fine rosewood sideboard and mirror which dominated the length of one wall. On it sat a chipped jug and an old bent oil lamp.

He looked around and sighed. 'This'll have to do.' he thought. The old white washed walls and the silence oppressed him.

He tossed the suitcase onto the bed beside him and opened it. There was little in it; a clean shirt, some underwear, a hair comb, his notebook and a service revolver. He took out a dog eared notebook. He had bought it when he worked for the council and had neatly written up all the signs he had painted; a sort of reference book. The book had also served to record his experiences on the Western front. He turned to a clean page and quickly wrote in it.

'I wish my babies were with me. I don't mean to hurt anyone.' He felt a lump in his throat and quickly shut the book. 'I can't start that now!' he said sharply. He rose, combed his hair, put his cap on and left.

The Grove Hotel was busy but the waiter found him a table next to the kitchen entrance and he ordered a pint of beer and a pork chop. Then he noticed the woman who had looked at him in the café at lunch time. She was sitting with her companion and when she saw him glance with surprise in her direction she smiled openly. Albert raised his glass and the woman raised hers.

When his chop arrived, he ate quickly, glancing all the while in their direction. The two ladies had finished eating when he arrived and now they finished their coffees, wiped their mouths and left, but the smile of the younger one remained with him.

He finished his meal and was getting up to leave when he spotted a pair of glasses left by one of the ladies on the table. Albert quickly picked them up and dropped them into his pocket.

He left the dining room and caught sight of the ladies seated in the lounge. Nervously he approached. 'I think you may have left these on the table. In the restaurant.'

The older woman looked at him suspiciously, as though he might have stolen them.

'Elsie, they are yours,' said the younger woman. She turned her smile back to Albert. 'Thank you so much.'

Elsie smiled weakly and thanked him too, half wondering if she should tip him.

Albert moved awkwardly from one foot to the other. 'You were in the tea shop this afternoon. I've not been long here and already we seem to have found the same places. I couldn't be rude without acknowledging you,' he said with a strangled voice.

She smiled again. She had a wide mouth set over a strong chin and hair that curled provocatively at her neck. He noticed that she had long slender fingers which were playing with the strap of her handbag.

'We can't stay long,' said Elsie looking at the younger woman. She was conscious that other people in the lounge were quietly looking at them, wondering what the rather dishevelled man would try next.

'My name's Albert, what's yours?'

'Trudie,' said the young woman confidently. 'And this is Elsie Cartledge'

'I don't know any Trudies,' he said, ignoring Elsie

'My mother was German.'

'Oh,' he said and fleetingly remembered with shame the German woman in the Belgian village who they had abused. He was thankful that he had not joined the queue to rape her. Then, they were no more than dirt caked frightened animals.

'Would you like to join us Albert?'

He said nothing and self consciously sat down in the vacant chair opposite.

'Are you local?' he asked.

'No, we came up from London. To visit the Baths. Miss Cartledge suffers from rheumatism and I agreed to keep her company. And what about you?'

She seemed very self assured and Albert suddenly thought how daft he must seem. She was a lady and he a dishevelled sign writer from a mining village in South Yorkshire.

'I liked Buxton when last I were here. In the war. 1917.'

'Very different then I should imagine. Were the baths open?'

'I don't remember. We were not billeted long. I didn't get to see much'

'So, now you want to make up for it?'

'Aye, summat like that. It's a lovely place and…' the words did not come easily.

'Don't forget that we are up early Trudie,' said her companion through tight lips.

'Of course not dear. But it's nice to meet interesting strangers. Buxton can be a little formal. What do you do, Albert?' she asked suddenly.

'Artist.' He paused. 'And sign writer.' He coloured up a little. 'I have to make a living as well,' he said with a limp smile.

'What do you paint?'

'Landscapes mostly, but they aren't very good. I don't really…'

His words trailed off again and he shrugged as he fought to find the words to continue the lie. He was no artist and had not worked in three months.

Trudie studied his face for a few seconds whilst Albert sat flushed with the embarrassment of one not given easily to small talk. 'Well, we really must go. Elsie's right, we have to be up quite early. It was lovely to meet you Albert and thank you for spotting the glasses.'

As they stood to leave he suddenly asked. 'Would you like a walk out tomorrow?'

Trudie paused and looked at her companion. 'I'm not sure.'

'I could call round for you. Are you staying here?'

'Yes, we are. I sometimes take a walk in the Gardens when Elsie is at the Baths.' she said, caught unawares by this awkward invitation. 'Our paths might cross then.'

'What time?' he asked a little breathlessly.

'I normally walk out after ten.'

'I'll wait near the entrance. Just after ten'

She said nothing and turned to follow the shocked Miss Cartledge up to their rooms. He could see her admonishing Trudie and wondered if she would really turn up on the morrow.

As he walked slowly down the stairs, his thoughts lingered on Trudie. 'Girls must all be like that in London,' he thought. 'Not afraid to talk to ordinary people'

For the first time that day, he felt more at ease with himself. His flight from home and the guilt of leaving his two daughters made him question if he really was doing the right thing by running. And now this woman, this self confident stranger who had no qualms about addressing him, added to his confusion. Perhaps there was life after all. Perhaps all the anxiety and anger of the last few weeks was a mirage, like the doctor had said. He smiled, straightened his shoulders and thought 'Bye heck Albert, she's a real lady an' all!'

As he stepped out of the hotel entrance a car passing by suddenly backfired just next to him. The sharp crack was amplified as it echoed through the enclosed colonnaded walk way running round the hotel. Albert let out a startled scream and threw himself to the pavement face down. There was a screaming noise deep within him. His breathing was short and his leg shook. His brain went into spasm as nothing but grey pain seared the back of his eyes. The warm feelings of a minute ago were completely smashed by the loud bang which was nothing less than a German shell landing close by, spraying him in mud and body parts.

A gibbering noise crept out of his shaking head as he fought to calm himself. He looked up gingerly, his face twisted with fright and saw a small knot of perturbed, whispering people had gathered.

'Are you alright?' asked a man in a bowler hat.

Albert did not hear him.

'Can we get a doctor? You look as if you have had a bit of a shock.' The man bent down. 'Here, let me help you…'

'No! I'm all right. I'm all right' and slowly Albert rose to a sitting position, sweating and still shaking. 'Yes. I'm OK.' He rose to his feet, dusted himself down and looked around without recognition. 'I'm OK. I'll be OK.' The last thing he wanted was strangers trying to help him; trying to tell him what he should do.

This was not the first time it had happened. He was shamed by it; he was left stripped of his dignity and it only drove him deeper into his despair. Quickly he moved off and headed back to the pub leaving the small knot of people staring in some concerned disbelief after him.

'Oh God,' he cried quietly 'Oh God, please leave me alone!'

5

1917

Albert Gibson and Jean Bairstow were married a few days before he was due to embark for France. It was a hurried affair but all their friends and family turned out to make sure it was memorable. They were married in the Wesleyan Chapel and had the reception in the Community hall.

Jean was eighteen, strikingly pretty and very shy. She had always looked up to him. Later, in her teens she had harboured a deep crush which had turned to a heart aching secret love. She was ill with desire which she could never express and hoped, every day, that Albert would ask her to step out with him.

The courtship was necessarily hurried. Now with the urge and desires of young adults, they could begin to seek out each others secret places. Albert felt a keen satisfaction that he was favoured over Harry Jackson; he was the alpha male in this town. She accepted him on first asking and he was overjoyed.

'You do mean it, don't you?' she implored, afraid that he just wanted to have his way with her before he went to France.

'Course I do. I've allas loved you. We can marry before I go.'

Their wedding night was spent in the local hotel. They were both young and unmannered in what was required, although uncle Peter had attempted in a rather drunken fashion, to advise him on the etiquette of the first sexual encounter.

'Tha's got to be gentle, lad. If she's not ready, then hang back a while. They appreciate it more if you take it nice and steady. Know what I mean lad?'

Their honeymoon was spent walking the fields and woods near where they lived. He identified bird song for her and showed her where the best wild flowers grew. They spent a day in Sheffield where Jean picked out a few things for their house, if and when they ever moved into one.

When Albert finally left to join his regiment, Jeanie knew instinctively that she was pregnant. She went back to work at Jackson's to await the return of her hero. She stayed on with her parents, occupying the same little room that had been hers since she had turned fourteen. It would be many months before she would see him again and then he would be another man entirely.

He got to France in January and the weather was bitterly cold; iron cold. Preparations were under way for the third great battle of Ypres and Albert spent his first weeks building the transport railway across the wasteland of northern France and Belgium that would support the big push. It was back-breaking work and he realised how out of condition he was.

His company were a mix of battle hardened regulars, and novices from the Reserve battalions. Building a railway wasn't the only job, as they were marched from one part of the front to the other, training, drilling, and preparing for the greatest test of their lives. His first letter home to Jean, in his best copper plate hand, was a shy rather nervous effort.

"My darling,
We are in a good billet at the moment and I am eating and sleeping well unless we are turned out at 3 o'clock in the morning to go on a march, which is often. The whole Regiment is moved about a lot. The Coy, is a good set of men and I have settled in well.

Tomorrow it is our turn to go up to the front, which will be my first time. I am not looking forward to it but some of the older men say to just keep my head down and I will be alright.

More important, how are you? I miss you very much and think about you all the time. I keep your picture in my tobacco tin to keep it dry. You would not believe how wet and muddy it can be sometimes.

Please tell my Mam and Marie and Arthur that I think of them too. And your parents of course.

Well, its' nearly time for us all to fall in. Then it's a short march up to the front trenches. I will write when we get back which should be in about a week, which is the time anyone spends up there before being relieved.

Write me soon with all your news.
Your loving husband, Albert.
P.S. Please send some thick socks as they are always getting wet.

There were many letters after that in a more confident and sometimes even defiant style, telling her of the frustrations of trench life but he omitted the horrors that he witnessed.

Jean wrote shortly after, with news of her pregnancy. He was overcome with happiness and although there was little privacy he found a quiet spot behind a hut, sat down and cried with joy.

She asked what they should call the baby and Albert sent

back '*...to call it Clementine, if a girl and George if a boy. I met a French lady in one of the towns we was billeted in and she was so kind to us. I liked her name right off and her husband was called George, but I love the way they say the names over here. When I see you I will try and say it like they do...*'

Albert was one of the lucky ones. He survived the patrols into 'no man's land', the patch of blasted country which consisted of barbed wire, shell holes and the dead. He also came out of the attack on Messines Ridge unscathed after the mines were detonated. No one had ever seen anything like the great explosion under the German lines, which sent tons of earth and body parts high into the air. The land around shuddered and the noise thundered and rolled slowly to the coast and beyond. Some men thought the whole world was blowing apart and prayed for forgiveness. Most just gawped in silence at the monstrousness of the event.

Albert's Division was in reserve and did not get into the attack until the afternoon, when most of the damage had been done. All he recalled later was the confusion, the noise, orders given and countermanded. But when they finally got through to the German positions, he thought he had arrived in hell itself. He and his comrades were carried along with the pressure of it all; there was no time to stand and stare as once more the bombardment of British artillery screamed over their heads and churned up the land just in front of them.

They took many prisoners that day and Albert would ever remember the looks of fear and despair on their dirty faces as they stumbled back towards the British rear.

And then the rat-tat-tat of German machine guns started up in angry reply which curtailed any celebration as he dug in once more.

Shortly after the battle he was given some leave, along with a promotion to Corporal but even that did not lift the strange uneasiness that came upon him whenever the shelling started.

It was four months since he and Jeanie had seen one another. Neither looked as they had when he marched off to war and it felt as if they were meeting for the first time.

'Tha looks wonderful,' he said hesitantly looking at the bulge that contained new life. She smiled coyly and said 'Thanks, I feel wonderful.'

Over the next few days she noticed a coldness in him. He was awkward, tongue tied and drifted off when she talked. She sensed no passion in him when they made love and at first she put this down to her size but he rarely put his arms around her or told her how much he missed her.

Things came to a head one evening when they were sitting in her mother's kitchen.

'Are you listening to me Albert? She said quietly 'I've been telling you about your young brother and I don't think you've heard a word I've been telling you'

'Sorry luv. I got things on me mind.'

'What things?'

'Oh, thinking about boys back ont' front.'

'Well tell me about it.'

'I don't think I can. It's too bloody awful.' He put his elbows on his knees and rubbed his face. 'Everything you read about in't papers is just lies. I've seen things you couldn't imagine.' Tears started in his eyes. 'I don't think I can take much more.'

She was stunned. Her hero, who had been feted round town was trying to tell her that he was through with it.

'But you have to go back in a couple of days.'

He sighed deeply. 'I know and I will do me duty, but, by God I hope it's over soon Jeanie.'

She looked frightened. 'You won't do anything stupid, will you?'

'No. I'm not that daft. There's many that might. We had a

fellow up for court martial for walking away from his post last month. He couldn't stand it neither and just walked off, away from t' guns. Not sure what will happen. Might go before firing squad.'

She leaned over and put her arms round him. 'You will look after the sen won't you? I love you too much to loose you now. And our baby needs a father.'

He sat up 'Ay. I'll come back.'

But the certainty left his eyes as soon as he said it. The remorseless noise of guns and the futility of what he was ordered to do had dulled his senses.

They took advantage of the weather to go on long walks. She still adored him and knew deep down that he loved her. But she also felt a barrier between them, forged by the war.

When he left to rejoin his regiment, he held her very close for a long time, not daring to say a word, burying his face in her hair and sobbing gently. 'I'll always luv you,' he said ardently. 'No matter what, remember that, won't you.'

'Of course. Just come back to us'

He pulled away and climbed into the train without a backward glance. Jean felt desperately sad for him and watched as the train pulled out until there was nothing but the puffs of smoke rising beyond the bend in the railroad. She trembled with fear. It might be the last time she ever saw him.

6
June 1922

Trudie came out of the Grove hotel at ten thirty five and saw Albert waiting by one of the many bath chairs parked up at the entrance to the Gardens. From afar, she looked him over and briefly wondered what some of her London friends might think of her going for a stroll with a sign writer. She was excited by the thought.

'Shall we walk?' he asked.

'Why not? It's a lovely morning.'

They paid to go into the Gardens and walked slowly along the path. She noticed that he was wearing the same clothes as the night before and guessed that he had little to change into.

They chatted inconsequentially for a while and walked slowly along the promenade in front of the Pavilion until Trudie said.

'You interest me Albert. I don't believe you are a painter.'

'Oh, why's that then?'

'I know painters, real painters in London, and you don't have the curiosity of a true painter.'

'I'm caught out then. Tha's right, I'm not a painter. But I am the best sign writer in Yorkshire. There's nothing I can't do.'

She laughed politely. 'And what exactly does a sign writer in Yorkshire do?'

'Anything really. I work for t' local council and there's always summat to put up, even if it's 'Keep off the Grass.'

'Are you married Albert?'

He hesitated. 'Sort of.'

She stopped. 'Sort of?'

'Aye, the wife and I don't get on and … well me being here is a separation like. We both needed to get away from each other for a spell.'

'Oh, how sad,' she said. 'Have you children?'

'Oh aye. Two girls, Beatrice and Clementine; wonderful bairns. I love 'em dearly.'

'What lovely names.'

'Aye. French. I chose them when I were over there. About the only pretty things there was.'

Then you'll be going back to them.'

'Oh yes, I hope so.'

'You don't sound very sure.'

He paused. 'Not easy when you've had a row.'

'No, I suppose not. But you do both still get on, don't you?'

'Not sure.' She could see that Albert was becoming a little agitated. The two of them stopped by the roller skating rink and watched people shrieking as they rushed past on the skates.

'Look can we change subject.' he said abruptly 'Tell me about you?'

'Not much to tell. I work up in London at a tedious job with an insurance company and live with my mother and Aunt Elsie who is at this moment dipping herself in the spring waters at the baths.'

'You don't sound very happy about it.'

'Oh I don't mind. She's very good to me. I owe her a lot. After my father died she came to stay. My mother is not very well, you see and she has become a good friend.'

'Very noble. The true Samaritan.'

'Yes, she is,' said Trudie firmly, thinking he was being face-tious.

'I'm sorry. I wasn't implying anything.'

'That's alright,' she said, smothering the discordant spark. 'Haven't you got a favoured aunt?

'Oh aye. Lots but they's all got big families of their own without bothering about out else.'

There was a strange intensity about Albert which she could not quite understand. He seemed nervous and a bit distant. They walked on in silence for a while.

'When the sun shines, this really is a beautiful place, don't you think?' said Trudie.

'Oh, aye. I was billeted here before being sent to France and loved it so much it were the first place I thought of when I had to get away. I think this park is the best I've ever been in.'

'That must have been difficult.'

'Difficult. How?'

'Well, if you fell in love with the place and then had to go off to the Front... from Elysium to Hades.'

Albert had no idea what she was referring to, but guessed it must be something to do with going from good to bad.

'In a way, aye. We don't have 'owt like this where I come from.' He looked around. 'Everywhere is so smart and the buildings grand. I'd seen nought like it and it just caught me imagination.'

They were walking passed the tennis courts and Trudie gestured to games in progress. They play the ladies championships here you know. It certainly has that over Bath.'

'Oh aye.' Again Albert felt out of his depth. 'I used to think about this Park an t' trees when I were in t' trenches. There weren't a tree in sight for miles. All blown up by artillery. Nothing but shell holes and barbed wire.'

'How awful. I can't imagine what it must have been like for you.'

'Pretty bad. But I was lucky. I came out alive.'

'Yes, you were lucky. I have known some who weren't quite so fortunate…'

'What, came out 'at trenches?'

'Not quite. A flyer. He was badly wounded.' Albert caught the change in her voice and was reluctant to dig any further.

They had reached the far end of the Gardens by now and Trudie turned. 'I need to get back. She worries a bit if I'm not around.'

'Oh,' Albert sounded disappointed. 'I were hoping we could go a bit further. Up in t' woods like. I like talking like this. I don't get much chance to talk to someone from London. Someone who knows so much.'

She smiled at him. 'There's nothing special about me, Albert. Just an ordinary girl from an ordinary town. And I really do need to get back.'

'Well, if we must.' And they turned and set off back round the Gardens and along Broad Walk, where Albert admired the old Victorian houses. They passed the great Hydropathic hotel, looking down across its own tennis courts.

'Why didn't you stay there? It looks grand.'

'Can't afford to, Albert.' She looked at him mischievously. 'Do you think we have money?'

'Well, you dress very well, I can tell that. And you live in London…'

'Oh, Albert, not everyone has money to burn, believe me,' she said with a light laugh which captivated him. 'I have to work hard for a living, like everybody else.'

When they got back to the Grove hotel, Albert was still reluctant to let her go. 'Could we meet up again? After lunch or this evening?'

Trudie frowned. 'I don't think I can. We have tickets to the Opera House for this evening. I promised Elsie.'

He looked crest fallen. 'I was banking on seeing you again. You see, you could help me.'

'Help you? How?'

He stared at her. 'I… I need a bit a' help. I'm not meself at the moment and talking to someone like you helps.'

Trudie felt a slight twinge of alarm. 'I'm sorry Albert, but I really have to put my Aunt first. That's why I'm here'

Words failed him for a moment. He was so sure that she would agree to see him again. They had got on so well. 'Oh, never mind. I'll work it out for meself,' he said bitterly, twisting his cap viciously in his hands.

'But, if it would help, I may be able to get away tomorrow, the same as we have done today. We could walk and talk then.'

Albert was now agitated. He seemed suddenly unsure of himself, impatient and his words were harsh. 'I'm not sure… I don't think I'll be here… I have to get back.' He looked at her with a sneer. 'You'se really all t' same, aren't you? No time for the likes of us!' His voice was sharp and threatening. He turned on his heel and walked quickly away. Trudie stared after him, astonished.

'How boorish' she said quietly to herself.

7

Nov 1917

The train from Dover was crowded with troops on leave. It was noisy and warm with the fug of cigarette smoke. They were crammed into the compartments singing and laughing with the relief of being back in Blighty for a few days. Many of them were already drunk and the Red Caps had eyed them suspiciously as they went aboard at Boulogne.

Albert sat quietly, jammed up against a couple of artillery men trying to protect his damaged arm and listened to their exaggerated tales of amorous conquests. Perhaps the artillery was luckier than the poor bloody infantry, he thought. There were a couple of other Sherwood Foresters, but he did not know them, and merely nodded acknowledgement. He was not in the mood to talk.

Albert had taken a piece of shrapnel in his left shoulder and sat with his arm in a sling, trying not to have it banged. The regiment had been in the thick of it at Poelcappelle and witnessed the worst of the slaughter. It was here that he won the Military Medal. But it did little to alleviate the memory of screaming men drowning in mud.

The journey from London had been painstakingly slow and Albert was tired and hungry when he finally got home.

'You've lost weight,' said Jeanie when she saw him. 'And your arm. What happened?'

'Nothing to worry about,' he said laconically 'How's Clementine?' he asked even before he shook out of his great coat.

'She's fine,' beamed Jeanie. 'Come and see.'

The baby was asleep, wrapped up tight. It was the first time he had seen her and the little pink face jutting out of the blanket gave him a sense of his true man hood.

'Your mam's coming over soon. I said I'd go get her when

you arrived.'

'Not yet. Let's just stop awhile. You an' me and the baby.'

Albert picked up Clementine and gently rockcd her in his good arm. Jeanie thought this was the happiest moment of her life. 'She's like you. Got your nose.'

'How can you tell?'

'Cos she has,' she said and kissed him on the cheek.

The family arrived and Albert played his part as the proud new dad. It was his mother who first noticed the change in him. No matter how hard he tried to put on a brave face, she could see the fear'd look in his eye, the slight twitch in his hand and sudden start at an unexpected noise. But the others, his brother and sister, uncles and aunts all saw only the brave man with two stripes on his shoulder and a ribbon on his breast pocket. Uncle Robert came and despite his hatred for the war, was secretly proud of his nephew. Uncle Peter was not able to come. His lungs were playing him up.

That night, Albert slept fitfully, tossing and turning, mumbling through some terrible dream which Jeanie could not decipher. When Clemantine woke, Albert shot up, startled.

'I'll go to her,' he said. For the rest of the night he sat with his daughter resting in his arm, gently rocking her back to sleep.

The following day Albert went over to see his uncle Peter in bed. His crumpled face lit up when he saw Albert and despite a bout of painful coughing, managed to welcome him into his overheated little bedroom.

Albert helped him sit up and waited until he had calmed a bit.

'Bye, look at you, lad. You're father would have been right proud of thee. Have you brought your medal to show me?' He was stopped once more by a coughing fit.

'I can come back a bit later uncle Peter if it would help.'

'No, no. I might not be here by then. No, lad I want to talk to you, find out what you've been up to. Now, lets have a little drink on your homecoming. In the cupboard, down here lad.'

Albert reached down and took out a half bottle of whiskey and poured some into a glass. 'I'll take bottle lad.' He tilted it to his trembling lips. 'Here's to you.'

'Aye, and you uncle Peter.'

No sooner had he sipped than he started coughing again and Albert looked with some concern as he coloured up and seemed to loose the ability to breathe.

'Are you all right?'

'Course I'm not,' he said sharply. 'I'm dying lad. Bloody coal dust got me at last. That's why I was keen to see you before you go back. Now, tell me about it.'

Albert paused. 'Oh, the usual thing, you know.'

'No lad, I don't know.'

'Well, we march up t' front go over, get shot, go back t' rear, have a bath, do some training or carrying stuff about and then get ready for t' trench again.'

'Don't you want to talk about it?'

'No, not much.'

'I can understand that.'

Albert looked at his uncle. 'We do lots of hanging about. Waiting. Just waiting to die basically.'

Uncle Peter took another swig from the bottle and wiped his lips with a shaky hand.

'You are OK aren't you lad. In yourself like.'

'Not always, no. Nobody is, except our bloody lieutenant who's trying to get us all killed as soon as possible.'

'Bit of a silly bugger is he?'

'Aye, you could say. If there's a job to be done, a snatch or mending barbed wire or scouting or summat, bloody Percy Bradstone bloody Smith is there, volunteering us.'

Peter noticed a thin line of sweat above Albert's top lip. 'But you're still here though. Must be doing summat right.'

Albert paused again. 'Do you think it's possible to hate a man and like him at same time like?'

'How d'ya mean?'

'He's a bastard. He's killed too many of me mates. And yet he's al'as first up, looking out for us. Takes us side against senior officers. Gets us decent food and cigarettes and things.' Albert paused whilst he brought the image of Lieutenant Percy Bradstone Smith into focus. ' He's a brave bastard an' we all hate him and admire him.'

'And looked out for you did he?'

'Aye. Sort of,' he said evasively.

'Follow your own instincts, lad. You do what you have to, to stay alive. That's all you can do. It's them bairns a' yours that's important. They need you.'

'I know but...'

'But what.'

'Your life's not your own in t' army. You have no idea.' His lip trembled and he looked away hoping his uncle would not see the shake in his hand. 'I can do everything short of walking away but if I'm meant to die...'

'None of that, lad! I won't have that kind of talk. You get yourself through this.' He put his thin hand on Albert's knee and tapped it gently. He noticed that Albert was touching himself; his head, belt buckle, pocket of his jacket, as in some kind of ritual. But he did not push him any further and then started another coughing fit. This time he asked if Betty his wife could come up.

'Hide bottle away lad,' he said with a wink. 'Tha'd best let me rest awhile.'

Albert left the little house and looked up at the window of the room he had just been in. He was not sure he would see his uncle Peter again.

The rest of his leave was spent with Jeanie and Clementine but the atmosphere was tense. They went round to his mother each day for their supper and the two women looked at each other anxiously.

'Everything alright?' she asked the two of them.

'Yes,' said Jeanie unconvincingly, remembering how Albert had uncharacteristically lost his temper the night before.

'Why can't you get this bloody washing hung up!' he had screamed after tripping over the basket. Jeanie was so shocked, she went quietly into the bedroom and cried. He came into the darkened room. 'I'm sorry luv. I'm not me sen. I don't like meself very much at the moment and I have to go back tomorrow.'

Jeanie kissed him as hard as she could, hoping to squeeze the poison from him. That night, after she had put Clementine down and made sure she was asleep, Jeanie got undressed in front of Albert, something she had never done before and stood in front of him. She was desperate to make his last night memorable; she wanted to give him something to remember. He made love to her but it was no more than an instinctual response which lacked any passion. But it would result in the birth of Beatrice nine months later.

On his last morning, he sat at the kitchen table and gently rocked Clementine on his knee. His arm was almost mended so there was little excuse for not heading back to his regiment which he would have done anyway, arm in a sling or not.

Jeanie thought that he looked even more good looking than he had done when last he was on leave. His face was thinner which gave him a square jawed look. And the aging around his eyes suggested terrible experience. His smile for Clementine was still bright and when he looked at her, she felt deep within him he loved her still.

'Albert, you will look after your sen won't you?'

'Course I will. I've got you two to look after. I promised me uncle Peter.'

'War will be over soon, won't it?'

'I bloody hope so.'

June 1922

Despite the sunshine Albert's room was gloomy and dank. He pulled out the suitcase once more and reached for the note book. On a fresh page he wrote about his walk in the Gardens that morning. He was intense and felt a sudden loathing for Trudie. 'Women like that! All done up. Don't know anything about the likes of us!'

Ruefully he said, 'I don't mean it Trudie, honest. I just want to explain it all to someone. I want someone to hear me.'

The notebook reminded him once more of home and he recalled the last meeting with his supervisor at the council office when he was given notice.

'Sorry, but we're cutting back, Albert. Not enough work,' the man had said.

But he knew that was not the only reason. There had been complaints. He was tardy. He was late. He was argumentative.

Albert put his head in his hands and rocked gently on the edge of the bed. His mind was a twisted bundle of painful emotions that he did not understand. One minute he cried desperately for the love of his two girls and in the next he wanted to murder the next person he saw in the street. On one occasion he had found himself with his hands round Jeanie's neck, trying to squeeze the screaming anger out of himself.

'Why don't you go away! Stop hurting me! It weren't my fault!' Tears and snot dribbled down his chin. 'There was nowt I could do!' he shouted.

He wiped his face with his sleeve and opened the notebook again. In large neat letters he wrote 'I'M SORRY.' Tearing the page out of the book, he propped it up on the sideboard.

Albert left in a hurry, out of the room and down the stone steps, passing a couple of gossiping women, who eyed him suspiciously. He hurried on out into Spring Gardens and walked quickly away from their curious tongues.

Everything seemed opaque, not quite in focus and on a

couple of occasions he bumped into people. He was heading for the Palace Hotel, a place of wonder five years previously.

The hotel rose above the skyline of the town and it all came back to him; hundreds of khaki clad men, lining up for the regimental photo in front of the Pavilion, laughing and joking. He remembered the camera man and his assistant running around, getting them all into the frame, tripping over one another. And his pal, Irish Mick, whispering to all those nearby 'Right, when I say the word, everyone lean to the left!' He saw the puzzled look on the photographer's face as half the line seemed on a slope. How they laughed! He laughed now, out loud, as he ran up the steps of the hotel and into the lobby.

'Can I help you?' asked a tall balding man with a sneer under his nose.

'No, not really. I just come in to have a look, like.'

The man looked at Albert's dishevelled appearance. 'If its staff you are looking for, there's the entrance round the back.'

'No. I were here five year ago. Just looking. Just remembering.'

He looked at the grand staircase down which loud men and women were descending.

'I would appreciate it if you did not stay if you have no business here.'

Albert froze and turned sharply 'Well, I might have business. I might be visiting someone important for all you know.'

'In that case I can ring for them if you give me their name,' he said authoritatively.

Albert paused and walked slowly up to the desk and in a loud mocking voice shouted, 'Don't fooking bother!' He turned and left through the knot of swanky guests staring open mouthed at his retreating back.

He walked out of the hotel and down the long path, cheeks burning. 'Jumped up bugger,' he said under his breath.

He stopped, and took a couple of deep breathes and was

conscious of the large slate dome of the Hospital looking down at him. Memories of soldiers, hundreds of them, some limping, some being pushed in wheeled chairs, others bent and twisted coming and going through the entrance.

Across the road was the railway station where he had alighted just yesterday; the one where he had left for France five years earlier.

He entered the booking hall and sat awhile watching people come and go. Again he was thrown back on the sights and smells of that day when he left; trains were crowded with men going to and from the front; big men, proud warriors. He began to sweat at the sense of being in a crowded place, unable to move or escape, with the shouts and haloo's and hissing steam and whistles and trundling baggage carts. Everyone looking at him, sneering and laughing. He had to get out!

Albert dashed from the ticket hall and ran back down Spring Gardens to the pub he had first entered the previous day. He took in deep lung fulls of air to steady himself before entering.

The landlord was standing behind the bar, as if waiting for him.

'Hello there! Enjoying your stay?' he asked.

'Aye', Albert wiped his forehead. 'Aye, I've seen what I need to see.'

The landlord pumped out a pint for him and Albert stood awhile, sipping slowly, looking around at the early evening tipplers. They were working men like himself, just finished for the day and stopping off before going home for their tea. Some of them would be back afterwards, happy to get away from the wife and crying children. Albert thought of Jeanie and the two girls and a shiver went down him. They would be frantic with worry now; the whole town would be wondering where he might be.

As he supped, he became conscious of a couple of men already quite far in their beer, arguing loudly.

'Keep it down lads!' shouted the landlord. 'There's folk here who like a drink without noise.'

'You're a bloody liar, Billy! We all know you never got anywhere near the fighting,' slurred a small weasely man in a dirty cap waving a finger under the nose of the man sat next to him.

'I did! You wouldn't know any case,' said the other man, waving a smoking pipe at him. 'You never even got to bloody France.'

'Course I bloody didn't! We all know that! And we know why.' He stopped to light up a cigarette with a drunken hand before continuing. 'Because I were making bloody explosives weren't I!'

'Aye and most of that were no good. Most of the buggers never went off!'

'I don't know do I? I just put bloody powder into the shells and packed them off. Some must have worked. Killed enough of those Hun bastards anyroad,' he said with a dribbly laugh.

Both men were noisily drunk. The regulars had heard this conversation many times before and studiously ignored them.

The landlord leaned in towards Albert. 'They's been at it ever since the end of the war, them two. The Grimes brothers. Brothers Grim, we call 'em!' He scoffed and wandered down to the other end of the bar to serve a customer.

Albert looked on and listened as the two men slurred at each other. He'd heard loose talk in other pubs before; pricked consciences, guilt, anger. He recognised his own distorted feelings in their words.

Suddenly, the small man in the dirty cap looked at Albert. 'Were you over there, pal?'

'Aye,' said Albert. 'But I don't shout about it.'

'We're not shouting. We're just making a point that not everyone had to be in the front line to have played their part. Some of us was doing important work back here. Do you get me?'

'Aye, I get you.' Albert turned away. He didn't like ignorant men who had no idea about what they were talking.

'Hey! Don't turn away, pal. I want to hear what you think. I'm talking to you. Now, do you agree with me, that just 'cos I weren't shooting at Huns, I'm not as important as you?'

Albert said nothing, although his hand was shaking. He waved at the landlord. 'Another pint please.' And then he started the ritualistic touching; head, belt buckle, top pocket of his jacket, over and over.

'You OK?' said the landlord noticing Albert's agitation.

'Yes, I'm fine. Just annoyed with them two...'

'Ignore 'em. We do!'

'I was over there,' the one called Billy shouted at Albert's back. 'Wounded an'all.'

'Ha!' His brother shrieked. 'Wounded? You? Wounded. Don't make me laff!'

'Yes! bloody wounded.'

Albert turned and eyed Billy Grimes. 'Where were you?'

'Arras,' Billy's eyes darted guiltily away from Albert and he knew instantly the man had been no where near the front line. He turned away once more.

'Where do I take a pee?' he asked the Landlord.

'Out th' back. Through that door.'

Albert wandered out. He no longer liked the pub or the people in it. It had turned against him. Best finish his drink and leave.

In the outhouse he felt himself shaking again. 'Christ, stop, please stop!' he said quietly.

Another man came in and stood beside him.

'Don't bother yourself about them. The little one, Billy Grimes, managed to get himself shot. Accidentally, if you know my meaning. Lost his big toe in the heat of battle.' The man laughed as he buttoned himself up. 'They's not worth the bother.'

Albert said nothing as he too buttoned himself and went

back into the pub.

Billy Grimes was at the bar, getting a couple more pints. He turned and limped back to his brother.

'D'ya get that crook leg at Arras?' asked Albert angrily.

'What's it to you?'

'Nothing I 'spose. I were wounded. Not as bad as you, like.' He sounded strangely menacing. 'Got me a medal an all. What did you get?'

'Fook all but a gammy leg and I don't know what you're getting at,' Billy Grimes said angrily as he slumped down next to his brother.

The two of them looked at Albert warily. His mood had changed. He was tense, staring at them menacingly, touching his 'magic' places.

He continued to stare until Billy Grimes shouted over. 'Have you lost something, 'cos I don't like your attitude.'

'Well that's too bloody bad.' Once more there was a noise deep inside him, exploding, ripping at him. He gripped the sides of his head and moaned.

The landlord watched anxiously. 'Leave it', he said. 'I don't want any trouble.'

'Shot yourself in the foot, did you?' shouted Albert 'Got your passage home did you?'

The pub went quiet, watching this agitated stranger goading the brothers. 'Is that it? Took your big toe off and left all your mates to die for you?'

'Look, that's enough. Sup up and leave,' said the landlord

'I will. Can't stand the smell of cowards!'

He drank his beer quickly, spilling some down his front. His hands were shaking.

'Look at him,' said Billy. 'He's shaking. Bloody frit! Must have got his balls shot off!'

Albert finished his pint and before anyone could do anything, he hurled the empty glass at Billy Grimes, hitting him in the forehead. His head rocked back and blood spurted from a deep cut over his eye. The landlord came round the bar with a stave which he waved menacingly at Albert. His brother knelt by Billy. 'Get me a cloth! He's dying.'

'He's not bloody dying,' said Albert scornfully. 'He's getting what he should have if he'd been a proper soldier!' The landlord had Albert by the arm and ushered him to the door. 'OK I'm going.'

Another man shouted. 'Someone's gone to get the police. Hold him!'

But Albert wasn't having that. He shook himself free and darted out of the door before anyone could stop him.

He ran hard along the street and crossed at a junction and ran up a sloping park in which was the war memorial. Panting heavily he ran up to the statue and dropped to his knees in front of the wing'd angel, the wreath of Victory held aloft in one hand and the sword of the Righteous in the other. He looked up into the face of the angel.

'Why?' He screamed. 'Why me?' He trembled, tears creasing down his face. 'Why did you leave me?' He spread out his arms in supplication, beseeching the statue to answer him. This was his hell, worse than death; to relive, over and over again the torment of all his dead comrades. They slept peacefully. He was here to carry their torment for an eternity.

He let out a long agonised cry, so deep, his very soul wept.

Unsteadily he rose from his knees and walked down some steps and stood in front of the Crescent which in its great mouth of an arc, seemed to mock him. He suddenly felt exhausted as if he were carrying some great boulder. He cut down a side street to avoid anyone who might be looking for him and found his way up to his dingy little room and stood, hanging onto the sideboard, staring into the mirror.

'I'm sorry!' he cried.' A vision of Jeanie and the girls flashed across his tortured mind. Faces and noises crowded in; mocking faces of Billy Grimes and Trudie, Clementine and Beatrice, all laughing at his failure.

Slowly he opened the suitcase and took out the service revolver and sat down on the edge of the bed. His face looked back at him in the mirror. It was the face of a million dead men, screaming.

And then everything went quiet. Light filled the room and he smiled. A great weight was lifting from him; floating up to the ceiling. 'Sorry,' he said quietly as he put the barrel of the gun in his mouth and pulled the trigger.

TRUDIE

1

June 1922

Trudie first knew of Albert's death two days later, when she read the lurid account in the local newspaper.

'Oh my Lord!' She gasped and turned pale.

'What is it dear?' enquired Elsie Cartledge.

At first she said nothing, too shocked at what she was reading.

'That young man we met. The one who found your glasses. Brought them from the table when we were having coffee the other evening. He's dead.'

'Oh, how awful. What happened?' said Elsie looking shocked.

'He shot himself. Here, in Buxton.'

Trudie's breakfast lay uneaten in front of her. She was too stunned to think of food.

'I must just go upstairs…'

'But you haven't finished your breakfast, dear…'

'I'm not hungry. I won't be long.'

In her room, Trudie sat at her dressing table and reread the account. 'And I turned him away,' she thought. She welled up and swallowed hard. 'The poor man. He must have been desperate.'

She sat for a long time, staring at nothing in particular, questioning her conscience. Could she have done anything?

Elsie tapped at her door.

'Come in Elsie.'

'Are you all right? I was quite concerned when you didn't come back down.'

'I'm alright now. It was such a shock, that's all.'

'Will you be alright if I go for my bathe this morning? I won't go if you don't want me to'

'Of course. I'll be fine. Don't worry.'

'Oh good.' She looked at Trudie for signs of discomfort and was reassured by her forced smile.

'You go and have a lovely soak. I might take a walk again. To clear my head.'

But Trudie was anything but comfortable. She had spent the best part of a morning two days ago, walking with Albert in the Gardens. She knew so little about him and the more she thought about him, the more she wanted to know.

'And the way he stormed off like that and all I could think was how rude he was.' The shocking event brought to the fore all her own confused suppressed emotions.

There was a thin sunshine when she stepped out of the hotel and headed for the Police Station. The day was like any other. People and traffic, jostling for space. The thermal baths were just across the road from the hotel and Trudie knew that Elsie would be in there for several hours, bathing, plunging and being massaged. Trudie was never sure of what good it did, but for Elsie, it meant the difference between life and decrepitude and, as she paid for her to accompany her, Trudie had no cause for complaint. Indeed, the town and surroundings were a pleasant change after the dust and grime of London.

'I've come about the death reported in today's newspaper,' she said matter of factly to the desk officer.

'Oh yes. What exactly can I help you with?' He was a large man with sympathetic eyes and the world weariness of one who had seen most of what people were capable of doing to themselves and others.

'The man, Albert Gibson. I was with him the day before he died.'

The officer lifted an eyebrow. What would this lady possibly know about Gibson who was one level above that of an itinerant.

'Were you now? Perhaps you had better come in and I will get the officer in charge of this particular case to have a word with you. Who shall I say…'

'Trudie Polesden. I'm staying in Buxton with my aunt. At the Grove Hotel.'

She was ushered into a small foul smelling room which contained a desk and several hard backed chairs. She sat down gingerly on the edge of one of them.

Presently, a large florid man entered. 'I'm Sergeant Nadin,' he said rather portentously. 'I believe you may have something to tell us about a recent death.'

'Well, I'm not sure I can tell you much about why he died or how, but I can tell you something of the conversation we had before the tragedy.'

Sergeant Nadin sat down with a wheeze and put his pudgy fingers on the table.

She spent the next forty five minutes with the Sergeant who laboriously wrote down what she quietly related. She did not however tell him of their abrupt ending or her annoyance. In the telling she was excitedly nervous and stopped on a couple of occasions to repress tears which remained close to the surface.

'Very interesting,' he said snapping his note book closed. 'He was obviously a very disturbed man when he shot himself, but we still don't know what drove him to it.'

'There was mention in the paper of an altercation in one of the pubs, just before he died. Is that the case?' she asked tentatively.

'Yes, it was. He was very aggressive and injured a man. An innocent bystander.'

'Oh! How awful. He seemed so inoffensive when we walked in the Gardens.' The sense of his delight with Gardens suddenly swept across her. 'Sergeant, would it be possible for me to see where he did it; where he died? You see, although we had only met in passing, so to speak, I would like to pay my respects, in some way.'

'Fraid not miss.'

But I may be able to tell you more…. He may have left an account of our meeting…. or something.'

Her request was quite spontaneous but now she was desperate to see where Albert spent the last minutes. 'I could be useful,' she said as her last throw of the dice.

Sergeant Nadin hesitated and drummed his fingers. 'She may still turn up something she's forgotten,' he thought.

When she entered the little room which had been scrubbed of the remains and effluvium of the dead man, she gasped. It was such a mean little place. 'No one should die in a place like this,' she thought. She glanced at the battered suitcase on the bed and wondered what it might contain.

'We are sending that back to his wife later. Not much in it,' said Sergeant Nadin from the doorway.

'Can I look in?'

'Yes, no harm I suppose. We will be clearing everything away, now the forensics people have done there stuff. He didn't have much with him.'

There was no harm in the contents any longer; the gun had been removed and now lay in the safe at the Police Station. She picked up the note book and flicked through it.

'He told me he was a very good sign writer. In Yorkshire.'

Slowly she walked round the room, trying to find something to absolve herself of the guilt she felt for dismissing him so abruptly. There was nothing of Albert here. The dingy little room was devoid of life

Just before she left, she spotted the sheet torn from the note book, a mere scrap which had been purposely left on top of the sideboard. It was specked with bloodstains, now brown, on which was written 'SORRY', in large capital letters. The hand was bold but distressed, reaching out in terror. Without the sergeant noticing she slipped the piece of paper into her gloved hand. It was only later that she thought the action may be illegal; stealing vital evidence. But it was a link with him and for that she was grateful.

Later that afternoon she said to Elsie. 'I need to go and see someone. In Yorkshire. I shouldn't be long if I catch an early train. I'll be back by evening.'

'Oh? Who?' said Elsie with a hint of annoyance.

'I want to see Albert's wife.'

'But what an earth for? I don't like you getting involved in something like this dear.'

'It's alright Elsie. I just think it would be a kindness to go and see her. I was practically the last person to speak to him.'

Elsie looked more hurt than shocked. 'Well, I don't suppose I can stop you. Do you know where he lived?'

Yes. The police very kindly gave me his address. Near Barnsley. It's something I just have to do.'

'Well, if you must, please be careful. You have no idea what you might find.'

Trudie smiled insincerely. 'I'll be very careful.'

2

August 1916

When the war began, Trudie was seventeen and, at the insistence of her father, was enrolled at a secretarial school, after which she joined the same insurance company that he worked with. The administration department was gradually denuded of the male workforce by the summer of 1916, which gave Trudie an opportunity to take on a bit more administrative responsibility than simply typing. It was still tedious but it proved that she was much more capable than she had been led to believe by her school teachers. It was not what she wanted despite her father's insistence that she had landed on her feet and should be grateful for the chance to build up a nest egg before she found a husband.

To relieve the routine she joined an art class and met people very different from her work colleagues; bright joyful people pushing at the boundaries of Edwardian stuffiness. They were an eclectic group who kept her amused and challenged and she delighted in their enthusiasms.

One evening, about six months after joining the class, she was invited out to dinner with one of her fellow students.

'We're all going out for something to eat and you must join us,' said Clare Robertson throwing on her coat at the end of their class. 'My brother is coming. You're sure to like him. He's an absolute sweetie.'

Ralph Robertson, "Robbie", was home on leave from the Royal Flying Corps and as soon as she was introduced, she fell for him. He was a typical product of a public school with an easy manner and good looks to match. A neat moustache sat under an aquiline nose and almond eyes which crinkled at the edges when he smiled.

There were four of them who squeezed round a small table at an Italian restaurant just off Drury Lane. Robbie met them at the door. He shook Trudie's hand and bowed slightly from the waist which she thought terribly gallant.

The evening rattled along joyously, helped by a bottle of Chianti and mountains of spaghetti. It was cramped and noisy and Trudie had to sit quite close to him.

'Have you been in France?' Trudie asked.

'I was with the Royal Engineers,' he said with a quiet soft tone which felt like melted butter. 'But I always wanted to fly and when the opportunity came up to transfer, I jumped at it. I've finished my training and go over with a new squadron in a couple of weeks'

Whilst his sister and Peter, the forth member of the party chatted, Trudie had Robbie to herself. She had dated boys before but this was grown up stuff with wine and conversation about real events. Little electric shocks ran up her spine every time he looked at her.

'It must be wonderful, flying over everything.'

'Yes. Everything is in miniature but I don't pretend for one minute that it is always fun down there. Our chaps are having an awful time of it. I just hope I can help in a small way.'

'Yes, I'm sure you can,' she said awkwardly, not knowing where to take the conversation next.

'And you?' he asked.

'Oh, not much to do with the war effort. I'm stuck in an office all day. But then your sister comes to my rescue twice a week with painting.'

'What's that I hear? interjected Clare. 'Robbie, she's the most divine painter. Frightfully talented...'

'Oh no. You'll embarrass me Clare.'

'But you are. Everyone says so. She'll be famous one day.'

'It sounds as if I will have to judge for myself. That's if you'll let me see your work,' he said hesitantly.

Trudie coloured up. 'But I have so little to show.'

'Oh nonsense. What about the painting you just finished. The one of Hampstead Heath. You could sell that for real money, Trudie.'

'You really are laying it on, Clare.' She turned to Robbie. 'Don't listen to her. I just dabble, no more.'

Peter chipped in. 'Why don't we have a little exhibition? We've all got masses of stuff we could show.'

'And why not have an auction of our work? Then we will see if your stuff is any good, Trudie,' said Clare, taking up the theme. 'The money can go to one of the soldier welfare funds!'

'What a great idea,' said Robbie. 'Perhaps you could invite that well known artist chap you know to open it...'

'Chris Nevinson? I'm sure he'd do it if I asked nicely. He's not long back from France. He's not been very well but I'm sure he'd want to help. He may even be our auctioneer.'

They all beamed with excitement. 'When shall we organise it?' asked Trudie.

'As soon as poss. If we advertise it in the Standard and put the word around I'm sure we could have something arranged within a couple of weeks.'

Trudie was as excited as the rest of them and hoped desperately that Robbie would not disappear to France before the auction.

As they left the restaurant, Robbie said cheerio and shook her hand. 'I hope we meet again. The auction possibly.'

'I hope so too,' she said hopefully and hung onto his hand for as long as she dared.

It was quite late and whilst Robbie, Clare and Peter hailed a taxi, Trudie went off to catch her bus, forstaying their protestations to take the taxi on to her house. Trudie's means were a lot more modest than theirs and was quite insistent on making her own arrangements.

She sat on the top deck, wistfully gazing at the lights of Piccadilly as it made its slow progress back to Bayswater where she lived with her parents.

'He's quiet,' she thought. 'Not out to impress. Not boastful. Lovely hands. I wonder if he's got someone already?'

Clearly he had not, for the next day. Trudie took a call at her office from Clare.

'Trudie, darling, can you talk?'

'Not for long. My boss doesn't like private calls.'

'Well, I won't keep you. It's Robbie. He wants very much to take you out to dinner this evening. Can you make it?'

Trudie was taken aback. 'Well... Yes, I'd love to but...'

'Oh good.'

'Where shall we meet?'

'Not us darling. Just you and Robbie. He's smitten and dying a thousand deaths. He's frightfully shy so I said I'd ask you.'

'Oh!… well, where shall I meet him?'

'At the Savoy. He says it would be far easier if he met you there instead of having you lurking outside a restaurant.'

She paused momentarily. 'OK. Tell him I will see him at 7.30. And please thank him.'

'Will do, darling. Have a wonderful evening and tell me all about it at our next class. Cheery bye!'

As she walked back to her desk, Trudie felt her cheeks burning.

'Is everything alright Miss Polesden?' asked her manager.

'Oh yes. Nothing to worry about,' she said with a broad smile.

3

June 1922

Trudie alighted at Doncaster station and caught a bus to the village. It was not difficult to find the house where Jeanie Gibson and the two children lived. Everyone was only too eager to point out the house of a suicide.

The small terraced house looked respectable. The window frames and front door had been recently painted and the door step brightly red-polished. She knocked gingerly with a couple of raggy children in close attendance.

'Is tha from t' Board miss?' One of them asked.

She turned and smiled. 'No. I'm just a friend.'

The door was opened by Jeanie. She looked dreadful. Her eyes were puffy with crying and she was haggard and thin.

'Jeanie Gibson?'

'Aye. What you want?'

'My name is Trudie Polesden.' she paused. 'I've come over from Buxton.'

'Aye?' Jeanie said suspiciously.

'May I come in? You see, I saw Albert the day before…the day before he died. We talked.'

Jeanie stared without knowing what to say. The last couple of days had been a haze, not knowing where she was or what to do; breaking down and frequently questioning whether she had misheard the policeman who had delivered the news.

She moved aside and let her in. They went down the corridor and into the kitchen. It was untidy and smelled of old frying.

'Where are the girls?' asked Trudie.

'At me mams. I come back to clean up a bit. But its' too much for me at moment.' She looked on the verge of crying again, 'Will you sit?'

'Thank you,' said Trudie

'I can put kettle on if tha'd like a cup of tea.'

'Thank you. That would be nice.'

Jeanie found two cups and saucers, items bought in Sheffield just after they had got married. She poured from the large brown tea pot and sat opposite Trudie. She looked washed out.

'I'm so sorry for what happened. You look as if it's hit you very hard. How are the girls?'

She turned dead eyes on Trudie. 'Eldest keeps asking where her dad is. Youngest isn't quite sure of what's happened.'

Trudie removed her gloves. 'I met Albert. We talked.'

'So you said. How's that then?' Jeanie said sharply.

'I was staying in Buxton with my aunt. Albert was dining at the hotel. He picked up a pair of glasses that my aunt had left behind on the dining table.' Trudie felt uncomfortable and suddenly thought for the first time that perhaps she was doing the wrong thing. What if Jeanie thought that Albert and she had done more than just talked?

'He seemed distraught. The reason I am here is because I think I may have been the last person to have a conversation with Albert. I came over to see if that might help you.'

'What did he say?'

Trudie did not recount everything that they had talked about, but told how he had talked in loving terms about the girls and Jeanie herself. 'He did say that the two of you had rowed and he seemed very upset by that.'

'Row? Aye, we rowed. The last year we seemed to be rowing all t' time. It weren't like that always. He changed an' I don't know why.'

Trudie sipped her tea and said a little more confidently, 'Tell me about it.'

Jeanie sat back lethargically. She was too tired to ask why this stranger was asking questions. 'I were mad about 'im. He were best looking lad in t' town and I used to spy on him. I'd even follow 'im just so's I could catch a glimpse of him. An he used to do t' same, so he told me. Used to try to catch a glimpse of me working in t' shop without me knowing. She wiped her nose and sniffed, 'So, you tell me, if he loved me and I loved him like that, like two silly love struck ha'peth, how come he turned so? I never stopped loving him.'

Trudie bent her head, not wishing to show how the words were affecting her.

'He said he loved us but he never showed owt. Just sat in t' chair or went t' pub. Ignored us. And if I said 'owt wrong, or summat weren't quite as he wanted, he'd start shouting. Real angry, like.'

'Had he been like that for long?'

'About a year after war ended. When he come back, everyone told him how great he was, getting medal an' all. We was all proud of him. Then after that, he just sort of slid down; lost his own pride. Started drinking and getting into scrapes and shouting at girls and me.'

'And his work?'

'Lost his job. And now we've nowt to live on.'

'He never got over the war; what he'd seen.'

'No. If there were any sharp noise, a long bang or even pit whistle or summat, he'd get really frightened; start this silly routine of touching himself. Said it were his way of keeping alive. Sometimes he'd throw himself ont' floor or hide somewhere.' Jeanie went quiet as she remembered the first time it happened; how he shook and cried and how he refused her help.'

'But why kill his self?' Jeanie looked imploringly, searching for an answer. 'Why do that to us? Why never talk to me about it?'

Trudie was stumped for an answer and said feebly 'Sometimes it takes a while to come out. If he never said anything, perhaps it was all boiling up inside him.'

'What were? He had nowt to worry about. Manager give him his job back when he come out of uniform. He had me and the bairns. So, why did he have to go and shoot hisself in bloody Buxton?'

'Jeanie, I know it's not much, but I thought Albert was a very brave man. He was obviously very hurt…'

'What do you mean!' Jeanie said sharply and for the first time seemed to recognise that there was a complete stranger in her kitchen.

'I don't know why you're here? What do you want?'

'I know how you feel. I've also suffered and I thought I could be of some help; some comfort.'

'Well, that's not what I need,' Jeanie shouted, tears once more falling down her cheeks. 'I've got two children to bring up on me own! Money! That's the help and comfort I need!'

Trudie felt uneasy.

'Is anyone helping you? With money?'

'Me mam an' Albert's mam help out wit' food. But rent's due at end of t' month and I don't know where that's coming from? Doubt I'll get a pension. They don't give money to widows of soldiers who shoot's the'selves four years after war's ended!'

'If you'd allow me, I could pay something.'

'Why? You don't know me? I don't know why you're here? It's not charity I want!'

Trudie bent her head and said quietly. 'I too lost someone to the war. Someone I love deeply. I know exactly how you feel. Albert may be dead, but you have memories and the children... You have a future. I want you to believe that.'

Jeanie sniffed and wiped her nose again. 'Without Albert? People already look at me wit' pity. "There's woman who's husband shot his self. Silly bugger, they say!'

'Will you let me pay your rent this month? I'd like to.' She opened her bag and took out the £10.00 she had brought with her and put it on the table.

'I have something else for you. From Albert.' She took out the scrap of paper that she had taken from the room. She straightened it out. 'SORRY' lay between them, pitifully.

Jeanie picked it up and stroked the words. 'Always was a good neat writer'

'I think he meant it.'

'Sorry? For me or him?'

'Perhaps both of you. He loved you, I know that. I heard it in his voice.'

'He told me about Buxton once. Said how he and his regiment had stayed there a short while before being shipped out. Full o' Canadians he said. But he kept saying, "I must take you one day, Jeanie. You'd love it. So green, with a lovely Park and hills all around. And a theatre. An' clean, not like this place, just one big slag heap.' She fell silent and looked down at her hands. 'But we never got there.'

They sat quietly for a while, sipping the strong tea.

'Can I stay in touch?' asked Trudie guardedly. 'Perhaps I can take you over to Buxton and you can see for yourself...'

Jeanie looked quizzical. 'Why? You don't owe me anything.'

'It's just... I don't really know. Albert's death shocked me.

Made me think about what we have done to all our men who went to war. Both of us have lost the only thing we really loved. I want to help, if I can.'

'Huh! There's a lot of us to help. Not sure what good you can do.'

'I'm not sure myself, but I want to try.'

After a while Trudie said, 'Well, I must be going. I told my aunt that I would get back in good time.'

They stood and Trudie held out her hand. 'Goodbye Jeanie. Things will get better. They must, for all our sakes.'

They walked to the front door.

'I hope you find what you're looking for an' all,' said Jeanie. 'Cause I just lost the only thing I ever wanted.'

Trudie was nonplussed for a moment, 'Yes. I hope so too.'

4

September 1916

'Where shall we go today? asked Robbie. 'I am completely at your disposal.'

It was a warm early autumn Saturday morning and Trudie thought it would be a shame to stay in town.

'Could we get into the country somewhere? Or at least find some greenery.'

Robbie looked every inch the flyer. His uniform now carried the wings of a pilot. Trudie was immensely proud and flattered to be escorted by such a dashing warrior.

'I know. How about going down to Richmond? We could hire a boat and afterwards walk in the Park.'

'That sounds wonderful.'

They made their way to the station and sat happily in a compartment to themselves. It smelled dusty, like all old carriages. She slipped her hand into his and beamed at him.

'Why do you make me so happy, Mr Robertson?' she asked playfully.

'Because you make me want to laugh and sing and dance, Miss Polesden. I can't help but think about you all the time and that conveys itself, by telepathy, which makes you happy.'

She shrugged up against him with delight as the train rattled and rolled its way through the suburbs of South West London and into Richmond.

'I'm so glad your squadron has been delayed. I'm sure its fate you know.'

'Only by a week, mind. Then its off and up into the sky!'

'I wish I were coming with you.'

'I wish you were. Not sure the uniform would fit you though'

Since their evening at the Savoy, their love developed like an uncontrolled wild fire. They met every day and seemed oblivious to the world around them. Both were novices. The first time he bent to kiss her, they were shaking so much, he missed her mouth completely and managed an ungainly swipe across the side of her face. But it did the trick as both of them laughed at the gaucheness of it. The second kiss hit the spot and both dived straight into love.

She put her head on his shoulder and smelled the bay rum which he had combed through his hair. The stiff serge of his uniform made her feel safe.

'Do you really think I could be an artist, Robbie?'

'Well, if the auction was anything to go by, I'd say it was a dead cert. Those two chaps were practically bankrupting themselves in bidding against one another.'

'But that was for charity. I'd love to do it properly but I don't think I'm ready yet.'

'You mustn't put yourself down so! Lots of people think you have a real flair.'

'There is one thing I want to do before you go.'

'Oh? What's that?'

'I want you to sit for me. I want your picture up in my room so that you will be with me whilst you are in France.'

'Gosh! Can't think of anything more ghastly than having to stare at my ugly mug.'

'Oh, don't worry, I'll paint out the imperfections! You will do it, won't you?'

He kissed her. 'Of course I will.'

'Good. We can start tomorrow morning.'

The day in Richmond was the happiest she ever had. Robbie was a strong rower.

'I was a wet bob at school. Raced at Henley one year.' he said as he removed his jacket and rolled up his sleeves.

He rowed them up to Twickenham, where they stopped for lunch at a riverside pub and rowed back again on the tide. Then they walked up the hill into the Park and sat under a large oak, soaking up the late afternoon sun.

'Oh, Robbie, is this real? I never thought anyone could be this happy.'

He took her in his arms and kissed her ardently. 'Trudie, shall we marry?'

She paused. 'Are you asking if that is a possibility or whether I agree with the statement.'

'Oh, you know what I mean! Will you be my wife?'

'Of course I will my darling. I never wanted anything more in my life.'

When they got back to London, the first person they told was Clare. Much to their surprise, she was not as enthusiastic as they.

'Of course, I'm delighted for the both of you but don't you think it's all a bit sudden? You hardly know one another.'

'Oh, we do!' implored Trudie.

'We wanted to tell you first before mother and father. What do you think they will say?' asked Robbie tentatively.

'Same as me I expect. It's all a bit quick. I know people are throwing themselves into marriage because of the beastly war, and I'm sure the two of you are desperately in love. But that doesn't mean all reason has to fly out the window.'

'We won't be able to marry for a while. I'm off to France in a week so we can't do anything until I get back on my next leave.'

They told Robbie's parents who, as Clare had predicted, were sceptical. But in these turbulent times, many parents found their children were not always being rational.

Telling Trudie's parents was another matter all together.

'We will go and see them tomorrow evening. After your sitting for me.'

'Aren't I supposed to go and ask for your hand in marriage? Your old man might turn me away.'

'Oh no he won't. He'll be delighted. But I'm not sure about you.'

'Me!'

'Sit down and I'll tell you something about my family.'

They sat and Robbie noticed a worried furrow across her forehead. He put his thumb across it to rub it out. 'No furrowed brow, darling. Not with me anyway.'

'Robbie, you need to know that my mother is German. At the beginning of the war, she had a terrible time of it. The authorities took her away as an enemy alien and quizzed her for three days. It was at that time when all the riots were going on and German shops were being broken up. No one knew what was happening and my father was so distraught. He was even taunted at work for marrying a German. It was horrible. I too had a beastly time at school. Name calling and such like. But it was mother who really suffered.'

She looked into his eyes to see what he was thinking. He kissed her hand. 'Go on, he said tenderly. 'I still love you.'

'Well, after her ordeal, she took to her room for a while. She refused to go outside and stayed at home. She seemed to have a seizure or something because she got very down. Couldn't understand why people had suddenly taken against her when she had lived here quite peacefully for twenty years.'

'How awful for you. How is she now?'

'She never was very strong. She has a nervous disposition which seemed to get worse. Her accent has never softened and so now she hardly speaks in case someone overhears her. She does not want to bring shame on us.' Trudie's voice begun to break. She could not help it when she thought of her mother, wasting away at home, sometimes with the curtains drawn.

'I hope that when we tell them, it will help her; give her a purpose to live for again.'

'Every mother loves preparing for their daughter's wedding, don't they?' said Robbie gently.

'I suppose so. It has been so difficult for us all and Daddy has coped wonderfully. I do so want you to like them!' she said almost desperately.

'Of course I will, you goose. How could I dislike her? She's your mother. Where she comes from doesn't matter one jot. In fact, I want to congratulate her on bringing up such a wonderful girl.'

Trudie hugged him. 'Thank you Robbie, I was a bit worried about what you might think. You really are the most wonderful man in the world.'

The following day, after Robbie had sat for his portrait, they went to the Polesden house to break the news. Mrs Polesden sat quietly and murmured congratulations. Mr Polesden was delighted for the two of them and shook Robbie vigorously by the hand. Everything he wanted for his daughter was coming right. Looking after his wife was a constant strain, but now he could smile again.

'We must celebrate! I think I can find something suitable' He went off to his small cellar where he kept a few bottles for happy occasions.

'Mummy, are you happy?' asked Trudie, slipping onto the settee next to her.

'Yes darling, of course.' She patted her daughter's hand and proffered a weak smile.

That evening Robbie captivated the Polesden family and even Mrs Polesden rediscovered her old spark. Trudie could not have wished for anything better.

The final week of his leave was a busy one with farewell dinner parties and long walks through the London Parks. He sat for her every day and by the time he left, the picture was taking shape nicely.

The final night was spent with Clare and Peter. He too had received his call up. The two lovers secretly wanted to spend the night together in an hotel, but Robbie thought it too indelicate to ask and Trudie was too well mannered to drop the hint. So, the last night was spent in a yearning frustration of unconsummated longing for one another.

It was a missed opportunity that she would always regret.

On a cold early morning in January, on a flight spotting enemy positions and artillery placements, he was shot down and crashed just inside allied lines. He had been in France barely four months. His jaw was snapped and half of it torn away. His scull was broken and an eye blinded. The clearing station to which he was first taken thought he would last no more than an hour or two. He did, but never to talk again and never to recognise the girl he had fallen hopelessly in love with.

5

1922

Buxton had lost it's charm when she got back from Yorkshire. The place itself was basking in rare sunshine but Trudie's mind was elsewhere.

'Ah, there you are dear,' said Elsie Cartledge. 'Did you have a nice time?'

'It wasn't that kind of trip Elsie,' she said a little too sharply.

'And how was the wife.'

'Devastated, as you can imagine.'

Elsie grunted, 'It was very kind of you to go but was there much you could do?'

'Not much, but I wanted to go.'

'Oh well. We leave tomorrow.' It was her final word on the affair and Elsie turned to more important matters. 'Are you packed dear?'

'Not yet. I'll do it after we've had dinner.'

Elsie did most of the talking at the table, telling Trudie about her day at the baths, who she had met and what she had seen.

'Oh! The sight of some people! I'm not sure that some of them should be allowed to bathe communally, they look so wretched. I took a private compartment this afternoon. It felt much more comfortable.'

Trudie was not listening. Her mind was still in South Yorkshire, seeing the figure of Jeanie Gibson; wondering what might become of her. With two young children, she would find life very tough. If only there was something she could do to help.

'When we get home I thought we might start up the bridge circle again. What do you think, dear?'

'What?' Trudie suddenly said. 'I'm sorry Elsie. Yes that would be a wonderful idea.'

'But not with me!' she thought.

Elsie had been a godsend to the Polesdens over the years. She was her father's sister and had moved into their house just after his death four years ago. She did not know what she would have done without her after her mother sunk into a deep melancholia.

She owed her a lot but at the age of twenty three, Trudie was not prepared to play bridge every week and pass around neatly trimmed sandwiches whilst they gossiped over the petty indiscretions of their neighbours.

Clare was her salvation. The two of them shared the grief of loosing Robbie and both were bonded in a common cause. The art classes became therapeutic; a way of painting out their anger and frustration. Trudie's work was now bolder, more colourful and direct, some said even angry. Her work was recognised and bought by a circle of admirers which gave her a small income.

The two of them left Buxton the following morning and as the train drew away, she looked back at the town and sensed that the events over the last three days were a catalyst. Albert's suicide had awakened a new purpose. Life was precious and needed to be nurtured; she needed to understand her role in the events that had overtaken her. There was a feeling, a yearning almost, that she was going to change. She did not know how, but the frustrations of the last five years had to be sloughed off. She was no longer going to be hemmed in by the duties she had formerly agreed to; she wanted to be a different Trudie. The first thing she would do would be to hand in her notice at the insurance company.

When they got back to London, she went straight round to see Robbie at the small private hospital which they had found for him.

'Hello Robbie darling,' she said quietly. He was sitting near a window in his wheeled chair. He turned when he heard her enter but there was no recognition. She took his hand.

'Well, Buxton is a pretty place. Have you ever been? Rains rather a lot. But Elsie loves it as she is inside one of the baths most of the time.'

She looked at his grotesque face with its collapsed jaw and eye patch. They had tried a false eye, but it made him look too ghoulish. She brushed the bit of hair over the scars in his scalp and sat back, smiling at him. All this physical destruction she had come to terms with. What she, and indeed no one was quite sure of, was if he recognised anything or anyone.

'Robbie, I've made a decision. About my life. Something happened in Buxton which affected me very much.'

She recounted her meeting with Albert and his suicide and her visit to Jeanie.

'Daddy left us quite well off. He was well insured and we have the house and my art is going quite well. So I can give up my job.'

Robbie just stared at her. On occasions, she thought she felt his hand twitch in recognition of something she said, but now there was nothing.

'You must be thinking, I wish she would get on with it! Well, I want to help people damaged by the war. I hate to see so much suffering. It's not right Robbie. That poor woman, the same age as me I should think, with a pittance to live on and two children to bring up and there are thousands like her!' Trudie became quite animated. 'What was it all for? All that slaughter. I need to do something! She looked longingly at him. 'Robbie. Do you understand?' His hand twitched very slightly, she was sure. She smiled and bent to kiss him. 'Thank you darling, I knew you would.'

Just then Clare entered. 'Trudie. I heard you were back. My you do look fresh and healthy. The northern air suits you.'

'I've just been telling Robbie all about it.'

Clare fussed about her brother, straightening the rug on his knees and patting his hand. 'You must tell me if it would do me any good, especially if there are any eligible young men whom might suit!'

'Oh lord, one only goes to Buxton for one's health. Men don't enter into it I'm afraid.'

'Then it's back to Eastbourne or I may even venture across to Dinard. I hear the place is respectable once more.'

Clare's love life had been a constant source of entertainment for both of them but, like Trudie, she felt it would be a betrayal if she forgot her allegiance to Robbie. They both knew that Clare would marry some day but Trudie, who had been betrothed to him, albeit for no more than a few weeks, seemed to accept that she would be his guardian for ever.

'Now I have some good news for you,' said Clare. 'I've got you another commission! Do you remember that funny little man who came to dinner a month ago; a business acquaintance of Father's? He wants you to paint his daughter.'

'But he knows nothing about my work and I don't do portraiture. Surely he's mistaken.'

'You promise not to be angry with me? I showed him some of your work and he was so enamoured of it, that he asked if you would be interested. And besides you did start Robbie's portrait'

Hanging above the mantle shelf was the incomplete painting of Robbie. There was an emotional depth to it which might have been smothered had she completed it. The painting was a representation of who he was now; not quite whole.

Trudie was taken aback. 'Well, I'll have a go. And what do I charge? What if it turns out to be a dud?'

'Oh don't worry about that. I'll help you there. I've told him that you have never done anything like this before but he is quite determined. So, you have to do it. It could be the start of something new!'

Clare's enthusiasm was infectious and she took her hand. 'You are good to me and I'm terribly grateful but I have a new life. I've just been telling Robbie. I want to work with a charity. Helping war widows.'

Clare's eyes widened in surprise. 'War widows! Where on earth did you get that notion?'

Trudie told her about her trip to Buxton and how she had been moved by the plight of Jeanie Gibson. 'I feel somehow responsible. If I had agreed to talk to him he might still be here and Jeanie would not be a widow.'

'But I can't see how you can be held responsible. A chance

encounter, that's all.'

'No, it's more than that. It was meant to happen and I let him down. Clare, you have no idea how distraught he must have been. He was hoping I would talk to him; help him in some way. But I didn't. I just walked away from him. Now I need to make amends.'

'Well, I never cease to be amazed by you darling. Becoming a good Samaritan.'

'Oh don't think that Clare. I'm really a very selfish person and I don't want to be seen as a do gooder either.'

'But you are darling. Just look at how you look after Robbie.'

'Only because I want to. Otherwise it's me I think about most.'

'Well, if you are set on it and there is anything I can do, you must ask. Father has lots of people he knows who might help as well. But you won't give up your painting, will you?'

'Of course not. It's what keeps me sane.'

6

Feb 1917

When Trudie got news of his crash she was numbed but hoped that his injuries were not life threatening. He was brought back to England and she and Clare were horrified at what they saw. He lay motionless, his head almost completely bandaged as if laid out ready for burial. His hands were carefully placed over the starched sheets and his legs straightened under the covers. The ward was as quiet as a chapel of rest, with other dangerously wounded men lined along either wall ready for absolution.

The girls could do little other than weep and hold Robbie's

hands. A Matron watched unobtrusively from a distance, ready to placate any outburst of emotion. She left them to absorb the devastation and then nodded to a doctor who had just arrived.

'I am so sorry ladies,' he whispered.

'Will he recover?' asked Clare. 'Will he be normal?'

'That we cannot say at present. His heart is strong but with head injuries, it takes longer to determine what might happen. There will be complications.'

'What complications? What can you tell us?' Trudie wiped away a tear.

'Well, we have relieved the pressure and removed bits and pieces from his brain. He is stable now but we may have to do a lot more work.'

'And what will he be like? Will he be alright?'

The doctor paused. This was always the hardest part.

'I'm afraid not. We think his speech will be affected and he may have other disabilities. He may loose some motor functions.'

'Motor functions?'

'He may not walk too well, and he may suffer epileptic fits.'

They all looked at the subject of their discussion.

'And,' continued the doctor, 'he lost an eye and suffered severe facial injuries.' He thought it best to let them know the full extent of the wounds. They would know soon enough. 'But he is still alive, thanks to the quick work of the medical staff at the Front.'

This was not the first or last time the doctor would have such conversations with the distraught relatives. 'That's as much as I can tell you at the moment.' He made to leave. 'If you need anything, please ask one of the nurses and if I have any further news, I'll let you know as soon as possible.'

They left after an hour and said nothing to each other, both wrapped in their own thoughts.

When Trudie reached home, she locked herself in her bedroom and wept uncontrollably.

'So short a time!' she cried. 'Why, why, why did you leave?'

She spent the following days in a fog of emotional turmoil. Tears mixed with anger and guilt were added to the weariness of sleepless nights. For a short while she went to the church in which she had been baptised but found little comfort. The priest who visited her was young and enthusiastic and despite the number of occasions he had comforted young widows and mothers, he seemed somehow the least appropriate person to confide in. What did he know of passion, other than his devotion to his Christ?

Clare was equally devastated and the two girls spent many hours together, questioning, arguing, and on occasions angrily shouting at one another.

'I don't care that you were going to marry him! I don't care if you loved him better than you loved yourself! He was my brother and… and he was part of me!' sobbed Clare.

She and Trudie were sitting on the bed in a large room, over-looking the sea front at Brighton where they had gone together for a change from the morbid daily atmosphere and routine of home and hospital.

'Sometimes I can't bear to look at you!' shouted Trudie. 'You remind me so much of him. I ache whenever I look at you. Am I to be tormented by you for the rest of my life?'

And then they would fall into one another's arms and swear undying fealty to Robbie. Their common cause, the purpose of their lives from now on, was to keep Robbie safe and comfortable; their penance for the unkindnesses of the world.

Brighton was some comfort. They forced themselves to break the routine of self pity by swimming in a cold sea, taking brisk walks along the Downs, going to shows which they invariably walked out of half way through and getting drunk in small scruffy pubs. But they still asked the same tormenting question day after day. Why?

7

1918

When Trudie's father died at the end of the war, another piece of her was torn away. Robbie had been bad enough but now her inspiration, the one who had first given her a zest for life was gone too.

'I think you should go up to see your father. He is very ill,' said her mother one afternoon when she returned from work.

Trudie hung up her coat and looked up the long flight of stairs. It had been like this for a week and each day he deteriorated. She did not want to go for she knew that her father was now close to death. For the last three days he had lain in bed, deliriously soaked, with the influenza that wracked his body. Slowly she climbed the stairs and entered the room set aside for him. She put on the mask, hanging by the door and approached him nervously.

'Hello Daddy. How are you feeling?'

His breath was short and his face the colour of cold porridge but he managed a smile. 'Not so good my love. You had a good day?'

'Yes thanks.' She did not go too close to his bed. He would have prevented her from doing so had she tried.

'Don't stay too long. I don't want you getting this dreadful cold.' The fever gave him a hideous look, like one of those medieval paintings of grey faced cadavers being readied for the grave and Trudie recoiled.

'Could you ask your mother to come up. Not feeling so great.'

Terrified, Trudie, backed out of the room. Her mother was already coming upstairs. 'Wait down in the dining room. I won't be long,' she commanded.

When her mother came back down she said. 'He's dying.

There is no sense in pretending otherwise.'

'Is he much worse? Than this morning?'

'Yes. Doctor Smith was in earlier and could not hide his concern although he still said there was hope.' The silence of the large dark house hung on the two of them. 'We must prepare ourselves.' Trudie took her mother's hand and they sat quietly on the settee in the fast approaching gloom of evening.

That night Fredric Polesden died, one of millions carried away by 'the Spanish flu' which had swept through the world, an influenza which seemed incapable of being stopped.

As she sat in her bedroom, she remembered her father with great fondness.

They often went out into the country side, where he would delight her with his enthusiasm for nature. 'Come on dear,' he would shout. 'Lets see what we can find in this pond.' And taking off his shoes and socks and rolling up his suit trousers, would plunge bravely into muddy places to see what could be found.

'Daddy! Daddy, over there!' She would shriek, pointing and jumping up and down. 'That yellow one!'

'I see!' He would wade over and with his pen knife, cut the stem of a water Plantain and bear it back to her, like her chivalrous knight.

Together, they would explore the world around them and she was never afraid to ask the awkward questions about where babies came from, or why there were poor people and rich people or why men had more hair on their faces than women. He always had an answer.

Tears coursed down her face as she thought of those days. 'Oh, Daddy, why? We never talked about influenza, did we?'

The funeral was a quiet affair with the Polesden family making up the bulk of the cortège. Her mother's family in Germany had never got to know them and now, after the devastation of defeat, were not likely to suddenly appear. She clung to the arm of her daughter and hid her tears under a black widow's veil. Trudie was heart broken for her.

'Mummy, just stay close to me. You don't have to say anything if you don't want to.'

The death of her husband pushed her even further into the depression that had formed itself like a miasma round her since the start of the war.

Trudie did her best to help. She would sit and listen to her when one of her many bouts of melancholia descended with tears and lamentations. Elsie too would spend hours with her and comforted both mother and daughter.

'Trudie, dear, I think we need to be very patient with her. She has never really got over being treated as an enemy alien, has she? Quite disgraceful, the way they treated her! Really, couldn't the authorities see the difference between your mother and an enemy spy?'

Trudie remembered what a fine woman she had been. From her she had inherited an aptitude and love of art.

'Now Schiller, there is a poet to rival your Shakespeare. And Bach! From him, all music flows.' she proclaimed with passion. 'You must learn German so that you can read all my favourite poets as they should be read,' she insisted.

But that all came to a halt after she had been treated like a 'German swine'; when she was spat at in the street and when people she called friends turned their backs. She was never quite the same after that. With the death of her husband, she became a recluse, tended by Trudie and Elsie Cartledge.

Now Trudie had two invalids to look after, neither of whom could communicate with her. She spent her days shuffling between the two of them with thankful interludes at the art studio. She was twenty years old and already thought of herself as an old maid.

'Oh, don't be so silly!' cried Clare.

'But how can I ever have a normal life?'

'Well, one day, you will meet someone...'

'How can I? Robbie is the only one I ever wanted.'

'Darling, life will go on. Your mother will get better too, surely.'

'I don't know,' she said wistfully. 'Some days she is a bit better and then others she just stays in bed. And Robbie… do you ever get a sign of recognition?'

Clare had to admit that if he had made a sign, she had not detected it.

'Well, at least you have your art.'

'Yes, there is that I suppose.'

8

1923

Trudie's first exhibition was at a small gallery just off New Bond Street and was a great success. Friends had rallied round and put the word about that Trudie Polesden, a coming young artist, was showing her work with all proceeds going to the War Widow's Benevolent Society. 'Buy one of her paintings now and you would have something that could only rise in value!' they trumpeted.

This was important to her. After the success of the Art class auction, which seemed a lifetime ago, she thought the same could be done for the Society. Any profits from the sale of pictures, after expenses, would be ploughed into helping the Jeanie Gibson's who currently survived at the whim of a mish-mash of Pension Boards and committees who decided the value or otherwise of human dignity.

'It's going well,' said Clare in one of the few moments that Trudie was not surrounded by eager patrons wanting to know more about her.

'Have we sold many?' asked Trudie excitedly. It was the

first time in months that she felt alive. She had got herself up in something glamorous and people remarked on how lovely she looked.

'Three so far, all bought by the same person.'

'Oh? Who?'

'The youngish man over there. The tall one with the moustache, talking to father.'

'I've never seen him before. Must have seen the advert in the paper.'

'He is rather good looking,' said Clare playfully.

'Well, why don't you go and talk to him then?'

'I think I will.' Clare weaved her way through the crowd and introduced herself to the new owner of three of Trudie's paintings.

A waiter approached and offered her a glass of champagne, which she took. The gallery was getting a bit warm and she had had nothing to eat or drink all day. The buzz and excitement with such a collection of people all talking about her work, made her quite dizzy.

Peter came up and congratulated her. 'Darling, you are a sensation!'

'Thank you Peter, but I don't think I deserve the hyperbole just yet.'

'But I've been eavesdropping and have heard nothing but praise. 'Waiting for Life' has caused a particular stir. Been snapped up already.'

'By the man talking to Clare?'

'Yes. Did she tell you?'

'Not that he had bought that particular picture.'

'Waiting For Life' had been painted shortly after Trudie's visit to Jeanie. It was a powerful sombre depiction of women and men waiting to hear news of loved ones at the Front and was stained with the emotion of hope and despair.

Trudie was swept away on a small flood of people all craving her attention. She was quite bemused with it all and frequently had no sense of what replies she gave to the numerous questions. She clung to her glass of rapidly warming champagne and was relieved to be rescued by Lady Riedsmuir, the Patron of the Society. Although she was flattered by the interest in her art, she did not want the exhibition to detract from what for her was it's purpose; to raise money for people like Jeanie Gibson. She had nearly invited Jeanie down and then thought she might be a bit overawed by it all. But she had resolved to take Jeanie over to Buxton.

'Lady Riedsmuir, what do you think?'

Lady Riedsmuir, large, bossy and completely devoted to causes which helped the poor, turned her smile on Trudie. 'My dear girl, I think this is wonderful. So original! I would never have thought of doing something like this, not that I have any artistic ability myself.'

'But I'm sure you know others who could donate things to the Society?'

'Oh yes, but when we have one so actively involved in the Society with such a talent, it means so much more! A stunning move which can do nothing but embarrass the Government to do more for these poor women. My Freddie would be turning in his grave if he knew the state we have got ourselves into.'

Freddie Riedsmuir, now dead, had been a prominent Liberal MP who had championed causes for the poor over many years. His wife, never one to hide behind her husband, picked up the flag of righteousness and marched on.

'Now I see lots of people just dying to talk to you. I'm sure they want to buy pictures!' Lady Riedsmuir squeezed Trudie's arm and propelled her towards a couple quietly waiting for a word with the artist.

The guests slowly came and went all evening and by ten o'clock, most of them had dispersed. Trudie was wonderfully tired with the success of it all. She kicked off her shoes and slumped down on a banquette in the middle of the Gallery.

'Oh, darling I'm so pleased for you!' said Clare. 'We must have raised a fortune. Peter says that at least six paintings have been sold and Charles says he has had expressions of interest from others who want to know what else you have.'

'But most of it is hanging on the walls here, in Charles' Gallery.' said Trudie yawning.

'Come on girls, I'm taking you out for a late supper,' butted in Peter.

'Oh no, I'm completely done in,' said Trudie. 'I just want to curl up in bed and sleep.

'But you must. You've had nothing all evening.'

'I know, but eating can wait. You two go on. I'll go back. If you don't mind, Clare, I'll stop off and see Robbie before I go home.'

Of course! I'm sure the staff will let you see him.'

When she got to his room, Robbie was in bed. She crept in. His eye was open. If he knew she was here he did not show it.

'Robbie darling, it's been a terrific success. Now we can really start on giving at least a few women some help. There will never be enough money for all we want to do but we've made a start and I'm so excited. You would have been so proud of me this evening.'

She squeezed his hand. 'I want to help Jeanie Gibson as soon as possible and will go up to see her and get things started. I want her to be my presence up there and help other women who have lost husbands. And fiancés of course. There will be such a lot to do, finding a place and organising things. Jeanie seems very capable.'

She looked at his scarred face. 'My poor darling, I wish you could share all this with me.'

Over the last few weeks, Robbie's condition had deteriorated. On two occasions he had suffered convulsions which scared them. He had developed a slight tremor as well. All of them begun to fear the worst.

She bent down and kissed him. 'I'm also doing this for you,

you know.'

She left his room shortly after, threw a cheery goodbye at the night staff and went out to find a taxi.

She climbed in and leaned back and said quietly to herself. 'I feel useful at long last!'

'Pardon miss?' said the cabbie.

She smiled. 'Just feeling happy for once.'

'And why not!' said the cabbie with a chuckle as he drove off.

Trudie met Jeanie at Buxton station the following week. It was a bright sunny day in September and she was pleased that the place was looking its best with an explosion of colour in the Gardens.

'How are you Jeanie?'

OK, 'spose. Thanks for sending me the money. And the fare to get over here. I wasn't sure about coming, but when you told me in your letter how successful the charity do had been, well I had to come and thank you.' For the first time since they had met, Trudie saw Jeanie's face light up. She looked more aware of the world, more confident.

'Shall we walk in the Gardens and than have lunch in the Pavilion?'

The Gardens were busy with a gay assortment of parasols and hats, prams and wheeled chairs. Children ran around noisily and couples walked arm in arm; it was a happy carefree afternoon in the sun. Jeanie looked about her in some awe.

'I see what Albert meant. It is lovely. I wish I'd bought the girls over with me.'

'But you could have…'

'Not this time. I just wanted to see where he spent his last hours for me sen. I can come over with them some other time.'

'How are the girls?'

'Clementine's at school and doing well. She gets down, 'specially when she sees other girls wi' t' dads. Beatrice is adapting quicker. Cheeky with it! You said it would take time. It will.'

They strolled slowly along the path. 'This is where Albert and I walked. And talked.' She wasn't sure if that was the right thing to say, but she said it anyway.

'What did he say? Tell me again, so I can hear his voice, here.'

"I'm a sign writer," he said. "Best in Yorkshire." And he said, "I love my two girls and Jeanie, my wife. But we've had a row." And I said, "will you be going back to her?" And he said "yes, probably." He was very confused, Jeanie. He wanted someone to talk to, to help him understand why he felt so... angry with everything.'

'So, do you think he came here to work it out like... that he never meant to do what he did?

Trudie stopped and took her arm. 'Oh, Jeanie. There is something I haven't told you. Can we sit?'

They sat on a bench opposite the fountain which sprayed a silver jet of water.

'It was a bit like today when we walked here and I think Albert felt easier in himself. But I let him down...'

'Let him down? How?'

'He said how he had enjoyed walking and talking to me and could we do it again the next day. He wasn't trying to pick me up or anything... he just wanted to talk. And I refused. Told him I had my aunt to think of. It upset him. He thought I was brushing him away and could not be bothered. He... he got quite agitated and he stormed off. That's the last I saw of him.'

They both sat quietly, caught up in their own thoughts, not daring to say anything. Trudie felt Jeanie's anguish. What must she think? Does she blame me?

At length, Jeanie looked straight at her. Trudie thought how pretty she looked with some colour in her cheeks, brought on, no doubt by her anger at what she had just heard. But Jeanie took her hand and squeezed it gently. 'Thank you,' she said quietly. 'You were the only one to listen. No one at home understood. I did me best, but he was so… He couldn't look at me, as if he hated himself and couldn't say anything to me. About how he felt. And I did nowt to get him help. Not that there was any.'

Both women begun to cry and people passing, looked away in embarrassment.

'Oh, Jeanie, if only I had met him again and talked to him, he might still be here…'

'No! No, he wouldn't. I don't think there was any thing any-one could do. He had been so…. agitated the weeks before. And then he were sacked. Because he weren't doing his job properly. And then he just up and left, creeping out at house so early that morning, like a whipped dog. Oh, if only I had listened more and seen how unhappy he was. No, it weren't you Trudie. You did more than me. You listened…'

'Not enough. It will live with me for the rest of my life.'

'And it's the rest of our lives we should be thinking on! I have the girls and you have your Robbie to look after,' Jeanie said animatedly. 'I want to help! I want to do something for Albert; something that will carry on. I want to help the Society to help others so that something good comes of his death.'

Trudie was astounded by this rush of resolve. 'Thank you Jeanie. I came up here thinking I could comfort you, but you have done more for me. Of course you can help. In fact I was going to ask you anyway.' Both of them laughed joyously and hugged one another.

'Well. I think we can finish our walk and then have a bit of lunch.'

This was a new beginning for both of them. The Society would grow into something far bigger than either of them could imagine and in the years to come, Jeanie would become the Patron of the War Widows Benevolent Society, winning the grateful thanks of widows in all walks of life. It would go on to support women of men lost in mining disasters, on the railways, in the steel mills. She would, in old age, be awarded the Order of the British Empire for her services to charity. But now she was grateful that Trudie was giving her something to hang onto.

The War Widow's Benevolent Society caught the imagination of the wider public, particularly when the papers highlighted 'the brilliant young artist', Trudie Polesden. And the Society was attracting attention from political quarters as well. What to do? She desperately wanted to spend more time with her paint brushes and also play an active role in helping the Society. Although Clare was only too happy to help out with social occasions, she was not cut out for the routines of charity work. Besides, she was now besotted with the man who had bought the three paintings at the charity exhibition, Percy Bradstone Smith

'He's so alive, Trudie. I know you'll love him as much as I do,' she gushed.

Trudie now rented a small studio and Clare watched as she deftly mixed paint.

'Has he proposed yet?' asked Trudie mischievously.

'Don't be silly! We're having far too much fun. Besides, he is too busy trying to get into Parliament.'

'Oh? I had no idea. Will he succeed?'

'He's winning lots of support, although father is not enamoured with his politics. He's on the Labour Party ticket.'

'Labour? He doesn't look like one of the proletariat.'

'No but he's frightfully intelligent. When he talks about his beliefs, he's very persuasive. He's more of a theoretical Socialist than a practicing one. He writes ever so clearly and simply about what needs to be done to get this country back on its feet.'

'Oh Clare, when were you ever interested in politics? Are you sure he's the one for you?' said Trudie putting down her palette and glancing artfully at her.

'I hope so. I do find him fascinating. And I'm not a complete dunce!'

Trudie smiled. Clare could be a bit of a butterfly, flitting from one love to another. Percy Bradstone Smith did not sound like her type at all.

'Anyway, he's dying to meet you. He wants to know more about the paintings he's bought. Says he may be interested in something else'

'But I haven't got any more work to show! I'm giving up most of my time to the Society.'

'Well, I hope you don't go to waste, darling. I think you have too much talent for it to rust away.'

Trudie did not answer. The Society, her art, her mother, Robbie and now Jeanie. How to get things into balance?

'I'm going over to see Robbie. Are you coming?'

'Shortly. I just want to finish this bit.'

Clare moved slowly to the door and then stopped and turned. 'You know he's dying, don't you.'

'Yes. I know,' she said without stopping her brushstroke. It was something neither had acknowledged yet.

As Clare left the room, Trudie put down the brush and gave herself over to contemplative tears.

'I know,' she said quietly. 'I know.'

It was almost seven years since Robbie's fateful accident and every day, Trudie had wished to see a spark which would indicate some hope; some miracle. Nothing. Just the occasional twitch of his hand which was probably just an involuntary jerk. Hope was fading. Things were crowding out the memory of those brief days they had spent together. She felt trapped. The poor creature sitting up in his room was slowly disappearing before her eyes and yet she could do nothing about it. She had sworn to be with him for as long as it took. Passion had been sacrificed to duty. Her sorrow was for herself now. She was trapped and the painting and the

Society were her way of pulling away from him. Robbie no longer belonged to her, or anyone. She found it more and more difficult to see him with his rictus smile and weeping eye. What was the point?

She finished off her painting and cleaned the brushes and then left the studio. She walked into the small park nearby and sat for a long time on a bench. She was demanding too much of herself. Something would have to give.

A week later she was summoned to Robbie's bedside by an anxious Clare.

'He's had another convulsion. He's also shaking uncontrollably. The doctor is up there at the moment. Oh, Trudie! What does it mean?'

'Is it worse than before?'

'Yes, oh much worse.'

The doctor descended the stairs and stopped in front of the two anxious girls. 'He's calm now. I've given him a shot so he will sleep.'

'How bad is he? Is he...'

'Well, he's not dying if that's what you are thinking. With brain injuries you can never be quite certain of what's happening up there.' He tapped his head to needlessly illustrate the point. 'Don't forget it's a miracle that he has survived this long.'

'And there is nothing more we can do?'

'Just keep him stable and warm. He turned to leave. 'Let's see how he is tomorrow and I might have a better answer for you'

The two women sat down quietly. 'Well, we carry on as normal I suppose,' said Clare.

Trudie looked at her without emotion or words.

They both went up to see him. He lay propped up on the bed with a rug thrown loosely over him.

'I'll stay with him for a while if you like.' said Trudie.

'Will you? I promised I'd meet Percy. You could join us later if you like.'

'I have some things to do at the Society. And I think I just want to paint.'

'Well, the offer stands and you haven't met Percy yet.'

'I know. But not tonight.'

'Trudie sat alone, looking at the sleeping figure. She pulled her chair a little closer and bent her head towards him.

'Robbie, darling, I don't think I can take much more of this. The uncertainty... the waiting and wondering and knowing that you will never get any better. I've been thinking about it for a long time. I love you so much but the memory of you strong and proud, rowing up the river at Richmond... I've had too much pain already, darling. First you, then Daddy and Mummy. And then Albert. Everything ends in tragedy.' She took a handkerchief and wiped her nose. 'I don't know if you ever hear me or recognise me; whether you ever have dreams and hopes. It's all locked away inside you. I'll never share those dreams. I want you to be happy darling, wherever you are and I want just the wonderful memory of you. Not like this, but when I first saw you, so shy and handsome.'

Slowly she stood, tears coursing down her face. She listened for anyone who might come in. 'Goodbye my darling,' she whispered through her tears. 'I love you so very much.' She took a pillow from under his head and put it over his face. She held it down hard for several minutes, sobbing. He did not move. She lifted the pillow and bent down to feel any breath. There was none. Carefully she replaced the pillow, kissed him and left silently.

PERCY

1

1923

'Here he is!' said Clare delightedly. 'Percy meet Trudie, Trudie, meet Percy.'

They shook hands formerly. 'Hello. I hear you splashed out on some of my paintings at the showing?'

'Yes, I did. They are quite wonderful.'

'Thank you. Have you hung them yet?'

'No. I have to think about that. These aren't any old paintings, are they? What you have done is more than good. They are special.'

Trudie was not quite sure of quite how sincere he was. He sounded genuine and she hardly thought that someone would spend good money on something they did not like, even if it was for charity.

'Well, I'm glad you like them...'

'Oh, I'm not sure I like them yet. But they have touched me. Deeply.' The intensity of his words unnerved her and she backed away from him.

'A lot of artists have represented the war as death and destruction, bomb blast, Armageddon. But you have touched upon something else; a woman's perspective.

Well, for obvious reasons...'

'I'm not trying to be clever. I really don't know enough about art but there is a lot of personal emotion that comes through. Emotion that one can only sense if one has been in the thick of it.'

'That's because I feel very emotional about the subject Mr Bradstone Smith,' she was not sure how genuine his comments were; he was too easy, too ready to share his insight.

'Clare has told me about her brother and your …engagement. I'm truly sorry that you never got to know him properly.'

'Thank you.' She now felt uncomfortable and looked to Clare to move the conversation along.

'You see, I told you he was fascinating,' chirped Clare, who had been looking at him as if he were a beautiful vision.

'And the one of Buxton, with the solitary soldier standing in the Pavilion Gardens…'

'You know Buxton?'

'Yes, I was born and raised not far from there. I take it that is Albert, who Clare has also told me about?'

'Yes. Yes it is'

'Very moving.' He said with the tone that was now beginning to annoy her. 'I was his commanding officer, you know'

Trudie's mouth hung open as she digested his words. 'You knew him?'

'Yes. Same company, same platoon. In fact I put him up for his citation at Poelcapelle. We were both lucky to get out of that one.'

'Well I don't quite know what to say. Apart from what a remarkable coincidence. Or did you know before you bought the pictures.'

'No. Just coincidence. But when Clare told me some of the details, I knew it had to be him. Of course I was unaware of what happened to him. Tragic.'

'Yes. Yes it was.' She was still stunned that he could so calmly tell her that he knew Albert. Albert was hers; her inspiration. How could he just barge into her world like this?

'And how are things going with the charity?' he asked, switching effortlessly from sincerity to warmth.

'Very well, thank you.' She caught her breath and regained

her composure. 'We have our first shop open in Doncaster.'

'Shop?'

'Yes, as a start, we thought it might be a good idea to sell clothing and household goods at very cheap prices. It's a club which widows join and contribute towards.'

'Sounds fascinating. You know my interests lie in that direction as well?'

'Clare had mentioned that you were trying to get into Parliament.'

'Well, I have missed the boat this time round,' he said immodestly, 'but I'm sure there will be opportunities at the next election.'

'Now come on you two, lets go and find lunch. You can talk some more there,' said Clare, anxious to turn the conversation in her direction. 'Peter's joining us as well.'

Trudie sat opposite Percy in the restaurant and tried to find redeeming features in his physical presence. He had a chiselled slender face with the sallow cheeks of one who needed more sleep and less alcohol. But his eyes were bright and curious and his fleshy lips were ever ready to flash a smile. Whether his looks made up for what Trudie thought his over familiarity on first meeting remained to be seen. She did not want to talk about Albert, and was at least grateful that he did not seem to want to either.

'Percy's taking me up to meet his people at the weekend, aren't you dear?' said Clare.

'Yes but I have to warn them about you first,' he said playfully.

'Oh you beast!' she said, cuffing him on the arm and he leaned across and kissed her on the cheek. 'But I told them you are quite harmless.'

'They do look in love,' thought Trudie. 'If only Robbie…' But she stopped herself in mid thought.

'I say, why don't you and Peter come up as well. Bags of room for all,' said Percy

'I can't I'm afraid. A prior engagement calls,' said Peter.

'Trudie?' he asked and she felt it was not quite a question but a command.

'No, I couldn't possibly. It's your weekend Clare.'

'Oh, go on darling. I need someone else to help me shut him up!'

'Yes, please do. I'm dying to hear more about the charity. Why don't you bring your painting things then you can wander off and paint another master piece. You do landscapes don't you?'

'Not much. But if I wasn't in the way...'

'That's settled then,' he said staring at her triumphantly.

The Bradstone Smiths farmed in Derbyshire not far from Bakewell. The closer the train got to the town the more her thoughts turned to Albert. She was not sure that a run over to Buxton would be a good idea.

'Do you know Buxton well?' she asked him, as the three of them sat in the dining car of the train.

'Oh yes. Many a desperate evening over there,' he said with a twinkle. 'Some very grand affairs at the Palace Hotel. But we always found it a bit parochial. Bit inbred, if you know what I mean.'

'No, I can't say I do. In fact we, my aunt and I, always found it very pleasant. Quiet and unpretentious.'

'As I said, boring.' He snapped his fingers at a passing waiter and ordered another beer.

'Well, I would certainly like to run over some time,' said Clare. 'It holds a very special memory for Trudie and it would be unforgivable if we could not see the place where it all began for you dear.'

'Oh, it really doesn't matter. I'm the interloper here. It's your weekend Clare and you have to decide what we all do.' She fixed Percy's eye, defying him to gainsay her.

'I couldn't agree more,' he said.

'That settles it then. We will go over and Percy can show us the sights.'

The rest of the journey was spent with Percy telling them of his childhood in Derbyshire and scandalous tit bits about the Devonshires and their numerous offspring, all of which hugely amused Clare and left Trudie irritated with his showing off. She suspected that he had never met the Duke and Duchess of Devonshire, despite the proximity of the Chatsworth estate to their land. But she was curious about the connection between Albert and Percy and how it might affect her.

When they arrived at Bakewell station, Percy's father was there to meet them with the car and after they had piled everything into the boot, they rattled and spluttered their way to the farmhouse.

'Farming isn't what it was', shouted his father over his shoulder as they bounced along. 'Country's gone to the dogs if you ask me. This new lot in government, are they going to fix the economy? Unemployment two million and rising! And we fought a bloody war to save this country! Now its going to wrack and ruin!' He kept up a constant stream of invective and Percy winked at Trudie, as if to say, 'Don't mind the old chap. It keeps him happy.'

His parents were a welcoming couple, delighted to have their son home, even if it was only for the weekend. And Percy was right about painting. She remembered some of the stark scenery; the dales and hills. They took her breath away and she was sure it would inspire her.

The next morning Percy suggested they walk some of the River Wye. 'We'll start off in Monsal Dale and see where that takes us.'

They took a picnic and Percy pointed out the landmarks he could remember from his childhood. 'Used to do a spot of fishing along here', he said as they walked by the stilled river. 'Haven't been here in years but now I see why we all went to war. Worth saving, all this.'

They stopped at mid day and whilst Percy and Clare set out the picnic, Trudie sat nearby and begun sketching some of the scenery along the river. Percy came over and looked over her shoulder at what she was doing.

'There is so much of it, I don't know where to start and end,' she said enthusiastically.

'That's good. Very good. Could I commission it? I'd like to give it to Ma and Pa as a present. They'd love it.'

'Of course, but I won't accept any payment.'

'But you must. It's what you do for a living.'

'Well, if you like you can make a donation to the Society.'

'Done!' He touched her shoulder in acknowledgement of the deal and a shiver went down her spine.

Clare spread out the victuals and Percy uncorked a bottle of wine. The sun was high and warm and the air still.

'How did you get into this charity lark,' asked Percy

Trudie told him of how she had felt the urge to visit Albert's widow. 'I needed to do something with my life. Especially after Robbie died.'

'We must have travelled along a similar road. There were too many Robbie's and when you think of how we treated the men in the trenches, well it makes me spit. That's why I want to do something. Politics seems to fit me. I can talk a lot, anyway.'

'Oh, you certainly can, darling. Very stirring as well. I've heard him, Trudie and he can certainly hold an audience,' said Clare proudly.

'Why the Labour party?' asked Trudie

'They are thinkers. They want to refashion the country and make it fairer. I think of the poor bloody infantry and those that survived are most probably in Queer Street now. They thought they were coming home to something better. The old men who run our country are completely outmoded; living in Victorian times. The war should have shaken them up but all they want to do is get back to how things were. It's not good

300

enough!' Trudie watched as he jabbed his points home. He may be a bit superficial, but she liked his enthusiasm.

'Darling, eat this lovely bit of pork pie your mother made. Food before speeches, I say.'

'You're right. I do talk too much. Must get it from the Pater.'

'I like to hear a man with convictions.' said Trudie. 'I think you are quite right. The rich just want to preserve what they have, regardless of who suffers for it.'

'Oh, not you too, Trudie. I thought we had come out for a lovely day in the country?'

'We have,' said Trudie placating her friend. 'But you can't ignore what has happened. If you come up to Yorkshire with me next time I go, you'll think differently too.'

'Dare say I would, but not today. Just for once let's be sybarites.'

'Steady on! A piece of pork pie and glass of iffy white wine hardly counts as a bacchanal. But then I do have two rather wonderful girls with me.'

'And what precisely do you mean by that?' said Clare, pushing him over. She started tickling him and the two of them rolled playfully whilst Trudie looked on wondering what his body must feel like.

'I think I'll take myself off and find another angle to sketch,' she said diplomatically

'OK,' said Clare sitting up suddenly. 'Let's finish lunch and I'll take this annoying person away so you can get on with his commission in peace.'

The two lovers wandered away and Trudie took herself up to a bank which afforded a wider sweep of the river and surroundings. The sky was scattered with bits of cotton wool, moving lazily across her eyeline. It was hazy and hot so she sat for a while under some shade taking it all in.

Then she saw a movement below near a clump of bushes. It took her a moment to realise that she was looking at Percy and Clare making love, oblivious to the world around them.

They were far enough away for her not to hear them, but the movements were unmistakable. Clare was giving herself willingly to this man. She was transfixed by the motion of their bodies and wondered if she would ever find herself clinging to a man with such abandon. She looked away, disturbed by her own carnal thoughts.

Later that evening when the two women found themselves alone together, Trudie asked. 'Did you enjoy the day?'

'Yes, wonderfully, I wish we could walk more of the river'

Trudie smiled, 'It certainly put colour in your cheeks'

On the Sunday they agreed to run over to Buxton, but not before morning service at the local church with his parents. 'You don't mind, do you?' Percy asked.

'Of course not, darling. It's part of the bucolic experience. I'll love it,' said Clare a little too effusively.

They all walked to church at Great Longstone and then back for lunch. It really did feel like they had hold of a thread of timeless history, the kind she had read about in nineteenth century novels.

At lunch, the men argued politics and Trudie found herself siding with Percy whilst Clare and his mother tried to bring the conversation back to more prosaic topics. Each time she looked at him, she thought back to the last afternoon with fluttering curiosity. He did not have his father's well grounded certainties of life, but in every other respect he was his image; convivial, argumentative, proud. He was a charmer but she could not help thinking that he was insubstantial; not yet the full man, despite his experiences of war.

They did not get to Buxton until 3 o'clock and had little time to get round all that Clare wanted to see. But she was happy to hang onto Percy's arm and listen to him expound on the more familiar sights; the Old Hall, where Mary Queen of Scots had stayed, the Pavilion, the Crescent with its hotels and the baths. Trudie was content just to wander along with them in her own little world which was suddenly broken by Percy asking to see where Albert had committed suicide.

'Why? I don't think I want to revisit it.'

'But I could put something together for the newspaper I freelance for. How our soldiers are still being let down. I could write up something about how you were inspired to start the charity of yours.'

'No,' she said firmly. 'No, I would not want that. Besides, it would not be fair to Jeanie Gibson. No I think it an awful idea.' She quickly walked on.

Clare was a little startled by the vehemence of her reaction.

'Well, I suggest we get back then and have some supper. We need to catch an early train back tomorrow morning,' said Percy who was not used to being denied quite so forcefully, particularly by women.

2

October 1917

Percy Bradstone Smith returned to his unit after his leave in a mood of angry resignation. He had a thundering headache which was to be expected after an all day drinking binge. He reported to his superior officer who took one look at him and said 'God, you look terrible. We're going in the attack day after tomorrow and I want you *compos*.' There were no words of welcome, no 'how did you enjoy your leave.' The captain was tired and anxious about the task ahead and was due some leave himself. He was in no mood to ease in a lieutenant with a hangover.

Percy slumped down onto a vacant cot and knew there would be little time for rest this day with final arrangements to be made. The enemy bombardment was fairly remorseless; they were jittery, not knowing quite if or when an attack would begin. The Sherwood Foresters would be moving up next day and he had to ensure his company were prepared; trenching equipment and rations handed out, packs stowed. He looked at the ceiling of grey canvas which constituted the roof of the old farm house that had been hit before he went on leave. It flapped slowly in the light breeze. It was too cold to sleep and with people constantly coming in and out he decided to write to his mother.

Dear Mater,

Hope I find you in fine order. Sorry I could not get over when I was back on leave but I really did not have an awful lot of time. Got in with Reggie Turnbull and his gang. You remember. He was the one at school who kept on getting into trouble. He's in some top job at the Ministry of something and far too important to be with us poor chaps here.

I have written to Annie but have not heard back for some time. Do hope she is alright. You couldn't go over there and see, could you? I'd hate to think that I had upset her again. It really is quite wretched not being able to talk to her...

As soon as he had finished and addressed an envelope, he fell back on the camp bed, wrapped himself in his great coat and thought about Annie, the girl to whom he was betrothed. He was confused. Did he love her or not?

Anne Russell's family had the estate bordering that of the Bradstone Smiths and they had known each other over many years. Percy's mother had always harboured a desire for young Anne and her son to form an alliance. Percy had been shipped off to Repton at a young age and each time he returned home on vacation, Anne Russell grew a little more interesting. When war was declared Percy fell in with thousands of other young men and joined the Officer Training Corps in his first year at Cambridge.

What were his feelings now? He had been carried away with the romantic thought of having his own sweet girl, waiting for him as he went off to war. He found her immensely attractive and each time he kissed her he wanted her. 'Is that all it was?' he mused. She really was not his type; had no conversation and few ideas; quite empty headed in fact. Is that why he had not gone up to see her this time? Why he had chosen instead to stay in London and gratify himself with a prostitute? But she was beautiful and he desperately wanted to do with her what he had done with the girl in a dismal little room in Kings Cross. If that were all, perhaps he was making a mistake and should write to end their engagement now. He groaned and turned over. 'Percy old chap, you're a bit of an idiot,' he said quietly.

He was suddenly interrupted by his sergeant who un-ceremoniously stamped into the room.

'Platoon ready for inspection, sir.'

Well, that was it then. Fun and games over. Time for death.

'Alright Sergeant Mullins. I'll be along shortly.'

He eased himself up and washed his face at the basin that stood on a rickety chair next to him. He brushed himself down, combed his hair, set his cap straight and went out into the murky Autumn chill, struggling into his great coat as he went. All thoughts of Annie faded as he turned to the business of readying the men for the next round of slaughter.

'We lost one yesterday, Sir. Abrahams. And Thomson was wounded,' said his sergeant unemotionally.

'Are we up to strength?'

'Nearly, sir. New arrivals arrived three days ago.'

'Good.' Percy looked at the men, two lines of them, heavy with rain sodden uniforms, standing grimly at ease. They looked as most soldiers did before battle; grim, sensate, nervous, scared.

'Well, let's look at them.'

The Sergeant called the platoon to attention and Percy walked up and down the line talking to the new recruits before addressing them all.

'So, gentlemen, this is it. No big speech; prepare well, and above all make sure you keep your weapons clean and dry.' He smiled ironically, knowing how impossible that would be. 'Get some food inside you and rest up when you can. It will be a long day tomorrow. He touched his cap in salute and turned to his Sergeant. 'I think they will do us proud, don't you Sergeant?'

'Yes Sir. They's all raring to go sir.'

'I'll bet they are.'Percy rubbed his hands together 'Tot each, Sergeant? Before we go in to clean the Augean stable once more?'

'Not sure we can, sir.'

'Oh, I think we can. Don't tell the Captain though, he might want some too.'

The Sergeant smiled. 'As you say sir.'

He turned and went back inside the house. A signaller sat with a telephone near him, waiting for any further instructions from Brigade.

'Can you make sure this goes in the next post?' Percy asked. He gave the man the letter to his mother and thought once more briefly about Annie. 'Have to do something soon I suppose,' he thought.

As he walked outside, he looked at the grey clouds which were ready to drop yet more rain. 'Just like the bloody German shells. It never stops,' he thought. 'Might not need to write to her after all if we don't get through this lot.'

Percy had cauterised his emotions in the midst of all the death. Two years before he had witnessed the worst of what man is capable of at Marmetz Wood. The sight of so many men being killed in the mud or hobbling back smashed and bleeding, inured him to the bestiality of it all. He could no longer distinguish one man from another; one death from another. It was all just one great rolling mass of flesh and filth, which lost its shape after time.

Like so many men of his class, this war had been his

opportunity for glory. He grew to accept that today might be his last and had a bargain with fate each time he faced bullet and shell fire. It was as if he were not really part of it; he was looking down on a vast Wagnerian tragedy, played in mud. He was fatalistic and a fearless gambler.

To his men 'e was a fookin' nut case' one minute and 'a bloody good bloke', the next. To his senior officers, he was 'a little too detached' but no one could decry his bravery.

The following morning, just before 6 a.m. the battalion was ready, lined up in the forward trench. There was a strong breeze which blew a drizzly rain into their faces. Amongst the thousands, stood Albert George Gibson, crushed alongside comrades smelling of rain damp and fear, his face almost buried in the wall of the crumbling trench, listening to the rumble and scream of British shells as they flew overhead. He mumbled a prayer to no one in particular and shook slightly. Quickly he touched his helmet, top button of his tunic, belt buckle and lastly, his left tunic pocket which contained his tobacco tin with the picture of Jeanie and her letters; his routine which would keep him alive if he repeated it often enough. He looked up and saw Percy, revolver in hand waiting to urge them all into battle and he cringed.

Percy looked at his watch and on the stroke of 6.00 a.m., on that dark, uncompassionate day, blew his whistle of death.

The leading companies of Foresters rose and scrambled as best they could over the collapsing trench and made off into the dark mud, following the sound of the artillery barrage which had been planned to creep ever forward, just ahead of the advance.

Percy stepped out, glancing from left to right, shouting in a strangled whisper for the line to keep in formation. He could see little beyond the soldiers either side of him, rifles at the high point. For the first fifteen minutes the enemy held fire. It made him frighteningly expectant. Barbed wire, shell holes and sloughs of deep mud forced a zig-zag path towards the enemy.

And then it started. All at once, a deafening sound of a thousand typewriters accompanied a wall of bullets which found their mark with unlucky accuracy. Percy threw himself to the ground as men collapsed around him. The thin slit of dawn showed him little but a deathly grey 'scape, blasted to hell with nothing but endless mud. But they kept moving.

Albert lagged behind the line a little, weighed down with the Mills bombs in a bag, strung round his neck. When the German machine guns opened up he flopped to the ground and cursed loudly. He got to a crouching position and moved forward again, only to trip over the first of many dead bodies. He had found his composure when leaving the trench but the sight and smell of the dead, brought back the sickening fear. He started to recite the names of the cup winning Barnsley team of 1912. 'Cooper, Downs, Taylor, Glendenning... Fook! Who's next! Cooper, Downs, Taylor, Glendenning.' Panic set in. 'Tufnell scored. I know that!' If he could not remember, it would be all over.

Ahead, he could make out few of his comrades, many of whom were either dead or by now lying in shell holes. The skyline showed the ridge they were supposed to reach, but he could see no one. The whizz of bullets, some of which zipped perilously close past his head or slurped into the mud close by, made him look for shelter.

The dulled light showed him a shell hole and he slithered over the lip and splashed, knee deep into oozing slimy water. Others were there already, including Percy, who was attempting to look over the edge.

'Steady on, sir, tha'll get tha 'ead blowed off!' said one of the men, crouching unashamedly in the water.

Albert looked at his mud caked gun and started to wipe the barrel, to no avail. Percy said 'Bayonet, Corporal. If it won't shoot, you can stick it in them.'

'Are they coming, sir?'

'No, not yet. They don't need to. They've got us pinned down and I don't know where the bloody hell we are. The Germans could be anywhere.' Percy dropped back down and stood in the water.

'Right, I want to establish contact with other companies. You two go left and you two go over there. And I want a runner to go back to the line with this.' Quickly he scribbled a note and handed it to another of the soldiers. The five of them hung back, grumbling, fearful of what awaited them. 'Off you go!' Slowly, they climbed up and disappeared, never to be seen again.

'Tha's sent them to their death, sir.' Albert was wild eyed. They were the only two left in the hole, along with two dead bodies and the noise of shelling and machine gun fire for company. Percy was conscious that Albert was acting strangely; touching parts of his clothing and mumbling to himself.

'Corporal, are you alright?'

'I can't remember, sir.'

'Remember?'

'The team, sir. I've got to remember them all!

'Corporal, what's your name?'

'Gibson, sir.'

'Corporal Gibson, we are going to get out of this, do you hear me? You've still got the grenades. You'll need them.'

Albert said nothing, but recoiled in fear. A shell threw up a great wump of mud next to them and they both ducked as it settled in a splatter around them. Percy shook Albert vigorously.

'Oh Christ!' said Albert. 'Oh Christ, Ah can't do it, sir.' He pushed Percy's hand from him. 'Leave me alone!'

'Oh yes you will!

Albert just stared at him and started to blub; a strangled snot noise that burbled up from his throat. Percy pushed Albert's helmet onto the back of his head and hit him, hard across the face.

Albert's eyes were bright with terror. 'It's mad sir. It's fooking murder!'

'Corporal, I have just given you an order. If you do not obey I will shoot you. Do you understand?'

The strike across his face and the threat of a gun being held to his head shook him straight.

'Now get out of this hole and go and throw some grenades!'

Percy was not sure if his order would settle Albert, but he hoped that he would automatically respond as he had been trained.

Just then, soldiers of the reserve companies started to arrive and several of them fell into the shell hole, Sergeant Mullins amongst them.

'Nice of you to join us, gentlemen but I fear the advance has stalled. Rain stopped play, so to speak.'

Sergeant Mullins edged himself forward. 'It's not good, Sir. We've lost most of the other officers and quite a few of our company as well.'

Best stand here, then.' Percy gingerly put his head over the lip of the crater. 'Any idea Sergeant, if we have a line of sorts? Is there any contact between us and other companies?'

'Hard to say. The whole line has stopped roughly where we are, I think.'

'Right. If we could only stop that bloody machine gun just ahead of us, it might give us some chance of making contact and we may be able to hold this line long enough for others to attack.'

'As you say Sir.'

Percy looked once more at Albert. 'Right, Mr Grenade Thrower, see what you can do'

Albert looked dumbstruck. 'I can't...'

Percy cocked his pistol. 'Them or me, corporal.'

Albert took deep breaths. There was a choking sound coming from deep within his throat. Slowly he wriggled out of his back pack whilst the half dozen soldiers looked on in trepidation, knowing that it could so easily be one of them going out to their death.

'Cooper, Downs, Taylor, Glendenning, Bratley, Utley, Bartrop, Tufnell, Lillycrop, Travers, Moore.' He looked up. 'I remember now.'

'I'll go with him, Sir,' said the sergeant.

Albert slipped the bag of bombs round to his back and the two of them slithered up the side of the crater with the help of a couple of soldiers, and were gone.

What remained of the company stayed, strung out in a series of shell holes for most of the day and as dusk fell, they made their way back to the lines with the help of Very lights and guides who bravely came out to lead them in. That any of them got back was in no small measure down to Sergeant Mullins and Albert, who, between them, silenced the German machine gun emplacement long enough for Percy to retreat to a line and link up with other companies.

Of the nine VC's awarded to Sherwood Foresters in the Great War, one went to Sergeant Mullins and Albert was awarded the Military Medal.

3

1924

'I really would like to write all this up you know.'

'What, for your paper?'

'Yes. I'm sure not enough people know about the plight of these women.'

Percy was sitting in Trudie's studio, a glass of whiskey to hand. Trudie was busy sorting through some posters she had promised to do for the Society. He had taken to dropping in unannounced, as did Clare.

Percy was no longer the slim army captain that had emerged from the war. He was not even the intriguing slightly dislikeable man she had met a few months ago. His face was fleshy and a little blotched, his eyes watery. But his sensuous mouth and eyes were still enchanting.

'Well, any good publicity would be very useful.'

'How about writing up the story of Albert's wife?'

'Jeanie? Not sure how she would take to that. Although she does deserve some recognition for what she is doing in the community up there. You have no idea what its like.'

'Well then. If the Government refuses to acknowledge that a man can be badly affected by the war years after it has happened, how can we ever understand what men went through?' He sounded passionate but Trudie was never quite sure how compassionate.

She held a sketch at arms length and squinted. 'What do you think?'

It was a picture of women and children playing happily but without any men. The caption said 'A Land fit for the Hero less.'

He pulled a face. 'Not sure. It needs something to make people question more.'

'Hmm. You may be right.'

'I am right! I'm getting a real hang of things now. Journalism suits me. It'll be a very sound platform for my political work.'

She hmmm-ed again. 'And is Clare fully committed to your passion for doing good?'

'Now, now. Clare is a godsend when we have to butter people up. She has a wonderful way of getting round the most awkward types who bore me silly. I have no patience with some of them.'

'So I have noticed.'

'He poured another drink and smiled at her. 'You're like me

312

a bit. Your face says it all and you don't suffer fools.'

She smiled back. 'Could I have a drink?'

He poured her one. 'Cheers,' she said and took a healthy gulp.

She put down the designs for posters and picked up a frayed book.

'Jeanie has leant me his diary; his 'black book' as she calls it.' She flicked through the curled pages of Albert's work book. 'He wrote some of his thoughts in it. And some of the things that he saw. She thought it might give me some insight into what he went through. And might help the Society.'

Percy held his hand out and she passed it to him.

The first half on the book contained the neat technical notes that he had laboriously written up as a sign writer. The second half was an account of his time at the Front. It wasn't comprehensive, but gave details of his movements back and forth across France and Belgium. It told of raids, work parties and battles, of blasted landscapes and destroyed villages that he could not name; of lice and dirt and dead comrades and officers. But there was little of himself. On the award of his Military Medal there was the single line entry for the 13th October, 1917. 'Told I have won the Military medal'

'He would have been in trouble if this had been found.'

'Why?'

'All these entries with where he was and where he was going. Give the Germans an idea about the movements of the Sherwood Forresters.'

The last few pages became more personal, more urgent. The final entry, written in his rented room in Buxton, was a scrawled message, '*I love you. I don't want to hurt you any longer.*'

'I wonder how he managed to keep hold of this all through the war?' said Percy.

'Can you remember what he was like?'

'Not really. He certainly didn't stand out in the crowd. But he overcame his jitters in that shell hole and proved himself.'

'So, he was not a coward after all. His death is even more senseless.' Trudie bit her lip. 'I should have done something!'

'No, he was obviously his own man, Trudie. But he was brave, I'll give you that.'

She smiled ruefully. 'Well, to think that we both met him at such… such dangerous times in his life.'

Percy stared contemplatively at nothing in particular as he flicked through the dog eared note book. 'Corporal Gibson. Your doomed angel who put you on the road to saving the poor and needy.'

'Not quite that.'

'Would you be doing what you are now if you hadn't met him?'

'Probably not. All I know is that he was a man from a part of the world of which I know nothing; a man whom I let down. Does that make sense?'

'And now you have sworn to gather up the lost and crippled and give them a better life.'

'You can be so cynical sometimes. We don't all do things for self aggrandisement. There is no ulterior motive. I don't know how Clare puts up with you.'

'I'm not sure she does, but love conquers all doesn't it?'

'I wouldn't know,' she said disdainfully.

'But you understand me. Too well, I think.' He casually put his arm round her and gave her a friendly hug. She smelt the whiskey on his breath and thought her breath must smell the same.

'Lets drink to our remarkable connection,' he said effusively and poured more whiskey into their glasses.

'So, Albert was just one of the millions killed, albeit some time afterwards. A line was drawn under it all in November 1918 and we were all meant to forget and just get on with our lives,' she said bitterly. 'I don't suppose officers mixed much with other ranks.'

'No, not much outside the confines of the job. That's why I became interested in what the Labour Party could offer after it was all over. I wanted to understand how we could treat people like Albert with such disdain, why it was so easy to use such vast numbers of people as canon fodder without remorse.'

'So you have rediscovered a conscious after all.'

'That's a bit below the belt.'

'You said yourself that there was no time for sentiment at the front. All that Wilfred Owen stuff and Rupert Brooke turns your stomach.'

'True, but it doesn't mean I can't understand what drove us all to perpetrate that madness, or to understand my part in it.'

'It looks as if we are both learning and we have Albert to teach us.'

'You might, with your charity trips up to Yorkshire. All those coal mines and endless mugs of tea. Where is Wombwell by the way?'

'If you were a proper journalist, or a potential member of Parliament, you'd find out where the Labour movement really lives. I thought you were a Socialist.'

'Oh but I am. One doesn't have to walk around in clogs to understand the plight of the unemployed.'

'Don't you?' She asked provocatively. 'I would have thought the least you could do is travel down to the East End and have pie and mash every now and again.'

'Now who's being cynical!'

'I can afford to be. You can't.'

He looked at her and felt a strong desire to know this woman better. She had a way of unsettling him.

'How much do you love Clare?' she asked suddenly.

'I love her dearly. Why?'

'Because I don't believe you do. I think you are a bit like Albert; damaged by the war and incapable of real intimacy. Do you get angry sometimes? I mean really angry, so you

315

could punch someone for no reason.'

'Where has all this come from? You're not one of these new fangled psychiatrists are you?'

'No, but you are very easy to read,' she smiled at him and once more he felt un-nerved.

'And what else do you read?'

'That yes, you feel very strongly for Clare and you think she would be helpful with your political career, if you ever have one…'

'Steady on! I'm not using her, if that's what you mean.' He slurped from his glass and refilled it, spilling some on the carpet which he rubbed in with his foot. 'Sorry about that. Waste of good whiskey.' He was by now a little drunk.

'We all use each other, Percy, don't you think?

'And you think I'm using you as well?'

'Possibly,' she said enigmatically. 'I can see that all this cynicism and bravado is a cover for something. I may be a substitute for any Socialist conscience you may have.' By now, Trudie too was a little drunk. She was not used to strong liquor. 'Were you ever frightened in the war?'

'Of course I bloody was,' he lied. 'We all were! And what's that got to do with me using Clare or you? War's over! It's time to move on.'

Oh, I just think that you don't know what you want from this life that you have been bequeathed. You are one of the lucky one's and you seem to me to lack… passion.'

'What bloody rot! I can be as passionate as the next man!'

'I don't mean love or sex, although I suspect you have never been in love. Not even with Clare. No, I mean passion for life; commitment to ideals and action.'

'Well, just because your conscience has been pricked and you want to save the world…'

'That's unfair! I didn't set out to do good. It just happened through circumstance. I used Albert to get something started.'

'And how are you using me?' he asked.

She looked at him and there was a charge of sexual tension between them.

'I want you to make love to me,' she said without a flicker of emotion.

He picked up his drink and took a gulp. 'You mean...'

'Yes. Why not? You have bags more experience than most men. I don't want to die an old maid you know.'

'But... Clare. I have got some scruples. And what about you? You are her dearest friend?'

'Oh, come on Percy, I don't think you have many scruples about anything. I've seen the way you treat people and I know you like women too much to ever stay faithful to Clare.'

He said nothing, his mind was racing. She was quite right. He had no real idea of what he wanted from life. Journalism, politics; these were fantasies. He could write, in fact he was quite good but too lazy.

'I suppose I should ask if you want me; if you find me attractive?' she said running her hand up and down his arm.

'Yes.' He said quietly. 'Yes, you are very attractive and yes I dearly want to make love to you.'

She took his hand and squeezed it gently. She leaned over and kissed him.

'This changes everything. You know that, don't you?'

4

Late 1917

'You are sailing very close to the wind, Captain Bradstone Smith.'

Percy was stood to attention in front of the Brigadier.

'It is not your place to contradict orders and certainly not your place to argue with the orders of the day. What do you think you are playing at?'

'I merely wanted to point out that the orders had failed to take account of the prevailing weather conditions, sir. Our men could not walk in the mud. They never got near the objective, sir.'

The Brigadier steepled his fingers and looked menacingly at Percy. 'This is not the first time you have queried orders. Your job is to execute orders, not question them.'

'Yes Sir.'

'You're a good soldier Bradstone Smith, I'll give you that but you have gained a reputation for being a bit too argumentative.'

'Yes Sir.'

'Why is that?'

Percy felt contempt for this man. He was pink faced and his bulbous eyes blinked continuously. He had heard that the Brigadier bred gold fish in civilian life and he looked like a large floundering carp now.

'I don't know sir. I have been here for quite a long time. Perhaps I have seen more than others.'

'Well, until you are in a position to make the orders, I would be obliged if you would just do what you are told. Next time you will be in real trouble. Understood?'

'Yes Sir.'

'Dismissed,' said the Brigadier curtly and turned his attention to some paperwork in front of him.

'Thank you Sir.' Percy saluted, turned with barely concealed disgust and marched out into the rain sodden street of the little town. Brigade Headquarters was four miles behind the line but still in range of German ordnance which came whistling in with a deathly scream every now and then. There was not much left of the village.

Two nights before, Percy had watched as a raiding party of thirty men had been caught cold, out in the middle of no where, barely able to move backwards or forwards whilst

German gunners spat a stream of machine gun fire into them. Those that made it into shell holes, sunk into the water. Two drowned. Of the thirty men he sent out that night, five were killed and thirteen wounded.

Percy felt sick thinking about it. He had let his men down badly and also lost Sergeant Mullins, V.C., the giant Londoner, worth more to him than any other man he knew.

He looked around the shell shot town and headed for a small estiminet. Its windows were gone and most of the insides had been gutted but the patron had set up a trestle from which he served sour wine and over priced brandy. The place was busy; an officer's only establishment which Percy would have avoided had he the opportunity to drink elsewhere. But this was all there was in town.

'A bottle, please,' he asked of the frightened looking proprietor who put a bottle of wine and glass on the trestle.

'No. A bottle of cognac.' He stared at nothing in particular and waited for the confused man to give him what he wanted.

Percy sat on a packing case which doubled as a chair. Two other officers looked at him and one asked gingerly 'I say old man, rough time?'

'You could say that, yes.' Percy was not in the mood for conversation. He was still seething at the idiocy of the raid; of his reprimand.

'You look a bit choked off I must say.'

The two were Guards officers in hand cut uniforms without any mud on their clothes. They had 'staffer' written into their clean shaven faces.

'So would you be if you had just seen thirty of your best men cut down needlessly! Cut down as easily as if the fucking idiot who gave the order had shot them!'

'Steady on old man...'

'And don't call me old man! I am Captain Bradstone Smith!'

They looked at him in alarm. 'Only trying to do the decent

thing,' said one of them wide eyed.

'Well, don't! Just fuck off and leave me be!' He took a swig from the neck of the bottle and wiped his mouth dramatically.

The two officers rose and without further comment, left. Others smiled ruefully at his tirade, and knew best to leave him whilst he drunk his anger out.

'Bloody Sergeant Mullins! I told him not to go out in front, the silly cunt!' he whispered to himself. He thought about what he would have to write to the man's wife. Mullins had shown him a picture of her and their two children. Their dad had lain out in the rain slowly bleeding to death, not making any noise until he had finally given out. What price for the hero?

He drank slowly and sullenly. He was a live hand grenade, just waiting for the pin to be pulled.

Eventually he got to his feet, very drunk and staggered to the door, still clutching the bottle with what remained of the brandy. Somehow he found his way to the dugout where he collapsed on his cot and fell asleep.

The following day half the battalion was pulled back. They had been in the thick of things for over two weeks and were due some rest and exercise and a chance to do a bit of training. Percy volunteered to stay in the forward positions and relieve other officers who had been wounded or due leave. The longer he stayed the longer he wanted to stay. It was said that he was now just looking for the bullet. He had no difficulty explaining to himself why he wanted to stay at the Front. He preferred the exhaustion of being amongst the dead and dying to the terror of leave when all you did was just think about what might happen when you got back from home comforts. On the Front, you did not have to think about the future.

His colonel saw him the following morning. 'I am ordering you on leave. It's high time you had a break from all this. I've seen too many chaps crack if they are up here too long. It's an opportunity to get back, get some training in some of the new stuff they are coming up with.'

'I know sir, and I'm not saying a break would not do me good. But I can't leave now. Not with the next attack coming up. I need to be with my troops, not now Mullins has gone. Then after that I am quite willing to get off and do some training, if you think it will do me good'

'You are one of my best officers, Bradstone Smith. I don't want to lose you as well. But you worry me. The Colonel rocked back in his chair. 'Why is that?'

'Couldn't say, sir. We all try to survive in our own way.'

'You've been out here since the beginning and with any luck you'll be here at the end; to celebrate, I hope. But I can't have you exhausted and losing your edge. You will take some leave. That's an order.'

She was waiting for him at the Charring Cross Hotel in the entrance, when he came striding in, every inch the officer.

'Hello Annie,' he said kissing her gently on the cheek.

'Oh, Percy,' she said shaking with emotion. She looked into his eyes which he crinkled at her. 'How are you, dear?'

'Fine. Just fine. I say, you look splendid. Prettier than ever in that dress.'

'I hoped you'd like it. I bought it 'specially for you.' He held her at arms length and looked her up and down with obvious satisfaction.

'Just wonderful. What say you to a spot of lunch and we can catch up. I'm starving.'

They went into the dining room which was full of officers young and old. The bustle and crush suggested that this was a popular meeting place for leave officers. They both chose from the meagre luncheon menu and he ordered a bottle of wine.

The conversation was a little stilted. Percy sat smoking a cheroot and listened patiently whilst Annie gave him all the gossip of home, none of which interested him much. She told him of the plans for their wedding for which no date had yet been set and which Percy seemed in no hurry to confirm. She was so excited at being with him that she failed to notice how little attention he was giving her.

They ate the unappetising food and Percy drank the wine which she refused. 'Darling, you're not going to drink the whole bottle. It'll make you tipsy,' she said with giggling admonishment.

'It keeps me happy.'

'But you have me to keep you happy.'

'I know and you remind me of what I've been missing all these months,' he said with little visible enthusiasm.

'It's going to be so wonderful!' she said and stretched out her hand to him.

'Let's hope the war ends soon. I can't wait to get home. I've been missing the old place.' he said convincingly.

'By the way, I hope you don't mind if we do a bit of shopping before we catch the train?'

'No, not at all.' It was the last thing he wanted to do with the few precious hours he had.

'Good. Then you can help me choose. I want a new coat and I also want to get something for you.'

'Oh no, no need there.'

'Oh but I do. We'll be married soon and I want you to look your best, so I want to get you some shirts and things. From a proper shirt maker.'

'Frightfully expensive…'

'That's alright. I have my allowance and I have spent hardly anything. Waiting for you.' And she leaned in towards him waiting for a kiss which never came.

They visited any number of elegant shops and finally found what she needed. It had taken most of the afternoon which, to Percy's great relief, meant they had no time to kit him out as well.

'The train goes in half an hour. We don't want to miss it, do we?' he said looking impatiently at his watch.

'Oh how annoying, darling. We should have made arrangements to stay up in town and done it properly. I do so want you looking your best when you come home.'

'Well there will be other times I'm sure but I really haven't got that long on leave.'

They caught a taxi to Euston. Percy seemed strangely distant, looking out of the window, whilst Annie gushed on.

'Are you alright darling?' She asked at length. All afternoon she had a growing sense that he was not quite with her but brushed it off as his antipathy for shopping.

'Yes,' he said unconvincingly.

'You don't seem very pleased to be here. We should never have gone shopping. It was silly of me to think that you would enjoy it.' She clutched his arm in desperation.

'Tired, that's all.'

'All that wine, I expect.'

'I do wish you wouldn't keep going on about it. It was just wine!' he said sharply

She opened her mouth in astonishment.

He pulled her closer. 'I'm sorry Annie. I didn't mean to snap. One gets so little time on leave.'

'That's alright. I understand,' she said coolly.

As they alighted at the station, she suddenly realised that he had no luggage. 'Where are your bags, Percy?'

'Oh, I didn't think it worth bringing anything home. Plenty of stuff there, even if it might not fit as well.'

She suddenly went cold. Standing rigid on the platform it came to her in an awful flash. 'You're not coming home, are you?'

He paused. Thoughts raced through his mind, all the things he had meant to say without hurting her, but she had pre-empted him. 'No. No I'm not.'

There was a tense silence. 'And us?' she stuttered.

'Annie, this is not the way I wanted to tell you. I was going to write and then see you on my next visit home…'

She was speechless, standing on the pavement outside the station. Her world had suddenly caved in.

'Lets go inside and sit down. I can explain better there.'

He led her in but she was dazed and had little comprehension of what was happening.

They sat on a bench. People swirled about them, but she saw no one.

'Look, being on the Front does things to one. I don't know what I want from you or anyone else. At any moment I could be killed. It changes one's perspective.'

She slowly looked up at him, dry eyed. 'You never wanted to marry me. Why tell me now, after three years. Three years I have waited with little to comfort me. And now this!'

'I am deeply sorry, truly I am.' Inside he felt nothing but a sense of relief that at last he had told her.

Tears were now trickling down her cheeks. The smell of steam and coal smoke reminded her of where she was.

'You monster!' She screamed above the noise. 'You utter fraud! I have given everything up waiting for you! And now you calmly break my heart without a second thought.'

Percy said nothing. What could he say? She was right. He had come to the conclusion that she was not for him. All those nights thinking not of her, but of what she represented; woman, any woman, sexual pleasure. He knew he would never marry her. And now he was putting it right.

'Look, you don't want to miss the train. I'll walk you to your compartment.'

'Why? Why wait so long?' she implored, trying to look into his face. How can you be so cruel?'

'I have been on the point of writing you many times. I don't know why. Selfishness I suppose.'

Annie blew her nose. 'I waited for you, prayed for you… I loved you… And now this.'

'Did you? Can you be sure you love me? Did we not just

drift into something... something that our parents wanted? We never really stopped to think about it. It was all done on the spur of the moment with me going off to war.'

'Oh don't say that!' she said bitterly. 'I have always loved you. I wanted nothing else all my life. And now... you've killed it.'

He rose. 'Come on, your train is over there. You can't miss it.'

She got up awkwardly, carrying the box containing her new coat. 'Just go! I never want to see you again!'

He watched as she handed her parcel to a porter who helped her into the train. He waited until the train pulled out.

'Well, that's that then,' he thought. There was a twinge of remorse, but nothing that could not be wiped away with a few stiff drinks and he made his way to the station bar.

When he returned from leave. A letter awaited him.

Dear Percy,
Really sorry to hear that things have been called off between you and Anne. Such a nice girl.

Needless to say that has caused one or two problems here. Your mother is upset and the Russell's haven't spoken to us. Don't suppose they ever will after this. Can't say that will give me sleepless nights though. Always found old Russell a bit pompous.

How are you old chap? Haven't heard from you in an age. We read such terrible things in the news although I am sure they still don't tell the whole story.

I have some sad news on that score. My cousin Arthur, who we haven't seen in ages, lost his son a couple of months ago. Must have been in the same show as you, or nearby. And old Peter, our herdsman, lost his youngest last week, but not through any direct action. Seems he contracted something and died. He was out in Mesopotamia of all places.

I read between the lines that this new offensive is getting a bit bogged down. I do hope you are managing to keep body and soul together. You have been in it from the start and we so much want to see you home. Can you arrange that? They say that this big push should wrap things up before long. We are praying for you.

We raised a glass on your birthday last week. Don't suppose you had a chance to celebrate much.

If you do get a chance, drop us a line. We do love hearing from you. And on your next leave, you must come up. For your mother's sake.

All the best old chap, Dad

Percy thought wistfully about the farm and all the people he knew, including Anne.

A year later he read in '*The Times*' that Anne Russell of Hassop, Derbyshire was to be married to someone with a title. He smiled contentedly.

5

1923

The late afternoon sunshine, sliding rapidly across the rooftops, glanced through the windows into the studio and gave the place a golden glow, picking out Clare, sitting naked on a chaise whilst Trudie captured her on canvas.

'It's getting a bit dark. I think we will have to stop.'

Clare rose and slipped on a silk gown. 'Thank you darling. I'm dying to see what you have done.'

'Not yet. I'll let you see it when I start painting you in. You really do have a wonderful skin tone and if I can catch that light we have just had, it ought to make something special.'

'Will you complete it in time for the exhibition?'

'Oh yes.' She packed away her pencils and charcoals and draped the canvas with a cloth. 'You are quite sure Percy's not going to explode when he knows you are modelling for me?'

'No. Why should he? It's my body.'

'Yes, but I thought he could be a bit jealous.'

'Yes, he can fly off the handle at times over the silliest things. Can a man be tolerant and jealous at the same time?'

'We both know he has an ego as big as a house. Perhaps he has no room for any other faults'

Both of them laughed whilst Trudie poured tea for them and Clare lit a cigarette.

'Where is he?'

'Sleeping it off, I should imagine. He had a luncheon appointment with some publisher and you know what they are like.'

'He seems to be drinking quite a bit. Does it worry you?'

'He seems to handle it. He's one of those men who holds his liquor.'

'Has he proposed yet?'

'Darling what is this, the inquisition?'

Trudie looked up a little startled. 'I'm sorry, I didn't realise I sounded inquisitorial. But I worry for you sometimes.'

'Worry for me, What an earth for?'

Trudie paused, weighing up the possible impact of her words. Clare with no clothes on was vulnerable.

'Do you think Percy is right for you?'

'What do you mean?'

'Is he intending to marry you? I am not being prudish Clare, but will he prove constant. Will he go off with other women?'

It was Clare's turn to pause. 'You sound like my mother. What on earth has brought this on?'

'Clare, I love you too much to see you unhappy…'

'But I'm not unhappy. In fact I couldn't be happier. He's wonderfully sweet to me.'

'I think his drinking might be a problem.'

'Trudie. I don't know what you are driving at, but you are beginning to upset me,' she said stubbing out her cigarette and pulling her gown tighter around her, as if seeking protection from this attack on her judgement.

'I'm sorry. After all we have been through I obviously feel concerned. You're more than a sister to me, don't forget.'

'Well there is no need. Now let's stop this. After all you concern me equally with no man in your life. What don't you like about Robert Ansty? He's rich, good looking and dotes on you.'

Trudie smiled, remembering the rather louche young man who had taken her out to dinner on the pretext of 'advancing her career' and then to a rather seedy night club.

'No, not for me.'

'Percy worries about you as well.'

'Does he? What does he say?'

'Oh, that it's time you found your protector, that sort of thing.'

'Men can be so silly. I'm only twenty four and I may decide not to marry at all. I don't think I like men very much anyway. Robbie was all I wanted. Besides, I have responsibilities to my mother.'

Clare sighed. 'Yes there is that, you poor darling. But he also thinks that you are a bit obsessive. About Albert's death.'

'Albert? What an earth has that to do with anything we are talking about? He's got a nerve! As if he hasn't got an obsession with the bottle.'

'Now you're being dramatic. He's as concerned for you as he is for me.'

'So, does he want to marry you?'

'I don't know. He hasn't said anything.'

After making love to Trudie, Percy did not know what to think. For the first time in his life he thought he might genuinely be in love. But she had refused to see him. Calls went unanswered and she was either not in or refusing to open the door when he called round. He was exasperated, and felt used. Clare was the last to suspect anything and put his moody hangovers down to the disappointment he had with the rejection of an outline for a book.

When he did finally see her he pushed his way into the studio and kissed her ardently. Trudie pushed him away.

'I've been thinking about you all week,' he said with a slightly demented look. 'Where have you been?'

She walked back into the main room and turned to face him.

'Why haven't you called?' he asked and Trudie thought he sounded like a third rate actor.

'I've been busy.' She kissed him lightly and held him off before he tried to undo her blouse.

'I haven't got very long. Got a piece to do for the paper.'

'Where is Clare?'

'At home I suppose. But it's you I want at the moment. I can't get the thought of you out of my mind.'

'Well, you can't have me.'

'But I thought…'

'You thought wrong.'

'It was you who initiated this if you remember. It was you who threw yourself at me!'

'Well, I've changed my mind. It won't happen again.'

'What! A woman doesn't take her clothes off and demand to be screwed if she doesn't enjoy it! And you certainly enjoyed it!'

'Yes I did but that doesn't mean I have to splay myself before you every time you tell me to. It doesn't work like that.'

He ran his hand through his hair and sat down heavily on the chaise. 'What is going on?'

'Nothing. I just wanted to know what making love was like. Now I know. End of story. Would you like a cup of tea?'

'No, I don't want a fucking cup of tea! I just want you!'

'Well, I'm sorry,' she said, pouring a cup for herself. 'What happened, happened because I wanted it to happen and I have no intention of repeating it.'

He looked around in desperation, looking for some argument that would persuade her otherwise. 'I just don't understand why you have changed? Why did you do it in the first place if you felt nothing for me?'

'I didn't want to stay a virgin all my life.'

'That's no bloody answer! What are you? You sit there with your holier than thou attitude, thinking you are the saviour of every poor bloody widow in the world, but you're nothing but a selfish bitch! Is this what you are? So eaten with guilt and jealousy?'

'Please Percy, I'm only doing this for the best…'

'Best!' He stared at her menacingly. 'I think this all goes back to that poor bloody soldier. You turned him down and I put him on his feet and you can't stand the thought of that…'

'No, no, it's nothing like that. I couldn't have done anything for him. You said so yourself.'

'But you could have spared him a few more minutes of your precious time!' He stood up and circled the room. 'And now you just want to play the angel without getting too close to anyone! All you are capable of is daubing paint and persuading some idiot to buy it for your charity and you don't give a damn about anybody!'

'Percy, that's not fair! I lost Robbie…'

'Robbie died like so many of us and there is nothing you could have done to save him! It's not him you are pining for, it's Albert Gibson! You're a fraud Trudie. The memory of Albert will live with both of us and you can't stand that because I got it right! I was the one that helped him!'

Trudie sat and listened dry eyed to his tirade, her face blanched and contorted. She had underestimated the consequences of her actions.

'I think you had better go,' she said solemnly.

'I am. I've got work to do.' He walked quickly to the door and slammed it shut behind him.

Trudie poured another cup of tea and went into her studio, and started mixing paint. 'He'll get over it,' she thought.

When Clare came round to the studio, later that day for her sitting, she found Trudie agitated.

'What is the matter darling. Who's upset you?'

'Clare, we need to talk.'

'Why don't I get ready and then when you are painting me, we can talk.'

'No. I need to talk now.'

They sat and Clare suddenly felt a slight chill. Trudie took her hand and looked into her eyes.

'You know that I love you dearly and always have your best interests at heart, don't you.'

Clare gave a cautious yes.

'You can't marry Percy.'

Clare tried to interrupt but was held back.

'He and I had an affair. A very brief one and I have told him that it will go no further.'

Clare sat dumbstruck. 'You had an affair?'

'That probably does not even adequately cover it. One night. That's all.'

Clare turned away and put her hand to her mouth as if intending to be sick. 'I don't believe you. Why would you make up such a thing?'

'It's true. It's for the best that you know.'

'For the best?'

'If he could do that with me he is capable of doing it with others, Clare. If you were to marry him, I know you would be desperately unhappy.'

'But you….. you my dearest friend. How could you. I can't believe this of you!'

'I had no other way.' she said quietly. 'You are in love with

331

him and I can't let you go through with it. I tried to warn you. The only thing I could do was to release you from him in the one way you would understand.'

'Release me!' Clare cried. Her face was distorted and ugly with confusion.

'You now know that he is unfaithful. He would do it again, in time. With other women. And then there would be recriminations and upsets. And what if there were children?'

Clare sat open mouthed, not believing that her dearest friend could so callously ruin her love; could cold bloodedly destroy her happiness.

'I'm not listening to any more!'

'Clare, please…'

'Don't touch me!'

'Clare, think of Robbie. Think of what he might have said. I know he would have agreed with me. Percy is too immature to take anyone seriously. I'm sure the war killed off any intimate feelings he has for anyone.'

'I must go!' Tears coursed down her face. As she rose she dropped her handbag and spilled the contents. Awkwardly she bent down to pick them up and fell to her knees, crying uncontrollably.

Trudie knelt to help and put a hand on her shoulder which Clare shook off. 'Don't!' she cried. She looked pitiful. Normally so chic, the news had despoiled her.

When she had left, Trudie sat down on the chaise and looked at the half finished painting of Clare, resting on the easel. She studied it for a long time. 'I haven't got the hands quite right,' she said, moving to take up the work once more.

For days afterwards, Percy struggled to understand what and why Trudie had acted as she had. Clare had sent round to his flat a long letter, explaining how she could no longer continue their relationship after what he had done, and wished him in hell. His drinking became more habitual and he found himself less and less certain of what he was fitted for. He became a drifter, supported by a meagre inheritance from an old relative. What writing he was capable of completing received good but pitying reviews.

'He writes with verve and insight but it appears that the pen is in competition with a lassitude that often wins out and stunts what could be significant work' were the words of a critic and friend.

Trudie's assessment that he was not the complete man came to him in the night when the brooding demons visited him. Not that people noticed, for it appeared to most that he had got over his war unscathed and had little else to bother him. But he and Trudie knew that he was not a man at ease with himself. The banality of peace time had frozen him to inaction. Perhaps he was unfit for civilised companionship. What she could not rob him of, however, was the knowledge that he had done the right thing in that shell hole at Poelcappelle.

It was some years before he met Trudie again. By then she was a good but not great artist, selling modestly well. The Society was well established and she still played an active role, appearing at fund raising events and donating pictures for auction.

One day Percy was browsing in a gallery when he was conscious that Trudie was watching him. She came over and they exchanged pleasantries. There was a sadness around her eyes he thought; something lost from her smile which he had remembered as a bright slash of welcome.

For her part, she was shocked by his bloated appearance and rheumy look.

'You look well,' she said unconvincingly.

'Not well enough, I fear.'

He took her to lunch and both sated their curiosity by picking delicately at each others feelings. He learned that she was unmarried but living with a female companion and no, she had not seen anything more of Clare. She still helped with the War Widows Benevolent Fund, and travelled abroad quite a lot, mostly to the South of France, where she helped run an artist's colony.

Percy had not lost his cynical edge. He told her that he wrote for various periodicals and was writing a memoir of his experiences in the war. She noticed that his hand shook as he took up his glass of wine.

'And apart from that I plough my furrow in this benighted town,' he said with deep resignation. He had not married, although got 'damn close.' Briefly the memory of her betrayal came between them and they veered away from any further talk of marriage. He asked after Albert's widow and she told him of Jeanie's efforts with the Society. The memory of Albert was still dear to both of them and Trudie told him of the memorial she had carved which had been placed in a quiet corner of the local Park in Wombwell. 'It was the least I could do to recognise the men who suffered after the war,' she said and Percy thought how little she really knew of unseen wounds.

'I never told you what happened to Albert at Poelcapelle, did I?'

She looked quizzical and then had a cold sensation. He was looking at her with pity.

'No. What happened?'

He took a deep breath and swallowed the remains of his wine. 'I nearly shot him. In cold blood.'

Quietly she asked why? She was not sure if she wanted to hear the answer.

Briefly he told her of the incident and how he had forced him out of the shell hole to silence the machine gun. ' If I hadn't, if I hadn't held that gun to his head, it would have been me who would have been dead. It had happened before; an officer being shot by his own men. I had to have discipline in the hole, else they would have shot me.'

Trudie was shocked. She held her fist to her mouth. 'You had to act like an animal! It wasn't good enough that the enemy might have killed him. You would just as easily have done it! The law of the jungle!'

'Everyone was your enemy sometimes, Trudie. I'm not proud of what I did, but it got him moving and he became a hero, a real hero. He saved the lives of a lot of his comrades that day.

'But you never said anything.'

'Of course not. I never told a soul. It was our secret. I owe him my life.'

And you never got in touch? Never wanted to see him again, after the war?'

'Oh no. Both of us knew what he had done and I was proud of him.'

If he had not been drinking so much, Trudie would have said that there were tears in his eyes but she could not be sure.

'When we got back to our lines, a shell came over and exploded just on top of the trench. He took a splinter in his shoulder, so off he went to have it dressed and then home on leave. I had him transferred to another battalion.'

'And you never spoke to him again.'

'No, never.'

'I… I don't know what to say.'

Trudie, you don't know the half of it!' he said bitterly.

'Oh yes I do!' she said sharply, her voice trembling. 'I have suffered every bit as much as you! Don't forget I lost Robbie; watched him take five years to die! Don't ever think I am any more innocent than you!' She looked away and tears sprung to her eyes. 'I too have sinned!' she said in a choked voice. 'I think I must go…too many memories,' she looked at Percy and fleetingly wondered if they could ever have consoled one another. It was too late now. Quickly she slid from the table and unsteadily said. 'Do you think I could…' The words stuck.

'Saved him? I doubt it.'
Goodbye Percy.'

He stood and they parted with a handshake. As they turned from one another, they both stifled tears of guilt. She had to get away from him. He was the dreadful past; the truth that she had put away; had almost expunged from her conscience.

Shortly afterwards she received a letter from him.

'My Dear Trudie,

Well, my secret is out. I never forget Albert Gibson, despite what you may think. How can I? But then I cannot forget the thousands of others who crossed my path; some to live, some to die and some to be heroes. We all have secrets. Keep yours safe.And please keep mine, in honour of Albert and his wife.

I hope you too find peace. None of us deserved what we got.

I wrote this poem when you and I first met and was told how he died. Its for you too.

Yours ever, Percy.

FOR ALBERT

There are no gifts for the valiant soldier,
No sweet memory for death's near neighbour
As a leak of rancour leaves its stain
And Ghosts step alongside the Victory train.
We bright faces, cheerfully mien'd,
Cannot say what assuages our pain,
But we remember each heart beat
Which touched another
With a word of love or a pull of the trigger.
We seek no rapture and cry no Hurrah
For killing Fritz and praising our Tommy;
But lie in wait for a blink of kindness
That says "You did well! You did so well."
We crave so little and need so much;
Not the shout of hello and a flag at the door,
But a mother to hear the low moan of despair,
Which comes on the night, year upon year,
And the scream that tires of waiting so long
'Til the call of the dead becomes a welcome song.

Percy Bradstone Smith, February, 1922

BIBLIOGRAPHY

Max Arthur, *Forgotten Voices of the Great War* 2002

Official History of the Sherwood Foresters

Mike Langham, *Buxton, a People's History* 2001

The Buxton Advertiser, 1914 - 1918

Niall Ferguson, *The Pity of War* 1998

Richard Holmes, *Tommy* 2004

Guy Chapman, ed. *Vain Glory* 1937

John Keegan, *The First World War* 1998